I0678142

TURN

ALSO BY ZACK MASON

Killing Halfbreed
Shift
Chase
Turn

TURN

Zack Mason

Dogwood Publishing
Lawrenceville, Georgia

Turn is a work of fiction. All names and places are either products of the author's imagination or are used fictitiously.

Published by Dogwood Publishing
Copyright © 2012 by Zack Mason

All rights reserved under International and Pan-American Copyright Conventions. Published in the United States by Dogwood Publishing, a division of More Than Books, Inc., Georgia.

Library of Congress Cataloging-in-Publication Data is available upon request from the publisher.

ISBN: 0-9787744-0-X
ISBN-13: 978-0-9787744-5-5

Manufactured in the United States of America.

9 8 7 6 5 4 3 2 1

First Edition: July 2012

Cover Design by Matt Smartt

This book is dedicated to
God,
the Creator of Time and Author of all Adventure

-and-

to Bill & Ruth Vance
who sowed the seeds of my faith
that have now grown into a harvest

-and-

to Jack L. Mason
who taught me joy

Previously in *Chase*
(Book II of the ChronoShift Trilogy)

- Mark Carpen loses his children in a tragic car accident.

- The father of the drunken teenager driver who killed them sues Mark for everything he has and Mark's wife, Kelly, abandons him.

- Mark turns his back on society and loses himself to live off the land in the Georgia mountains.

- While wandering, Mark discovers an empty shed in the middle of the woods. Inside, he finds three watches with very unusual features.

- The watches turn out to be time-travel devices. They latch onto the wearer's wrist and can only be removed at death.

- Using one of the watches, which Mark calls a shifter, he can jump through time at will, but only 6 times within 24 hours.

- Mark uses the shifter to become a multi-billionaire within months.

- Then, he returns to the day of the accident to save his kids. To his great frustration, a strange and powerful force firmly prevents him from stopping the accident no matter what he tries. Mark is devastated anew.

- Mark forms a company called ChronoShift and recruits fellow special forces soldiers Hardy Phillips and Ty Jennings to become time shifters with him. Together they save thousands of innocent people, stopping violent crimes and tragedies before they happen.

- Mark hires Savannah Stanford to be their in-house historian and office manager.

- At one point, Mark saves a stripper named Laura Kingsley from an assault. He becomes infatuated with her and they date.

- Laura turns out to be only interested in material gains. When she realizes she cannot dominate Mark, she breaks it off. She then takes up with Hardy. Mark's fury over the betrayal causes Hardy to temporarily separate from ChronoShift. Soon, she leaves Hardy as well.

- Alexander Rialto, a senior IRS investigator, begins to investigate Mark's tax history. After 15 years of continual investigation and frustration, Rialto finally discovers Mark's secret.

- A bitter Rialto kills Ty in the year 2027 and takes his shifter for himself. He uses it to kill Hardy, taking that watch as well. Then, using Hardy's shifter, Rialto recruits for himself an army of time-traveling, former mafiosos whose primary objective is to destroy Mark Carpen. Many of these "hirees" have personal reasons to hate Mark. Among them is Laura Kingsley, Mark and Hardy's former girlfriend, who almost successfully gets them killed on behalf of Rialto.

- As Chase unfolds, an all-out war breaks out between ChronoShift and Rialto's crew, which begins to call itself Dark Shift. While Rialto has superior numbers, Mark and his friends have superior training. Neither side is able to fully get the upper hand, for as soon as one member is killed, others may shift back to save them.

- As Chase concludes, Hardy and Ty have been gassed and captured by Rialto. They lie unconscious and dying on the cold floor of room tailor-made to trap time shifters like them. Mark cannot shift in to save them without getting himself killed.

- Before Mark is able to devise an alternative plan, he is unexpectedly summoned by the Secret Service to an audience with the President of the United States.

Like Secret Codes?

The author has been given exclusive access
to ChronoShift's website while it is under construction.

1. Go to www.Chrono-Shift.com
2. Login: 09071890
3. Click "Account Access" to solve a special riddle.
4. Under "Alerts," click on the Level 3 Alert and look
   closely to see if you can solve the code.

"Oh! Do not attack me with your watch.
A watch is always too fast or too slow. I cannot be dictated to by a watch."

- Jane Austen

Chapter 1

"Time is the longest distance between two places."

~Tennessee Williams

June 2ⁿᵈ 2014, Washington DC

The ride to DC was a silent one.

Secret service agents were used to intimidating those they crossed, not the other way around, and Mark's greeting had just about scared the bodily fluids out of these two, not to mention the bitter taste of bile in their mouths they were surely tasting from the embarrassment of the one having been forcibly derobed.

Still, Mark hadn't had a choice. Rialto and his men posed too great a danger, and on the heels of Ty and Hardy's disappearance, Mark's suspicion level had to be at red alert levels.

He'd left Savannah back at headquarters with instructions to not leave the building for any reason. He'd return to reassure her he was okay once this was over.

Mark stared at the agents. He'd learned nothing from the pair of tight-lipped men and his suspicions regarding their truthfulness only added to the tension in the car as they rode from Boston to Washington. No matter how authentic the men's credentials were, this could still be a trap.

Mark's finger constantly hovered near his shifter, ready at a moment's notice to jump times and escape, even if that meant shifting out of a car moving at fifty miles per hour.

A small sigh of relief escaped his lips when he actually saw the White House peeking through the trees that surrounded it. His lingering doubts as to whether these were really agents of the President instead of Rialto dissipated. Now, his concern turned to what possible reason the president would have for summoning him.

It obviously had something do with his watch. There was no other reason that would cause the president to summon Mark, but how did the president know about the shifters?

Wrought-iron sentry gates parted as if on cue for their black sedan. The driver parked the car in a circular drive which served as a drop-off area under the portico of the West Wing.

Both agents stepped out of the vehicle and Mark followed. Two Marines in full dress opened the doors to the lobby as they approached.

The lobby was a formal affair. White, beige, and darker brown marble tiles created a mosaic of earth-tones throughout. White columns, antique tables and couches, and classical paintings added to the foyer's solemnity.

The agents stopped and motioned for Mark to turn around.

One frisked him thoroughly while another retrieved a detector wand to look for undiscovered weapons. Mark was impressed with their professionalism in spite of the embarrassment they'd suffered at Mark's hands back in Boston.

Two more agents stood at a distance, their hands on their guns. There would be many other unseen security features in this entrance room, some of which Mark could guess, some he could not. One such feature was the three dimensional x-ray machines built into several of the door frames visitors would pass through. Other secret service agents in hidden monitoring rooms viewed these images intently, looking for anything out of the ordinary. Every room in the building could be locked down on a moment's notice.

At first, he thought they were taking him to the Oval Office, but instead they turned several corners and passed through a number of small offices, finally arriving at a steel elevator. Agent number one pushed the down button.

Mark stepped back and shook his head assertively.

"Sorry, gentlemen. I'm not going down in that thing."

Each agent retreated a step in sync with his motion like cats alerted to a potential danger.

The elevator doors slid open with a quiet shuffling of metal. The lead agent seemed to be debating whether or not to forcibly throw Mark into it.

"I'll go down one floor, no more," Mark clarified, "and only by stairs. No elevators."

He was worried about the limitations of his shifter. Faced with a virtual army of government agents, it was his only escape route. Mark preferred not to be underground when he shifted. He knew from experience the device could handle a certain depth of earth, but he didn't know the limit of its abilities. If he descended beyond what the shifter could overcome, he could suddenly find himself locked fast in solid dirt, which would mean certain death. Or the shifter might just refuse to work at all, leaving him vulnerable in whatever situation had prompted him to try and shift out in the first place, which wasn't much better.

And shifting in an elevator was a definite no-no. It was the easiest place to get trapped. No, he wasn't about to get into an elevator that might take him down who knew how many floors.

The lead agent's body relaxed as he gave up the unspoken plan which had been forming in his mind. He seemed to have been advised as to the nature of Mark's watch to some degree.

He nodded and moved away, speaking in firm, hushed tones to someone over his lapel mike. After a minute, he returned.

"Mr. Carpen, we'll wait here for a moment."

He didn't offer Mark a seat. After a few minutes passed, the agent touched his ear piece with one finger and responded with a gruff "Roger that." He motioned toward another door which led to a stairwell.

They descended a flight of stairs and then entered the smallish office complex which occupied the first basement level of the West Wing. The agents guided him through the halls to what was a large conference room outfitted with the latest technology in video and teleconferencing equipment. A large rectangular table filled the center of the room. It was ringed by black leather office chairs on rollers. In one of those chairs, at the end of the table and directly in front of one particularly large video monitor, sat the President of the United States.

President Nelson James was a man of stately appearance. He looked presidential, which hadn't hurt during election time. His jet black hair, peppered with touches of grey, was neatly groomed. His suit was a dashing, dark blue, and a red power tie adorned his neck. He flashed a large smile as Mark entered the room, but he did not stand up, nor did he offer his hand.

Another man in his fifties and a similar business suit sat to the right of the president.

"Welcome to the Situation Room, Mr. Carpen. This is Burton Howard, my National Security Advisor." The President motioned for Mark to take a chair with an open palm, an invitation which Mark declined firmly. His refusal irked James visibly. The president was not accustomed to open defiance, yet Mark was not about to make himself vulnerable.

Mark had no idea why the leader of the free world had sum-moned him so mysteriously, nor why he was being viewed with something bordering on hostility by the Secret Service. It was always possible that Rialto had gotten to the man. Or perhaps the government had discovered the shifters on their own and now had some other nefarious purpose in mind. Either was a very real possibility.

Whatever was going on, Mark was primed to react and shift out at the first sign of a threat.

"If it's okay with you, Mr. President, I'd prefer to remain standing," Mark explained in a weak attempt to mollify.

The president nodded. "Mr. Carpen, thank you for coming so quickly."

"Did I have much choice?"

The president laughed. "Yes, I am sorry for the short notice. I'll get right to the point. Does the name Alexander Rialto mean anything to you?"

Mark tensed, instantly on full alert. His hand slid to his shifter. All four protective agents tracked the movement by touching the butts of their pistols.

The president held up a palm. "Relax. Everybody, just relax. I take it you know him?"

"I do."

"What, may I ask, is your connection to Mr. Rialto?"

"A better question would be how you know about him? And how do you know about me?"

Nelson James' face momentarily turned a bright shade of pink. "Sir, I will remind you that I am the elected leader of this nation and you will answer my questions, not the other way around. What is your connection to Mr. Rialto?"

"We are enemies, sir."

The president studied Mark's eyes, looking for any deceit lingering behind them. Satisfied, he continued, "Why, *specifically*, are you enemies, Carpen?"

Mark snapped to attention, suddenly feeling like he was back in boot camp. "I am a former US Marine, sir. He is a greedy, former IRS agent." Mark's voice turned a shade harsher. "That and he murdered a good friend of mine."

"I see." The president sighed and leaned back in his chair, rubbing his forehead with his fingers. "You asked how I knew about you? Rialto gave me your name."

"How did you meet Rialto?"

"Well, to be honest, he just *poof*...appeared in my office one day." James spread his arms wide in exasperated amazement.

"In the...uh...in the Oval Office?"

"Yep. Just popped right in, smack dab in the middle of a meeting with some of my cabinet leaders. Secret Service went berserk, of course. Rialto just disappeared and reappeared behind each agent, and took each one of them out. Next thing I knew, he was behind me, whispering in my ear, demanding I call them off. Said he just wanted to talk."

Mark nodded knowingly. "What did he want?"

"Said he wanted me to use the full power of the government to freeze your assets and prosecute you for whatever crimes we could come up with."

"Me?"

"Yes, you, Mr. Carpen. He showed me his little wrist watch, explained what it could do. He offered to take me back in time, if you can believe such a thing..." Eyeing the pewter watch on Mark's own wrist, he continued, "Well, I guess you *can* imagine. Anyway, I obviously declined to go anywhere. I'd already seen a front row demonstration of his abilities.

"He said you were an enemy of the state, that it was the government's duty to persecute such men."

"What did you say?"

"That I hadn't heard your name before and that before I committed to anything there would have to be an investigation... Well, he didn't like that. Threatened my life if I didn't do exactly what he wanted. Said he could kill me, or plant evidence to get me impeached, or go back in time and prevent me from being elected. Didn't really matter to him. He gave me a week to decide and then *poof*...he was gone again."

James leaned forward in his chair. "Tell me something, Carpen. What are the limits of Rialto's capabilities? Can he carry out his threats? Why shouldn't I do what he's asking?"

Mark soaked in everything he'd learned and considered the situation.

"Theoretically, Mr. President, he can do all of things you mentioned, and *more,* frankly. He can travel back or forward in time at will. He has access to unlimited financial resources. If you try to kill him, he's got six others with similar devices who will shift in and save him before your men even lift the gun that would have shot him. You can't get rid of him."

"Excuse me, you said.....*shift* in?"

"Shifting...that's what I call it. When you use the watch, it feels like you're shifting through time."

"And you have this ability too, I suppose?"

"Yes."

"And you also have others to back you up in case something happens to you?"

Mark nodded.

If a stern Secret Service agent can look worried, all four of the agents in the room did now. A bead of sweat broke out on the president's forehead.

He pushed a button on the intercom on the table in front of him. "Shelley, will you please turn the air up in here." He turned back to Mark.

"Sir, I said *theoretically* he can do all those things, but I expect, in your case, he cannot."

James' expression sharpened. "What do you mean?"

"In our experience, there are certain events which cannot be...altered. Major historical events especially tend to fall in that category, which would include presidential elections, assassinations, or impeachments."

"Why not?"

"Sometimes, my team and I will run into a historical event which resists every effort we make to change it. For example, once I tried to stop the Lincoln assassination. There was some mysterious force that would not allow me near Lincoln's box in Ford's Theater at any time close to the shooting. And I mean, there was no way around it. I was physically prevented from walking into the box. My shifter would malfunction if I tried shifting to the right time while in the box. This force was unstoppable. It became clear that the Lincoln assassination was not something we could undo."

"Are you talking about *fate*?" President James sounded incredulous. "You want me to trust that *fate* will keep that maniac from being able to hurt me, my presidency, or the country. You're off your rocker!" His nose crinkled in distaste.

"Hey, don't yell at me. You're the one who dragged me here. I'm not the one who bounced around your office taking out Secret Service agents."

The president drew back into a steely calmness that belied the fear and suspicion boiling beneath. "Mr. Carpen...yes, I did bring you here. And the fact that a time-traveling terrorist named you as his enemy makes me tend to believe that you are on the right side of this, but I've either got to comply with this man's demands or find a way to stop him."

"I thought the United States had a policy to never deal with terrorists."

"We never met one that could jump through time at will."

"Look," Mark growled, "You wanna know how I got into this mess? My kids were killed in a car accident." Mark waved his wrist in the air contemptuously. "*Now*, I've got this time travel device, this big beautiful, should-be-able-to-undo-your favorite-tragedy device stuck on my wrist, but do you think I was able to save my kids with it?" Mark's voice broke. Water welled in his eyes. "They were just five and three," he whispered.

"I don't care what you call it. Fate, God, the universe. Something steps in every time I try to stop that car accident. You can mock if you want, but it's real, and if you make light of it again, I'll throttle you, agents or not," he motioned blindly at the four guards.

"Okay, let's remain calm, Mr. Carpen. I'm sorry. This is all just so hard to believe."

"I didn't bring you into this, Rialto did."

"So, you don't believe this mysterious 'force' will allow him to do anything that would change my being president, or endanger the country...why?"

"I don't know why. My guess is that it would affect too much. We seem to only be able to alter smaller threads of history, things that don't affect a whole lot."

"What is this force?" The president asked.

"We're not sure. Ty thinks it's God..."

"Who's Ty?"

"Ty Jennings, he's one of my partners. Hardy thinks it's a natural law of the universe that automatically prevents paradoxes from being created."

"And Hardy's another partner?"

Mark nodded.

"I would think changing small things in history would be as likely to create paradoxes as the bigger events. What's your opinion?"

Mark shrugged. "No idea. Don't care at this point. It is what it is."

"How many of these watches are there?"

"Rialto's team has seven that we know of. As far as how many my team has...that's classified."

"Classified?"

"As soon as I leave this room, your National Security Advisor and probably just about every other member of your administration is going to tell you these watches are a tremendous national security risk and that you need to take action to secure them. I assure you that every member of my team is a loyal supporter of the United States, but we have no intention of being locked away for the rest of lives, prodded and poked as prisoners in some sterile government laboratory, or having our hands lopped off just so you can get at our watches."

"Why would we lop off your hands?"

"The only way a shifter will come off somebody's wrist is when they die — or if you cut off their hand."

The president frowned. "Surely there's another way."

"See. You're already thinking about it, how you can harness this new power. The government cannot be entrusted with something like this. It would be misused." Mark's tone was firm.

"And you *can* be trusted?" The president snorted. "I don't think..."

"So far we've done pretty well."

Nelson James leaned back in his chair again, digesting everything he'd just learned. His was not an easy position.

Mark grimaced, remembering a detail he needed to share with the president. "Mr. President," he added, "now that we've discussed why Rialto shouldn't be able to do anything to you, I do need to qualify that statement. There is a remote possibility he could, though I really do believe it's remote."

"Go on," James commanded warily.

"We visited the Kennedy assassination once. I'm sure you're familiar with all the conspiracy theories surrounding it..."

The president's face was dead-pan.

"It turns out Alexander Rialto was one of the shooters behind the fence on the grassy knoll."

James exchanged glances with his National Security Advisor.

"Okay...that actually helps clarify something for us, something that has never been clear since that day."

"Which is?"

"Sorry, now it's my turn to say 'that's classified'."

"As if I couldn't go back and figure it out myself. Just tell me."

"Suffice it to say, we do know who the real shooters were that day, at least we've always known who two of them were. The identity of third man was always a mystery. Oswald really was a patsy, just like he claimed. The two real killers were punished appropriately, out of the public eye of course, as well as those who'd backed them. But that third shooter has always been an enigma — The Mysterious Gunman Who

Got Away. Perhaps after all this time retribution is finally in sight."

"That won't be as easy as you think."

"We'd kind of already figured that out. So, how do you suggest we stop Rialto?"

"If I had an answer to that, he'd be dead already. As it is, the only reason I'm not dead myself is because our technology matches Rialto's, and every time he's tried to take us out, it ends up in a draw."

James winced, concern etching the lines of his forehead deep in the artificial light.

"The only way I know," Mark offered, "would be to find a place and time where every member of Rialto's crew is simultaneously present and take them out with high-powered explosives. There can't be any mistakes, though. If just one of his crew escapes, he'll be able to shift back in time and stop the explosion before it happens. Rialto is aware of this risk though. He's not going to do something stupid like call a team meeting now." Mark shook his head. "I really don't have any good answers for you."

President James steeled his expression and stared into Mark's eyes for what seemed an eternity, searching for something.

"Mr. Carpen, I know a lot more about you than you think. I've had all your records pulled, as well as Rialto's. I already knew about your friends, Jennings and Phillips. To be honest, we've been watching you, and my agents tell me that the security and anti-surveillance techniques you've employed at your headquarters are top of the line and quite effective. We've only been able to intercept a few snippets of your conversations on the street.

"And those we only got by using a lot of manpower. You are very hard to track...I guess for obvious reasons," he said, pointing to the watch.

"Anyway," he continued, "I don't know as much as I would like, but I know enough. I know you're on our side, and obviously, Rialto is not. You're former military, as are your friends. Would the three of you consider coming out of retirement and joining an elite Special Ops team for the United States which would operate in...uh...realms previously unknown. Your first and primary mission, of course, would be to stop Alexander Rialto from doing anything he might be planning."

Mark reddened. He was embarrassed they'd been followed around Boston and hadn't picked up on it.

"We'll think about it."

"That's all I can ask." The president smiled.

Chapter 2

This is the same place, love
No, not the same place we've been before

"Gravity"

~ *Vienna Teng*

Moments after the Secret Service agents escorted Mark from the room, a side door opened to a flood of people in suits. A couple of younger men took seats away from the central table and opened up their laptops, fingers ready to document the meeting word for word. Christopher Swanson, the Secretary of Defense, took a chair next to the National Security Advisor, followed by Chuck Tanner, Director of National Intelligence and head of NSA. Stephen Patowski, Chairman of the Joint Chiefs of Staff and Barbara McNair, head of Homeland Security, both sat rigidly on the opposite side of the table.

"Needless to say, this meeting, as well as the contents of the conversation you just heard, are classified Top Secret," began the president. "I would also like to personally add that this information is not to be shared with anyone outside this room, not even your Deputy Secretaries, is that clear?"

Everyone nodded.

"Are those devices for real?" Swanson asked. "I mean, time travel is supposed to be physically impossible. How do we know this isn't some kind of disinformation op?"

"It's real," the president affirmed, nodding once. "Not some smoke and mirror show. I watched a guy disappear and reappear before me on cue. Video footage shows the same. My agents saw it. Some of our more sensitive electro-magnetic monitors picked up some unusual electrical activity."

"If this guy Carpen has another one of these devices, how could you just let him walk out the door?" The Secretary of Defense continued. "He's a walking threat to national security."

President James smiled. "We do still presumably live in a free country, Chris. He hasn't committed any crimes that we know of."

"That we know of..."

"And...how exactly did you expect us to hold him? His finger never wandered further than an inch away from that watch of his. One push and he'd disappear to another time. No, this is a whole new technology, a weapon we have no defense for. At least, not yet."

Patowski of the Joint Chiefs spoke up. "Mr. President, we need to nail this thing down."

"Yes, general, we do. But again, how? We have no way of containing these people short of killing them, and by all appearances even that would prove very difficult considering their escape capabilities. We can't even locate them if they've got a mind to evade us. They could hide in our past, or in some year in our future. In either case, we can only reach them in our present."

"This is a nightmare." Barbara McNair dug her fingertips deep into her temples, massaging them in tight, small circles.

"This is a whole new ball game," said the DNI. "Do we need to bring in the CIA?"

"No. Langley's been leaking worse than a rubber raft filled with porcupines. We're going to keep this very close to the vest."

"So, what do we do? Just sit on our hands and hope Carpen takes Rialto out for us from the goodness of his heart?" Swanson was exasperated.

"There's a bit more than that involved, I'd bet," the president answered.

"What do you mean?"

"I got the distinct impression Mark Carpen would have strangled Rialto on the spot if he could have gotten a hold of him, whether we approved or not. Plus, Carpen's a patriot at heart."

"How do you know that?"

"You don't get to be president without having a certain instinct about people, Chris. I saw it in his eyes."

"Even if you're right, how do we know he'll be successful? How do we know Rialto won't come out on top?"

General Patowski interrupted. "Carpen's a Marine. I'd put my money on a Marine any day."

"Plus, we'll give him all the help we can," the president added. "We can't let a rogue, former IRS agent dictate what the United States of America will and will not do, time travel watch or not."

June 1st 2014, outside New London, CT

Rows of long, dried grass waved rhythmically before the weak wind, their yellowed blades bowing in soft arcs as if beckoning Mark to come into their domain.

Mark stared at the field. His friends had both disappeared into that field and neither had come out on the other side. They were either still in there, or they'd shifted out to another time while inside. Either way, he wasn't about to get any closer to it.

Hardy and Ty had to have been captured. That was the only explanation for them not showing up at headquarters.

Originally, one of Rialto's assassins, Vincent Torino had set some explosives under a train rail here in New London, Connecticut and triggered them right as a commuter train was passing over the package. The three of them had guessed the train wreck was just a set up to lure them out into the open. Rialto knew they couldn't stand by and watch hundreds of innocent people die without doing something about it.

And, of course, Rialto had been right. Before the president summoned him, Mark had shifted back and successfully disarmed the bomb Torino set before anybody got hurt. He'd asked Ty to follow the assassin as he left the scene and Hardy to follow Ty. Knowing Rialto was expecting them, Hardy's job had been to keep Ty safe from any potential ambush as he pursued the assassin.

Which obviously hadn't worked since both men were now missing.

The only way Mark could free them was to find out where they'd gone. Fully aware he could be walking into a trap, Mark had shifted back to follow Hardy from a distance, but he had to do it in a way that would not trigger whatever ambush Rialto had planned. Hardy and Ty were probably supposed to serve as bait to get to Mark. Rialto couldn't win unless all three of them were incapacitated simultaneously.

Wary of someone sneaking up on his back trail, Mark only followed Hardy for short distances before he shifted, covertly relocated himself, and then intercepted Hardy's path from a new angle. Occasionally, Mark also caught glimpses of Ty and Torino.

There really wasn't much chance the two of them were just lying there in that grass — much more likely they'd shifted to a different time, but he'd have to get closer to find out for sure. He needed to be within 100 feet of their departure point for his shift detector to pick up their shift signal so he'd know when they'd sifted to.

He returned to his vehicle and calmly changed into field

camouflage. He shifted back to around the time they'd disappeared and then slowly crawled his way through the grass on his belly. He never saw Ty, or Torino for that matter, but he did finally spy Hardy.

Half of him wanted to warn Hardy off from the pursuit, but it didn't seem like the right move. Rialto had some trick up his sleeve and if they wanted to disarm it, they'd have to trigger it first. Otherwise, they'd never really know what they were up against. Plus, Rialto could easily have posted snipers around the perimeter, ready to take them both out as soon as Mark revealed himself.

No, for now, he had to keep a low profile and let this play out. If things went badly, he could always shift back to this time and warn Hardy then.

Mark watched discreetly as Hardy scouted the field, looking for hidden observers. He stepped within ten feet of Mark's prone body, but never saw him. Mark grinned. He'd be sure to razz Hardy for months over that one.

An electric hiss sizzled the air, marking his friend's disappearance from this time. Mark checked his detector. It read June 1, 2009.

Easy enough.

Still, Mark could take no chances. He would take the word 'precaution' to a whole new extreme. If Hardy and Ty were prisoners, Rialto only had Mark left to kill for the game to be up.

If he were Rialto, he'd have had sniper upon sniper, backing each other up, stationed around this field at this very moment just to take Mark out.

So far, he hadn't seen anybody, but that didn't mean anything. They could have shifted in while Mark was crawling through the grass, just waiting for him to emerge.

Rialto's largest weakness was his arrogance. If Mark ever succeeded in beating the man, it would be because of his overinflated ego.

Mark crawled back to the edge of the field, careful to avoid disturbing any of the grass in an unnatural way as he moved. Once safely there, he shifted, not to the past, but to a random day five years in the future. He simultaneously employed his jammer so no one could follow.

The field looked pretty much the same in the future, though the patch of earth on which he stood was now somewhat bald of grass. Turning his back on it, he walked toward town, making sure he was as far away from the field as possible before shifting back to June, 2009.

When he re-approached, he wanted to come in from far enough away to spot most snipers.

Covertly, he made his way back to the field one last time, circling around it more than was really necessary, covering every angle to make sure he would not, could not, be surprised, ambushed, or sniped. For now, he just wanted to view the field, to see what could be seen.

And what he saw *was* surprising. In 2009, in the middle of that field, stood a squat, squarish concrete structure. It had no aesthetic adornments to pretty it up. Just thick, rough, windowless, concrete walls surrounded by several rows of electrified fence high enough to suit a prison, curling razor wire running along the top of every row. A small, simple door broke the monotony of the face of the building, but nothing else altered its surfaces. The roof was dotted with an overabundance of what looked like air conditioning compressor units.

Maintaining an undetectable profile, Mark advanced into the field toward the fence line. Three different rows of electrified mesh fence blocked his path, each thirty feet away from the other. Another thirty feet space lay between the innermost fence and the building. Several enormous electrical transformers stood within that inner fence line.

Torino had been bait. He'd lured Ty to follow him into a shift to this year, which would have landed Ty right smack dab in the middle of that building which looked more secure than a supermax facility. The building was large enough that when Hardy shifted from a distance to follow Ty, he would have arrived inside the building as well. Soon after today, Rialto would probably raze the building to the ground to hide all evidence of it so the field would appear undisturbed in 2014.

How was Rialto holding them in there? Why didn't Hardy and Ty just shift right back out? A better question was how Mark was going to get them out?

If he shifted into the building to rescue them, he'd most likely become trapped as well. And from the outside, he'd have a difficult time getting past those three fence lines without being detected. Surely, Rialto had cameras stationed around the building and any breaks in the fence would likely set off an alarm.

Parachuting into the zone between the inner fence and the building was a non-starter. The space was too small. The roof was big enough for a parachute landing but was made of solid concrete. Breaching it would be impossible. Plus, they likely had some kind of sensors or cameras up there too.

The only way in appeared to be the front door, and he grimaced at the thought of the number of guns that were most probably pointed at it from the inside, ready for someone like him.

He slid forward a little closer to the edge of the tall grass in order to get a better look. He could go a few more feet without exposing himself.

His attention was caught by a red glow in the corner of his eye. It was his shifter. In shock, he stared at it, realizing it had become inoperable. Involuntarily, his breathing deepened.

Having his shifter shut down in this place at this very moment was like being a quadriplegic in the path of a ravenous lion. The initial panic was difficult to tamp down. Instinct pushed him to flee and seek cover, but he remained transfixed on his shifter's red display. Slowly, the wheels of thought creaked into motion, and understanding clicked into place. The last vestiges of panic melted away.

He wiggled backward about twenty feet and smiled as the shifter blinked back to operable mode. An idea began to form.

He was going to need more equipment.

***

May 7th 2008, outside New London, CT

Mark whistled the Battle Hymn of the Republic as he dug. He was now in 2008, a time when Rialto's concrete prison was still under construction. It was late in the afternoon, and all the construction workers had gone home for the evening, leaving the site wide open to his mischief.

Rialto would have been smarter to post guards around the property throughout the construction. Now was the opportune time, a uniquely opportune time, for Rialto to strike and take Mark out of the picture once and for all.

Yet his plot had a number of weak links that Mark could exploit. Weak links that could only have been discovered with strategic planning and thought, combined with a good bit of patience and prudence. If Mark had gone barreling in after Hardy, that would have been all she wrote, for sure. He would have been trapped with his friends, all three of them at Rialto's mercy.

Yet, once again, Rialto's arrogance, his inability to believe anyone else was as smart as he, did him in.

Perhaps Rialto was simply waiting for Mark to make the first move and reveal himself. If so, he certainly wasn't going to be very happy with the first move Mark had chosen. And Mark didn't intend to reveal himself either.

He drove his trowel deep into the bottom of the trench at his knees and scooped out another pile of dirt. He had excavated a small void underneath the massive electric cable which would service the prison and had just been laid this very day. The workers would cover it up tomorrow.

But not before he'd buried a significant amount of C-4 explosive under it along with a wireless trigger. He wrapped the C-4 and the trigger in several black garbage bags and laid them in the hole. Then, he covered the package with dirt and tamped it down until it looked natural and undisturbed. No one would discover his handiwork and he wouldn't need it until next year.

He shifted forward to 2009 again when Hardy and Ty were trapped and slowly circled the building at a distance until he was behind it, taking great care to remain unobserved. He lay prone on his stomach, camouflaged in an uncut portion of the grass. That was another error on Rialto's part. The grass should have been cut low everywhere to prevent someone like him from using it as cover.

The object of his focus now was a large piece of electrical equipment situated next to the massive transformers. Larger and structurally different from the transformers, he guessed it was a power generator which would kick in should the main power source be cut off.

The RPG-29 he pulled out of his black, oversized duffel bag was shoulder-mounted, and could penetrate the armor of most tanks. He loaded it, took aim at the generator, and pulled the trigger.

The sizzle of burning air ripped the otherwise quiet morning as it rocketed towards its target, leaving thin tendrils of smoke behind as it flew.

Mark had never used this model of RPG before. Today, he wasn't really able to verify its reputation since the generator had no armor to speak of, not at all like a tank.

The explosion was impressive though. Jagged shrapnel flew up and out far enough that Mark wondered if he shouldn't have positioned himself further back.

A hunk of twisted, smoking metal was all that was left of the generator. At least one of the transformers looked to be out of commission as well. Another machine was arcing electricity and making harsh grinding sounds like some terrible, maniacal robot. A few seconds later, it blew itself apart.

Mark withdrew a small triggering device from his pocket. It was already armed, so he just activated it with a swift punch of the finger. Now, a much larger explosion rocked the morning's peace. Plumes of dirt shot up near the road, showering everything within range in trickles of soil and stone. The wireless trigger had worked just fine, even after being buried for over a year.

The C-4 had shredded the only electric lines running to the building, and he'd just taken out what appeared to be the only generator with an RPG. Unless he'd miscalculated, Rialto's prison was now completely without power.

Mark had timed the explosions to occur ten seconds before Ty shifted into the building. That would hopefully be enough.

Slowly, Mark backed out of the grass. He'd head back to headquarters and find out.

Chapter 3

When the dawn seemed forever lost
You showed me your love in the light of the stars

"Dante's Prayer"

~ Loreena McKennitt

Mark's spirit lifted as the elevators doors slid open to reveal the beaming faces of his two friends. Ty and Hardy had their feet up in a couple of leather recliners. They'd been waiting for him. Savannah came in soon after, also smiling.

Ty stood and retrieved a soft drink from the mini-fridge which he tossed to Mark.

"We got a couple of pizzas in the oven," he said.

Mark couldn't believe his eyes — their shifters could pull off such miracles, it still amazed him at times.

"So, what happened?" He asked.

"Ty followed Torino to this empty field, and I followed Ty," Hardy explained.

"Yeah," Ty added, "Torino shifted back to 2009, so I did too."

"Even though I said not to."

"Look, I 'followed' him to 2009. You said to follow him. I wanted to have more info."

Mark decided to let it go. "And?"

"I landed inside this huge concrete room filled with some kind of nerve gas. Fast working too. Felt it hit me right away. When I tried to shift out, I couldn't. My watch was red, man. Inoperable."

"What else was in the room?" Mark interrupted.

"Nothing, just concrete everywhere, except for the floor, that was metal."

"The floor was metal?"

"Yeah. Then, just when I decided I'd bought it, a couple of explosions rocked the entire building from the outside. When I looked at my shifter again, it had changed back to normal operational mode, so

I didn't skip a beat. I booked it out of there."

Mark turned to Hardy.

"Don't look at me. I followed Ty from a safe distance. I watched him shift out and then he shifted right back. I never saw the building he's talking about."

Mark stared at them. Obviously, they had no memory of the previous reality, of the both of them being trapped in Rialto's prison.

So, how did *he* remember? Was it because he'd been the one who changed the history while they'd been part of the history changed? In all their previous cases, they remembered both histories just like him. But then, in those cases, they'd also been involved in changing the history, not as a part of it.

Mark turned to Savannah. She smiled at him knowingly. She remembered. But then, she'd also been part of the undoing of it. She had not been "in" it.

The philosophical implications of what they did for a living were too much too handle sometimes. It was better to block those kinds of questions out of your mind and just act. Let others ask how and why.

"What is that fantastic smell?" Mark asked.

The sweet aroma of baking chocolate percolated in the air.

"Brownies," Savannah said. "And they're probably ready, but you can't have any till after the pizza." She slipped out of the room to check on them. Moments later she returned with platters full of steaming pizza and plate thick with rich brownies.

"I'm glad you're back, Mark," She said.

"Thanks."

"Mark, I think I know who our mystery man is," Ty said. "You know, the one on the roof you shot who went after Hardy that time."

"Yeah, who is he?"

"Hugh Plageanet. You remember. From 1863."

"Hugh...." Mark snapped his fingers in recognition. "You're right! That *was* him. I didn't recognize him in the modern get up. How did you know?"

"He was in a sniper's roost covering Torino as he snuck out of New London."

"I guess you didn't just leave him up there."

"Nah, took his weapon and trussed him up, but I'm sure they'll rescue him."

"Okay, so, we now know the identity of all seven of Rialto's team. Do we suspect he has any more?"

They all looked around at each other. The question was key to their survival. Unfortunately, they had no way to answer it in an absolute way.

"I wouldn't think so," Ty offered.

"Why not?" Mark demanded.

"Dunno. Just seems like we would have run into them by now."

"Until now, we thought there were only three of them."

"Don't forget," Hardy said, "Rialto gets his shifter off Ty's future self, after he kills Ty. If we can somehow stop that, we can stop Rialto before he ever gets started."

Mark grimaced. "I told you, We can't stop it. I already tried. You've got no idea how hard I tried. It isn't something we can change." He cursed. "Man, you just torment Ty with talk like that...and me."

"It's okay, Mark. I'm okay with it," Ty replied.

"How can you be okay with it?" Mark asked.

"I've made my peace."

Hardy shrugged his shoulders. "Mark..."

"Yeah?"

"There may be some hope."

"What do you mean?"

"You know how I've been spending time with Abbie back in the 1600's."

"Yes."

"Well, Abbie's young cousin was recently kidnapped by some Indians, the same Wampanoag tribe we fought in King Philip's War. I tried to save him, and at first, I couldn't. We tried every trick in the book, but nothing worked. You know how sometimes it's like God steps in and won't let us..."

"God? I thought you didn't believe in God, Hardy. I thought you said it was just the universe automatically preventing paradoxes."

"Uh...well...I'll talk to you about that later. Anyway, *whatever* it is that sometimes holds us back, it was sure doing it then. I could feel it loud and clear, but Abbie wouldn't let me give up. I just kept at it and all of a sudden — we saved him. Somehow, we broke through. It was like the force stopping us suddenly lifted its hand."

Mark glared at him long and hard, his expression unreadable.

The silence in the room grew unbearable. They all knew memories of Mark's own children and the fatal accident which stole them from him were flooding his mind.

Mark finally broke the silence.

"I've never told you guys this, but a little while ago, I shifted to

Washington DC in 1990 so I could take Rialto out before he'd ever heard of us. God, or the universe, or whatever you want to call it, wouldn't let me. I fired at him a good seven times from point blank range — every shot missed. *Every* shot missed."

"Look, Mark...all I'm saying is that Abbie and I broke through it. We saved her cousin. I don't know what that means for Rialto...or for other things, but I had to tell you."

Mark's gaze dropped to the floor, his forehead creased with intense contemplation.

"Meeting adjourned," he muttered.

"What?" Hardy asked.

"Meeting adjourned," he repeated more loudly, "I need to think."

"What about Rialto? We need to come up with a plan," Ty said.

"Later."

Mark gathered up some papers and receipts in a manila folder Savannah had brought him and walked out of the room, leaving Ty and Hardy staring at each other in disbelief.

He went straight to his quarters and began tossing whatever clothing items he might need in an olive-green duffel bag. He'd grab the right equipment from the armory downstairs and be on his way before anybody knew he was gone. He was going back to Georgia.

***

Before he'd even made it to his car, Mark's phone rang. It was Bobby Prescott, their in-house physicist. He'd discovered a new feature to the shifters. As he explained the feature, Mark couldn't help but notice how opportune this revelation was for his mission at hand.

Mark zipped over to ChronoShift's hangar. He'd called ahead and had the pilot warm up the Gulfstream. He used the secret tunnel in the mechanic's ditch to get into ChronoShift's second and more secret hangar. That hangar contained an immense historical armory filled with era-appropriate money, weapons, and clothing, and briefing reports for every era in every western country for the past 500 years. Mark hastily loaded up with numerous items he thought he might need before boarding the plane. This time, he would succeed. This time, he *would* save his kids.

Mark's leg never stopped bouncing in nervous anticipation throughout the flight. They couldn't land soon enough for him. He had instructed the pilot to land at Briscoe Field, the local airport in

Lawrenceville, GA. Memories flooded back as brief jolts and squealing rubber indicated they'd touched down.

Mark remembered coming here years ago with Kelly and the kids to watch planes take off. They'd eaten lunch at the Flying Machine, a restaurant located right off the runway.

Several of the terrorists that brought down the Twin Towers had taken practice flights at Briscoe Field to prepare for their evil mission, including Mohammad Atta, their ringleader. Mark had considered shifting back before September 11 to stop them, but he could guess how successful he'd be. Probably had as much chance of changing that as he had the Lincoln assassination — which meant no chance.

Still, Hardy had given Mark new hope. If Hardy had been able to save that boy, then perhaps Mark could save his own children if he just tried a little harder. And if he could somehow save his kids now, the next thing he would do is shift back to 2001 and kill Atta on this very field before flying back to Boston.

Mark hadn't brought the others along because he didn't want anyone dissuading him. He didn't need the negative thoughts. He didn't even want suggestions. Frankly, he didn't want any input at all. He just wanted to save his kids.

If he could save Daniel and Brittany, *everything* would change. He'd be back with Kelly. Of course, the shifter would disappear from his wrist because then he never would have been in the woods that day to find it.

He'd lose all the wealth he'd built, but who cared? Daniel and Brittany were all the treasure he'd ever need.

Of course that meant Ty would still die in Vietnam, and Mark would never meet Hardy...but he pushed those thoughts from his mind. He couldn't afford to think about things like that. If Ty never had a shifter, then Rialto would never get one either.

It was the perfect solution. Save his kids, save the world from Rialto.

This time, he wouldn't take no for an answer. He would fight and fight until he broke through whatever force was stopping him. The same way Hardy had.

Within five minutes of the plane rolling to a stop, Mark was in the Enterprise car rental facility securing transportation.

Stephen Chadwick was the name of the teenage football star who had gotten behind the wheel drunk in the middle of the afternoon and killed them. By the time he met his friends at the local all-you-can-eat pizza buffet in downtown Lawrenceville, he'd already been drunk for several hours. Then, in a fit of sloshed stupidity, Chadwick whipped his car into the road right in front of Mark and then inexplicably slammed on his brakes. There had been no time for Mark to stop. Their vehicle smashed into a ditch, flipped, and both Daniel and Brittany had been killed instantly.

Chadwick, it turned out, was the nephew of the governor of Georgia. The teenager ended up paralyzed and Chadwick's father, the governor's brother, sued Mark for millions. The records of young Chadwick's DUI mysteriously disappeared and Mark lost the lawsuit. Mark's ensuing depression combined with the negative publicity surrounding the case cost him his job. The stress on his marriage had been unbearable and Kelly finally walked out. He didn't blame her. He'd only been surprised she had stuck around as long as she had.

Back then, Mark had been a man defeated with nothing left to live for, which is why he'd abandoned everything and fled to the North Georgia mountains in search of a fresh start — as a forgotten hermit hiding out in the woods and living off the land.

That was all before Mark had found his magic watch. One day, after several months of being on his own, Mark had stumbled across an old shack in the middle of the woods. Inside, he'd found the shifter, and that had changed everything.

Once he understood the power the watch held, Mark began using it to build up massive amounts of wealth to prevent himself from being victimized again. He began saving people from rape and murder before it happened. He visited amazing historical events in person and brought medicine to sick kids decades before it was available.

The one thing he'd never been able to do, however, was save his own children. No matter what Mark had tried, something had always gone wrong to thwart his plan. At first, the glitches had just seemed highly coincidental, but later they became so improbable it defied explanation. The last thing he had tried was to wait outside the pizzeria with the intent of pouncing on Chadwick right as he emerged. All Mark needed was to delay the teen for just a few seconds and the accident would be avoided. However, in that crucial moment, when Chadwick had first stepped outside, Mark had tried to jump into action, but some strong, invisible force had pinned him in place, virtually paralyzing him. Needless to say, Chadwick had gotten away.

After that, Mark had given up, believing the universe, or God, or whoever it was controlling these things, was blocking him from saving Daniel and Brittany. This belief fostered a bitterness in Mark toward God so great that it dwarfed even the anger and hurt he'd felt when Daniel and Brittany were ripped from him so roughly.

Now, he had new hope.

Hardy had given him hope. Unexpected hope. Hope, frankly, that a big part of him wasn't sure he could believe in.

After persisting, Hardy had "broken through" whatever mysterious force had been holding him back and they'd saved the boy.

The possibility, even the mere slightest possibility, that Mark might be able to do the same was a temptation which he could not — would not — resist.

Fantasies of seeing them alive again, laughing, playing, happy, set his head swimming.

Chapter 4

Breathe life into this feeble heart
Lift this mortal veil of fear

"Dante's Prayer"

~ Loreena McKennitt

Frustration set in almost immediately as he pondered the possible tacks he might take, realizing some of the simpler solutions like taking an RPG to Chadwick's care were not viable. He didn't want to hurt or kill anyone, and large explosions were somewhat uncontrollable in that respect. He didn't even really want to hurt Chadwick if he didn't have to, though he wouldn't hesitate if necessary.

Still, he could use explosives in other ways. The night before the accident, he knew that Chadwick's car would be parked on the street in front of his house.

So, Mark shifted to that night and planted some C-4 under the teen's car since no one would be nearby to get hurt. Yet, when he tried to set it off, the remote detonator failed.

Then, he tried doing the same thing with his own Camry in his old driveway the night before his previous self would get in it. Same result. Failed detonator.

Next, Mark called a bomb threat in to his children's school so the officials would let the kids out early, but the receptionist simply laughed at him and hung up. *Who in the world ever heard of a school laughing off a bomb threat?*

After that, Mark "borrowed" a police car and uniform. He planned to block off Clayton Street with the vehicle in an effort to redirect traffic, but the police cruiser broke down several blocks away from the scene.

Mark felt the crushing weight of fatalism pressing down upon him again, bending his shoulders toward the ground and depressing his spirit.

This was part of it. The discouragement.

He had to resist the discouragement. He forced himself to focus on the fact that Hardy had broken through. Hardy had *done it*. The disbelief washing over him now was just part of that immobilizing force's efforts to stop him. He had to shake it off.

He redoubled his efforts, manufacturing energy to buoy up his spirit.

Mark tried to locate Chadwick's alcohol stash so he could taint it ahead of time, but with no success. He tried twenty-seven different ways to get at Chadwick before the accident. Nothing he tried worked. Mark tried blocking Chadwick's Celica in right before the accident with other stolen and rented vehicles, but none of them would start at the crucial time. He even ran into the Mexican supermarket next door screaming about some drunken teen in the pizzeria next door calling Mexicans racist names, and he was quite explicit in his choice of words. He was sure this would induce some retribution against Chadwick, but the Mexican patrons just looked at him like he had a third eye.

Mark sat down on the curb in front of the shopping center to think.

He decided to go straight to the heart of the matter. He'd break Chadwick's driver-side window, let himself in, and sit in the teen's car, waiting for him. There would be witnesses, and that was all the better. Let the police come. The disturbance would delay the teen long enough to make the crucial difference. Heck, the police might even haul the boy off to jail for public intoxication.

He couldn't stand.

His mind was sending the appropriate signals to his legs, but they weren't moving.

The fatalistic weight that had been bearing down on him now burst through his feeble mental attempts to hold it back and reigned firmly, occupying his mind like a conquering military force. He kept telling his legs to straighten, but they wouldn't, and deep down, he knew he wasn't going to be able to stand. The force wouldn't let him.

Jaws clenched, he turned his face to the sky and shook his fist. It wasn't some mysterious force out of Star Wars that wouldn't let him move, it was God.

Deep within, he knew he wouldn't be able to leave this post until he decided not to go forward with the plan. He would stay rooted here for hours, if not days, if he had to. He did not want to give up. He wanted to break through the force as Hardy had, but he just couldn't muster the strength. It felt impossible. It was too strong, like the invisible hand of a giant holding him to the sidewalk. Holding him firmly.

The tiny sliver of hope he'd been grasping snapped like a thread. In his mind, he saw Daniel and Brittany's laughing faces dissipate like morning mist before the dawn, like pixels on a computer screen fading until nothing remained.

All hope was gone. There was no chance for a redo. No way to change this history. He just didn't have the power.

He gave up.

***

The way that it was and could have been surrounds me
I'll never get over you walkin' away

"Tonight I Wanna Cry"

~ Keith Urban

Mark looked over his living room in silence. His old living room that is. In his old house. Where he'd lived with Kelly.

The abandoned space which had once upon a time witnessed so many happy memories, but had been empty of life for too many years.

Right after their divorce, Kelly had sold the house back to him, though unknowingly so. She thought she'd sold it to some real estate investment company, but Mark had been behind the dummy corporation.

He'd bought the house right after he'd become a billionaire and left it empty ever since. This was where they'd last lived as a family and he preserved it. Since then, he would drive out to the house every now and then, just to sit and remember what true life had once been.

Remembering wasn't hard. Enduring the pain the memories brought was. Still, like some wayward masochistic junkie, he kept returning time and time again to get another fix of painful heartbreak.

Shutting his eyes, he focused on the soft hum of the air conditioner. Its peaceful whir was so low, so calming, he could almost hear their laughter again...

The house smelt as unused as it was bare. Rays of sunlight streamed through the windows, tiny particles of dust dancing in its beams. The worn carpet looked inviting. It'd be nice to lie down here and sleep for a while on the familiar beige rug. He could pretend he was home again, at least for a while in his dreams.

With trepidation, Mark raised his wrist, index finger hovering over the button. These peeks into the past were like an addiction he couldn't shake. *Why did he keep doing it?* Nostalgia could grow into an invisible tumor, hurting deep down, revealing its damage only rarely. His had grown into a gluttonous beast of a cancer.

He set the shifter to a random date during the years they'd owned the home. He pressed the red button down, but only halfway, using the viewing feature Bobby Prescott had discovered.

A window to the past opened before his eyes, like a movie projected on a screen. The room was filled with their furniture again, but still empty of people. Looked like no one was home.

He tried a different date and struck gold. This time, Kelly sat in his recliner, a novel in her hand. She was wearing her reading glasses and her dark hair was tucked gracefully behind one ear. She'd built a fire in the fireplace. It looked cold outside. He wasn't sure where their kids were, but it must have been one of those rare days when she'd gotten a chance to relax by herself.

The kids being gone was probably a blessing. It really hurt whenever he saw them. Still, he was disappointed.

A flood of memories came rushing back. He smiled through the tears forming in his eyes. It would be so good to go back. Why not? Just for one day wouldn't hurt anything. All he had to do was push the button down all the way. Just one more millimeter and he'd be there.

He knew he couldn't. He could return physically, but never emotionally...nor relationally.

"Have you ever gone back to her?"

The voice startled him so much he jumped. His finger came off the shifter, and the window to the past closed like a monitor powering down.

Savannah was there. Somehow she'd snuck in behind him without him hearing. *How had she known he'd be here?* What was she doing here?

"Crap, Savannah! You scared me!"

"Sorry, I thought you heard me come in," she apologized. "Hardy told me you'd been coming out here." Her gaze penetrated, all the way to his heart.

"Have you ever gone back to her?" she repeated.

"You mean, have I ever gone back and pretended to be the old me?"

She nodded.

"No."

"Why not?"

"I don't know."

Quietly, she listened with him for a moment, letting the silence of the house envelope them like a blanket. The silence of a life long gone.

"Mark," she whispered, "You've got to let it go."

I know, he thought.

***

Mark heard the hollow echo of her car door closing outside. He deeply appreciated Savannah. He could never have made it through the past few years without her. Hers was a quiet, but solid strength. She had such a gentle spirit, it refreshed him every time he took the time to confide in her. *Why didn't he do that more often?*

She was right. Absolutely right. He had to let go. He couldn't get the past back.

He didn't understand, he didn't even pretend to understand, why his life had to be the way it was. It just was.

A simmering hatred burned deep within, a resentment born of frustration, of confusion, of insecurity and doubt. He tamped it down, tucking it away inside the folds of his soul so he wouldn't have to deal with it. It would fester there like an unlanced boil, but he didn't know how else to deal with it. He was in a battle with God Himself, and there was no doubt as to who was stronger. Mark couldn't win the fight, but neither could he forgive.

At least he could take Savannah's advice and try to let go. Maybe that would end it. But it was hard.

Mark studied his living room for a moment longer, taking it in one last time, breathing in the lightly dusty air of his home. He moved from room to room, dwelling on the fleeting images of happier times. The sight of the fireplace triggered a memory of Daniel taking his first step. They'd rushed over to catch him, afraid he was going to fall and hit his head on the corner of the hearth. He imagined Brittany lying in her bed, ready for him to kiss her goodnight after the bedtime story. He could still see them playing on the playset out back. A thousand memories passed through his mind, and he strained into the depths to recover thousands more he'd forgotten. This would be the last time he would come to this house.

He could also see Kelly. Their memories together, the life they'd shared. The exchanged glances when the kids did something cute, or said something unexpectedly uncouth which needed correction but made them want to bust out laughing. The candle-lit dinner she'd prepared one time in front of that same fireplace.

It was time. The ache would recede once he'd left.

He moved to go and hesitated inside the door frame, looking back one more time into his home. He would never truly be at home again. It took all his effort, but he reached out, flipped the light switch off, and closed the door behind him.

He looked up into the sky. Its deep blue hue was very similar to that of the day of the accident. He breathed in and out several times, filling his lungs with cool air, invigorating like a fresh start.

He stepped onto the sidewalk and something slammed into the back of his neck. The whole world turned black.

Chapter 5

Cast your eyes on the ocean
Cast your soul to the sea

"Dante's Prayer"

~ *Loreena McKennitt*

Mark woke up to the rude throttle of an outboard motor. Groggily, he tried to shake the haze from his thoughts, but his movements were restrained by something. The strange motion rocking him from beneath meant he was probably on a small boat of some kind.

He squinted painfully in the bright sunlight. He was on his back. His left wrist appeared to be tied to a tie-down at the back of the vessel so he couldn't pull it down. His right was also restricted, apparently tied to something beyond his head. He couldn't twist far enough to see very well in that direction. There was something heavy wrapped around his feet.

"Yer awake. Good," A gravelly voice growled.

Mark peered over at the man sitting to his side. Randall Cook, a man who had shanghaied Mark once before back in 1814 and now worked for Alexander Rialto, grinned like the cat's meow.

"Man, you guys never give up do you?" Mark groaned, wishing he could rub the throbbing ache at the back of his head. "Why bother? You know my friends will come after me again."

"Don' be so sure," Cook smiled thinly, "We don' think ye'll be gettin' outta this'un."

Mark surveyed the situation more closely now that his eyes were adjusting to the sun. What he could see from this angle was limited, but it was enough.

"Graves," Mark muttered.

Stanley Graves sat beside the outboard motor, steering the boat. He ignored Mark, focusing instead on the waters straight ahead.

"Who else is here?" Mark asked. "Rialto?" He strained to see who was at the front of the boat but couldn't quite do it.

"Mr. Torino be here as well," Cook giggled.

Vincent Torino and Stanley Graves were professional assassins that Rialto had recruited from the Boston mafia. Cook was just a thug and buffoon.

Mark examined the odd weight on his feet more closely and was surprised to see his lower calves descending into solid blocks of poured, hardened concrete.

"Where are we?" Mark demanded.

"Lake Sydney Lanier," Cook gleefully obliged. He resented Mark for the way he and Hardy had bested Cook back in 1814 aboard the HMS Huntingdon, though if anyone had the right to a real grievance it should be Mark since Cook had shanghaied him in the first place.

Mark stifled a groan, knowing it would only encourage the trio. He understood what they were planning. The urban legend about the mafia fitting their victims with cement shoes and throwing them overboard apparently wasn't so mythical.

The outboard motor sputtered as the boat slowed, eventually coasting to a complete stop. Torino peered in every direction across the gently rolling waters. The sound of the water lapping against the gunwales, which normally would have been a soothing sound, instead lent itself to a special kind of terror. Mark fought down his irrational fear. He needed to focus on the problem at hand.

"Lake's pretty low, nobody's out. Looks like we're clear," Torino said. He turned to Cook, "Knock him out before you cut his restraints."

"No," Graves interrupted, "Just stun him. He should experience this."

On the assassin temperament scale, Graves tended to fall a little more toward the psychotic end of the spectrum, while Torino was clearly the more professional.

Torino's look was blank. Empty of emotion, other than clear disapproval. "We're going to do this right," he stated.

"Ah think Graves is right. Let 'em suffer, I say." Cook loved the idea.

"All right," Graves offered, "How about we lower him into the water with a rope tied to his shifter arm and truss his other arm down against his leg. There's no way he could shift then. And it'd be painful."

Torino looked disgusted, but he nodded. There wasn't much way Carpen was going to find his way out of this one, but you never knew. Torino had learned to always err on the side of caution. These two buffoons didn't get that, but he wasn't going to win the argument.

Cook tied Mark's arm tightly to his left leg before he cut that arm loose from the boat's tie-down. It left Mark in an odd-looking, hunched over position with his shifter arm twisted behind him. Next, Cook moved to the front of the boat to cut Mark's other arm free. He and Vincent Torino held his wrist down against the wood while Cook brought the knife up and cut Mark's bond. They were going to tie a much longer piece of rope to his wrist to lower him slowly as Cook had described.

This would be his only chance. If he didn't do something right now, he wouldn't be around much longer to think of anything else.

Graves was too far away from his feet to do much, and Mark's feet were too heavily weighed down with concrete to kick anyway. Cook and Torino would be expecting him to try and rip his wrist from their grasp.

It was now or never. With one mighty exertion, he twisted and threw himself feet first up and out in an attempt to get over the gunwale and into the water. He landed awkwardly on his side with his hip still in the boat, but his feet had made it over the side. The weight of the concrete pulling toward the water put tremendously painful pressure on his pelvis due to the odd position.

"Grab him!" Torino yelled to Graves.

Mark heaved himself up and out again. One more massive body hop and his hips made it over the edge. The gunwale dug under his ribs like a thick, blunted knife. The only thing holding him out of the water now was Cook's and Torino's grip on his arm, which was slowly slipping. The weight of his body combined with the concrete was pulling him toward the water in powerful way and they were having trouble hanging on.

Mark yanked hard once and successfully ripped his wrist free. The pain from the gunwale in his side evaporated as his body sliced into the water like a bullet. He hastily snatched a big breath and caught a glimpse of the surprised and dismayed faces of his attackers before the water covered his head.

Visibility was less than three feet in the murky water. If they had tied his hands behind his back or knocked him out, he would have been a goner. As it was, he still faced very difficult circumstances.

The concrete was causing him to plummet down through the water like a rock. There was no way he could break the concrete off, or free the arm that was tied to his leg for that matter. Swimming up was impossible with the extra weight.

He only had one chance. He'd grown up in Georgia and knew that Lake Lanier was a man-made lake. The Chattahoochee River was dammed up by the Army Corps of Engineers some time during the late 1950's. He would drown unless he could shift to a year before the lake was formed.

Desperately, he gripped his left leg with his free arm and pulled himself forward in the water until he was almost in a sitting position so he could read the display on his shifter through the lake's silt. He used his free hand to change the target year to 1950. He didn't have time to change the settings further than that.

Still, he had a major problem. If he shifted before he touched the lake's bottom, he'd arrive in 1950 in mid-air, crashing to the ground with no parachute. But he most likely couldn't wait that long. He could already feel the water pressure building, squeezing his skull and threatening to burst his ear drums. Lake Lanier had depths varying from ten to two hundred feet, and he had no idea how deep it was here. Presumably, Rialto's men had taken him to a deeper section of the lake. His body couldn't survive a depth of two hundred feet.

His air was running out too. He let himself drop as far as he could stand, hoping to hit bottom before he shifted.

The water pressure reached crushing levels, pressing the air from his lungs which trickled out in tiny bubbles that raced back to their home at the surface. The sharp piercing in his eardrums became unbearable. His body screamed for oxygen. He sensed the periphery of his vision turning black. He couldn't wait any more.

He shifted.

He panicked when the water surrounding him did not disappear as it should have, though it did suddenly brighten under the illumination of new sunlight. The water pressure abruptly lifted, and he sensed he was falling much faster now. At first, he didn't understand what was happening, but then he saw the water around him was falling too.

Mark slammed into the ground on his side, and a great jarring pain shot up through his spine and hips. A deluge of water washed over him and then melted away into the soil like a flash flood.

The fall had knocked the wind out of him. He lay like a guppy gasping for breath in the receding waters. The double blow of having to hold it for so long followed by getting roughly winded made death by asphyxiation a real possibility.

After what seemed an eternity, his breath finally started to return.

When Mark had shifted, he must have still been at least twenty to thirty feet above the lake bottom, because that was about how far he'd fallen from the sky. The shift had brought along a massive amount of lake water with him.

They'd already known you could bring solid objects as large as a horse with you on a shift, though a horse seemed to be about the limit. They also knew that gasses like air surrounding the person doing the shifting were ignored by the shifter, but they'd never had an experience with liquids before. Liquids were apparently a different story. The shifter didn't ignore liquids like it did gasses, and it brought along a lot more of it than it would have if it had been in solid form.

The massive, round sphere of water which had followed him from the 21st century had acted a little bit like a cushion, softening his fall, not by much but perhaps just enough to prevent serious damage. He sensed no broken bones, just panicked lungs. Slowly, Mark assessed his surroundings while his respiratory system recovered.

He was in somebody's back yard.

"What is it, Frank?" A scared, female voice called from inside the house.

The screen door creaked open. An obviously befuddled middle-aged man poked his head through the opening. His eyebrows crossed and his mouth dropped slightly agape. The forgotten coffee cup he held in his hand tilted as his fingers unconsciously loosened, spilling brown liquid on his shoes and evoking a curse.

Frank had a crew-cut and wore a white undershirt marred by a couple of faded yellow stains. His wife soon joined him at the door. Her hair was up in pink curlers.

She turned back toward the interior of the home, keeping one suspicious eye on the sopping-wet man lying hogtied and cemented in her yard. "Billy, get back. Go to your room," she said to some unseen child.

"You too, Madge," her husband said. "Get back in the house. Call the police."

She obeyed, disappearing like a ghost fading into nothingness. The man stepped warily down his back steps one at a time, eyes darting back and forth, searching for more clues as to what was going on.

"Who in the heck are you, mister? What are you doing there?"

Mark strained his eyes up to meet the man's gaze, which was quite difficult in his forced position. His fingers were busy trying to undo the knot holding his wrist to his ankle. He refrained from giving into the temptation to answer the last question with sarcasm.

"It's a prank," Mark croaked, "Just some friends — pulling a prank."

A part of the knot was underneath Mark's hand that he couldn't see, and it was proving impossible for him to undo without help.

"Give a guy a hand?" he asked.

The man stepped back and crossed his arms. "That's a bunch of B.S., son. Pardon my French. Who's gonna set their friend's feet in concrete? Seems to me yer in a sore bit of trouble."

"Okay, fine. You're right. It was the mafia. The mafia did this to me, and they're still around. Can you help me get out of here?"

After studying Mark, the man must have decided he approved of what he saw. He went in the house and came back out with some scissors.

"I told Madge not to call the police. Name's Frank Peck." Specks of gray dotted the sides of his head. Mark guessed he was in his late forties.

"Perry...Bud Perry." Mark gave the first name that popped into his mind. It wouldn't do to have his name show up on any historical records for Rialto to find in the future.

Frank snipped the rope in a couple of places before Mark finally felt the slack indicating freedom. Quickly, he undid the rest of the knot and rubbed his wrist, freshly appreciating what a gift mobility was. His feet weren't going to be so easy.

"You got any tools over there in that shed we could use to get these off?"

"Maybe. If not, Lawson will have some. He's my neighbor. Works for the county."

Frank helped Mark to his feet. He followed Frank slowly toward the shed. Each step required a lot of strength to lift the over-sized, cement shoes. Deep, block-shaped indentations in the damp earth stamped the ground behind him as he went.

"Where ya from, Perry?"

"Uh," Mark almost replied with 'Boston,' then though better of it, "Lawrenceville."

"How'd you get mixed up with the guys who did this to you?"

"Long story."

Mark struggled along as fast as he could. The next time he saw Torino or Graves, he would be sure to show them just how much he appreciated this little stunt of theirs.

"Where did all that water come from?"

"Can we just get this cement off?" They were almost there.

"Sure, sure." Frank said, but he didn't look appeased. No, he looked like Mark had just ticked him off. At least, he was still helping. That was what mattered.

Frank helped Mark hop onto a tool bench so he could work on his feet. He rummaged until he found a set of well-used rock chisels and a ball-peen hammer, then set to chipping away at the thinnest sections of the cement. After about fifteen minutes, a good sized crack formed on one side of Mark's right foot, so Frank started on the other side.

The shed door swung out and Madge stepped in. She'd cleaned herself up some; gone were the pink curlers, replaced by bouncy, brown curls.

"I tried to get Joy to call the Sheriff off, Frank, but she wouldn't."

"Why not? Just tell him we don't need him."

"She said he was already on the way."

"Fine. I guess it doesn't matter. You're not worried about the law, are you Bud?" He asked.

"Nah. No problem."

Inside, he was stressing. He had to get these concrete boots off and move out before the Sheriff arrived. If Rialto somehow guessed he'd shifted out of the lake, and if there were a police report from the 1950's about some man showing up in the Peck's backyard drenched and wearing concrete shoes, Rialto would come back here and finish him off while he was still vulnerable.

Madge went back in the house and after what seemed an eternity, Frank enlarged the second crack enough the concrete on his right foot split in half. Mark pulled the two halves apart, let them drop, and brushed the cement flakes from his bare skin, relieved by the feel of cool air reviving his freed flesh.

The faint wail of a siren howled in the distance.

"Quick, give me the hammer," Mark said.

Frank handed it to him and Mark launched into starting a new crevice on the block enclosing his left foot with a fury. He'd never worked a hammer so feverishly in all his life. All Rialto would have to do is shift back to the moment he'd landed. With his breath knocked out of him, Rialto could take Mark out before he'd recuperated enough to think straight.

"Frank, hold the Sheriff off as long as you can, okay? Buy me some time."

"Are you sure you're not in trouble with the law?" Frank was worried now.

"Hold him off okay. Just for a minute. And promise you won't mention these cement shoes. Tell him I was tied up, that's all."

"Why?"

"Just promise me, okay?"

"Okay, fine." Frank slipped out the door.

The siren grew louder and louder, like the torturing notice of an oncoming air raid when no one knew when the bombs would begin to fall. He swung the small hammer faster and faster until he'd made a crack on one side which extended almost all the way down to his foot. He began on the opposite side, but hadn't gotten very far before the siren shut off abruptly. A car door slammed shut, followed by Frank greeting somebody in the front yard.

He had to get out of here, now. No more time.

He leapt down from the tool bench. A jolt of pain shot up through his knee due to the unexpected pressure the uneven levels of his feet made on his legs. He grabbed up all the sections of busted concrete he could and limped out the door.

With only one concrete shoe intact, he found he could make a little better time hobbling along, but not by much. He pushed himself toward the fence line marking the back of the Peck's property. Thankfully, it wasn't very far.

Mark launched himself up and over the fence, throwing the concrete pieces before him. The chunks of cement cleared the fence easily, but the added weight of the remaining shoe threw Mark's balance off. Instead of sailing over to land on his feet again, Mark landed on top of it, his freed foot over, the cement shoe still behind. The fence rails dug painfully into his stomach, almost taking the wind from him again.

He needed to catch his breath and gather his senses. This was not like him. He was in a state of mild panic, so worried about what Rialto might do to him next that he wasn't thinking straight. The close call with the lake had gotten to him, more than he cared to admit. The feel of that murky water closing over his head like a deep, liquid tomb had been terrifying.

With a great heave, Mark flung his other foot up and over, this time overcompensating for the weight. The concrete boot sailed over at head level, flipping him comically onto his back on the other side of the fence. He landed with a thud.

He stood back up, dazed. Time to get his act together. A creek ran behind the property lines of all the houses on this street. Mark hobbled hard and fast across Peck's neighbor's property and continued into the next house's territory. He chucked the broken pieces of cement into the creek here, doubting they would be searched for, much less found.

When this was all said and done, he would travel back to the day before this one and give Frank and Madge some money, tell them to help a man if he appeared in their back yard the following day and to keep their mouths shut.

Mark saw a large boulder jutting out of the creek about twenty feet ahead and stumbled toward it. He climbed up and sat down on top. He slammed his left foot repeatedly into the rock as hard as he could. Twisting pains cried out in his knee and he had to adjust the angle several times to avoid damaging it. With one final mighty blow, he succeeded in cracking the side of the cement shoe opposite the crevice he'd already made, and the block broke cleanly into two pieces.

He shoved the pieces of concrete into the water and dropped off the rock. A sharp pain pierced his foot. He'd broken something, but it didn't seem so bad he couldn't keep going.

He ran.

Chapter 6

Any shift into the future would bring a monstrous lake crashing down on his head, so he could only shift into the past, and he didn't want to waste a shift right now. You never knew how many you would need, especially if Rialto showed up.

His immediate focus was to get out of this valley as fast as he could so he could shift forward to modern times and return to headquarters. He jogged for several miles until he was sure he'd left the Sheriff behind.

The run hadn't done his foot any good — it was swelling and starting to ache. He stumbled across a gravel road that wound its way through some dense forest and followed it until it spilled out onto a paved two-lane highway. Mark limped along the shoulder. The grass was much easier on his bare feet than the asphalt.

He drew his cell phone from his pocket and flipped it open. Of course. His dip in the lake had killed it. Great. Not that he could use it in the 1950's anyway, but after he shifted forward to the future, he'd still have to hitchhike until he got to a phone.

Ahead, a smallish brick building materialized like a wavering mirage in a desert. The sign hanging from its roof line set his stomach growling.

3 Gables
Beer
Fine Food

The 3 Gables probably referred to three miniature window structures attached to the sloped roof on the front of the building. They were kind of pitiful looking actually, at least by any modern standard. It could only be his tremendous hunger that made this place look so appetizing.

The waitress wore a crisp, neatly pressed uniform. Her tight wavy hairstyle looked like something out of the movies. She was pretty, but looked like she'd been around the block a time or two. She frowned disapprovingly at his bare feet and looked surprised by the sight of his swollen left, but Mark placed his hands together in front of him as if praying or pleading and gave her his best puppy-dog look.

The start of a smile broke through. She glanced around at the restaurant's other patrons, who actually numbered quite a few and appeared to be some of the community's more professional members. Deciding he wouldn't cause much of a stir at the back of the dining area, she led him to a table there and brought him a platter filled with hot fried chicken, mashed potatoes, and corn, all of it home-cooked. The ice-cold lemonade was the best part. He had several glasses of that.

Feeling revived, Mark thanked her and left some money on the table to pay for the meal along with a substantial tip. The bills were soggy, so he wiped them on a napkin to try and dry them first.

Mark, Hardy, and Ty had all made it a habit to always carry a special wallet on them which held moderate amounts of dollars dated from a number of different decades. You never knew when you might have to shift to the past unexpectedly, and they'd gotten sick of getting stranded without the right spending money pretty quick.

Mark moved on down the highway. He figured he probably only had a few more miles to go till he could shift, but the clouds opened up, so he took cover under some trees. In spite of the refreshing meal, Mark wasn't feeling so good.

His foot was now an ugly, bruised purple and had grown to half again its normal size. Whatever he'd broken was more serious than he'd realized. He touched his forehead and detected a slight fever. Infection. He really needed to get out of this valley.

He stood back up and a new pain, or perhaps a pain he'd been ignoring, sent an electric shock up through his leg. It almost knocked him back onto his haunches, but he had to keep going.

The drizzle plastered wet, thick strands of hair to his forehead. His shirt stuck to his back like cold paper-mâché. After another two miles, the pain in his foot became unbearable. He began shivering uncontrollably, which he feared was more from the fever clouding his mind than the rain.

He stumbled forward. A muddy road turned off the highway and about two hundred feet up it stood an old clapboard building bare of paint. A tiny steeple on top revealed it to be a church.

He could keep going or he could take shelter. Continuing on wasn't looking so good.

He turned onto the mud path. The waitress had said today was a

Monday, so no one should be there. At least, he'd get out of the rain.

Frankly, he didn't care if he had to break down the front door to get in or bust up some of the pews to make a fire. He needed warmth and God hadn't done him any favors.

A hand-painted sign on the side of the church announced all the information anyone might need to know. It read:

Spencer Hill Baptist Church

Sunday School 9:45
Service 11 AM
Preaching 11:45 AM
Evening Service 3 PM
Preaching 3:30 PM

Rev. A Booker
Pastor

Mark ascended the three steps in front and tried the doorknob. To his surprise, it turned. He swung it open. The faint illumination of several candles spilled out, casting an orange glow over him through the doorway. An older man in a rumpled black suit sat at a desk near the front studying a book. When he saw Mark, he got up and came forward.

"Yes? May I help you?" he said.

"Uh..."

The pastor noticed Mark's condition and then saw his foot. Wariness gave way to concern as he reached out to take Mark's hand. Mark shook it.

"Rev. Booker at your service."

"Mark. Mark Carpen."

"You look like you could use some help, Mr. Carpen. Come with me." He laid an arm around Mark's shoulder and led him to a pew, setting him down next to a kerosene heater. Its warmth felt good, like it was soaking deep into Mark's bones.

Pastor Booker disappeared for a little while and Mark was in too much of a fog to think much of it. He soon returned with a plump, middle-aged woman. The two of them moved Mark to a back room, brought the heater with them, and set him on a cot.

The next two days were a series of broken fragments of cognition fading into one another like misplaced splices in a film. Some woman mopped his forehead repeatedly. A doctor examined his foot and caused him great PAIN. He vaguely recalled the pastor reading the Bible and preaching to him.

On the third day, Mark awoke to clarity of mind and an empty room. That probably wouldn't last, he guessed. Someone would be along to check on him soon. His fever had broken and his foot was wrapped tightly in clean medical bandages. It was time to move out.

He took his time as his limp was more pronounced. He hoped to not undo whatever setting of bones the doctor had managed to achieve. Mark had half a mind to walk all the way to the towns of Buford or Gainesville just to be absolutely sure he was far enough away from the lake to shift, but his condition wouldn't permit it. Instead, he climbed the highest hill he could find and scanned the countryside.

He saw not just one, but three communities dotting the valley below, along with a plethora of farm buildings scattered throughout. All those people would be displaced within nine years from now. Houses, barns, businesses, whole towns would be swallowed up forever by the flood waters once the Lanier Dam was finished.

Surely, he was high enough. If not, he could always swim to the surface now that he wasn't weighed down by the mafia boots.

Mark shifted forward to 2014. The valley was suddenly replaced by the millions of gallons of water which made up Lake Lanier. Gentle waves not more than a couple inches high lapped at a shoreline not fifty feet away from where he stood. Spencer Hill Baptist church was underwater, unless they'd torn it down before closing up the dam. So was the 3 Gables diner for that matter.

Luckily, he'd chosen a hill that hadn't become an island in the middle of the lake. Instead, he found himself standing in the middle of a campground. RV's, tents, and grills surrounded him on all sides. No one seemed to notice the insta-man who'd suddenly appeared among them.

He'd ask around. Someone here would give him a ride to town.

Chapter 7

"Events in our lives happen in a sequence in time, but in their significance to ourselves they find their own order the continuous thread of revelation."

- Eudora Welty

When Mark hobbled out of the elevator wincing with pain, Savannah's eyes grew big as saucers.

"What happened, Mark?" She ran over to him, and propped her shoulder under his arm to help him to the couch. The bandages Pastor Booker had wrapped around his foot had helped keep the swelling down, but he could feel it pressing against the wrap. He'd done his best to stay off it, but there was only so much he could do. At least, the pain was dulled from what it was.

"Rialto broke my foot. I mean, *I* broke my foot...but Rialto made me do it...oh, never mind."

"Why didn't you go see a doctor?" She sat him down on the sofa.

"Rialto's still out there. Can't take a chance on leaving a paper trail. Can you call one and have them come here please? It's more secure."

"Sure, Mark." She left to go make some calls.

Hardy walked in as she left.

"Hey, Hey! What's going on, man? What's up with your foot?"

"Rialto."

"What happened?"

"They ambushed me. Torino, Graves, and Cook. Fitted me with some concrete shoes and tried to throw me overboard into Lake Lanier."

Hardy whistled. "Wow, that is a tricky one. How'd you get out of that?"

"How'd he get out of what?" Ty walked in.

Hardy explained while Mark winced down a new shooting pain running up his leg.

"I didn't give them the chance. Threw myself overboard before they could so my hands would be free," Mark explained. He told the whole story about his deep-lake dive and how Frank Peck had helped him out of the concrete.

"That was some quick thinking," Ty offered.

Mark shrugged.

"So, is the doc on his way? You don't look so good."

Mark nodded. "Savannah went to call him. Listen, could one of you guys go back down there and give the Pecks some money the day before I shifted into their backyard? Tell them to help when I show up, etc. I don't want to forget later and I don't really feel up to it."

"Hmmm, Georgia, 1950's, let me think," Ty grinned big. "I volunteer Hardy."

Hardy grunted.

"Probably wise," Mark said. Ty was a big African American who'd experienced much of the turmoil of the Civil Rights movement in the 1960's first hand. Mark had shifted back to 1968 to recruit Ty while he was still a marine in Vietnam.

They were well aware that not everybody in Georgia back then was racist, but in the south in the 1950's, you had too much of a chance of guessing wrong.

"Thanks, guys."

"For what?"

"For being my friends."

***

July 7th 2014, ChronoShift headquarters, Boston, Massachusetts

"Hello?"

"Mark Carpen?" a smooth, professional female voice asked.

"Yes."

"Please hold for the President?"

"I'm sorry, what..." She was gone, replaced by a hollow silence on the other end. A few moments later, a click indicated a receiver had been picked up somewhere else.

"Mark?" It was President James.

"Yes, sir."

"We've had some new developments."

"I'm listening."

"I need to talk to you, but this is not a secure line."

"Understood."

"There are a couple of agents outside your building with a secure sat phone. I'd appreciate it if you'd let one of them in to give you the phone."

"Tell them to come into the lobby and follow my instructions." Mark hung up. He didn't disrespect the president, he actually had high regard for the man, he just had no time for interruptions which didn't pertain to his mission. The government, no matter who was running it, tended to think they owned you, especially if you had something they wanted. Mark's shifter, however, made him as slippery in their hands as a wet bar of soap greased with Crisco. He would serve at his pleasure, not theirs.

He descended the short flight of stairs. Ty, Hardy, and Savannah followed close behind. Mark unlocked the lobby's front door and watched the two secret service agents come in on the security cameras. They weren't the same two agents who had come for him before, but he imagined their co-workers had warned them about all of Mark's security measures.

The rest of their headquarters was completely secure from intrusion. The building itself had been decked with thick, solid steel plates throughout its walls. Vents and other small openings were covered with similar steel grates. The windows were bulletproof and transmission resistant, i.e. no one could point a laser listening device at the building and listen in on their conversations. Anti-eavesdropping devices had been installed on all their telephone and electrical wiring, as well as electronic jammers which prevented wireless bugs from transmitting signals outside the building. The most unusual part of the elaborate security system were small shift detectors hidden in ceilings and floors. These sensors would set off a silent alarm if anyone besides the three of them tried to shift into their haven and could only be manually reset by Mark.

The building only had one other entrance besides the lobby, which was via an elevator that descended into several sub-levels connected to the sewers beneath Boston. Of course, they'd put even more shift sensors down in the sewers.

In short, no one could break in or shift in. The building was impenetrable, barring human error, as they'd seen when Laura had gotten the drop on Ty recently.

The door between the lobby where the agents waited and the rest of their headquarters was as thick as a bank vault. Computer-controlled, heat-seeking automatic weapons were hidden behind the walls of the lobby and plastic explosives, which could be remotely detonated, had been installed under the flooring. Mark could activate either system with the push of a button.

Speaking into a microphone, Mark asked "You got the phone?"

One of the agents silently held up a black satellite phone.

"Lay it on the table in the corner."

The table was outfitted with an X-ray machine like those used at airports. He examined the image of the phone's guts, looking for any circuitry that looked out of place. For all he knew, Rialto could have been holding the president hostage and forcing him to make the call just to get these agents in with a bomb. Or, he could have been playing a recording of the president's voice.

The phone looked as expected though. It was just a phone.

"Okay, put it in the tray."

Mark pushed open a security tray like those used at bank drive-thrus. The agent placed it in the tray and Mark retracted it.

The agents immediately turned around to leave. The first one bumped up against the front door, expecting it to open easily, but Mark had locked it after they entered. He pushed a button absent-mindedly to let them out.

"Huh. I kind of expected it to be red." He smiled, looking at the others.

They chuckled nervously. The stress of the situation was written across all their faces. Rialto posed an ever significant threat to their well-being. Until he was taken care of, their only safe haven was this building, and cabin fever was really starting to get to them.

Now, the U.S. government was trying to pull them into service. While that didn't bother Savannah too much, it got under Hardy and Ty's skin about as much as it did Mark's. From their military experience, they knew how the government operated.

The phone rang. Mark pushed *Talk*.

"Hello?"

"Sorry for all the trouble, Mark. Like I said, we've had some developments." The president sounded upbeat in contrast to his words.

"What happened?"

"Mr. Rialto paid us another visit. He popped into the Oval Office during a meeting with Senate and House leadership. 'Bout scared them out of their suits. Not that he's not getting to me too. I think Lee's getting an ulcer from thinking about it."

"Who's Lee?"

"Head of my security detail. Doesn't have a clue how to protect me from something like this."

"I'm not sure he can."

"I know. Listen, it was kind of a good thing he showed up when he did. Saved me a lot of explaining and incredulity on the part of congressional leaders. That's probably why he chose to show up when he did actually. To streamline things."

"What did he say?"

"He gave us a list of demands. Threatened to cause a major war in the Middle East, the likes of which would dwarf anything we ever saw in the 20th century."

"How does he plan to do that?" Mark asked, seriously incredulous. These shifters were powerful, but starting a war? Mark hadn't even been able to save Lincoln.

"He says he's got the Ark of the Covenant."

"The Ark of what?"

"The Ark of the Covenant. You know, 'Raiders of the Lost Ark', Indiana Jones and all that. The golden chest that Moses built which held the 10 commandments."

Mark shook his head, not understanding. "How's he going to start a war with that?"

"The Ark is the holiest object in the Jewish faith, but it disappeared from history thousands of years ago. If it were discovered again, it could ignite a religious war between Israel and the Arab nations."

"And you believe that would happen?"

"I've spoken with Prime Minister Alon in Israel. He was quite nervous at the prospect. I take his opinion on the matter very seriously."

"But why? How could one artifact cause a war?"

"There are many orthodox and conservative Jews in Israel who are ardently waiting to build the Third Jewish Temple. The only thing many of them are waiting on is the unveiling of the Ark of the Covenant. There are apparently prophecies predicting this will happen someday."

"So? Let them build it."

"To build it would require tearing down the Dome of the Rock, the third holiest shrine in Islam."

"Oh."

"I'm assured by experts down at Langley that even the appearance of the Ark on the world scene could ignite a Middle Eastern conflict which could easily morph into World War III. Not to mention the skyrocketing oil prices and other inconveniences which would result."

Mark took the information in, processing the full implications of it.

"If Rialto really does have the Ark, we're in a bad spot," the president continued, "I can't imagine what would happen if he elected to give it to a Muslim nation like Iran."

"What do you want us to do?"

"I need you to find out if Rialto really does have the Ark, and if so, go back and stop him before he gets it."

"What were his demands?"

"He wants $50 billion wired to several bank accounts in the Caiman Islands and Switzerland immediately. He also demanded 20% ownership of the Federal Reserve."

"The Federal Reserve? How can he own a part of the government?"

"The Fed's not part of the government. It's a private bank."

"You've got to be kidding me."

"No, I'm not. Needless to say, we can't give him part ownership of it. Even if we wanted to, I just don't know that I could make that happen. My influence only goes so far. The president is not king, you know."

Mark glanced back at his friends. They were watching him intently, having only been able to follow his half of the conversation, but understanding the gravity of it. His decision would determine their future, their well-being. Rialto was a formidable enemy, truly the only one on earth who was capable of harming them — and had the *will* to.

They had to overcome the man somehow. If they didn't, he would end up destroying them. This seemed as good a lead as any.

He turned back to the phone. "Okay, we'll do it."

Mark heard a sigh of relief on the other end of the line even though the president tried to mask it.

"Good. Your service is appreciated, Mark."

"Don't mention it."

"Listen, I took the initiative to get as much info out of Israel as I could. I mean, it is their lost relic after all. They should know something about it."

"And?"

"I spoke with the director of Mossad and the director-general of the Israeli Antiquities Authority. Both of them recommended we start by talking with Benjamin Rosenberg of the Harvard Divinity School. He apparently knows more about the Ark than anybody. Why don't you start by paying him a visit?"

"Thank you, Mr. President."

"No, thank *you*, Mark. I mean that. Please keep me updated."

The phone line clicked dead.

Mark turned to his friends. His face hardened.

"We are going to take Rialto out, once and for all."

Chapter 8

Savannah had taken a couple of graduate courses with Professor Rosenberg and knew him, so she went along with them to the interview.

Rosenberg was an amicable enough man, dressed in tweed, twiddling a pair of thin-rimmed spectacles in his fingers as he spoke. Mark mused how men like him all too often seemed to match the stereotypical image of what a college professor was supposed to look like. He thought there must be some kind of unspoken dress code subconsciously imposed by colleagues.

Rosenberg's office, however, belied the stereotype. The books on the shelves were arranged neatly. Papers were not strewn about chaotically, but filed in several folders stacked in a short pile. The furniture was recently polished and the light scent of lemon Pledge was detectable. Similarly, the floor was waxed, the rug immaculate. He was a neat freak, almost military in his cleanliness.

A light shade of brown tinted his otherwise pale skin. He was balding, but the hair on the sides of his head had been neatly trimmed.

Rosenberg professed his pleasure at being able to meet them, but his eyes said something entirely different. Perhaps they'd interrupted an otherwise busy schedule.

"Professor, I sincerely appreciate you carving out some time for us," Mark said.

"Well, when the President of the United States calls and asks you to make time, you tend to find it," he laughed. Once more, the smile didn't quite make it to his eyes.

Seeing this, Mark got straight to the point. "Well, I won't waste it then. We need to know everything you can tell us about the Ark of the Covenant and where it might be today."

The professor raised an eyebrow. "So...are we treasure seekers?"

"I'm not at liberty to say..."

"Yes, the president told me it was a matter of national security."

"It is. Any discretion would be appreciated."

"What do you know so far?" Rosenberg leaned back in his chair, let out a little sigh and laced his fingers behind his head.

"Not much."

"I bet you know more than you think. Who hasn't seen *Raiders of the Lost Ark*? Anyway, the Ark of the Covenant is the holiest object in Judaism. God ordered Moses to build it while Moses was up on Mt. Sinai. It was a hollow chest made of wood, with a lid, all of it overlaid with pure gold, both inside and out. Rings on the sides held long poles, also covered in gold, which were used by the priests to carry it about. Anyone who touched it directly instantly died."

Mark's eyes widened. Hardy grunted a "Huh?" Ty bore an expression like he'd heard all this before and Savannah was nodding like it was also familiar material to her.

"They would die?" Hardy asked.

"Yes, God told Moses to place His Law, or possibly just the 10 Commandments, inside the Ark, along with Aaron's staff and a jar full of manna."

"Forgive my ignorance, but who was Aaron? And what is manna?" Mark asked.

"Ha!" The laughter actually reached Rosenberg's eyes this time. "That's exactly what manna means: 'What is it?' While the Israelites wandered in the desert for forty years, God provided them with a heavenly bread that appeared like dew on the ground each morning and they collected it for food. At first, they didn't know what it was, so that's what they called it, *Manna*, or 'what is it?'"

"Aaron was Moses' brother, the first High Priest of Israel," Ty added.

Mark shot him a look.

"Anyway," the professor continued, "As I said, the Ark was greatly revered. It was the only object in the holiest room of Moses' Tabernacle. Later, it became the most important item in God's Temple in Jerusalem. The room where it was housed was called the Holy of Holies. It was believed that the Ark was the footstool before God's invisible throne in the Temple. The Bible reports that the *Shekinah*, eh, that means the physical manifestation of God's glory, indwelled the Temple and rested between the cherubim on top of the Ark."

"What are Cherubim?" Hardy asked.

"Angels," Savannah offered.

"That's right," Rosenberg continued, "Sometimes, the Israelites would carry the Ark before them in battle, believing God Himself was leading them, and they attributed their success to it, to God. One time, the Philistines captured it and..."

"How could the Philistines capture it if God was with them?"

"Israel had disobeyed Him, and their punishment was to lose the battle. Anyway, the Philistines put the Ark in the temple of their god, and several times they came in to find the statue of their god fallen on the floor before the Ark as if bowing to it. The second time the head and hands of the statue had been cut off by a mysterious force. The Philistines also became afflicted by a great plague and eventually returned the Ark to Israel to rid themselves of it."

"So, what happened to the Ark? Where is it now?" Mark asked.

"It was last mentioned in the Bible during the reign of King Josiah around 621 BC. That was right before King Nebuchadnezzar of Babylon destroyed Jerusalem in 586 BC. Some scholars believe Nebuchadnezzar melted it down for the gold value, but that is really very unlikely."

"Why?"

"A number of reasons. First, it was the practice of ancient kings to preserve the relics of the gods of the peoples they conquered as a symbol of the supremacy of their god over the other gods. An example of this is seen in the Book of Daniel where King Belshazzar, one of Nebuchadnezzar's descendants, brings out the golden objects that were taken from God's Temple in Jerusalem and uses them in a drunken feast. God judged him for the act and Belshazzar was killed that very night by the invading Persian army. What is remarkable is that the lesser objects had been preserved and not melted down, strong evidence the Ark would not have been melted down either. But, the Ark was not mentioned in that account, nor was it mentioned years later when the king of Persia gave the Jews permission to return to Jerusalem to rebuild their Temple and returned their holy vessels to them.

"No honest scholar who knows what they're talking about believes Babylon or Persia ever got their hands on it. Which means one of two things happened. Either priests smuggled it out of Jerusalem before the siege by Babylon, or the priests hid it in a cave system underneath the Temple Mount. There are, in fact, Jewish legends supporting both possibilities."

Mark leaned back in his chair. This was getting good. Ty and Savannah had both tilted forward, paying closer attention now.

"One legend says the prophet Jeremiah was warned by God about the coming destruction of Jerusalem by Babylon and commanded him to remove the Ark and hide it in a cave on Mt. Nebo just across the

Israeli border in what is now the country of Jordan. There's not much support for this theory in the scholarly world. Mt. Nebo has been scoured a hundred times over with nothing to show for the effort.

"The other Jewish legend says that when Solomon built the first Temple, he had a special platform built underneath the Ark that could be lowered by the priests into a cave system and hidden there should Jerusalem ever be attacked. This is quite possible."

"Are you saying the Ark is still in a cave under the Temple Mount?"

"The most likely scenario is that the Ark was hidden underneath the Temple, but it may or may not still be there."

"How could it still be there after all these years without anybody finding it?"

"There is an elaborate cave system within the Temple Mount — the area is quite large — and for the past 1300 years, it's been controlled by fanatical Muslims who won't let anybody explore them. Plus, if it had been hidden there, the Jewish priests would have filled in any access points with a large amount of rubble to protect it. Tomb robbers don't always get the goods."

Savannah held up a finger, "Wasn't there an excavation in recent years that found something?"

"Yes, several of Israel's leading rabbis conducted a secret excavation for 18 months starting in 1981. They claim to have seen the Ark in a cave, but were stopped right before reaching it when Muslim authorities discovered their work and shut them down."

"So, do you think that's where it is?" Mark said.

"No one knows for sure. But, there's more. A lot more. Have you heard of the Templar Knights?"

They all nodded.

"Well, they've been the subject of many a fanciful tale, like those portrayed in the *Da Vinci Code*, but one tale that is true is the story of their origins. When they first began, there were only nine Templar knights. These were men who took an oath of poverty and swore to fight for God's kingdom on earth. They traveled to Jerusalem with the intention of protecting Christian pilgrims who were being assaulted by Muslim bandits on their way to Israel. In 1119, King Baldwin II of Jerusalem gave them permission to station their headquarters on the Temple Mount.

"After that, the Templars seemed to spend a lot more time digging than they did protecting pilgrims, and it wasn't long before the Templar Order became wealthy. Very wealthy in fact. By the year

1300, they had become the most powerful financial institution in Europe and perhaps the world, acting like an international bank of sorts. Some people believe they may have found the Ark of the Covenant under the Temple Mount and brought it back to Europe.

"Other scholars think the Templars found nothing because they believe the Romans took the Ark when they conquered Jerusalem back in 70 AD. That theory really isn't very plausible though. There is a monument in Rome called the Titus Arch which was built to honor the sacking of Jerusalem by the Romans. It depicts the holy objects removed from the Temple in Jerusalem and brought to Rome. The Ark isn't in the picture."

"Wow," Mark said. His head whirled as he tried to process all this information.

"And that's not all," Rosenberg continued, a mischievous smile lighting his face, "I mentioned the last reference to the Ark in the Bible was in Josiah's reign around 621 BC?"

"Yes."

"Let me throw a wrench in the works. That biblical reference only refers to "the ark," not "the Ark of the Covenant". The last full reference to it in the Bible as the "Ark of the Covenant" occurs before the end of King Solomon's reign around 930 BC. There is a well-known account in the Bible in which the Queen of Sheba comes to visit King Solomon because she's heard of his great wisdom.

"Sheba is modern day Ethiopia. Ethiopians have a legend that the Queen of Sheba and Solomon went to bed together and she bore him a son. This boy, Menelik, came back to Israel at the age of 22 to sit at the feet of his father to learn. According to the legend, which is not in the Bible, when he saw Solomon worshiping pagan idols, he stole the Ark and took it back to Ethiopia for safe keeping. The claim is that after Menelik left with the real Ark, Solomon had a replica made, which is the "ark" mentioned later during the reign of Josiah. That is why it's only referred to then as the "ark" and not the "Ark of the Covenant."

"There is a lot of evidence that before Christianity, Ethiopia was a very Jewish nation. Very soon after Christ, much of the country became Christian. Ethiopians believe that all of their kings, even up through the 1950's, were direct descendants of Solomon through Menelik. In the city of Axum, there is a holy building where it is said a high priest guards the Holy Ark. This priest never leaves the building's small compound and never lets anyone in. He stays there for life."

Rosenberg leaned forward in a slightly aggressive pose, a playful grin plastered on his face. "Is that enough theories for you?" he asked.

Mark shook his head in an effort to recapture all the info. "So, either Babylon destroyed it, Rome took it, or Jeremiah hid it on..."

"Mt. Nebo."

"Right, Mt. Nebo. Or it's still under the Temple Mount...or the Templars took it to who knows where in Europe. Or it's in Ethiopia."

"You got it. You should also know that many students of the Knights Templar believe that group morphed into the Masonic Lodge in the 14th century. If that's true, any western government could have the Ark, including the U.S. government."

Mark, Ty, Hardy, and Savannah all exchanged glassy-eyed stares as if they were each developing migraines.

"Professor, you're the expert. Where do *you* think it is?"

Rosenberg leaned back once more and removed his glasses. He pinched the bridge of his nose tightly and then, in a more relaxed manner, massaged it. "The Babylonian destruction and Roman capture theories aren't very likely. I also think the Jeremiah legend is just that, pure legend. That legend has been adapted to conceive all kinds of crazy theories, even to the point of saying Jeremiah brought the Ark to ancient Ireland.

"It could still be under the Temple Mount. Still, if I were a betting man, I'd place my money on either Ethiopia or the Templars."

"Really?" Hardy seemed surprised.

"Yes. In spite of the fact that I am not usually a fan of conspiracy theories, both possibilities have a lot of circumstantial evidence to back them up. It could be either."

He stood and pulled a couple of books from his library shelves. "Here," he said to Mark, "These books can give you a lot more information than I could in a couple of hours."

***

Mark stood at the top of the granite steps. Ty was on his left and Hardy and Savannah were back and to his right. Stoic white columns lanced upward on either side. Mark surveyed the green courtyard before them in silence. He should be descending the steps, but he was deliberating.

"What did you think, Ty?" Mark asked under his breath.

Ty gathered his thoughts. "I don't know. I was surprised by the theories he believes are correct."

"Why?"

"Not sure, seemed like they would have been the least likely, but he didn't think so."

A couple of undergrads were tossing a football back and forth in the grass. One of them missed a catch and went running after it.

"Yeah, but the way he explained it — it made sense," Mark said. He looked to Savannah.

"He's a very respected professor, both here at Harvard *and* internationally," she said.

"He was recommended by Mossad," Hardy added.

Mark grimaced. "That could be as bad as it is good."

Hardy shrugged, which made Mark snicker. It was an all-too familiar gesture of his.

"Hardy, Savannah, I'd like you two to start researching the Knights Templar. Figure out where it could be today if they did get their hands on it. Ty, you and I are going to Ethiopia."

Chapter 9

Axum, Ethiopia was a sleepy village, ancient in its roots, made grand through legend. Tall trees with dark green boughs distinguished the area belonging to the town from the rest of the verdant valley in which it lay. Low-lying hill ranges rolled in the distance.

Old ruins of a bygone kingdom filled the town's center. Obelisks and steles testified to the greatness of that kingdom. Still functioning churches proved its heritage remained intact even now. All of these structures were constructed of granite, some with a lot of ornamentation, others had none. One of the largest obelisks had fallen over at some point and now lay broken in several large sections like the crooked spine of an ancient dinosaur.

While the center of Ethiopia's holiest city seemed frozen in antiquity, it was surrounded by tin-roofed shanties and streets full of the throngs of people who kept the city alive with their daily activity.

Mark stuck out like a sore thumb in Ethiopia, but the number of tourists in Axum reduced his signature to the point he didn't draw too much attention. Ty, on the other hand, stuck out just because of his sheer size. He had dressed in a worn out T-shirt and slacks to blend in with the other local men. Though his skin color matched, his bearing, the way he carried himself, and the fit tone of his oversized muscles set him apart. He was as much a foreigner as Mark in the eyes of the people here.

The Chapel of the Tablet stood before them and many believed the Ark of the Covenant could be found within its walls. According to the Ethiopian legend, King Solomon's illegitimate son, Menelik, brought the Ark to Axum, which was once the capital city of the kingdom of Sheba.

There were two St. Mary of Zion churches, one on either side of the chapel. The older one was adjacent and much closer. It held Ethiopia's most treasured and holiest relics.

The Chapel of the Tablet itself wasn't much to write home about architecturally. It was a small, square building built of granite blocks. Each side of the building had a pair of double windows covered in a decorative blue iron work and surrounded by yellow and green trim. Only one side of the chapel offered an entrance to the building. On the other three sides, the space between the windows had been filled in with stacks of lighter grey stones. Each side sported a small decorative arch at the top center of its facade, and a small spherical dome could be seen coming up from the center of its roof.

There was a basement level built with a much less ornament, but it was only accessible from the rear. From that side, the squarish upper Chapel looked like the second floor of a larger building. From the front, it was the only portion of the building visible above ground.

A high priest lived within its walls and was the only person allowed into the room which contained the Ark. Other priests could enter the courtyard, but they could not go into the Holy of Holies without being killed. Others, even young boys, could enter the courtyard to perform general maintenance on the building and its grounds. The high priest, however, was the only one allowed to see the Ark and he could never leave the grounds. He would not name a successor until on his death bed.

The security around this squat building was pitifully small if indeed it contained what was perhaps the most sacred relic in the history of all mankind. A ragtag group of guards armed with automatic weapons were stationed outside the flimsy, iron fence which separated the Chapel courtyard from the public. These guards were a relatively recent addition to the building's security.

Mark and Ty lounged in a couple of stiff-backed wooden chairs in front of what passed for a sidewalk café in Axum. It was really just a small neighborhood shop which had a couple of chairs and served coffee.

"Doesn't look like much, does it?" Ty asked.

"It's definitely the best looking building around. The church over there's bigger, but not as well taken care of." Mark pointed at the large dome of the newer, larger St. Mary of Zion church.

"How in the world are we going to prove if the Ark is in there or not?"

"What?" Mark laughed. "You don't think a bribe would work?"

"I tell you what, these people are clearly sincere and passionate about their city and their Ark tradition. The security may be light, but they probably don't need much. If word got out some foreigner broke into that chapel, I have a feeling there'd be a mob of angry citizens to answer to in no time."

Mark nodded. "Yeah, they believe the Ark is in there. That's for sure."

He paused. "The Chapel of the Tablet was built sometime in the late 1940's or 50's to house the Ark by Emperor Hailie Salassie. So, there wouldn't be anything here in the 1930's. I thought we could just shift back to that decade, walk over to where that Chapel would be, and then shift forward to the present to see what they've got inside."

"Why not just barge in right now and shift out before the mob forms?"

"Something about that makes me nervous."

"What's the matter, Mark? What could make you nervous? I thought you didn't believe in God."

"Never said that. Never said *that*. Sure...sometimes I'm not sure He's there. If He is, I've got a few bones to pick with Him. What I've never liked is your talk about fate."

"It *is* scary, the idea of seeing the Ark in person," Ty said. "If it is in there, and if it is what the Bible says it is, and if nothing's changed in the past three thousand years, we could be killed by God Himself for the intrusion."

"I'd almost welcome that sometimes." Mark's face darkened. "That's a lot of 'ifs' by the way."

"Maybe. For me, the only real 'if' is if it's in there and not something else. I believe the Ark is what the Bible says it is, and I don't believe it's powers would have changed."

Mark looked skeptical. "So, if it's in there, then we're going to die for sure?"

"I'd think so."

"All right...So, why don't you go in, Ty? It'd be dumb to put both of us at risk. If you don't come back, I'll shift back and warn you not to do it."

"Thanks," Ty muttered.

"No, seriously. We know *you* can't die."

"And just how do we know that?"

"Because Rialto kills you in the future, remember, and I haven't been able to undo it. That means you can't die yet."

"Doesn't the fact that I'm killed in the future prove the Ark isn't in there? Because if it was, I'd be killed during this plan."

"We won't know unless we try. Maybe you'll bounce off when you try to shift in, like we do when we try to go too far into the future. Or when I tried to save Lincoln."

"I thought you didn't believe in all that fate stuff."

Mark clenched his jaws.

"Who knows," Ty added. "Maybe it *is* in there. Maybe I don't die because I'm a Christian."

"Fine. Forget it. I'll go."

"No, no," Ty laughed, "I'll go. I'm just giving you a hard time."

"Well, don't. It isn't funny."

***

The high priest of the Chapel of the Ark in Axum took regular strolls out of the stone building, but he never left the grounds or passed the limit imposed by the wrought-iron fence. One had to imagine being cooped up in such a small space for your entire life would be difficult unless aided supernaturally.

These outings of his were probably just to get some fresh air and see something of other people if nothing else.

Mark and Ty had carefully noted a time when the high priest left the sanctuary and stayed outside for more than twenty minutes. That should be enough time for Ty to look around without being disturbed.

They had done more research too. The Ethiopian word for the Ark of the Covenant was *tabot*, and most Ethiopian churches had a replica of the Ark which contained wooden or marble tablets representing the Ten Commandments given to Moses and stored inside the Ark. The problem which plagued students of the Ethiopian Ark theory was that *tabot* was also the word used for the tablets on which the commandments had been carved. In fact, the technical name in Ethiopia for the chests which contained the tablets was actually *manbara tabot*. Therefore, no one knew for sure if it was the Ark itself inside that Chapel, or just a replica of the stone tablets given to Moses.

Ty was about to find out first hand.

He shifted back to 1930. Looking around, he was surprised to see not much had changed in Axum over eighty years. It was slightly less colorful now. The Coca-Cola signs had disappeared along with all the other modern advertising posters that would be pasted on storefronts in the future. The most glaring difference was the absence of the Chapel and the large dome belonging to the modern Church of St. Mary of Zion.

Ty made his way over to the empty lot where the Chapel would stand. The day was ending. It was late in the afternoon and any people left in the streets were busy heading home. The ancient and smaller Church of St. Mary of Zion stood resolutely to his right. It was the current home of the holiest Ethiopian *tabot*.

Ty centered himself in the empty lot, mentally recalling roughly where the Chapel would stand. He shifted forward to 2014, to one minute after the high priest had left the building for a stroll around the grounds.

The difference in floor height caused Ty to stumble as he shifted in. He found himself inside an ornate chapel draped in antiquity like many of the alcoves found in some of the more prestigious Catholic cathedrals. The walls were a deep burgundy. Golden relics, cups, trinkets, and other treasures dotted small shelves on each wall. Censers filled with burning incense rose from each of the four corners of the room, hung from golden chains which ran to the ceiling.

He was surprised to see a golden Menorah to his left. On his right was a golden table covered with a number of flattened loaves of bread. In front of him stood a small golden table, an altar of sorts, which held some burning coals. The strong fragrance of incense wafted up from it as well. Beyond the golden altar of incense was a doorway covered by a burgundy veil. Just like the Holy of Holies.

Ty saw nothing in this outer room which resembled the Ark. A spiral staircase in one of the front corners by the entrance led to the basement level and something lay beyond the burgundy veil. Those were the only two places it could be.

He guessed the lower level housed the high priest's living quarters and anything of real interest lay beyond the veil.

A sudden and unexpected feeling of dread and fear washed over Ty as he reached for it. What if he were about to intrude on God's holy sanctuary?

Chapter 10

"We say we waste time, but that is impossible. We waste ourselves."

- Alice Bloch

A group of middle-aged women draped in white shrouds hustled by as Mark waited. He tapped his foot nervously on the chipped concrete. Time could stretch itself out mercilessly when you were waiting for something, especially if you were waiting on some*body*.

Ty was taking entirely too long. He had a shifter. He should not have been gone for more than just a few seconds unless something had happened.

He was just about to stand up when he saw his friend's large, familiar form moving toward him through a crowd of people. Ty's expression was neutral, unreadable.

"So?" Mark asked.

Ty shook his head. "It's not the Ark."

Mark sensed something move behind him.

He twisted sharply in his chair in response. The shopkeeper had leaned forward, a look of concern etched on his dark, wrinkled forehead. With all the tourists around, he must have picked up a little English over the years and was trying to listen more closely.

"Let's take a walk," Mark suggested.

Ty agreed and they moved off.

"What did you see?"

"The outer room of the Chapel is very interesting. It's set up in the same way Solomon's Temple was and even had replicas of all the same furniture."

"But no Ark?"

"Not in that room, but there was a smaller room beyond the main room, separated by a thick veil. Again, just like the Jewish Temple. And I did see *an* ark when I peeked behind the veil."

"A peek was enough? How can you be sure it's not the real one?'

"Because the Ark behind that veil isn't solid gold like the Ark of the Covenant. This one's made mostly of gold, but it has numerous small sections of inlaid marble as well. It's also got crosses of all sizes carved in both the gold and the marble. The Ark of the Covenant would not have any crosses on it. Nor any marble for that matter."

"Very true."

"Also, the cherubim on top of the lid didn't look quite right. If I remember right, on the real Ark, the cherubim were beaten into shape out of a single piece of solid gold. And their wings were touching on the real Ark. These angels looked like they'd been formed from various pieces of metal, and there's a space of about a foot between their wings. We can check to be sure when we get back to headquarters."

"Forget that, we'll check on it before we leave Axum. I don't want to have to fly back here a second time."

A soccer ball rolled to a stop at Ty's feet. He picked it up and tossed it back to some kids playing in a vacant lot.

"Even if I'm wrong, there's still the issue of the crosses."

"What if they did have the Ark originally, but Rialto took it years ago and what you saw was a replica they made to cover up the theft?"

"The ark I saw looked pretty old."

"How can gold look old? And what if Rialto stole it hundreds of years ago? For that matter, he could have even taken it a thousand years ago."

"Do you really think that if we can't stop the Lincoln assassination, God is going to let Rialto steal the Ark of the Covenant before He's ready? Doesn't make sense."

Mark spewed a puff of air through pursed lips in disgust. "Ty..."

"Okay, fine. Look, even if Rialto stole it from the Ethiopians a long time ago, they would have known what the original looked like. Why would they add marble and crosses to the replica? Why wouldn't they imitate the original as closely as possible?"

"Okay, I guess you're right." He pulled out his cell phone. "Let's see what Savannah thinks."

After a few rings, she picked up. "Hello?"

"Hey, it's Mark." He explained to her what they'd discovered. "So, what do you think?"

She thought silently for a moment. "I'll run it by Professor Rosenberg, but I think Ty's right."

Mark pinched the bridge of his nose between thumb and forefinger. "How exactly are you going to run it by Rosenberg without telling him about our special watches?"

"Oh...yeah. Well, I'll find a way," she replied cheerily.

"Fine. We're gonna go ahead and head back to the airport here. Call me if Rosenberg has anything unexpected to add."

"Sure, Mark. Be safe."

"Bye."

He hung up and turned back to Ty, who looked like he was about to bust out laughing.

"What's that silly grin for?" Mark demanded.

"Nothing."

Ty tried to smother the smile, but only managed to tone it down to a smirk.

***

Professor Rosenberg had been non-committal in his assessment, which struck Mark as odd. Granted, they weren't able to share the nature of their technology with him, so Savannah had to tell him they'd learned of the marble and crosses from a friend of the high priest. Still, he'd been reluctant to declare the matter settled even if the account of marble pieces or crosses were accurate.

They, however, had no time to waste and Ethiopia looked to be very unlikely as a viable option at this point, at least from their perspective. It was time to follow the thread of the Templar Knights, the other candidate theory Rosenberg considered probable.

Mark and Ty rejoined Savannah and Hardy back at head-quarters. It was comforting to have such a secure facility to fall back on whenever they needed it.

Savannah had set up a large whiteboard on an easel in the large meeting/recreation room where they spent most of their time. Through extensive research, she'd uncovered as much as she could over the past few days regarding the Templars and the legends of the Ark, and now she'd prepared a presentation to get them all up to speed.

"The Templars are an enigmatic entity," she began.

"Hold it, hold it." Ty held up his hand. "What in the world does that mean?"

"Uh...mysterious. I mean, they're a puzzle, a riddle."

"You're going to have to dumb it down for some of us, Savannah."

Hardy jumped in. "Can't handle a little educated vocab, Ty?"

"Did you know what she meant?" Ty responded.

Hardy pressed his lips together.

"Thought so," Ty said.

"Shut up, both of you!" Mark ordered. "Go on, Savannah. Ignore these louts."

She'd blushed a light shade of pink, but took up a red marker and began writing a number of names, places and dates on the board as she spoke.

"As I was saying, the Templars are a *mysterious* organization. They were founded by Hugues de Payens in 1119 AD, around the time of the first crusade. They were unusual in that they were a monastic order — uh, that means they were monks — but they also considered themselves soldiers. The classic images of medieval knights wearing white cassocks with a red cross in the center are Templars.

"Hugues de Payens founded the order for the purpose of protecting and defending Christian pilgrims from Muslim attacks as they made their way toward Jerusalem. The Templar order was founded in poverty at its beginning and they initially relied on donations to survive.

"The first Templars were only nine men with no resources. They arrived in Jerusalem with the stated purpose of defending pilgrims and amazingly, King Baldwin of Jerusalem granted them the right to base themselves on the Temple Mount in a building that is now called the Al-Aqsa Mosque.

"Thereafter, strange rumors began to swirl around the Templars. They apparently spent much more time excavating underneath the Temple Mount than they did actually protecting pilgrims. Today's legends circulate around their diggings and the fact that soon after their arrival on the Temple Mount, the Templar order suddenly became very wealthy. They eventually became what is considered to be the first international banking system. Pilgrims from Europe could deposit gold with the Templars in their home country and the Templars would give the pilgrim a letter of credit, like a check, which they could cash with other Templars in Jerusalem.

"By 1300, the Templars owned great estates and castles all over Europe and were wealthier than any of the European monarchs. King Philip IV of France was so indebted to the Templars that he began a campaign to destroy them. He coerced the Pope into helping and had most of the Templars in France arrested and executed, including the order's Grand Master, Jacques De Molay. Templars in other countries fled similar but less effective persecution in their respective countries, but thereafter, the order disappeared forever from the pages of history.

"Other orders purporting to be the successors of the Templars popped up in several different places, but none of them had the power or wealth of the original Templars. Many scholars believe that many of the Templars fled to Scotland where they morphed into what is known today as the Masonic Lodge. Other Templars found refuge in Portugal and formed the Order of Christ."

Mark raised his hand to interrupt. "So, where do the legends with the Ark come in?"

"Well, most legends surrounding the Templar Knights pertain to *something* they may have found while digging on the Temple Mount, something which could make them suddenly and extravagantly wealthy. Some legends have them finding the Holy Grail, in others the treasure is a collection of scrolls damaging to the Vatican which they used to extort the Vatican for money. Some modern conspiracy theorists say the Templars found evidence that Jesus never died and married Mary Magdalene and that she bore his children whose descendants later became the kings of France and other European kings. They say the Templars, and later the Masonic Lodge, were protectors of this "Holy Blood" line. This theory was popularized recently in books like the *Da Vinci Code*."

"I remember Laura reading that book," Hardy said, "She told me a little bit about it."

Laura Kingsley was an ex-stripper that Mark had saved from a serial rapist. She and Mark had dated for a while, but she'd broken up with him and took up with Hardy for a few months. Her leaving Mark for Hardy had carved a deep schism between the two friends for a time, but that was all moot now. Rialto had recruited Laura. He'd given her a shifter and now she worked for him against all of them.

"From a scholarly perspective," Savannah continued, "books like the *Da Vinci Code* are a bunch of rubbish. Not only is there *no* evidence to support its claims and *ample* historical evidence supporting the contrary, but authors who write those books have had to seriously and *intentionally* twist and distort historical facts just to make their theories even plausible."

Savannah paused, her brow creased in concentration. "While all that is true, I've researched the Templars and their history thoroughly, and if they did find something on the Temple Mount, the most likely object would have been the Ark of the Covenant. None of the other objects theorized would have been hidden in the Temple Mount in the first place. Only the Ark could have been hidden there and only the Ark would have been hidden so well as to require years of excavation to recover."

"Do we have any evidence they did in fact find the Ark?"

"The evidence is mostly circumstantial. It's largely based on the fact that the Templars were originally poor, but once they set up camp on the Temple Mount and devoted themselves exclusively to excavating it, then they grew dramatically wealthy. What made them so wealthy? If it was indeed something they found under the Temple Mount, the most likely candidate is the Ark of the Covenant."

"That's the only evidence there is?" Mark was incredulous.

"Well, the Ark is *somewhere*, and we now know that somewhere isn't Ethiopia. Historical evidence seems to indicate neither Babylon nor Rome got a hold of it when they each destroyed Jerusalem, which can only mean that at some point in the past, somebody hid it.

"So, where would they hide it? The tunnels underneath the Temple Mount are the most likely place. And if it was hidden there, it's either *still* there or someone found it. If someone found it, the Templars are the most likely culprits."

"Do you believe that?" Mark asked.

Savannah stared at her hands as she laced her fingers together. "It's possible. Professor Rosenberg certainly thinks it's the most likely scenario."

"If the Templars got it, where could it be now?" Hardy asked.

"After studying the various legends, I've found four possible locations. Many believe it's near the Rosslyn Chapel in Scotland, others in some cave in the mountains of Languedoc, France. A lesser known possibility is a system of tunnels under Hertford, England. One of the books Professor Rosenberg gave me tried to establish the Ark was buried in the Burton Dassett Hills in England, though that author had the Templars digging the Ark out of Petra in Jordan, not the Temple Mount."

"I can see why the location of the Ark has remained such a mystery," Mark said.

"Yeah, but we've got tools no one else has had before," Hardy noted.

"Savannah, can you prepare some briefs for each of us?"

She nodded.

Mark stood.

"Let's get started."

Chapter 11

"All my possessions for a moment of time."

- Elizabeth I

November 14th 1891, Rennes-le-Chateau, France

The dark grey stones at Mark's back chilled him even through his several layers of clothing. Their dreary color matched the slate sky of this cold morning. What he wouldn't give for a steaming cup of coffee right about now.

The view of the valley below was breath-taking from up here in Rennes-Le-Chateau — at least it was on sunnier days when the vale was brightened by bluer skies. He knew because he'd already been here on a number of different dates in search of answers. Even facing the flat greyness before him, the sight was still impressive.

The valley lay long and pristine, undulating with endless rows of small hills and low mountains. It looked like it went on forever. He did not know his target, the Abbé Bérenger Saunière, but Mark thought the man must enjoy living here.

The village itself was humble. It was not much more than a smattering of old country houses that already felt antique now in 1891. Besides the homes, the community consisted of a few shops, a convent, and the church, which was clearly in a state of disrepair. No rhyme nor reason dictated the orientation of these buildings. It was as if someone had just thrown them down on the hill, and wherever they landed, there they stayed.

The resulting maze made hiding out incognito much easier for Mark. He was dressed as a peasant from late 19th century France, which basically meant his clothes were simple cotton affairs (but would have been linen in the summer). He had long johns under his shirt and pants, and a jacket on top of that. He'd chosen grey colors for his attire so he'd blend in even more against the ancient stone buildings and pewter sky. Between the color camouflage and his choice to appear as a man of low status, Mark hoped to remain as unremarkable as possible, which would allow him prolonged surveillance.

Still, Rennes-le-Chateau was a small village. The residents would easily know a stranger from a local. He could only hang out for so long before being questioned, and French was not a language in which Mark could claim any proficiency so he wouldn't be able to pass off a credible cover story. He needed invisibility.

Bérenger Saunière was the *Abbé* of the church of Rennes-le-Chateau and had been since 1886. A hundred years from now, his name would become legendary as the man who had possibly found the secrets and lost treasure of the Templar Knights. Critics claimed Saunière was nothing more than a con man who got rich selling masses. They claimed the legends about him were started by a local restaurant owner in the 1950's in order to drum up business. If so, it had worked. Rennes-le-Chateau became a major tourist attraction by 2011.

A couple of things were clear to any historian who researched the subject. First, Saunière was a Catholic priest who became inexplicably wealthy, even building a tower, which was more like a small fortress, on the precipice overlooking the beautiful valley behind Mark. It was designed to be Saunière's library, and there was no way he could have built it on his salary.

Second, this area was one of the prime candidates for any lost Templar treasure because the Templars had fled through this region in 1307 while running from the persecution of King Phillip IV of France. The Templars were rumored to have made their escape through these mountainous passes with a hoard of treasure, yet neither treasure nor Templars had ever been found or heard of again.

Third, Saunière had commissioned and installed some unusual and quite interesting decorations on the church of Rennes-le-Chateau, one of which was a Latin inscription over the door that read *Terribilis est locus iste*, meaning "Terrible is this place."

Those three facts were enough for many desiring to believe that Saunière had in fact found the Templar treasure and rehidden it. They viewed the strange inscriptions around the church and its grounds as clues, a road map to the treasure that just needed to be deciphered.

Critics, however, pointed out the gaping holes in the sparse circumstantial evidence.

Mark's mission today was to discover what Saunière had really discovered in the recesses of his church. The legend said that when he began restoring the church, Saunière found some parchments hidden in an ancient, hollow column supporting the altar. Mark had already popped in and out of Rennes-le-Chateau on different days and years and, with a little deductive reasoning, had determined today was the day Saunière would discover those documents.

Of course, Rennes-le-Chateau was not the only possible Templar stash. For efficiency's sake, Hardy had gone to England to investigate a couple of the other possible locations up there while Mark checked out the Saunière legend here in France, and Ty had gone to Jerusalem to see what he could find out about the Temple Mount.

A light morning mist wafted up and swirled in short-lived, tumbling curlicues as a lone, dark figure made his way toward the church. It was Saunière.

If Mark were able to speak French, his options would be more varied. Since he didn't, he found himself limited to surveillance for the moment. Saunière reached the church door, unlocked it, and disappeared inside.

Mark moved closer, careful not to draw attention should prying eyes be watching from a neighboring house. No one else was on the deserted streets. Mark walked to the rear of the church and stationed himself next to a stained glass window in the center of the back wall, which was the central window directly behind the altar. There was a small hole in the corner of the colored glass through which he could peer in unobserved.

Whatever else this priest might be, he wasn't afraid of hard work. He was apparently doing a lot of the restoration himself. His long, black cassock already had several thick streaks of grey stone dust smeared into it. Mark watched as the man flitted to and fro, moving stones and furniture here and there. After about an hour, Saunière crossed the sanctuary to the stone altar and placed his hands on its edges.

The altar was basically a massive stone slab resting on two squarish pillars. All of it was heavily worn, adorned by pre-medieval symbolism. It looked to be very old. With a tremendous effort, the priest heaved upward once and, amazingly, the heavy slab lifted off one pillar and began sliding down the edge of the other. Another push from the priest and it slid all the way off onto the stone floor where it struck with a loud, resonating boom, followed by a pluming cloud of mortar dust. That the slab survived the fall in one piece was only due to its thickness.

The slab now leaned against the short pillar farthest from the priest, making it lean toward him precariously. The priest got in the slab's center and pushed it fully upright on one side. Then, with a good bit of struggle, he walked it little by little until he'd moved it completely out of the alcove. He rested it against one of the supporting columns of the church.

Next, he returned to the short stone pillars which had been the altar's base. He approached the first one, squatted, wrapped his arms around it in a bear hug, and began walking it in slow half-circles over to join the altar's top. Then, he went for the second pillar.

Saunière squatted and wrapped his arms around this one too. Then, as his nose touched the pillar's upper edge, he suddenly released it and stood back up. Peering into its hollow center, his sallow eyes lit with a new light.

The priest reached his arm into the hole and withdrew two yellowed scrolls sealed with red wax. He reached back in again and fished for a minute before his hand came back up holding a glittering gold necklace fitted with large precious gems. Hastily, he shoved his fist back in, and this time it emerged with a loose ruby. He held the ruby up to the window's light for examination.

Mark jumped back. He thought Saunière might have spotted him through the window.

No alarm was raised, however, and the priest simply slipped the jewel into a pocket of his cassock. The gold necklace followed and then he was peering at the scrolls. Mark guessed the man would probably not open those here, and he was right.

All restoration work completely forgotten now, the priest examined the hollow in the pillar one more time to make sure he hadn't missed anything. Then, in a panicked afterthought, he hurriedly glanced around the church to see if anybody had been spying on him. Seeing no one, he checked the other pillar for loot, but didn't find anything else. Finally, he hurried toward the front doors of the church, both scrolls clenched in one fist.

Very Interesting.

Saunière *had* found a couple of scrolls in the altar, and they *did* have something to do with treasure. Now, Mark had to figure out if it had anything to do with the Ark.

***

Saunière was French, and that was Mark's biggest problem. He didn't speak French. The only way he was going to find out what was on those scrolls was to ask the priest outright. The language barrier was the first problem, getting Saunière to answer truthfully was the second.

For all his training in the Marines, Mark had never had to

interrogate someone using an interpreter. This would be a first.

He'd have to go to Paris to recruit someone who spoke English as well as French. And they'd need to be from this century. He wasn't going to bring someone back from the future and give away the secret of the shifters just to ask Saunière a few questions.

Instinct told him he should find a mafia type, some unscrupulous fellow from the dregs of Paris who would intimidate answers out of Saunière, maybe even rough him up some. Finding a 19th century French thug who was fluent in English might prove difficult though. Plus, the brute force method left no guarantee the answers would be truthful, and potentially, said mafia guy could come back later and rob or kill Saunière after he understood the level of treasure involved.

Perhaps there was a better way. A man Saunière respected, maybe an authority figure in the church such as a bishop, might be able to elicit the truth peacefully in the form of a confession. That was an interesting solution.

First, Mark would need to sneak a peek at those scrolls in person. He might avoid having to speak with Saunière at all that way depending on what they contained.

Saunière had a live in maid/caretaker by the name of Marie Denarnaud, so Mark had to wait until both of them were out of the house to sneak in and plant some tiny wireless spy cameras around the home. They revealed that Saunière had not been very sophisticated in hiding the scrolls. They were in the center drawer of his desk.

The priest had taken extra care to hide the jewels; he'd pried up a loose board in his bedroom floor and dropped them in the void.

When the house was empty again, Mark went in and retrieved the scrolls. He pried the board in the bedroom up, pulled out the two pieces of treasure and studied them.

The ruby was just a ruby. Albeit quite a large one. The necklace, however, was stunning in design and beauty. Mark was no expert, but he didn't think it looked thousands of years old. It was definitely very antique, but the style seemed too recent to be that ancient.

He slipped the jewelry into his satchel. In Paris, he'd find an expert who could help him decipher the scrolls and date the necklace authoritatively. If not, he could always pop forward to his home time and get a modern university to look at them. He'd return the items here in no time and Saunière wouldn't be any the wiser.

Chapter 12

The old man hunched over his desk looked like an ancient scribe in the flickering yellow candlelight. He studied the object intensively for a several minutes before he finally leaned back and sighed exaggeratedly.

"*Definitivement*, zees ees un anteequitee."

His accent was so strong, Mark could barely understand what the man was saying. Mark guessed some part of that had been English.

His blank stare prompted the old man to repeat himself. Mark got it this time. He was saying the bejeweled gold necklace was an "antiquity."

"How old?"

"Heh? Ah, *oui, Quel âge a-t-il?* Eez vuree old. *Pas plus que sept cent ans.* Eh — no more zan seven hoondred yeers."

"How do you know?"

The elderly antique dealer held up his eye loupe for Mark to examine the metalwork. Mark took it and studied the magnified image of the gold piece.

"See zeese marks, zees tooleeng vas not used unteel zee Meeddle Age. May-bee, twelve hoondred AD."

"Can you decipher the scroll?"

To get at the contents of the scrolls, Mark had had to break the red wax seals. He would melt new seals on them later so Saunière wouldn't know anything had changed.

One of the scrolls was a map of some sort. Mark guessed it was of the valley area surrounding Rennes-le-Chateau. That in itself did not match with legend.

The story spread by Noel Corbu, the 20th century restaurant owner, and others was that Saunière had found three scrolls, two of which contained genealogies of King Dagobert II, an ancient king of France. These legends mentioned no map and Mark knew Saunière hadn't found any genealogies.

The second scroll did have writing on it which Mark thought was Latin, but the letters were all run together. Regardless, he couldn't have made it out even with proper spacing. His knowledge of Latin made him look like a professor of French by comparison.

This antique dealer was supposed to be one of the best experts in ancient artifacts to be found in Paris during the late 19th century, which is why Mark had sought him out. He had not shown the man the map, just the second scroll.

The old man shook his head slowly after another quick glance at the ancient text.

"I am, *comment se dit*, no *erudit*. I no scholar. You moost take to zee uneeversitee *de* Paree. Zees ees Lateen, you vant Monsieur Gerard. He ees scholar een Lateen. Vuree intelleejent."

Mark rolled the scroll back up. If he'd made that out right, he was supposed to go to the University of Paris and find one Professor Gerard, expert in Latin. Good. He'd had about enough of this guy's accent anyway.

***

Professor Gerard was haughty and hurried for time, but his schedule opened up mysteriously when Mark offered to pay him in gold for a couple hours of it.

The Latin had been complicated by the fact it was not written in complete sentences, or even sentences with normal meaning. The scroll actually turned out to be a list of directions and distances, four sets of them to be precise. At the end of each set was a random word: horse, beehive, turtle, and triangle.

Mark guessed the list was to be combined with the map and would lead its user to four distinct locations on the map. There was a conspicuous black dot in the center of the map and he figured the directions and distances were to be measured from that dot. Dashed, arching lines at random locations were probably hills and other terrain lines. Once the general area depicted by the map was identified, finding the four stashes would be easy.

The distances were in roman *uncia*, which translated to "inches," and were obviously supposed to be measured on the map itself, not in actual distance. Mark had no idea what the words horse, beehive, turtle, or triangle referred to. They had to be code for something.

Regardless, the only part of this whole deal that was matching up with the legend so far was the fact that Saunière had found some scrolls and a little bit of treasure. The "coded" scroll was supposed to have been a code referring to King Dagobert II's treasure and some reformation era paintings, not the simplistic list Mark actually had in his hands. That combined with the dating of the necklace to the 1200's by the antique dealer left Mark skeptical as to the rest of the legend.

Mark shifted forward to the 21st century and made color photocopies of the two scrolls. He then reformed the wax seals as authentically as possible and returned them to Saunière's desk. The gold necklace and jewelry he put back under the loose board in Saunière's bedroom.

Let the priest keep his treasure. Mark already had more wealth than he could ever use.

Next, Mark compared modern satellite topographical maps of the terrain around Rennes-le-Chateau with the photocopy of the scroll map. After a bit of twisting and turning the papers and using different scales on the satellite maps, Mark found a pretty close match of topography. When he was finished, the black dot was centered right over the church where Saunière had found the scrolls.

This was far too easy.

Mark decided to follow the "horse" directional/distance set first. He plotted it out on the map in inches, and then programmed his GPS to take him as close as he could get to those coordinates by car. He walked the rest on foot. At the end of his little journey, he found himself halfway up a hill in the valley. He was on private land, but there weren't any farmhouses nearby, so he shouldn't be disturbed.

He slowly turned in a full circle, searching for some sign of what he was supposed to be looking for.

There was nothing. Nothing but rolling green grass and large, grey rocks scattered across the fallow field. He started walking in increasingly wider circles.

Finally, he saw the "horse." Mark's angle with regard to one of the larger rocks had changed and now it looked exactly like a giant horse head, ears and all. There was nothing unusual about it other than its shape. It wouldn't budge, and there was nothing else out of the ordinary nearby.

Mark shifted back to 1889, which was two years before Saunière found the scrolls. He wanted to see the site before the priest ever got to it. Now, next to the "horsehead" rock on the hillside was a pile of loose rocks. Mark began pulling the rocks out one by one.

The rock pile was deeper than it appeared from the surface. It continued below the grass line into the earth by about two feet before Mark found a large stone slab. He dug around the slab's edges and wiggled it until he had loosened it enough to get it free. The squarish, flat piece of stone was enormously heavy, but Mark managed to pull it out by himself. Behind the slab was a narrow, dark opening that led into a cave of some sort.

Mark pulled a Maglite from his backpack and scurried into the small tunnel. It immediately opened up into a larger cave which was about fifteen feet deep and almost tall enough for him to stand straight up. The deep, wet smell of old must greeted him.

A couple of rotting wooden chests sat against the back wall, their boards crumbling, loose, and bowing. The only thing holding them together was the rusted iron clasps and bands encircling them. Flashes of golden glint twinkled through large cracks between several boards as Mark's flashlight focused on the chests.

They were likely to crumble at his touch if he tried to open them, but he had no choice. He needed to see what was inside.

He tugged up on one of the lids, but it resisted stiffly. Slowly, he increased the pressure until it gave with an unoiled shriek. One of the hinges snapped, but the chest remained intact. Inside, it was filled to the brim with gold coins, a few jewels, and a number of other pieces of gold jewelry. The second chest was similar, but had a larger ratio of jewelry to coins. The coins were not consistent in type and looked like they represented a plethora of countries and denominations.

The necklaces, bracelets, rings, and even a tiara or two were unremarkable aside from their great beauty and worth. They didn't seem any older than the first necklace he'd taken to the antique dealer for analysis.

Mark took a couple of the pieces and placed them in his rucksack. He also scooped out a handful of coins, making an effort to get a fair representation of the different faces peering out at him from the golden piles and poured those into his bag too.

Then, carefully, he lowered the lids back down and crawled out into the afternoon air. He replaced the slab, covered the cave entrance once more, and piled the smaller stones back into place. Last, he slung loose dirt over the rock pile to restore its untouched image.

Mark shifted forward to the 21st century and drove back to Paris to have the coins and jewelry dated. This modern antiquity expert was quite animated over the fantastic collection Mark presented and insistent on knowing where Mark had gotten it, but Mark wasn't about to give away any more information than he had to. When the dealer saw that, he eventually gave up and just rattled off his analysis.

The coins were real gold and represented currencies from a wide variety of kingdoms, ranging from France to the Byzantine Empire to even Jerusalem. However, the large majority of them were French coins dating from the reign of Philip IV, the king who'd wiped out the Templars. Many of those coins were clipped, i.e. somebody had trimmed the edges off in an effort to debase the coinage. This had been a common practice during Phillip's reign and thus confirmed the authenticity of the coin collection even further.

The Templars had served as an international banking system for travelers. Pilgrims could leave their gold with the Templars in one country and retrieve an equal amount, minus a fee of course, from another Templar depository in whatever city was their destination. The wide variety of dates and regions represented in this coin collection indicated this could very well be part of the Templar treasure which was lost during Phillip IV's persecution of the warrior monks. A similar suspicion shone behind the antiquity dealer's eyes, which is why the man had pried so hard for more information, but he was more likely to get blood from a stone than a drop of info from Mark.

The bracelet and the ring couldn't be identified by region, but the tooling marks once again indicated they were fabricated some time between the 12th and 14th centuries. The idea that Saunière had discovered a map to the lost Templar treasure was actually looking quite true.

However, if the other stashes on the map weren't any larger than this one, the total *amount* of treasure might not be that great. And Mark had still not found any connection to the Ark of the Covenant, or, for that matter, even any artifacts dating older than the Middle Ages.

Chapter 13

One by one, Mark searched the other three locations. The "turtle," like the horse, turned out to be a turtle-shaped rock. At some point in the past, the "triangle" had been broken in half. In 1889, the pieces were separated by a couple of feet, but it was still identifiable. The "bee hive" wasn't just one rock, but a collection of tiny rocks in an odd-looking formation which had been shaped to look like a bee hive and fitted into the lintel of an ancient tomb as adornment.

In each case, the shaped rocks marked a cave or tomb which held or had held Templar treasure. Turtle cave and Triangle tomb still held their treasures. Both were similar collections of coins and jewels to those of Horsehead cave. He initially got excited about the find in Turtle cave because it had three chests instead of two, and several gilded swords to boot. The third chest contained a number of unique ivory sculptures. The antiquity dealer said the ivory pieces were older, probably from the 8th or 9th century, and had originated in Yemen.

Still not old enough.

The Bee Hive tomb had been robbed some time before 1889. Whoever's bones it held had long since returned to dust, and only a few rotting slivers of splintered wood strewn about the floor hinted at the chests that might have been stashed there before.

He was ready to give up on this particular thread to the Ark. More and more, he was becoming convinced the Templar treasure hidden in these hills had nothing to do with the ancient Hebrew relic. These treasure stashes were simply last minute repositories where the Templars had rushed to hide their wealth while fleeing persecution.

Still, the fact remained the Templars *had* hidden treasure here. He had to exhaust the possibility the Ark had been, or still could be, in this valley somewhere. The only way to be sure was to continue shifting back until he found a time when the Bee Hive tomb had not yet been robbed.

Further and further back he went. He grew increasingly uncomfortable the more centuries he crossed. For Mark, his shifter was a life jacket. If he got into a dangerous situation, he could usually pop right back out just by hitting that magic red button that would pull him home — or rather, to his home time.

However, the watch shut down for longer and longer periods the further back in time you went. It looked like he was going to have to go all the way back to the 14th century to find a time when this particular tomb had not been robbed, and that shift would make his "life jacket" unusable for somewhere between three to four minutes, which wasn't much if you're reading a book, but an eternity if an enraged knight is bearing down on you with a sword.

Which was exactly what happened when he decided to try a shift to 1308 AD.

As fate would have it, he wasn't alone when he arrived. An extremely agitated horse reared up on his left, legs flailing, terrified by the static electric hiss of the shift and the sudden appearance of a human whose modern smell was alien to a medieval stallion. Mark threw himself into a roll to the side to escape the sharp hooves seeking to crush his skull.

As he came out of the roll, he realized he'd finally identified when the tomb had been robbed. They were robbing it right now. Or...maybe they weren't robbing it. Maybe the treasure belonged to them and they were just recovering it.

When he arrived, two large men had been in the process of removing rocks from the pile around the tomb and whirled at the sound of the hiss and their horse's alarmed whinnying. They wore heavy brown cassocks split down the middle like robes. The ties on these "robes" hung loose, which allowed the sides to flap open as they moved, revealing their true attire underneath. White cassocks emblazoned with a large, red cross in the center.

They were Templars.

In this year, 1308, Philip's persecution was still in full force. So, the brown robes must be to hide their identity from a prying public. They'd apparently loosened them as they dug to expose their Templar wardrobe for the retrieval of their order's treasure. Perhaps a hastily-conceived, symbolic gesture.

The panicked cries of their steed had focused their attention on Mark like a laser.

"*Magie étrange!*" One of them yelled, waving his all too real sword in the air. "*Attrapez-le!*"

To Mark, the words were gibberish, but the aggressive rage in their faces was clear. Mark was moving before the second Templar could respond to his friend's call to arms, but before he'd gone ten feet, the second knight had pulled his sword.

Mark drew his .45 from the holster under his leather jacket. He'd been shifting to such a wide variety of eras, he hadn't bothered to change his attire to match the times.

He had no desire to kill either of these knights, so he aimed for the dirt at their feet. The explosive retorts of his pistol sent both horses fleeing from the scene at full gallop. Medieval horses were not only unfamiliar with the smell of modern man, they'd never experienced gunfire either.

Dirt sprayed into the faces of the knights as the bullets dug into the ground. The knights dove for cover in opposite directions, unsure what strange weapon they were facing.

This gave Mark the time he needed to scramble for cover behind a rock a short distance away. Panting to regain breath, he snatched the laminated "Shut Down" card he always carried with him from his back pocket. Bobby Prescott, his in-house physicist, had given it to him. It was a listing of the shifter shut down delays he could expect to face, depending on how many centuries he had crossed. He ran his finger down the list until he found the right line.

"Crap."

3.84 minutes.

He'd shifted seven hundred years into the past, which meant his watch would be shut down for 3.84 minutes, and he still had at least three of those minutes remaining.

He could hear the Templars whispering fiercely on the far side of the rock, though they were keeping their distance for the moment. They were speaking French and he could only make out a word or two, though several times he heard them mention "Philip." Well, *Philippe*, that is.

A loud and sudden war cry let Mark know these professional soldiers had finished whatever debate they were having.

Mark glanced at his watch. Still red.

"Crap."

Scrambling to his feet, he raced from behind his rock for about twenty feet and then turned to face them. They were wild eyed, determined to dispatch this strange magician sent by Philip the Persecutor.

Mark crouched and expended an entire clip at the ground by their feet. This time, they were, unfortunately, completely unfazed by his superior weaponry. Either that, or they didn't care if they were killed so long as they got a blade in him in the process — or maybe they didn't recognize the little splashes of dirt as being deadly — or maybe they thought Mark had terrible aim and wasn't a threat. Whatever they were thinking, he was not going to have time to reload.

For all the weight of their chain mail, these knights were unbelievably swift. It was all he could do to stay ahead of them. For a full two and half minutes, the Templars chased Mark in circles waving their swords menacingly in the air as he struggled to stay ahead of them. He checked his shifter every five seconds for a reprieve. He was starting to feel like he'd shifted into a bad Three Stooges movie. If Hardy or Ty could see him now, they'd be laughing their rear ends off.

Finally, his shifter's display blinked from red back to its normal transparent state and Mark's finger was on the button faster than a dog on a piece of raw meat.

And just like that, he was gone. He could only imagine their faces.

***

Most likely, the Templars had originally deposited that stash of treasure in the Bee Hive tomb in 1307 while fleeing Phillip. For some reason, they'd apparently come back in disguises in 1308 to retrieve it. But if so, why hadn't they cleared out the other three stashes as well?

Regardless, now that he knew when they'd come in 1308, it was a simple enough thing to travel three months prior to their visit and check out the tomb before they returned.

When he did, he just found more of the same. Chests filled with gold and jewelry. The only difference was that this stash had an extra chest overflowing with silver objects, a canvas bag full of brass utensils, and a few swords. Mark grabbed samples of each for modern day testing.

Once again, the results were the same. All were from the Middle ages, and nothing was unique. No sign of the Ark.

Yet, there was one last 't' to cross.

Chapter 14

November 15th 1907, Rennes-le-Chateau, France

The grainy afternoon turned dark as storm clouds rolled in. Mark hadn't realized it was going to rain today, but he wasn't about to cancel now.

The few inhabitants of Rennes-le-Chateau who'd been out were hurrying back to their homes ahead of the expected downpour.

Mark's agent slowly made his way down the cobble-stoned street. His black robes billowed against his sides amidst the growing gusts of wind. He was tall and unbent, almost regal in appearance. A bishop of the church.

Except he wasn't. He was a bilingual actor from a theatrical company in Paris. Mark had dressed him in the appropriate eccles-iastical robes and prepped him on what questions to ask — without giving too much away of course. Mark had already paid the actor a handsome sum to play this role today, and he would receive an equal amount if he performed to Mark's satisfaction.

Mark closed in on Saunière's home. He passed in front of the church and spied a white notice nailed to its front door. Icy pellets of rain brushed his face like cold, metallic fingertips. A chilling wetness pierced his scalp as the rain began to drip through his hair.

The notice was an advertisement regarding masses. He'd seen an identical copy of this advertisement and its translation during his research on Saunière. Many modern historians had speculated that Saunière's real source of wealth was the trafficking of masses, which was when a priest charged a significant fee to perform a mass on behalf of an individual, from which that individual was supposed to receive some kind of spiritual blessing. In other words, the priest would bestow God's blessing, but only for a price. It was despicable corruption like this that had provoked Martin Luther to launch the Reformation.

That Saunière had in fact trafficked masses was evident from notices such as this, as well as the ads he placed in Catholic magazines across France. Regardless, Mark now knew a good bit of the priest's wealth did in fact come from the Templar treasure. Whatever he'd gotten out of trafficking in masses was just extra.

But had Saunière found anything else besides gold coins over the years? Today was 1907, twenty years after the discovery of the scrolls, and whatever Saunière was going to find, he should have found it by now.

Mark's "bishop" reached the front door of Saunière's home and was let in by the priest. Mark waited out of sight along the side of the abode and pointed a directional listening device at the glass panes of a window in the sitting room. The device used a laser to pick up tiny vibrations in the glass created by sounds inside the room, including conversations.

He was recording the conversation for later translation. When he received the translated transcript later, it would read:

"...sorry, who did you say you are again?"

"Bishop Tournier. I have just recently been appointed over the diocese of Carcassonne."

"Oh. I had not heard of your appointment." Pause. "What happened to Beausejour?"

"It was quite sudden."

"Oh."

"Abbé, I will not waste your time. I am here regarding the unusual wealth you seem to have come into."

"That again? You are a quick student. At least Beausejour was patient..."

"What do you mean?"

"He at least waited several years to falsely accuse me. I will tell you what I told him. My income is from the performance of masses, just like everybody else."

"Abbé, I know you pulled two scrolls from a pillar in the church here. I even know what the scrolls said. One was a map of the valley, the other was a list, written in Latin."

"You can't know those things," Saunière hissed.

"Do the words 'Horse, bee hive, turtle, and triangle' mean anything to you?"

"How can you possibly know that?" he squealed.

"I know much. Yet, there is no need to fear. What treasures you have found will remain yours. No one will demand restitution or even know of this conversation. I am simply here to ask what you did find. I have need of knowing."

Silence.

"It is time to confess, *Abbé*."

"I...I found some treasure buried near a rock that looked like a turtle, okay. That's it. The bee hive tomb was empty. I never found the horse or the triangle."

The rest of the conversation revealed little more. Saunière's wealth had been a combination of what limited treasure he had found combined with his sale of masses. This was officially a dead end.

***

April 30th 2014, Paris, France

Mark met the actor back in Paris and paid him the rest of what Mark had promised. Then, he shifted forward to 2014.

He contemplated staying in Paris for a day or so to recoup. The weather was beautiful, he was tired. It was a pleasant city.

After the bone-chilling rain of Rennes-le-Chateau in November, the warner April climate and the green grass under his feet were a welcome change. He stood in the long Champ de Mars park, facing the immense Eiffel tower and listening to the antiphonal song of several birds in a nearby tree.

Mark sat on a bench and let the warm sun soak into his skin. He decided to check in back at headquarters and see what was going on. Let them know his plans. Savannah answered.

"Hey, Savannah. Any news?"

"Yes, actually." Her voice was soft, soothing in its familiarity. "Ty called in, said to cancel whatever you were doing and meet him in Jerusalem."

"In Israel?"

"Is there another Jerusalem?"

He laughed. "Right. Stupid question. Did he say why?"

"He said to tell you you'd see why when you got there. He didn't want to elaborate over the phone."

"Okay — have you heard anything from Hardy?"

"Not yet."

"All right. When he checks in, tell him to meet us out there too."

It looked like his few days in Paris would have to wait.

Chapter 15

Hertford, England was gloomy. Perhaps on a sunny day it would have a different feel, but today the flat grey skies overhead draped a deadened pallor over the whole town. Like it could rain any second, yet wouldn't give you the satisfaction of actually doing it.

It was an old town, full of history. Hardy had taken time to grab a beer at a sidewalk café. He'd inquired with the waiter and several passers-by about local lore, but hadn't had any luck.

So far, all he knew was limited to what Mark and Savannah had told him. In 1307, when Philip IV's persecution began, the Templars fled Europe and their enormous hoards of treasure were lost in the sands of time. That treasure had been hidden somewhere, of that there was no doubt.

They'd had it. No one had found it. Ergo, it was still out there waiting to be found.

Mark had tasked Hardy with exploring two of the prime candidate sites for the Templar's golden stash, Rosslyn Chapel in Scotland and Hertford, England. Hardy had decided to explore Hertford first.

In the early 14th century, the Templars had large holdings in Hertfordshire, England, and it could be argued that Hertford was one of their centers of operations at the time. It was also well known the Templars had constructed an extensive labyrinth of tunnels, centered around Hertford Castle, which extended in all directions under the town. In 1309, the King of England, Edward II, imprisoned four Templar knights in Hertford Castle, convinced they were hiding much treasure somewhere in the tunnels.

Unlike Philip IV, Edward II never persecuted the Templars with the fervor of his counterpart in France. In fact, the imprisonment of these four knights was one of the rare instances when he actually arrested some of them, which spoke to how strongly he felt they were hiding something. He believed they'd buried a casket filled with gold, silver, and jewels somewhere near the castle.

Edward II had never found the treasure, but Hardy Phillips had an advantage the King of England never had.

Hardy took a short walk around the town square, observing details regarding the layout. He knew the names of some of the streets and other locations associated with entrances to the tunnels, but how far he could get in modern times would be limited.

Since 1309, even the general layout of the streets had changed. Houses and buildings had been erected, torn down, and erected again. Tunnels underneath could have been added, blocked off, or even filled in.

He decided he would travel back to 1307, the year the persecution began in mainland Europe and follow the Templars as they began stashing their hoard. That would be easier than a hit or miss search in the tunnels today.

Hardy began searching for a quiet corner where he could shift unnoticed.

***

Randall Cook hacked the phlegm from the back of his throat and spat onto the sidewalk. A middle-aged woman walking by saw him. She shriveled her face in disgust, hurrying to get out of the sailor's sight.

Randall had not been able to relax ever since Carpen and Phillips had yanked him out of the 19th century and shoved him face first into the modern world. He was thankful Rialto had taken him under his wing, and even more grateful the man had given him a shifter, but Cook still preferred the simpler life he'd known in the royal navy.

The dirty looks he used to get from the more genteel class two hundred years ago had been bad enough. A sailor was frowned on in any century, but now in the 21st century, everybody had their nose up in the air at him. Making him feel uncouth seemed to be their favorite past time.

In this time, everybody took *baths* — or showers as they called them — and they took them *every day*. These people smelled unnatural. They reeked of perfumes, colognes, lotions and balms, or not at all. In his opinion, a man should smell like God intended, and you should know he was coming before you saw him.

Rialto insisted Cook participate in this stupid "shower" ritual every morning, and he gave in, not because he liked it, but because Rialto would kill·him if he didn't. Rialto viewed him as highly expendable and Cook had no doubt he would replace him at the drop of a hat. Rialto also insisted he keep himself groomed nicely. He was required to keep his hair trimmed and wear freshly laundered clothes every morning.

The result was atrocious. The man in the mirror was a man Randall Cook had trouble recognizing. Just the sight of it made him want to go get drunk. It felt like he was putting on airs. Still, he had to do it. Rialto said he had to blend in with the rest of the people in the 21st century.

It must be working because Hardy Phillips sure hadn't noticed him as he walked by.

Rialto had somehow gotten a hold of the flight plan for ChronoShift's corporate jet. After that, it had been a snap to intercept Phillips once he landed in London, but Cook's orders were to follow, not attack. He *was* somewhat surprised that Phillips hadn't spotted him yet.

He'd lost some weight too since Phillips had last seen him and that probably helped as much as the short hair and clean clothes. Cook couldn't stand 21st century food. It was either tasteless, fake, or too sugary. Even the ale had something off about it, not to mention being too watered down. He avoided food as often as he ate it, except when he shifted back to the 1800's for some relief.

Anyway, that stupid, uppity woman had seen him spit, but Phillips was still clueless which was all that mattered. Randall followed his enemy down the street to his rental car.

Phillips withdrew a large, black duffel bag from the vehicle's trunk and ducked into an alley.

Randall stopped. He leaned back against a storefront, one knee half-cocked as he lifted a foot and placed it against the wall, the image of a man relaxed. From his pocket, Cook withdrew the small detector device Rialto had given him.

Sure enough, Phillips suspected nothing; he hadn't even activated his jammer. Cook's detector picked up Phillips' shift signature without a problem. The display said Phillips had gone back to 1307.

Why 1307?

Randall briefly considered asking Rialto to have Randolph DeCleary continue the pursuit instead since the former knight was more familiar with that time period. Cook had never been back that far himself and wouldn't know what to expect.

Nah, on second thought, he couldn't let Rialto perceive him as useless. His position was precarious enough as it was.

Rialto *had* given him clear instructions though. Before he used his shifter to follow someone across time, he was supposed to distance himself from that person's departure point. So, he would walk just outside of town, shift from there, and then return to this spot in the Middle Ages. That way, if he had to attack Phillips for some reason and then Carpen came along later to figure out what had happened to his friend, Carpen wouldn't detect Cook's secondary shift because it would have been done too far away.

Cook's main mission was to figure out what Phillips was up to. Once he'd done that, Rialto had given him permission to kill Phillips if he thought there was some way to do it without Carpen interfering. He hoped he could find a way to do that. He really did.

He studied the shiny paper card Rialto had given him. Rialto had called it a *la-mee-nay-ted* chart, though he didn't get what that meant. They'd taught him how to use it, though, and he saw that if he shifted to the 1300's, his shifter would shut down for four minutes.

Because of that, he decided to shift in a few hours before Phillips' arrival time. That would give Cook plenty of time for his own shifter to reset and get back into town before Phillips arrived. When Phillips did materialize, he'd be at Cook's mercy for a full four minutes. The thought made his mouth water.

Still, he would have to follow the man in 1307 first. Though once he understood Phillips' purpose, he could go back and get him while Phillip's shifter was inoperable.

He needed to get a change of clothes first — and grunge his hair up some. These 21st century pieces would stand out like a sore thumb back then.

Chapter 16

"A time to rend, and a time to sew;
a time to keep silence, and a time to speak"

- Ecclesiastes 3:7

October 17th 1307, Hertford, England

Hardy felt that odd, yet familiar, wrenching sensation as he almost shifted into the middle of a workbench. He found himself standing in the backroom of a medieval blacksmith shop.

Sharp clangs of iron on iron rang out from the front of the building where the forge was presumably located. He was alone back here for the moment amongst an odd assortment of metal scraps and other unusual metalworking tools. Thankfully, the shop had a back door which would allow him to slip out unobserved.

First, he unzipped his duffel bag and removed a long white cassock emblazoned with a bright red cross. He slipped it over his head and hooked a broadsword onto his hip belt. He tucked a dagger in the belt and switched out his socks and shoes with leggings and hand-worked leather boots.

He lifted the cassock, hung an Uzi on a specially made underarm sling and slipped a Glock pistol into a holster on the opposite hip, then let the cassock fall back down to conceal them. It was loose enough no one should notice. Lastly, he grabbed a leather pouch that would go over his shoulder like a rucksack. He tossed a Bic lighter and a couple grenades inside.

That should do it.

Hardy stuffed his old clothes in the duffel bag and zipped it up. He hid it under a sack of grain and some tools.

If it were discovered, it would not be a problem. Aside from the stitching on his clothes, there was nothing modern inside. If not, all the better. He'd retrieve it later.

He slipped out the door and into the street.

He sighed. It was still gloomy. More grey skies. He really didn't like this town. There was something off about it. Something depressing.

He had planned to stroll through town toward the castle looking for Templars disappearing into the tunnel system. Now that he thought about it though, that didn't seem like a very good plan after all. He could wander for years and not be fortunate enough to spy a Templar using one of the secret entrances. Still, what else was he going to do?

The castle was only a few blocks away. Hardy approached it confidently. A helmeted soldier stood guard at the gate, pike in hand. The guard was slouching, but when he saw Hardy's Templar uniform, he straightened as if someone had shot a bolt up his spine.

Hardy assumed an air of self-importance and blew past the soldier without acknowledging him in the least.

Crisp air cooled his skin as he entered the keep. A real Templar knight sat just inside the entrance way at some kind of a writing desk. He stood as Hardy entered, a puzzled expression creasing his visage when he failed to recognize the visitor.

"Salve frater, kan ich helpe thu?"

The greeting was a mixture of Latin and antiquated English. Hardy thanked God Mark had made him sit in on some of those Middle English classes a while back. Once upon a time, he and Mark had accidentally shifted back to 1100 AD and ended up saving a young boy named Robyn from a noose he didn't deserve. They had strong reason to believe that boy had grown up to be the famed Robin Hood, but they had never returned to know for sure.

That time Hardy had spent in the 12th century would now help him understand most of what was said to him here, but that didn't mean he could speak it. If he opened his mouth, his broken accent would be a dead give-away.

Hardy gently folded his hands together, as if praying. He closed his eyes and dipped his head in reverent greeting without uttering a word.

"Ah, thu spekest nat Engelisch, frater?"

Mark translated mentally. *You don't speak English, brother?*

Hardy shook his head.

"Ich see. Alors, ais-tu fué de France?"

I see. Are you fleeing France then?

He shook his head again.

"Alamanni? Veneto? Castiliano?"

Hardy didn't get the first two, but he recognized the third as a reference to Spanish. He knew enough Spanish he could probably get by. The Templars were a large international organization, so the fact he didn't speak English shouldn't alarm them.

"Bueno! Commo está, fermano?"

Good! How are you, brother?

Great. Of all the luck, this guy spoke Spanish too, and old Spanish at that. Hardy's modern Spanish wouldn't work after all.

Hardy lifted a finger to his lips in a shushing gesture.

"Perdoname, fermano. Está ayuso un voto de silencio?"

Forgive me, brother. Have you taken a vow of silence?

Hardy nodded, relieved the man had interpreted his gesture correctly.

"Benvenido. El señor del castillo está en Londres, pero buscaré al Fermano Lawrence. El le saludaré propiamente."

Welcome. The lord of the castle is in London, but I will get(?) Brother Lawrence. He will greet you _____.

Hardy hadn't understood that last word, but it had something to do with how he was to be greeted. The Templar signaled for Hardy to have a seat in a chair against the wall and scurried up the stairs to get Brother Lawrence.

Hardy's only chance was now. It wouldn't take them long to uncover his ruse and he needed to be inside the castle unobserved.

The most logical place for any entrance to secret tunnels would be near the stairs. He moved to the stairwell and ran his fingers over each stone searching for some kind of crack or loose rock that might indicate a hidden entrance.

Nothing.

The pattering of two sets of unhurried footsteps echoed from further up the stairwell. Hardy snatched a torch from the wall and moved to the center of the room. He hit his shifter, transposing himself to the dark solitude of 3:00 AM. Daylight would have facilitated the search, but doing so undetected was more important, and the best time to do that was when everyone else was asleep.

The torch's flame blazed with a low roar in the now blackened hall. He swung it in wide circles, looking for something that would stand out as being out of place. Glints of light reflecting off an iron drainage grate in the center of the floor caught his eye.

He moved to it and tugged up on the grate. It lifted easily from the recessed stone ledges that supported it. Shining the torch down into the hole revealed what appeared to be short series of stone steps descending further into the darkness. The first step, however, was a six-foot drop, which perplexed him. *How would you get back out after you went down there?*

Hardy leaned over the hole's edge and peered further inside, using the torch to reveal what it could. The steps didn't go very far before ending in a blank wall with a small semi-circular drainage hole in the center of its base.

If this was an entrance to the tunnels, there would have to be some secret release on that wall, but he wasn't willing to risk it. It could be nothing more than what it appeared: a drainage basin. There had to be another way in.

He stood back up and contemplated his options. In addition to the stairs, dark hallways led off in three directions.

A sudden, distant cough startled him, but it was the cough of someone asleep — or trying to fall asleep — upstairs.

He had no desire to go up there. Most of the sleeping quarters were likely to be on the next level, plus any entrance to a secret underground labyrinth would by necessity be on the ground floor.

Hardy moved into the center hall, the one that seemed most likely to take him to the heart of the keep. He passed several smaller doors along the hall and eventually came to a large two-story library. The library's walls were adorned with hundreds of small, diamond-shaped cubby-holes filled with scrolls and many straight traditional shelves lined in leather-bound books. A couple of tall rolling ladders stood at attention, ready to grant their users access to the books at higher levels. Four oversized study tables were the only furniture in the room. There were two sets of candles on each one.

Hardy lit all the candles, which basked the room in a warm glow. He would need all the light he could get.

Everybody knows there's always a secret passage in the library, he laughed to himself.

He examined each of the bookcases and scroll racks for some sign of an ability to move, but found nothing. He approached the large stone fireplace and thrust his torch inside the hearth. He stopped short.

Could it be that easy?

A small, metallic catch jutted out from the hearth's left interior wall.

The day's embers were no longer glowing. They'd been extinguished for several hours, so the lever should be cool to the touch, but you certainly wouldn't want to grab hold of it with bare hands if a fire was going.

He pulled it down and was rewarded with a solid click.

He fully expected the back wall of the hearth to open, but instead, the bookcase to his immediate left noiselessly swung outward a few inches. He pushed it open the rest of the way. A long tunnel lay beyond.

Hardy blew out all the candles on the study tables. No need to burn their library down while they slept. He stepped into the tunnel and swung the bookcase shut behind him.

***

Randall Cook watched Phillips bypass the sentry without a word as he entered the castle. Cook dropped his gaze to his own garments and cursed. He didn't have a Templar outfit he could use to gain access like that. He ducked out of sight and shifted forward to later that evening.

The night was enshrouded in deep shadows under a new moon with only the stars to witness his movements. The castle loomed large and dark in the inky black. Cook slinked toward the keep and tripped on a protruding cobblestone which sent him skidding forward, scraping the side of his face on the rough surface of its wall.

He cursed again and continued his creep toward the drawbridge. He finally stationed himself a few steps behind where the sentry had stood earlier that day.

He hit the return button on his shifter. The static hiss of Cook's shift startled the guard, who appeared right in front of Cook, exactly as planned.

The sentry tried to turn to see what was going on, but Randall slipped his knife into the man's spine before the guard could complete his turn. He clamped his hand over the sentry's mouth, and as the man collapsed limply, Randall guided his body silently into the moat.

Suddenly, something vibrated in his pocket. It was his shift detector. Phillips must have shifted to another time while inside the castle. Cook examined the detector's display. It showed three in the morning. He grinned. Whatever Phillips was after, he must be getting close, which meant Randall could soon finish the guy off. This was fun.

Chapter 17

Hardy found himself immersed in a system of endless tunnels that seemed to branch off in all directions. How in the world was he going to locate anything of consequence down here? It would take days to explore these man-made caverns, maybe even weeks depending on how far they went.

Thankfully, right inside the entrance to the first tunnel behind the fireplace, he'd found a pile of unused torches. The Templars probably kept a stash there for convenience. There also seemed to be other torches mounted on the walls sporadically throughout the tunnels which meant he wouldn't have to worry about losing his light.

He wandered for about twenty minutes or so and ran into several dead ends before encountering anything besides tunnels. He emerged into a large, circular room which had more tunnels running out of it in so many directions, it was like spokes on a wheel.

A thick stone ring in the center of the room looked big enough to be some kind of well. Strange carvings and paint markings filled the top foot of space near the ceiling all the way around the walls like a medieval, decorative border.

From deep within one of the tunnels, an orange light glowed.

Torch light.

Someone else was down here with him.

Quickly, Hardy dropped his torch to the ground and stamped it out.

In the darkness behind him, a foot scraped against a loose rock. Hardy snapped his head around and slipped away from where he'd thrown the snuffed out torch.

Someone else was in the room. Someone who had followed him without the aid of a torch for light. From the sound of it, they were about fifty yards back.

He would have to handle this without the help of his shifter. It was dangerous to shift underground.

He moved to the wall adjacent to the lit tunnel and peered

around its corner. Two Templars stood about a hundred yards down, and one carried a torch. Their attention was fixed on the tunnel wall they were facing.

Was the man behind him a Templar too? If so, why was he following so discreetly without raising the alarm?

Hardy's eyes were adjusting to the dark at a painfully slow rate. Noiselessly, he circled the room until he reached a position right beside the tunnel that led back to the library. He kept his back to the wall the entire way.

He drew still.

And waited.

Whoever it was, they were still in the library tunnel and taking their sweet time coming out. They had to have seen him extinguish his torch and couldn't know where he was at the moment.

Another brush of a foot against stone, this time much closer.

At last, he sensed a shadow passing by in front of him as somebody cautiously emerged. He could barely make out the form of a head in the dim, residual light coming from the opposing tunnel.

Hardy reached out and clamped a firm hand over the mouth of his pursuer. He wrapped his other arm around the man's throat and yanked him backward and off balance.

The flash of a small yellow glow caught Hardy's eye as his victim frantically thrashed his arms up in instinctive defense. The glow came from his follower's wrist and matched a glow on his own.

A shifter.

It had to be Rialto or one of his men. Hardy instantly dropped his arm from the guy's throat and slipped his hand under the man's arm, leveraging it back into a painful Half-Nelson so the man would have no hope of getting his hands close enough to each other to activate his shifter. Hardy released his other hand from the man's mouth but swiftly pressed his forearm hard into the attacker's throat before he could make a sound.

The man struggled and bucked, but to no avail. Hardy's grip was firm.

Once the man fell unconscious, Hardy laid him gently on the floor, not so much from mercy, but to keep the Templars in the other tunnel unaware.

Hardy flicked open his lighter and held the flame close to his pursuer's face.

Randall Cook.

It figured. Of all Rialto's men Hardy could have gotten the

jump on, Cook was probably the easiest. The former sailor had no formal training. He was just a crude, strong brute.

This was not good. Not at all. Somehow Rialto's crew had picked up his trail and followed him here. Who knew how many others were down here with them right now. Hardy needed to take serious evasive action right now to hold the rest of Rialto's men at bay.

The last thing they wanted was to reignite the fruitless shifting wars they'd been through recently with those guys. Rialto would have the upper hand in any conflict just because of his superior numbers. Mark, Ty, and he would need a serious advantage before they'd be willing to provoke another direct battle against those odds.

But first, he needed to see what those Templars were up to.

He untied the rope around his waist he was using as a belt holster for his sword and dagger and rolled Cook over onto his face. He pulled the sailor's hands behind his back and tied them securely with the rope. He'd just as soon kill the guy, as that's what Cook most likely had in mind for Hardy once he figured out what Hardy was up to, but killing the sailor would only assure Rialto would come to Cook's rescue. If Hardy left him tied up, Cook would eventually get loose and Rialto might or might not pursue.

Hardy crossed the room once more and felt around for his extinguished torch. He used his shifter to move forward 24 hours before relighting it, but when he shifted, he was sure to employ the jammer this time so neither Cook nor Rialto could follow with their detectors.

A day later now, the Templars were gone and so was Cook, which meant the sailor had in fact woken up and gotten away as expected. Hardy moved down the tunnel, trying to remember exactly where the Templars had been working.

The tunnel walls were built with thick, sand-colored stones graced by sporadic hues of rose. About a hundred yards down, Hardy found what the Templars had to have been looking at. A poem of sorts was carved into the wall.

THE SERCHER HÆR DORST WEL
FER THE WEL OF SOULES SHALE REVEL
ALE THATE WHECHE BITH DESIREE
TAKE SAUNS AVERICE AND GÆTH THINE WEI
ER CURSES TERRIBILES UPON THIE FEL

Sounding the words out in his mind, Hardy could make out the gist of their meaning. The word "sauns" threw him for a minute, but then he decided it must be a version of *sans*, which is French for "without." The word *desiree* was also French for "desired." From the sprinkling of French terms, he guessed the author was probably some Templar with origins in France. Still, who knew. Middle English was heavily influenced by Norman French.

> *The Searcher here does well*
> *For the Well of Souls shall reveal*
> *All that which is desired*
> *Take without avarice and go thy way*
> *Before terrible curses upon thee fall*

The Well of Souls? Why did that sound familiar? The poem had to be referring to some kind of treasure. The word "desired" together with the reference to avarice and curses must be alluding to some Templar stash.

The treasure must be down here somewhere. This was a Templar stronghold and King Edward II had been sure there was a treasure hidden away in these tunnels.

And so far, Hardy had only seen one well.

He hurried back up the passage toward the circular room. He peered inside the well with his torch and leaned over its edge to see how deep it was. Less than two feet down, it ended in dirt.

That was odd.

He pushed himself back up.

He examined the well more closely on all sides, looking for some kind of markings or writing, but the only markings in the room were the string of symbols lining the upper edge of room's walls. He leaned back over the well's edge and stabbed his sword straight down into the dirt several times. A real knight probably would have been horrified by this abuse of his blade.

About a foot down, he struck something that sounded like wood.

He laid the torch on the well's low stone wall next to him, balanced it so it wouldn't fall, and jumped inside the ring. Then, he began scooping dirt out with both hands. In just a few minutes, he'd uncovered several worn, wooden planks. Symbols were carved deeply into their surface. Symbols which matched some of the symbols carved into the walls of the room.

He spent a few minutes pushing the remaining dirt around to

make sure he'd found all there was to find. The symbols on the planks had an obvious starting point. In order, they read:

Hardy shone the torch around the room. Tongues of flame flared and flickered as he examined the wall more carefully. A number of the symbols were present on the wall, but not all of them. There was no bird, no knife, and no water. Of the ones which were visible, only the fruit symbol was not directly over a tunnel.

The most obvious approach seemed to be to first follow the tunnel underneath the tree symbol and see what he saw after that.

As he made his way down the passage, shadows melted before him in the face of his torchlight, solidifying again behind him as he moved. He passed several side tunnels and was encouraged to see each entrance was indeed marked by a small symbol carved into the rock over it. Above the third such entrance, the outline of a bird glinted down at him.

He turned into it and soon found another tunnel marked with the fruit symbol. Any question that he was on to something was dissipated by a dull grey wire he spotted halfway down that passage. It stretched from wall to wall about six inches off the floor.

A trip wire.

It had been dulled to blend in better with the flagstones beneath it and did not glimmer in the torch light. It would have been *very* easy to overlook if keeping an eye out for trip wires and booby traps hadn't been so ingrained in his subconscious that it had become second nature. Without his Delta Force training, Hardy might not have seen it in time.

What exactly would happen should that wire be tripped was not clear. Explosives were not something you had to worry about in the 14th century. Unless this was Rialto's handiwork, of course.

It was always possible Rialto had already discovered whatever was down this tunnel and rigged some nasty surprises in anticipation of Hardy's search.

He didn't think so, though. This wire ran to an eye bolt in the wall which definitely looked medieval in its craftsmanship. A couple of suspicious, inch-wide holes in the wall and a row of odd looking stones in the ceiling just past the wire loomed ominously. He didn't know what, but something bad would happen if he kicked that wire.

He stepped over it and continued until he found the knife symbol, and then the cross. In the tunnel marked by the cross, he paused before some unusual flagstones in the floor. They were raised up about half an inch above the rest. Again, lines of inconspicuous holes dotted the wall in sync with the strange stones. Every raised flagstone in the floor had an accompanying vertical row of holes in the wall parallel with it.

Hardy stepped back and examined the whole system. Images of Indiana Jones frantically running through the ancient temple in *Raiders of the Lost Ark* came to mind, poison darts spewing from the walls as his racing feet hit the wrong stones in the floor.

He retreated about a hundred feet before he found a loose stone on the floor he could use. He carried it forward to the first unusual flagstone.

Stepping back to what he considered a safe distance, Hardy heaved the stone so it fell on top of the curious flagstone. The wall to his right burst open in a shower of rock shards and splinters. An iron portcullis raced from the wall, slicing the tunnel in half and slamming into the opposing wall with a shudder. When all had stilled again, he moved forward and pushed against the grille, trying to slide it back into the wall from where it'd come, but it wouldn't budge.

It had been spring-loaded and some catch had been released by the flagstone setting it free. The slot in the wall from which it emerged had been coated with some kind of plaster that matched the color of the surrounding wall to camouflage it. Now that it was fully extended, some kind of locking mechanism had fallen into place so it couldn't be pushed back into its hole. There had to be a reset lever somewhere releasing the lock, but he couldn't find it.

It was ingenious. If the gate struck the hapless victim that set it off, piercing them with the sharpened arrows adorning its left edge, all the better, but it didn't have to hit the unsuspecting person directly to be effective. If they got caught behind it, like he was now, they were essentially blocked off from pursuing whatever treasure lay beyond. If they found themselves on the other side, they'd be locked in until someone let them out.

Hardy raised his wrist and shifted back two hours. The portcullis was now back in the wall, unreleased. He proceeded on, careful to avoid stepping on any of the undesired flagstones. If one of those gates slammed into him, his shifter wouldn't be much help.

In the tunnel marked by the sun, he spotted what he hoped was the last of the booby traps. The flagstones here seemed randomly uneven as if the mason who'd laid them hadn't cared for any kind of excellence in work.

However, the stones running along the walls looked normal, indicating there probably weren't any nasty surprises waiting to fly out from them.

No, the trap here would be different. Due to the unlevel nature of the floor, Hardy guessed there might be a pit below those stones supported by some kind of weak wooden frame that wouldn't be strong enough to support a man's weight. So, he stuck to the edges by the wall and had no problem.

The last tunnel, the water tunnel, was very short. He saw no booby-traps, no unusual stones in the floor, and this worried him.

The tunnel ended in an enormous, gleaming heap of gold and silver. Light from his torch danced in shimmers off the various pieces. Chests, chests, and more chests brimmed over with gold and silver coins. Other chests were filled with jeweled items. Gold and silver cutlery and other food service items filled the floor from wall to wall and between the chests. A narrow path wound through the piles all the way to the rear wall. The sheer amount of treasure here was enormous. It looked like a dragon's lair.

Ever mindful of unexpected traps, he carefully made his way through the hoard, eyeing the various items, inspecting them for some sign of the Ark of the Covenant. Everything he saw seemed to be of more recent, medieval production, not that he was an expert on dating antique utensils, but the Ark and any accompanying service ware from Solomon's Temple would stand out from the items he was seeing. Being at least several thousand years older, their style and craftsmanship would vary wildly with pieces from 13th or 14th century Europe.

Engraved in the bare rock wall that formed the tunnel's end was an inscription:

IN BENGEO HERTE
HÆR RESTE IN PART
HOLI FATED
AWEI REMEVED
GREAL SILVER SHADED

FRO STONCROS
TWOE UNDRED PASE
STEORBORD A TEIME AND TEIMES
HEVEN SHEUETH THE WEI

Hardy had not come prepared to take notes, so he had no way to copy the script down. He studied the inscription as closely as he could, searching for some less obvious symbols or scratchings. There didn't appear to be any.

The lines were some kind of verse, but as a whole, the message didn't make much sense to him. He'd just have to memorize it as best he could for now and come back later to make charcoal impressions if needed. If Savannah couldn't decipher it, he was willing to bet someone at Harvard could.

He began shuffling some of the treasure around. This stash was huge; much larger than he'd expected. It had to represent the majority of the Templar wealth in England.

Still, there was nothing that looked especially old or fit the description of any of the utensils from Solomon's Temple. He scoured harder, shuffling every stack tall enough to hide an object as large as the Ark, or another secret passage.

Nothing.

Hardy pressed his back to the wall, slid down till he was seated on the cool, stone floor, and let out a tired sigh. He'd actually gotten his hopes up with this little treasure hunt the symbols had led him on. The booby-traps had gotten his blood pumping, but the Ark was not here.

Savannah would hopefully know somebody who could translate that inscription once he got back to the U.S., but he'd have to check in first to see if Mark still wanted him to go up to Rosslyn Chapel in Scotland.

Chapter 18

With a quick slash of the hand, Alexander Rialto swatted a fly from the air. It had been annoying him for a while with its malevolent buzzing, distracting him from the task at hand.

"You lost him, huh?" he sneered at his hand-picked, 19th century thug.

Randall Cook couldn't stop the slight tremor that rolled through him under the pressure implied by the innocent-sounding question.

He did not like Rialto. The man made him feel like some deck swabber. Ever since Rialto had thrown him on that electrical pad just to test some equipment, Cook had understood his place in the pecking order. He was expendable — and that made him mad.

He'd been the purser back on the HMS Huntingdon. The Huntingdon's captain had even put him in charge of acquiring new "recruits." That had been a good life. He'd been free then, even if he hadn't had much money.

Here in the 21st century, Rialto treated him like he was barely good enough to take out the trash.

He missed life on the sea. He had half a mind to just walk away from this time travel business, but he couldn't. If he ever failed to perform as required, Rialto could set off some explosives in his watch with the push of a button that wouldn't leave much to feed to the fishes. And he couldn't remove the watch without lopping off his own hand.

Rialto had tempted him with unlimited wealth and revenge on those upstarts Carpen and Phillips. That was why he'd slipped on the watch. It had sounded like a dream, but it was really a nightmare, a trap, and he'd walked right into it.

Now, he was as good as Rialto's slave. His helplessness made him boil.

And there was something about Rialto that scared him to death.

Randall Cook had never been afraid of getting rough before. He'd bust a few heads sooner than take lip from anybody, but there was something cold and sharp behind Rialto's eyes. Something deep that seemed to grow harder and darker every time he saw the man. His chiseled features looked even sharper than when he'd first met him, like a knife poised to strike, only held back by the whim of its wielder.

A bead of sweat rolled down his temple, wetting his hair with an uncomfortable tickling sensation.

"At least you've been bathing and keeping your hair cut."

"That actually made me stand out more back then..."

"Are you criticizing my policy?"

Randall shook his head. "No," he growled.

"How did you lose him?"

"For the last time, he got the jump on me an' knocked me out. When I came to, he was gone."

"When did he shift to?"

"Don't know. He must have used his jammer."

"You didn't go back to be sure?"

"Uh..."

"No matter, if you had, you and Phillips would only have gotten into a shifting war, and you'd have lost. Your error was letting him see you. If you hadn't gotten caught, we could have set up an ambush or something."

Cook pressed his lips together.

Rialto sighed. He raised a cup of tea to his lips. "And you have no idea what he was doing back then in those tunnels?"

"No."

"Hmm."

Rialto contemplated what he'd learned, which wasn't much, thanks to this primitive goon. If he knew Mark Carpen, there was no way he could live with the threat of Rialto and his crew constantly looming over them. Carpen wouldn't be able to rest until he did something about it. Of course, the same went for himself. He could not accept the risk Carpen and his team posed to himself. One way or the other, this would end with the permanent elimination of one of them from the playing field.

If Carpen's priority was getting rid of Rialto, what in the world did a 14th century English castle have to do with it?

"Cook, you're done with surveillance. Get on the next plane to Israel. Hook up with DeCleary and Laura; they're already over there. See what you can do to help them."

"What about Phillips?"

"We'll handle Phillips." He paused. "And you'd better not

screw this one up. Clear?"

Cook grunted his acknowledgment and walked out.

***

After arriving in Jerusalem, the first place Ty went was the Temple Mount. It was central to all the theories regarding the Ark they were currently pursuing.

Ty walked its perimeter, as much as he could at least with modern walls and buildings not always cooperating with the ancient path.

The Western Wall was amazing. Orthodox Jews, and others of less devout persuasions, came here to pray, their heads bobbing incessantly as they made supplication to God in the place closest to the original Holy Temple available to them. Muslims still ruled the Temple Mount itself and it was off limits to any Jew who would visit for religious purposes.

Hopeful individuals scribbled prayers to God on tiny pieces of paper and stuffed them in whatever cracks they could find in the wall.

Ty stayed for a few minutes, watching a sight he'd only heard of until now. He felt at peace here, seeing the people of God worship their Creator. Even if they didn't recognize Jesus as their Messiah, Ty knew the prophecies and that it was only a matter of time before they did.

He moved on, circling around to the south. He bought a ticket to visit the southern steps area and found himself in an area littered with archaeological digs, most of which seemed to be inactive. Broken, crumbling walls and paths formed neat rows of narrow rectangles. A trained archaeologist could probably tell you what they had once been, but he had no clue.

A long, tall stone wall divided the area south of the Temple Mount in half and extended quite a way. It emerged from an ancient addition to the Al-Aqsa Mosque that protruded from the Mount's wall.

The only activity here was a small dig going on several hundred feet away from the wall. It looked like a bunch of university students were running it.

Ty walked toward them, curious as to what they were working on. It seemed so unremarkable, young men and women on their knees, dusting off stones with brushes, toting small pails of dirt to be sifted before being removed from the site. A few pottery shards were lined up on a rustic table.

One bronze-skinned youth had apparently taken a break and was relaxing with his back against a knee wall, Coke in hand.

"Taking it easy?" Ty joked.

The man removed his dark sunglasses and lifted a hand to his brow to block the newly blinding sun so he could see Ty more clearly. He was older than Ty had first thought, definitely not a youth, maybe somewhere in his mid-thirties. The man flashed a quick smile.

"I've been here since dawn. These jokers," He waved a hand at his co-workers, "Just got here. They were up too late partying."

His Hebrew accent was thick, but pleasant. Ty liked him.

"Are you students at the university?"

"They are. Hebrew University, Institute of Archaeology. I'm their professor."

"Oh...sorry."

"Not a problem. I look young for my age." He thrust his hand out congenially. "Daud Zahavi."

Ty responded in kind. "Ty Jennings."

"Nice to meet you, Ty. What brings you to Israel?"

"Just touring, I guess."

"You with a tour group? I know a lot of the guides."

"No, it's more self-guided, you could say. I'm researching whatever I can find out about the Ark of the Covenant."

"Ah, the *Ark*...You aren't the first, and I sincerely doubt you'll be the last. Yes, the Ark *is* fascinating. Are you one of those optimistic individuals who thinks they're actually going to find it?" He grinned.

Ty blushed.

"Ha! You are! Sorry, didn't mean to make fun. It's just that if I had a shekel for every amateur I've met who thinks they're going to be the one to find it when no one else could, well..."

"If nobody believes it can be found, it won't."

"Touché. Have a seat, Ty." He patted the ground next to him. "You want a Coke?"

Ty nodded and sat. Zahavi got up, fetched a soda from a cooler nearby, and popped the top. He handed it to Ty.

One of the students called up. "Hey, Daud, can we take a break now?"

Zahavi cupped his hands and called back, "I'll let you know when your penance is done. And that's Professor Zahavi to you for the next couple of hours at least."

The students were sweating but they chuckled at the banter. Zahavi turned back to Ty.

"So, you want to find the Ark. Where have you looked so far?"

Ty told him about the Ethiopian theory they'd discounted, careful not to give away too much information, and their current theories regarding the Templar Knights.

Zahavi shook his head. "You're barking up the wrong trees, my friend." He took a swig from his can. "There may be something to the Templar legends, I mean it does seem like they must have found something up there while they were digging." He jerked his head back, gesturing toward the Temple Mount. "But they didn't find the Ark."

"How do you know?"

"Look, we know where the Ark is. We just don't know *exactly* where it is." He tilted his head quizzically, "Being a serious student of the Ark as you are, I'd think you'd know all about that. I mean, it's not a secret really. Pretty public."

Ty shrugged, but his eyes were wider than they had been a few minutes ago.

Zahavi turned his watchful eye back to his students. "Yeah, I guess if you've been listening to a bunch of Templar kooks, you wouldn't know. Ever heard of the Dead Sea Scrolls?"

"Yeah, don't know much about them."

Zahavi checked his watch and stood, brushing the dust off his slacks with neat sweeps of his hands. "You should read up on them. Might change your angle of study a bit. Sorry, but it's about time I got back to it." He bobbed his head toward the dig. "Can't let these youngsters have all the fun." He held out his hand.

Ty took it but didn't let go immediately.

"I'd really like to meet with you when you've got more time," he said.

Zahavi looked reluctant. He withdrew his hand. "I don't mean to be rude, Ty, but I am pretty busy these days. If you'll give me your email, I'd be happy to send you a list of good books which would get you started."

"I'd make it worth your while of course," Ty assured him.

Zahavi nodded and laughed. "No need to pay me. If you're that serious about it, I'll make time. Just seemed like you were an amateur with those Templar theories."

He handed Ty his card and walked over to his students, jokingly chastising them for their slow work.

Ty moved on, Zahavi's words digging into his thoughts, upsetting his understanding of where they were going with their search.

Chapter 19

This is a song that nobody knows
I couldn't begin to describe how it goes

"When There's No One Around"

~ Garth Brooks

In Jerusalem, the most mundane of buildings felt sacred. The Old City was a lot smaller than Ty had imagined, and its winding, narrow streets whispered hints of ancient intrigue. This afternoon, as the sun inched toward the horizon, golden rays bathed Jerusalem's stone facades in a warm glow, oranges, pinks and yellows sparking from the undertones of the local limestone used throughout the city.

It was a city like no other. He could see why people fell in love with it, why they fought over it, why so many were inspired just by being here. It was God's city.

Ty had been dressed as a tourist, but now he'd changed to the attire of a Falasha Jew in order to reduce his "signature." He wanted to blend in. He rested in a chair in front of a tiny café, nursing a Turkish coffee. For as long as he'd been here observing, watching the flow of people come and go, a tourist with a money belt and camera draped around his neck would have stood out far too much.

He wasn't sure he was really looking for anything in particular, more just taking in the pulse of the city and thinking.

He'd done some limited research after his conversation with Daud Zahavi and was more intrigued now than ever, but he decided he'd meet with Zahavi again first before he called Mark. He needed to hear the Hebrew professor's full theory as well as his evidence.

In that moment, a passerby caught Ty's eye. He was a large, tall, blonde-haired man. Too old to be an international student and he walked with rigidity foreign to any tourist. Everything about him screamed military. And he looked familiar. Very familiar.

Something clicked in his mind. It was Randolph DeCleary.

DeCleary was *here*.

Now.

Ty tensed, instantly alert for unseen threats. He discreetly swiveled his head, checking his six for any sign of an ambush. Was he being followed by Rialto's team or was this purely coincidental?

Ty had taken every precaution at the hotel and in his wanderings to avoid detection, and he should have spotted someone following him. He knew what to look for.

Was DeCleary here looking for the Ark too? If so, there had to be others.

He watched the out-of-place medieval knight tug in annoyance at the collar of his polo shirt as if it were no better than sandpaper against his skin. Green shirt, khaki pants. Easy enough to keep an eye on.

Once DeCleary turned out of sight into one of the winding side streets, Ty stood and laid fifteen shekels down on the table, nodding to the merchant so he would see the payment. He marked the time and moved off in the opposite direction from DeCleary.

He wasn't about to follow any of Rialto's men on his own. The situation screamed ambush. He needed back-up. Calling Mark could no longer wait.

***

Ty shook hands with his friends as they met him in the parking lot of the Ben Gurion airport. It felt like an eternity since he'd seen them, though it hadn't been really that long ago, at least for him. He'd been on mission for four days now, but it had been a week for Hardy, and almost a month for Mark.

The marvels of time travel. He wondered if these time disparities weren't throwing off some internal clocks they weren't even aware they had.

"How's it going, guys?" Ty smiled.

"*Tres bien*," Mark replied.

"*Icham goed.*"

"You haven't gotten any better at Middle English, have you?" Ty asked. Hardy's imitation of the extinct language was horrible.

Hardy shook his head ruefully, trying not to crack a smile, and tossed his bags in the back of Ty's rented SUV. They'd already made arrangements with a contact here in Israel for any weapons they might need, but they'd brought along some regionally-appropriate historical attire, similar coinage, and info booklets for different eras since they had no idea what years they might have to shift to.

"Good to see you, Ty," Mark said, "Fill us in."

"I may have a new lead on the Ark, but the bigger issue is that DeCleary's here in Jerusalem. Saw him myself. Hop in and I'll give you the lowdown on the way to the hotel."

***

The cool night air felt pleasant on the skin after a full day of heat. Mark, Ty, and Hardy made their way up the pavement toward the stone and glass building which housed the Hebrew University's Institute of Archaeology in Jerusalem.

"Now, tell me again. Why exactly are we busting our butts to find this golden box nobody's seen for three thousand years?" Mark asked.

"What could be cooler than using the shifters to look for the Ark?" Ty said. "It's better than Raiders of the Lost Ark."

"Yeah, really," Hardy agreed.

"What did you do? Drink some of Ty's Kool-Aid?" Mark was incredulous. He rolled his eyes. "Oh, I forgot. You've been living with Abbie back in the 1600's. I can't believe you dropped your atheism for a girl."

"It's not like that, Mark. It's different — I'm different. Something changed me."

"Sure, sure." Mark's face tightened.

"You've been living with Abbie?" It was Ty's turn to be incredulous. "I never thought she would...I mean I thought she was..."

"...A good girl. Of course, she is. No, I'm not *living* with her. I built a cabin next to hers. Been hanging out with her while we've been avoiding Rialto. She's been teaching me."

"So, we're brothers now?" Ty grinned.

"Brothers." Hardy smiled back as they opened the door to enter the building.

"Congratulations, man. I mean it." Ty slapped Hardy on the back.

"We may be getting married."

"What? Wow! That's awesome!"

"Thanks, man."

"Yeah, congratulations," Mark muttered.

Hardy and Ty shot each other a knowing look, and Ty shook his head imperceptibly.

"Please tell me we're not just looking for this thing because it's cool," Mark said.

"No, it's for the same reasons you gave us when we started, Mark. Rialto's after it because he either wants to spark a war in the Middle East or to blackmail the United States. Either way, we have to stop him. Also, since we know *he* is looking for it, being on the trail of the Ark is the best chance we have of crossing paths with Rialto and putting him out of commission permanently. The cool part is just an added bonus."

Mark grunted.

"This should be it," Ty said.

A name plaque next to the closed office door read "Daud Zahavi" in muted bronze letters. They knocked and a muffled voice behind the door beckoned them to enter.

The archaeology professor didn't look the part. He was young and dashing, dressed in slacks and a hip dress shirt like he was headed out for a night on the town. Not the typical tweed jacket one would expect, especially after interviewing Rosenberg at Harvard.

"Hello, Professor Zahavi." Ty extended his hand. "These are my friends, Mark Carpen and Hardy Phillips."

"Please, call me Daud. Or, David, if you prefer. Let me get some more chairs." He left the room and quickly returned with two wooden chairs which he placed next to a third in front of his desk. "Sorry, I wasn't expecting anyone but Ty."

He sat behind the desk and folded his hands in his lap, leaning back slightly. The office was cramped, but modern in style. Full bookshelves lined every free wall and neat stacks of papers and manila folders topped much of the desk.

"Thank you very much for meeting with us, Daud. Mark and Hardy are as interested in the Ark as I am."

"May I ask *why* you're so interested? It can't be much more than a hobby if you're still chasing those Templar theories."

"Ty said you suggested we read up on the Dead Sea Scrolls?"

Zahavi wrinkled his forehead in concern, not missing Mark's evasion of his question.

"Well, I will tell you what I know, but I must warn you not to attempt any kind of a dig without getting a permit from the Israeli Antiquities Authority. And I must add, I don't think you'll have much luck knowing where to dig even then. Not that they'd be willing to give non-Israelis a permit to dig for the Ark anyway."

They waited.

"According to 2 Maccabees, which is part of what Protestants refer to as the Apocrypha, Jeremiah the prophet removed the Ark from Solomon's Temple before the Babylonian destruction of Jerusalem in 586 BC along with several other items of religious and historical significance.

"For centuries, scholars viewed that account as nothing more than legend — at least until the discovery of the Dead Sea Scrolls, that is. In the late 1940's and early 50's, numerous depositories of ancient scrolls were discovered in several caves surrounding an area called Qumran. During the Roman Occupation, which you would probably refer to as around the time of Christ, Qumran was inhabited by an isolated group of monk scholars called the Essenes. The Essenes had access to a lot of ancient documents which are no longer available to us, and these earthenware jars filled with their scrolls was a great boon to archaeology.

"Two of the scrolls, however, stood out as distinctly different from all the others. The most fascinating scroll of the two was made of copper, not papyrus. It was difficult to open at first — they were afraid of destroying it — but when they finally did and scholars got to read it, they discovered what they'd found was an incredibly detailed treasure map.

"This Copper Scroll describes, in detail, a long list of treasures that were secreted away from Solomon's Temple, presumably before the Babylonian invasion, and gives directions to find each item. It tells the reader how to find a silver chest containing the vestments of the high priest, the Tabernacle with all its treasures, and even the Ark of the Covenant. The sands of time have lost to us many of the place names mentioned by the scroll, but one archaeological team has successfully used the scroll to discover at least two of the many treasures listed.

"Another scroll discovered in 1950 is referred to as the Ibex Skin Scroll, or the Temple Scroll, which is a long and very detailed set of instructions as to how to rebuild the Temple of God and re-institute the daily sacrifices once the treasures described in the Copper Scroll are found. Both of these scrolls are clearly much older than the Essene community and all of the other scrolls found.

"Then, if that were not enough, in 1952, in the basement of a museum in Beirut, Lebanon, scholars discovered two ancient marble tablets which had been originally discovered on Mt. Carmel. The text on these tablets was carved in bas-relief style, just like the Copper Scroll. Bas-relief means the letters protrude outward rather than being engraved into the material.

"These Marble Tablets begin with 'These are the words of Simon the Levite, the servant of the Name, in the year 3331 of Adam.' The account goes on to describe how five holy men, Simon the Levite, Hezekiah, Zedekiah, Haggai the prophet, and Zechariah the Prophet hid the treasures of God in different locations in the wilderness. Then, the five men compiled a series of writings to lead future Israelites to the hidden treasures at the appointed time. The writings mentioned are the Copper Scroll, the Temple Scroll, the two Marble Tablets, and a Silver Scroll. The Silver Scroll has yet to be discovered, but we've got all the others. Haggai and Zechariah were significant enough as prophets that their writings have been preserved as part of the Bible.

"Still, many scholars felt there had to be more info out there somewhere and there was. In 1992, the long, lost writings of Rabbi Naftali Hertz were found. These writings are called the Emeq HaMelekh, or "The Valley of the Kings." Rabbi Hertz wrote these documents in 1648 in Amsterdam. He had access to some ancient versions of Talmudic tradition that have also been lost to us today. His writing, "The Valley of the Kings," confirms exactly the account in 2 Maccabees of Jeremiah hiding the Ark in 586 BC. The ancient Talmudic traditions he cites also confirmed the account of the five prophets stashing the rest of the treasures in the desert and documenting their locations and that of the Ark. He says they recorded the locations on a Copper Scroll, a Silver Scroll, a Scroll written on the Skin of an Ibex, and two Marble Tablets. Later, more ancient documents were found in Egypt which confirmed these accounts a third time.

"The bottom line is this: most scholars, at least those who don't have an anti-religious agenda, know exactly where the Ark of the Covenant is, because the Copper Scroll tells us."

Mark leaned forward. "And where is that *exactly*?"

"In the Cave of the Column by the River of the Dome."

"And where is *that*?"

"Good question. That's what I meant when I told Ty scholars *do* know exactly where the Ark is...yet we *don't* really know exactly where it is either. Nobody knows where that cave is other than it is supposed to be somewhere on or near Mt. Nebo and the valley of Achor. Jeremiah himself sealed the cave up and said no one would find it again until the time of the Messiah when God gathered His people back to Himself."

"What does *that* mean?"

"Those who believe say that when Israel is gathered as a nation once more and the Messiah has come, the Ark will be found."

"Well...Israel is a nation again."

"But the Messiah has not come," Zahavi countered.

"Some believe He has," Ty interrupted.

"Didn't it say until the 'time of the Messiah'? You didn't say till *after* the Messiah has come," Mark noted.

"That is technically correct," Zahavi agreed, "All the writings refer to the day of the coming of the Messiah, which means near or during the age of His coming, not necessarily after."

"I thought you didn't believe in this stuff, Mark," Ty commented.

Mark waved him off. "So, no one knows where this cave of Jeremiah's is?"

"No, not exactly. There are even some who think we've misidentified which mountain is Mt. Nebo."

Mark leaned back in his seat hard, letting out a sigh of exasperation. He didn't want to be pursuing this fabled treasure any longer than he had to.

"And the theories that the Templars discovered the Ark under the Temple Mount a thousand years ago?" Mark asked. "Those theories seem pretty credible."

"If the Templars found something underneath the Temple Mount, it certainly wasn't the Ark. Jeremiah hid it 1,500 years before they even existed. Who got you so turned on to these Templar theories anyway?"

"Professor Rosenberg of Harvard," Mark replied.

"Professor Rosenberg? Professor *Benjamin* Rosenberg?"

Mark nodded and it was Zahavi's turn to sit back in his chair. His face grew stern.

"I...uh...hmm." He looked puzzled and angry at the same time. "I'm not sure why he would...."

"Do you know Professor Rosenberg, Daud?" Mark asked, trying to soften the suddenly charged atmosphere. Zahavi had proven to be a treasure trove of useful information and he didn't want the flow cut off.

"I'm sorry, but I'm afraid we're going to have to cut this interview short," he said.

"Why?"

Zahavi shook his head. "Yes, I know Rosenberg, and...I'm just going to have to check on a few things before I talk with you guys any further."

Mark already had his phone out and was dialing. "Excuse me,

do you mind if I make a quick call?" He stood and slipped out of the office without waiting for the answer.

Zahavi's expression took on an added nervousness at the suddenness of Mark's departure. He stared at Ty and the other burly sentinel facing him silently from their chairs.

"What's that about?" Zahavi asked.

Ty shrugged. Hardy sat motionless, waiting. Their presence felt menacing to Zahavi now. All three men were strong and muscular, with an air of professionalism and discipline that came naturally to those in the military, or ex-military. There was plenty of room in their loose clothing to conceal weapons. He'd thought Ty was just your average American tourist, which is why he'd agreed to meet with him. The other two were a surprise. Now he found out they had been speaking with Rosenberg, which meant they weren't amateurs, and the look in their eyes was one of supreme confidence...and purpose.

He slipped his hand under the lip of his desk as inconspicuously as possible and pushed a button which triggered a silent alarm. Israel was a dangerous land where violence could be expected around any corner at any time. Every office was wired with extra security precautions such as this. Private security officers would already be racing toward his office now with weapons drawn. He just had to stall these men for about five minutes.

"I saw that," Hardy grinned.

"Saw what?"

"That." Hardy pointed to the desk. "You got a silent alarm under there?"

"Security will be here in less than two minutes, you might as well slip out now."

"It's all right," Ty smiled. "We'll wait."

Their calm confidence was unnerving. Very unnerving. Mark returned to the room just as the phone on Zahavi's desk began ringing. It had to be Security wanting to see if he was all right.

"Shall I?" Zahavi asked.

"Most definitely," Mark waved congenially as he sat back down. "Go ahead."

Zahavi picked up the receiver.

"Hello? Uh...yes. Yes, I'm fine, Prime Minister, how are you?" He pinched the bridge of his nose between two fingers. "Yes, I understand. Yes, sir. Of course, sir. Thank you, sir." He hung up, his face visibly paler than minutes before.

"Um...that was Prime Minister Alon. He said I am supposed to lend you whatever assistance I can."

"Sorry we had to pull out the big guns, but we need this info," Mark said consolingly, "We're here on official business."

"So I gathered."

The door behind them suddenly burst open. The dark space was filled by two burly security guards. Their faces were tense and their pistols up, pointing directly at the backs of Zahavi's visitors.

"Hands behind your heads!" One of them shouted.

Zahavi raised a hand. "It's okay, guys. False alarm."

"You know we can't just leave sir. Hands on your heads, now!"

"You'd better do it," Zahavi whispered to Mark, leaning forward.

Mark, Ty, and Hardy all lifted their arms and laced their fingers behind their heads. Zahavi noticed all three men wore the same odd-looking watch. He stood, arms out and visible as well, and moved slowly around the desk.

"Look, gentlemen, it was a misunderstanding, let me come outside and explain."

The guards wavered and then finally acquiesced, lowering their guns. The trio kept their hands in place so as to not raise an alarm. Zahavi left the room with the guards, conversed with them for a moment and then returned alone.

"You can put your arms down now." He sat back down. "Sorry about that. We are in Israel and I have no idea who you are."

"Understood," said Mark. "You can't be too careful. Now, as you were saying? You know Professor Rosenberg?"

Zahavi nodded. "Yes."

"How do you know him?"

"Benjamin Rosenberg used to be on staff here at the institute. He is an excellent scholar and an expert on the Temple and its artifacts, especially the Ark of the Covenant. That's why I am so surprised it was he who turned you on to the Templar theories. He knows better."

"Maybe he learned something new since he worked here? Something which could have changed his mind about where it was?"

Zahavi shook his head. "Not likely. Those Templar theories are a crock, something we laugh about around here."

"*Why* then? Why would he intentionally throw us off?"

"I don't know. That's why I didn't want to talk to you anymore. If he was trying to mislead you, then he must have had a good reason. I figured he suspected you were working for the enemy."

"The enemy? Which enemy?"

"Uh...let's see. The Arabs, the Palestinians, Iran, Hamas, Hezbollah, Russia, you name it, they're our enemy."

"No, he would have had no reason to doubt our backing. He got a call directly from the President of the United States."

"I don't know then. I can't believe he'd be worried about you actually finding it. But then again, maybe the US government being involved in an official search for the Ark worried him enough to not take any chances. It certainly does me. I mean, of course America is our strong ally, but we could not trust the Ark even in her hands."

"Still, he is an American citizen, is he not?"

"Yes, but look...there may be other organizations involved. Rosenberg's actions combined with the phone call from the Prime Minister are very conflicting to me. That's all I'm going to say on that subject. If you want to know more about Rosenberg, I suggest you talk to him about it yourself."

"Fair enough. What else can you tell us about the Ark?"

"I've got some materials that may be of help."

Zahavi rose and collected several books from the shelves along with a manila folder filled with some articles he'd copied from *Biblical Archaeology Review*. In his cabinets, he had more — much more — and even better information, but he wasn't about it give it to them. Not until he could speak with the Prime Minister's office again, *and* Rosenberg, to see what was really going on and how much help they really wanted him to give them. The U.S. government should not be involved in a search for the Ark of the Covenant. That was the prerogative of the State of Israel and no one else. *Anyone* else would be extremely dangerous.

The crude maps and lightly researched books and articles he was handing over should satisfy these men as to his cooperation, but they wouldn't help them significantly. If Prime Minister Alon really was adamant about him giving all the aid possible, Zahavi could always mail them more later.

Chapter 20

They descended the stone steps leaving the Institute.

"So, what was all that about Rosenberg?" Ty asked. "Did he send us on a wild goose chase on purpose? Why would he do that?"

"He's probably Mossad," Hardy said.

Mossad was Israel's version of the CIA, only more effective, more efficient, and more deadly.

Mark grimaced, "Yeah. His actions would fit perfectly with an agent working for Mossad.

"Let's think about it. If you were the Prime Minister of Israel and the President of the United States requests help on a matter Israel considers vital to national security, but you want the U.S. to stay out of it, what would you do? You wouldn't want to buck the president publically, so you refer them to a highly respected professor you know will send the Americans on the wild goose chase, all the while pretending to cooperate fully."

"Then, why did the prime minister call Zahavi just now and tell him to help us?

"Because I had just called the President James. He said to call if we needed any help, so I did. He probably got on the horn with Prime Minister Alon and asked him to call. Alon had no choice but to comply for the moment. Even then, I doubt Zahavi gave us everything he knows."

"What if Rosenberg's not Mossad? What if Zahavi is wrong, or crazy?"

"I tend to think he knows what he's talking about, but we should go back and verify once and for all what the Templars found under the Temple Mount just to be sure."

***

They had not forgotten about Randolph de Cleary. They needed to know what Rialto was up to before they started popping in and out of modern Jerusalem like some kind of time-traveling prairie dogs. Ty showed them the intersection where he'd seen DeCleary.

They set their watches to twenty minutes before Ty had first observed the former knight so they could prepare to tail him before DeCleary reached the intersection.

The plan was for Ty to follow the knight a short way through the winding streets. Then, Mark would pick up the tail as Ty peeled off. After Mark had followed for a time, he would turn off and Hardy would continue the surveillance.

The plan was to repeat the pattern for as long as it took to find out where DeCleary was staying and whether any other Rialto men were in town.

They shifted back, spotted the knight, and then after their target passed through the intersection, they followed him out of the Old City and into the more modern section of Jerusalem to the west. Hardy was the active pursuer and doing his best to keep up when Randolph suddenly took a hard right into a secluded alley.

Hardy turned the corner to follow, and then, to his dismay, saw the large knight facing him, feet apart, ready for battle. DeCleary stood firm, a long broadsword looming ominously in his right hand.

Hardy stopped short.

"How in the world did you get that sword into Israel, DeCleary?"

"Shut up and fight, you cur."

"My friends are right behind me."

Randolph snarled menacingly and charged, sword raised high. He growled unintelligible medieval expletives as he closed the short gap between them. With no time to think, Hardy parried DeCleary's descending sword arm with a forearm block and then followed it up by slugging the knight in the stomach with the other hand. His fist felt like it had hit a bag of rocks.

DeCleary's body plowed through Hardy as if he were a child. He'd forgotten how powerful the knight's brute strength really was.

DeCleary planted a foot behind Hardy's ankle and slammed the hilt of his sword into his forehead, which sent Hardy sprawling. He slid several feet across the cobblestone street on his back before he came to a stop. Streaks of white hot pain shot through his skull. He rubbed it. *Had the knight actually cracked the bone?*

Randolph growled and charged again, ready to stomp Hardy into oblivion. Hardy rolled to the side but saw he wasn't going to be able to get out of the way in time.

A sudden cry from the alley's entrance caused the knight to pause.

Out of nowhere, Mark slammed into DeCleary's mid-section like the cavalry coming to the rescue. Instead of the expected *oof* and expulsion of air, DeCleary batted Mark aside like a fly. His friend had encountered the same bag of rocks under the knight's shirt, but the distraction had been enough to give Hardy time to scramble up to his feet.

A stone sailed through the air and slammed Randolph squarely in the forehead, which was the first thing that seemed to faze him.

Ty followed the rock in like a whirling madman. He launched himself at the knight's head, his fists a crazy blur as he whipped blow after blow into the big man's skull. Mark dove into DeCleary's side again and drove the knight backward. Then, he landed several punches on his kidney.

DeCleary tripped over something under the backward pressure and crashed flat on his back with the full weight of Mark and Ty on top of him. Now, Hardy pounced too, adding to the melee. Even with the weight of all three of them, the knight's strength was so great it was a struggle to keep him pinned.

"His arms!" Mark yelled. "Keep his arms apart!"

Hardy grappled for the knight's right wrist and secured it. Mark took charge of the other. Even with Mark and Hardy holding his wrists to the pavement and Ty pretty much sitting on his head, the knight wasn't giving up. He bucked for everything he was worth, arching his back wildly in an attempt to throw his subduers.

"Hardy! Send him back to kingdom come!"

Hardy caught on right away. He kept his full body weight on DeCleary and yanked at his wrist until he could see the face of the knight's shifter. Desperately he played with the buttons and had gotten the target date set all the way back to 1020 BC when Mark yelled again.

"Wait! DON"T PUSH IT!"

Hardy froze his finger.

"Ty! Knock him out!"

The knight bucked even harder while Ty grabbed a loose stone and slammed it down on DeCleary's head. He had to hit the knight again before his body finally went limp.

"Is he out?"

Ty pulled an eyelid back and examined his pupils.

"Yeah, he's out."

"Everybody off."

All three of them slowly stood and moved away from the unconscious man.

"Find a stick."

Ty picked up an iron rod lying against a building and handed it to Hardy.

"You got the date set far enough back?"

Hardy nodded.

"Hit it."

Hardy extended the rod toward Randolph's shifter, but stopped short.

"This is metal, it might conduct the signal."

"Throw it then."

Hardy did and missed. The second time the rod struck the red button.

With a hiss of electric static, Randolph DeCleary faded from sight.

They stood in silence, considering what they'd just done. This was something new.

"How far back did you send him?" Mark asked.

"1020 BC," Hardy said.

All three men simultaneously pulled their laminated cards from their back pockets which showed how long a shifter would shut down based on the number of centuries traversed.

Ty whistled.

"Wow, good work, Hardy! *420 years.*" He slapped his friend on the back.

"Yeah, assuming Prescott's chart is right."

"It is," Mark said. "We won't have to worry about DeCleary ever again. He'll die of old age before his shifter starts working again. And Rialto's not going to go get him either. He'd get stuck back then too."

For the first time in a long while, Mark smiled a sincerely felt smile.

"Let's go," he said.

Chapter 21

"There is never enough time, unless you're serving it."

- Malcolm Forbes

Randolph DeCleary's head felt like it had been run over by an army of horses. He groaned audibly as he rolled from side to side in a vain effort to shake the splitting headache. After a while, he finally dropped his hand from his forehead and staggered to his feet, still shaking his head back and forth. If he could just get rid of the fogginess in his mind.

He sensed he was alone now.

The surrounding landscape shocked him in its complete unexpectedness. Gone were the houses, apartment buildings, and shops. Gone were the streets and alleyways. In fact, the city itself was gone.

Instead he saw endless fields, some of them filled with mid-season crops, though most lay fallow. The grass covering the hills was lusher, more green than one would ever expect to find in Israel. There were even a few splotches of forest dotting the horizon.

Where was he?

He turned his head and finally saw Jerusalem, or rather what was left of Jerusalem.

Was that Jerusalem? It was so much smaller. There were no surrounding villages filled with concrete houses. Instead, a thick stone wall encircled the tiny settlement. The entire city appeared to be limited to just the top of one small hill and it looked very primitive.

When was he?

Groggily, he examined his right hand. He was relieved to see his fist still gripping his sword. He lifted his arm, hefting the sword, thankful for its familiar weight. He checked his left. The shifter glowed red.

He knew that happened sometimes when you traveled back too far. Every time he went back to his home time, it would shut down for about twenty minutes.

He checked the display. Through the red glow he translated the numbers into a year he could make sense of: 1020 BC.

It took a minute for the full shock of that date to run through him. Rialto had always been concerned about how long the device would shut down if they traveled back too far. If traveling nine hundred years shut it down for twenty minutes then surely three thousand years wouldn't be more than an hour.

Still, Rialto had seemed to think it would take longer. He hoped it wouldn't be out of service for more than a few days. He'd just have to make due until then.

Carpen and Phillips had done this to him — and their Moorish armorbearer. He would make them pay once he got back. Their despicable cowardice was affront to his honor. Three on one! *What cowards.* He spat on the ground in contempt.

Their inability to fight honorably seared him with a stronger determination to destroy them, and he vowed to do so as soon as he got back.

Some movement in the distance caught his eye. It looked to be a group of men.

He peered through the haze and realized they were actually closer than he had originally thought. Some were on foot, but three pairs of them rode in odd-looking carriages.

As the group drew closer, DeCleary recognized the iron beasts from one of the history books he'd perused one afternoon in Rialto's library. The book had called them chariots. The chariots were pulled by a team of horses and looked like they would be a formidable piece of armor for the men riding. In each car, one of the men held the reins and drove the horses. The other held a sword in one hand and what looked to be a spear in the other.

After another minute, they were close enough he could see the men afoot were armed too. Each had an iron helmet, a short sword in hand, and a shorter dagger stuffed in their belts. This was a light cavalry unit, about twenty strong. Thankfully, he didn't see any archers.

A few more minutes and he'd see if their intentions were hostile or not. There wasn't anywhere nearby he could run for cover, not that he would have considered such a thing.

He didn't have to wait long to find out. A sharp shout from their captain sent all three of the chariot drivers into a whipping frenzy and the stallions charged his direction in a mad rush. The armored chariots would be on him in no time.

Two of the chariots lined up in parallel. They would each pass within a few feet, one on each side with him in the middle. The third chariot dropped about forty feet behind to clean up anything the first two missed. The infantry men were jogging as fast as they could behind the cars and would arrive soon after they passed.

As soon as the first chariots were in range, the spear man on Randolph's left side let his weapon fly. Randolph waited for exactly the right second and then, with a flourishing sweep of his sword, deflected the spear in mid-air. It clattered impotently to the ground.

With his other hand, Randolph flipped his dagger out of his belt and flung it at the right-hand spear man where it buried itself in his chest. That man crumpled over and toppled from his chariot before it reached him.

Seconds before the chariots passed, flashes of light glinting off rapidly rotating blades attached to the hubs of the chariots' wheels caught his eye. The razor sharp blades would slice through his legs mid-calf if he didn't compensate.

Deftly, he leapt over the blades as they passed, but did not miss the opportunity for a slash with his sword at the driver of the left-hand chariot. His blade struck the driver in the neck, ending his career permanently. The spear man of that chariot grabbed wildly for the reins to maintain control. The driver of the right-hand chariot was too busy trying to do the same to pose any further threat for the moment.

The third chariot was the worry now. The unit's captain held the weapons in that one. Randolph scooped up a large rock and chucked it at the captain's driver, but it missed.

The captain hurled his spear at Randolph with an amazing velocity, but Randolph dodged it effortlessly. He whipped another rock the driver's way, striking home this time, right on the man's temple. The driver stumbled, collapsed forward limply, and the reins fell from his hand.

The captain glanced at his driver, but didn't have time to worry about him as the chariot was now almost on top of its target. Once again, Randolph made sure to keep clear of the vicious rotating blades attached to the wheel and met the attack.

The captain swung a sweeping blow toward Randolph's head, but DeCleary caught his wrist and twisted the blade away. Simultaneously, he used the captain's weight against him as the chariot kept moving and flipped the captain out of the chariot, landing him hard on his back in the dust. The fall clearly knocked the wind out of the leader of these attackers, but just to be sure, Randolph stomped his stomach hard.

The captain crumpled, gasping for air, unable to pursue more battle with the large stranger.

Behind DeCleary, the first spear man had never fully regained control of his horses and was thrown from the chariot when a wheel struck a rock and tumbled over. He avoided injury, and raced back to the battle. The driver of the second chariot abandoned his vehicle, diving out at almost full speed and rolling to a stop. He'd grabbed the sword of the man with the dagger in his chest and was also rushing to the fight. The infantry soldiers were upon Randolph then and the fight degraded from an elegant dance into a mad melee.

Randolph took down two or three men at a time with broad sweeps of his sword, which was significantly longer than theirs and gave him an advantage. As the recently footed charioteers reached his rear, he dropped to one knee, twisted, and made at broad cut behind him. His blade cut deeply into the legs of one of the charioteers and dropped him like a rock. Startled, the other backed up too fast, tripped and fell. Several fruitless slices from the foot soldiers parted the air above his head. He rolled out of the pack and stood again to face the group a few feet outside their perimeter.

They regrouped and attacked again, trying to surround him, but their numbers were dwindling along with their morale. He still had a few tricks up his sleeve and proceeded to use them.

Their will to fight seemed to melt away when he nearly decapitated one of their friends and in the same motion knocked another unconscious with the heel of his hilt.

The remaining men backed off then, panting, swords limp. Four of them still stood. Of the fallen, most were dead, some were wounded, and a couple unconscious.

The captain finally regained his breath and stood back up. He leaned on his sword, holding his side and respiring hard. He straightened, lifted his sword skyward and motioned to his men to back off while he moved in.

If nothing else, the man was brave. Randolph held his hand high, breathed in and out several times deeply, and then pointed at the captain.

"Get your breath, man. I'll wait," he muttered.

The captain looked back at his men, puzzled. They conversed in some unknown, guttural tongue, but the captain seemed to understand. Randolph wasn't out of breath and he wanted a fair fight.

Once the captain fully recovered, Randolph waved him forward, smiling.

The captain moved in. His stance said he was more skilled than his soldiers, but it wouldn't matter. DeCleary had been trained for fighting since birth. Well...at least since he was four.

The captain faked to the right and sent a terrible blow toward Randolph's left side. Randolph parried it without effort, made a counterattack at the captain's legs, which the man was barely able to block, and landed a third blow solidly on the captain's well-armored mid-section.

On the dance went. Randolph didn't want to hurt the captain; he respected him for his honor and bravery. He'd wetted his blood lust already, so now he was just enjoying the sport of the fight.

The captain became increasingly flustered and more determined when trained blow after trained blow were frustrated by the stranger.

Randolph moved with increasingly less effort with every exchange. He made sure all of his attacks landed on sections protected by the captain's armor.

After a while, the captain realized what Randolph was doing, but also realized he was not mocking or having sport with him. The stranger was not withholding any strength from his blows, nor laying insulting taps on his helmet with the tip of the sword.

Finally, when the captain appeared to have no more energy for the fight, Randolph brought the battle to an end by bringing his blade to a full stop underneath the captain's chin as if to pierce his throat.

The captain let his sword arm go limp, resigned to his fate. He had lost.

His men yelled and moved in, but he waved them off.

Randolph observed all this with admiration. His opponent was a man of honor.

He dropped his own blade to his side and waited.

The captain stared in the medieval knight's eyes for a full minute, searching for the truth of his intentions, for some sign of trickery or hatred.

Finally, he dropped to one knee before Randolph, bowing his head. His men followed suit.

Chapter 22

To gain entrance to the Al-Aqsa mosque without unusual scrutiny, Mark, Hardy and Ty dressed as devout Muslims. Even with Hardy's hair dyed black, he and Mark received a few extra glances their way, though Ty drew no special attention. It didn't matter, they wouldn't be here long. They just needed to get inside long enough to shift.

The interior of the ancient domed building was filled with pillars in neat rows. Five times per day this mosque overflowed with Muslims coming here to pray, and even now men were scattered throughout the facility bowing their heads to the ground as they repeated the *Shahadah*.

None of this mattered to Mark. Their purpose was to separate from each other and shift as soon as they'd reached opposing corners of the mosque.

Mark took the left corner, and Hardy and Ty grouped together in the right. All three stayed behind the worshipers who were facing the front of the mosque.

A flash of static and they were suddenly in the dark, nine hundred years earlier. They'd chosen to come in at night so as to reduce the likelihood of being intercepted by any Templars on site.

As soon as he transitioned in, Mark quietly slipped away from his corner, covering the red glow from his shifter with his sleeve. Hardy and Ty would be doing the same.

A hundred and forty pillars stood in rows throughout the mosque, all of them topped by arches. The resulting atmosphere was a view of seeming openness blocked endlessly by many half-walls and columns, leaving plenty of places one could hide if needed.

Mark pulled a pair of infrared goggles from under his tunic and stuffed his white skullcap in his pocket. The goggles revealed walls and barriers he could not see with his own eyes, as well as the heat signatures of anyone nearby.

He moved to the right. Two bright, man-shaped orange glows

at the opposite side of the mosque indicated Hardy and Ty's location. Ty separated from Hardy and took a more centric position.

All three advanced in sync, working their way toward the front of the building.

A large orange mass glowed close to the front, near where an altar would be if it were a church. The features of the unknown mass remained indistinguishable until they drew closer. It turned out to be twelve men stretched out asleep on the floor.

Mark had only been expecting nine. History books were universal in the assertion that the original group of Templar knights was only nine strong. Nine men had occupied the Al-Aqsa mosque, renaming it Solomon's Temple.

Perhaps three of these shapes were servants or aides of some kind.

Regardless, they were all sound asleep for the moment and it was best they stay that way. Mark signaled and moved to the left, searching for a staircase. Anything of interest to them would be on a lower level of the building.

The staircase wasn't hard to find. A stone spiral of steps wound down from the left front corner of the mosque into a deeper darkness. The three friends descended.

They didn't see any more heat signatures down here, so each flipped off his infrared goggles and turned on a flashlight to begin searching for signs of digging.

Another narrow set of roughly-hewn stone steps — though this set was straight, not spiral — led down another level and bottomed out in front of a rough door in the wall which looked to have been created through a haphazard and hasty removal of stones. Definitely not a planned passage.

Once they passed through it, they found themselves in an ancient tunnel which at one point had been stuffed full with debris. The Templars were clearing it out. It looked like they had already removed an inordinate amount of loose stone and rock.

The tunnel ran for about fifty feet before it turned. After the corner, it branched off in two directions. And that was not the last fork they encountered. They were surprised to see the tunnels beneath the Temple Mount seemingly went on forever, branching into new paths here and there, sometimes recombining. No wonder the Templars had dug for so many years.

They walked each branch, following its path until it ended in a pile of debris, losing hope with each one they checked off the list of possibilities. Some of the branches terminated after only a few feet, others went on for several hundred with numerous turns along the way.

After several hours, they'd exhausted almost every possibility. Each and every tunnel they'd followed had ended in debris.

There was one more promising passageway which opened into several successive wider chambers before it came to an end just like the others. The walls of these chambers held some interesting inscriptions, but they couldn't read them. Hardy snapped a few photos to take back to Savannah for deciphering.

Still, in the end they found nothing. Either the Templars had not reached their treasure yet, or there was no treasure to be found.

***

"Yes, Mr. President, we're making progress."

Mark waited while the president responded. They were back at headquarters and Ty, Hardy, and Savannah sat around the boardroom table, listening to the one-sided conversation while Mark reported in to the leader of the free world.

"No, sir. Yes....No....We believe Prime Minister Alon may not be providing all the help he could....No. No, we think Rosenberg may be Mossad...Yes. I don't know why. It may be Israel isn't too keen on an American team searching for their most precious national treasure. Yes....Of course, I understand." Mark turned to Savannah. "What about the materials Professor Zahavi gave us?" he repeated.

Savannah waved both hands once reaffirming what she'd already told Mark.

"No, sir. Those documents were mostly useless. Just a repetition of what Zahavi already told us, about the ark being hidden by Jeremiah in some cave near Mt. Nebo."

Mark fell silent.

"No, sir, that wouldn't be very practical....Teams of archaeologists have been searching in that area for decades. We would need better info first to narrow down the search....What? No, we can't go back to the time of Jeremiah....It's a feature of the shifters. They can't go back that far. That's right, Rialto can't either."

Mark listened some more.

"Yes, sir. So, we have your permission? Understood. We'll get it done."

Mark hung up the phone.

"What did he say?" Ty asked.

"He was happy to hear Rialto couldn't shift back any farther than we could. Said he would call Prime Minister Alon and put more pressure on him, but that we should do whatever we have to to get the information from Zahavi. He is taking this very seriously. The Ark of the Covenant in Rialto's hands could be used to spark the bloodiest religious war in Middle Eastern history. He considers Rialto a direct threat to the national security of both the United States and Israel."

"Why doesn't he just tell Prime Minister Alon what's going on?"

"He doesn't want to tip his hand about our abilities to Mossad."

"Yeah," Hardy said, "The last thing we need is Israel trying to kidnap us to get a hold of this technology."

"True," Mark nodded.

"And when we've served our purpose?" Hardy asked. "When our usefulness to the Unites States of America is at an end? What then?"

"We'll cross that bridge when we come to it," Mark said. "Savannah, how can we find this Ark?"

"I don't know, Mark. Its location has stumped scholars for over two thousand years. This information Zahavi gave us is interesting...but it doesn't have much in the way of specifics."

"You agree Zahavi's theory is the correct one though? That the Templars didn't get it?"

"Yes," she nodded.

"Then, what kind of information could Zahavi be holding back?"

She thought for a minute. "The White Marble Tablets that were found at Mt. Carmel — they mention four records created by the men who hid the Ark in 586 BC. The Temple Scroll was an instruction book for re-instituting the services in a rebuilt temple. The Marble Tablets describe *how* the Ark and the other treasures of the Temple were hidden by Jeremiah and the others. The Copper Scroll was a detailed list of treasures and the locations where they'd been hidden. The problem has always been that many of the place names described in the Copper Scroll have been lost to the sands of time and no one today knows what they're referring to."

"Go on," Mark said.

"Well, *one* of the records made by those men has never been found. The Silver Scroll. What if the Silver Scroll is the other half of the treasure map, so to speak? What if the Silver Scroll is needed to correctly interpret the locations described in the Copper Scroll?"

"You're right," Mark smiled. "Each of the records contains different information than the others. Whatever is on the Silver Scroll has to be different from the others and it has to be information that will help somehow in locating the treasures and reinstalling them correctly in the Temple again. Since the Temple Scroll fully describes how to re-institute the services, the Silver Scroll must have something to do with locating the treasures. What else could it be?"

"So, if we find the Silver Scroll, we can find the Ark?" Ty asked.

"Sounds like it," Hardy answered, "At least we'll have a much better shot at it."

"All right," Mark said, "Who wants to go with me to pay Zahavi another visit?"

"Count me in." Hardy flopped his arm up.

"Ty will you stay and help Savannah research some more? Keep her safe from Rialto?"

"Sure."

"All right, let's go."

***

Once again, the weather in Jerusalem was deliciously pleasant. And once more, it was sunset. The golden-pink hues dominating the cityscape warmly colored its streets and filled it with a tangible aura of timeless nostalgia.

Sunset was the perfect time to pay Daud Zahavi a visit. Catching him at the end of a long work day would yield better results than early on when he'd be fresh from sleep and a morning coffee.

"I still say we should..."

"We're not going to kidnap the man, Hardy," Mark interrupted.

"I'm just saying...the president practically authorized us to do whatever we needed to. We'd get a lot further a lot faster if we just did some simple tricks, maybe a little..."

"The guy's not the enemy, man. He's doing what either of us would do in his situation, protecting the national security of his country."

"I know, I know. So, what's the plan?"

"We'll see."

They entered the Institute of Archaeology and walked to Zahavi's office.

Mark knocked.

Zahavi's face fell visibly when he opened the door and saw who it was.

"Come in," he said, though he didn't look the least bit glad to see them.

Mark and Hardy stepped into the small office, closing the door behind them. Mark motioned for Zahavi to stop moving.

"Stay away from that silent alarm behind your desk," he ordered.

"Look, I don't know why you guys are here. I've told you everything I know."

"You know why we're here, and we both know you haven't told us everything."

"If you know that, then you also know there's no way I can tell you anymore. Not unless you're planning on torturing me," the professor scoffed.

"Well, Hardy had suggested that..."

Zahavi paled. Mark held up a hand.

"Don't worry. We're not going to. Look — just keep your eye on me for a minute."

Mark pressed his shifter and disappeared into thin air.

Hardy hung his head and slowly shook it back and forth as the static dissipated. He couldn't believe Mark was showing Zahavi the shifters.

A second later, Mark materialized once more. If Zahavi had paled before, he was whiter than a Russian ghost now. A tremor ran through his legs and he stumbled back a step. It looked like his body was searching for a seat independently of his mind.

"Wha..." He stammered.

"Yeah, I know," Mark said nonchalantly. He held out his arm. "Here, take my wrist."

Zahavi just stared at Mark, rooted in place like a concrete pylon.

"Come on."

Something in his voice must have inspired some confidence because the professor reached out warily. Mark hit the shifter as soon as contact was made and the pair of them were suddenly standing in open air.

It was now morning and the air was being moved about by a dry breeze. The slope of the hill on which they stood was rocky and free of buildings of any kind. Jerusalem was still there, but it no longer looked the same. Much more rustic.

Not a blade of green grass was anywhere to be seen, just dusty, dry terrain. This was the Palestine of Mark Twain's travels, the Palestine of the mid-1800's, not the reborn Israel of the 21st century.

Zahavi's body finally gave out. He fell back and landed on his rear, mouth agape in shock.

"You're gonna catch some flies in that maw," Mark said.

The professor shut his trap, quickly trying to regain some sense of himself.

"Where are we?" he stammered.

"1850."

"18...what? What are you talking about?"

"We didn't move anywhere. We're still where your office was...eh, where it will be. We're just in 1850 now instead of 2014."

Zahavi shook his head in combined disbelief and confusion.

"Yeah, I know. It's a lot to take in. Come on, let's take a walk."

Mark began to descend the hill. Zahavi followed.

A short stroll through the streets of 19th century Jerusalem made Mark's case for him without having to say another word. The dress of the people, the complete lack of electricity or any sign of modern technology. Either they'd just traveled through time, or Mark had instantly teleported Zahavi to some Palestinian theme park. A very authentic theme park.

Or, it could be a massive hallucination. Maybe Carpen had sprayed some kind of nerve agent into his face.

Zahavi pinched himself several times.

"It's real. You're not dreaming."

The look on Zahavi's face was a mélange of anger and bewilderment.

"Look, don't get peeved. Any time you're ready, we'll head back. I had to show you why you should trust us. We have technology that allows us to travel through time at ease."

Zahavi gulped. "Why are you showing me this?"

"We aren't the only ones who have this technology. There's another group led by a man named Alexander Rialto. He has threatened to use the Ark of the Covenant to spark a holy war in the Middle East against Israel. Thus, the President of the United States has tasked us with finding the Ark first, before Rialto can get his hands on it. Obviously, anyone with the ability to travel through time has a serious chance of finding it."

"So, why don't you just go back to when it disappeared?" Zahavi stared blankly at several houses. His mind was still having trouble accepting what he was seeing.

"Our technology doesn't allow us to go back that far."

"I see." He really didn't.

"Even with the amazing advantages we have, it's still like looking for a needle in a haystack. We need some guidance from you to narrow down the search."

"I can't help you," Zahavi mumbled mindlessly. "The Ark belongs to Israel, not the United States."

"Look, we don't want the Ark, man. We want to stop Rialto and we need to know where he's going to be looking. I promise, we'll give the Ark to the Israeli government the moment we find it, if we ever do."

"I don't know."

"What kind of proof do you need?"

"How do I know this Rialto guy isn't actually the good guy? How do I know you're not the ones I should be worried about?"

"If we were the bad guys, wouldn't we have just tortured you from the start instead of showing you what we can do?"

"I guess."

"Look, let me take you back. You can think about it. We've got all the time in the world."

Chapter 23

"Time cools, time clarifies; no mood can be maintained
quite unaltered through the course of hours."

- Mark Twain

It took Professor Daud Zahavi several weeks to wrap his mind around the idea of time travel. The possibility of it excited him, but his scientific training had drilled into him the dogma that such things were an impossibility.

Mark shifted with him a couple more times and Zahavi was finally on board. He promised not to reveal their secret to anyone in exchange for Mark making himself available every now and then to help Zahavi with "on the scene" archaeological investigations, the kind of "live" research no other archaeologist in the world could ever dream of doing.

It turned out their theory regarding the Silver Scroll was shared by Zahavi. When it came right down to it, his knowledge narrowed down their search grid a good bit for the location of Jeremiah's cave, but it wasn't enough. They needed the Silver Scroll.

Their last hope was a small tidbit of information in the dregs of Zahavi's handwritten notes: an obscure reference in the writings of an even more obscure Jewish scholar from the mid-1800's.

At least, it was a place to start.

The tidbit was a brief reference to the Silver Scroll in the writings of Solomon Schechter. Schechter founded the United Synagogue of Conservative Judaism in 1913 and was a major contributor to modern-day conservative Judaism. Schechter was also credited with bringing to light an amazing treasure trove of ancient Hebrew scrolls found in an ancient synagogue in Cairo, Egypt. His discovery was what brought to light most of the information available today about the hiding of the Ark and the tablets and scrolls which had been stashed by Jeremiah's men.

However, what had caught Zahavi's eye was not that discovery, but another small reference in Schechter's writings to the journals of an unknown rabbi from San Francisco. Schechter had heard this other rabbi's journals made mention of the mysterious Silver Scroll, but Schechter was never able to find anyone who'd actually seen the journals.

The unknown rabbi was one Jacob Gould, a private man who had led a synagogue in San Francisco in the late 1870's. A talented scholar, Gould had been offered a position in a more prominent synagogue in New York City and had set out east by stage coach in 1880 with all his belongings, including his books and journals.

Unfortunately, his stage was attacked along the way by Apaches somewhere in New Mexico. Gould was killed and all his journals were either lost or destroyed.

Which made it simple. All they had to do was get a hold of Gould's papers before the Apaches did.

Ty opted to remain in Boston again, allowing Mark and Hardy to take the lead once more. Surprisingly, Savannah wanted to come along on this trip. The idea made Mark a little more nervous than he expected; she wasn't exactly the warrior type like Abbie. Mark didn't like any distractions on a mission and he didn't want to have to worry about her safety.

Still, Savannah held a quiet steel in her spirit that wasn't immediately obvious, but neither could it be denied. She was not as direct and aggressive as Abbie, a much more subtle soul, yet in many ways just as determined.

Plus, they were just going to the Old West. Sure gunslingers were the norm, but all that was calming down by 1880 and women were a protected species in the Old West by the unspoken code of the cowboy. Even the worst of outlaws shied away from hurting a woman.

A little less testosterone might actually be a nice for a change, he reasoned.

***

Long, green grass rolled in waves before the wind as it traversed the endless rounded hills. The landscape was pure beauty. One of the most beautiful Mark had ever seen. Savannah seemed captivated by its serenity as well.

Hardy was checking his weapons.

"Man, we already checked those three times," Mark commented.

Hardy didn't look up from the bolt assembly he was inspecting.

"Dude, we're about to take on Apaches. Haven't you heard what they used to do to their prisoners?"

"They don't have a chance. And if even by some fluke they did capture us, Ty would get us out."

"Overconfidence has been the downfall of many a man — not to mention armies. And how many times are they gonna rip my fingernails out before Ty figures out what to do? By the way, I'm not a big fan of getting staked out alive on top of an ant pile in the middle of the desert either."

Mark grimaced. "Good grief, man, we have a lady present."

"I still don't think you should have let her come along."

"I'll be fine, Hardy," she said demurely.

"Just keep your head down when this thing gets going, okay?"

She nodded.

"You wouldn't even remember the torture," Mark said to him. "Once Ty saved us, the history would reset and there'd be nothing to remember."

"How do you *know* we wouldn't remember?"

"Just shut up and keep checking your weapons. Sorry I said anything."

Mark lifted the binoculars to his eyes and scanned the horizon. They'd visited the soon-to-be battlefield several times already to observe the Apaches' line and method of attack. In a few minutes, the band of warriors would sweep in over a nearby hill from the northeast. Uncharacteristically, these Apaches would save their war cries until they were right upon the stagecoach to preserve the element of surprise.

The first volley of arrows would take out both the driver and the guard riding shotgun. After that, it only took a few minutes for the wild riders to fully decimate the passengers, steal what they could grab, set the coach afire, and tear off again back over the hill. Jacob Gould was just unlucky to be one of the passengers on board today.

Right on time, of course, the Apaches topped the ridge at full speed. They were already stretching their bows back to let the first fusillade of arrows fly.

Mark and Hardy knew which of the attackers would fire the shots that killed the driver and his guard, so they swept those braves off their mounts with a few well-placed rifle shots before they could launch their arrows. Two more shots and a total of four Indians were laid out.

They had debated whether or not to use modern guns with silencers, but in the end they opted to stick with their well-established policy of only using era-appropriate weaponry when possible. They had, however, planted a good bit of dynamite between the attackers and the coach — just in case.

It turned out not to be needed. When the sharp cracks of Mark and Hardy's rifles reached the Apaches' ears and they saw four of their number tumbling from their mounts in quick succession, the rest of the riders turned tail in full retreat. They no longer had the element of surprise and had already sustained great losses. Not the kind of battle Apaches preferred.

Upon seeing wild-eyed Apaches, even retreating ones, combined with the gunshots, the stage driver began snapping his wrists and whipping his horses into a frenzied run. The coach bounced along the broken path precariously. Its top-heavy frame looked like it might tip over or come apart any minute. The driver wouldn't overdo it though. A tipped stage would be the worst of all scenarios for him.

Mark, Hardy, & Savannah mounted the horses they'd brought along and followed at a leisurely pace. The driver would slow down whenever he felt the threat was sufficiently abated. The stage would stop for rest in the next town, and that's where Mark would find Jacob Gould with his journals.

***

The next town over turned out to be Cottonwood, New Mexico. It was a dusty town set right in the heart of a good-sized valley filled with lush grass. Perfect for raising cattle. Smaller vales ran off in a number of directions. The people were pleasant enough, though reserved in a pioneer, Western sort of way.

Gould and the rest of the crew from the stage were in the hotel restaurant, taking a meal and soothing their strained nerves. An Apache attack was nothing to laugh at. They knew they'd been rescued, though they had no idea by whom since they'd been in such a hurry to put massive distance between themselves and the scene of the would-be slaughter.

Mark wasted no time, not that he ever was one to sit around twiddling his thumbs. He approached Gould's table. The stage driver and another young lady were sitting with him. The guard who'd ridden shotgun was nowhere to be seen.

The young woman was a looker. Jet-back raven hair flowed straight and long with hints of heavy curls at the tips. Her eyes were a striking green, accentuated by lily white skin. It would be considered a very pretty complexion here in the 19th century. She was in her early twenties and Mark thought that if she lived in his century, she would probably be one of those girls who spent half their week in a tanning salon. It was a pity so many people couldn't appreciate original beauty in the form God made it.

Where had that thought come from?

"Howdy! Glad to see you folks are all right," Mark said in his best western drawl.

Gould looked up sharply. He was still a bundle of nerves.

"Has word of what happened gotten around town so fast?" He asked.

"Nah, it wuz me and my partner who shot them 'Paches fer you." Mark pointed at Hardy, who'd stayed by the bar. Hardy tipped his hat in acknowledgment, but didn't come over.

"Well, my goodness! Thank you, sir!" Gould hurriedly stood and shook Mark's hand. The girl's face lit up and she smiled genuinely. Her teeth were white and bright surrounded by rosy red lips. She'd received good dental care growing up and probably came from a family of means.

The driver studied Mark. He was more trail savvy and thus more cynical.

"Have a seat, have a seat," Gould said, pulling out a chair. Mark joined them.

"Doesn't your friend want to come over?" Gould asked. "We'd be happy to buy him lunch."

"He's fine. Likes to keep to himself. Glad to see you folks are all right is all."

"Gus went to tell the sheriff about what happened," the stage driver offered. The comment was meant to warn as much as inform.

"I'm Jacob. Jacob Gould."

The girl offered her hand to Mark in a very feminine gesture. "Rachel MacKenzie."

Mark leaned forward to take it. "Mark Carpen," he responded.

He turned to the driver, not that he was interested, but he had to keep up appearances.

"Zeke Smith," the driver uttered grudgingly.

They settled into a pleasant conversation, Mark explaining how they'd come upon the stage and seen it was being followed. They discussed the potential horrors of being captured by savages like the Apaches. The driver relaxed as the conversation progressed, deciding Mark and Hardy were no risk. Mark finally steered the conversation in the way he wanted it to go.

"So, where are you headed?"

Gould spoke first. "I'm actually on my way to take a teaching position at a university in New York City."

Mark looked impressed. "Really? Which one?"

"Uh...the Jewish Theological Seminary." He looked embarrassed.

"Wow, are you Jewish?"

The rabbi visibly tensed. Anti-Semitism was very real in the 1800's. "Yes, I'm a rabbi."

"That's wonderful! I've always been fascinated with all things Jewish. What is your area of expertise?"

The man looked surprised, but he relaxed and smiled. "The period of the Babylonian Exile."

"Isn't that when King Nebuchadnezzar destroyed Jerusalem and the Temple?"

"Yes. You certainly seem to know your history, young man."

"Ma raised us on heavy doses of Scripture."

"I see."

"You know, I've always been fascinated by the Ark and what might have happened to it."

"It's funny you should mention that..."

Gould went on to explain how he'd researched that very topic himself extensively. Slowly, Mark probed him with questions to discover what the rabbi knew, discretely guiding their talk to the subject of the Silver Scroll.

It turned out Gould didn't know that much about it after all, other than he'd seen it referenced in the writings of another Rabbi from Amsterdam. He couldn't remember the name of the Rabbi off the top of his head, but said he had the details written down in one of his journals. Mark said he would love to know more about it, so Gould offered to go get the pertinent journal.

After he'd left, Zeke Smith excused himself and the young MacKenzie woman followed suit. Mark got up and moved to the bar to join Hardy.

A new man came into the restaurant then and sidled up to the bar. Mark noticed something different about him the moment he stepped inside. He was muscular, but lean, confident, but not cocky. The hard, chiseled look of his face said he wasn't a man to be messed with.

"You the gents that saved the stage back there?"

"Yes," Mark said.

"Well, sir, I believe some thanks are in order then. We get along with most of the Apaches 'round here, but we've had a roving band of young Mescalero warriors plaguing us lately."

The man stuck out his hand.

"Jake Halfbreed."

"Halfbreed? That's an unusual name."

"I like it."

"So, Mr. Halfbreed, are you the Sheriff around here?"

"You can call me Jake. No, I'm a rancher. Sheriff's name is McCraigh."

"How long have these Apaches been bothering you?"

"They started raising Cain a few weeks ago or so. Haven't touched my cattle yet, but they took some of Hartford's last week. Sooner or later they'll pick on the wrong person. Sounds like maybe they did today." He smiled.

Mark liked this guy. He was no-nonsense, direct and straight to the point. He noticed Halfbreed wore his guns low, like a gunslinger — yet he said he was a rancher.

Some commotion from the street broke the cadence of their conversation. Halfbreed pushed himself away from the bar and moved swiftly to the door. Mark and Hardy followed.

"Why'd you spit on me, Jew?"

A rough-looking cowboy was harassing Jacob Gould, blocking his path back to the restaurant. Gould's journals were tucked under one arm.

"I...I did no such thing," Gould stammered.

"Yeah, you did. Now yer gonna pay for it. I'll need a gold piece to get these boots shined up."

Gould was white in the face, glancing nervously back and forth for help. Rachel MacKenzie stood to Mark's right on the boardwalk, hands clasped tightly as the scene unfolded.

Those journals were the whole reason Mark was here, so he wasn't about to let some cowboy do something crazy which might ruin them.

Before he could step into the street, however, Jake Halfbreed called out.

"Jenks, leave the man alone."

The man whirled to face Halfbreed.

"You got no part in this, Jake."

"I said, leave him alone."

"What are you, a Jew-lover? Why this no-good scoundrel

spat..."

Jake scooped a stone from the ground and whipped it like a bullet toward the bully. It struck him square in the side of the head. He had moved so fast, Mark had barely registered seeing him pick it up. Jenks collapsed in a heap, groaning in the dust. Halfbreed moved to the fallen man and swung a fist downward, knocking him unconscious with one strong punch to the jaw. One by one, he lifted Jenks' boots and let them drop back to the dirt. No spittle.

"Sorry about that, sir," Jake consoled the open-mouthed Gould. "He gets out of hand sometimes."

Mark looked over at Rachel MacKenzie. She was watching Jake with a doe-eyed admiration that was hard to mistake.

"I think he's married," Mark muttered her way, pointing at his own ring finger to emphasize the point. The young woman looked puzzled and then blushed a bright shade of pink.

A stocky man wearing a star came running up the street. He stopped by the unconscious cowboy.

"What's going on, Jake?"

"Jenks was getting rowdy. Had to put him down."

"Figures. Ain't the first time."

Sheriff McCraigh tipped his hat apologetically at Gould and then waved to another man in the crowd to come help him. The two of them began dragging the cowboy up the street, presumably toward the jail.

Nice town, Mark thought.

Chapter 24

Rabbi Gould's journals referenced a collection of writings called *Emeq HaMelekh*, which means "The Valley of the Kings." The writings were written by Rabbi Naphtali Hertz in 1648 in Amsterdam, Holland. It turned out Gould had remembered wrong. He had not actually seen the "Valley of the Kings" writings, but had read another work which referenced them.

The *Emeq HaMelekh* basically told the same apocryphal story as 2 Maccabees, with the prophet Jeremiah and others hiding the Ark. What *was* different was the Silver Scroll was mentioned by name, which is why Gould had taken note of it. It was unusual.

Of course, this meant a trip back to 17th century Holland, so without a moment to waste, Mark, Savannah, and Hardy were soon on their way, leaving Cottonwood, New Mexico behind.

***

July 1st 1649, 11:17 AM - Amsterdam, Holland

It wasn't hard to locate the residence of Rabbi Hertz. The Jewish population of Amsterdam at this time, while significant, only numbered about 1,700. It had actually been much harder to locate an interpreter who spoke English well enough they could understand him.

The interpreter knocked firmly on the door as Mark, Savannah, and Hardy waited a few steps below.

Amsterdam in the 1600's was quite charming. The Rabbi's home mirrored much of the other homes along the canals in what was the city's golden age. If anything, it was actually a little smaller than others in the row.

His house was long, deep and narrow. It had four full stories topped by a single window, which hinted at a tiny attic room squeezed between the two sharply angled lines of the roof's peak. The facade was all brick, rust red. Grey stone accents dotted the corners of its front door and windows. Another large band of stone divided the lower floors from the attic level.

After a few moments, a teen-aged servant girl answered the door.

"Is de Rabbijn thuis?" The interpreter asked her.

"Wacht hier, tevreden." She curtsied and disappeared back inside the house.

After a few minutes, she returned to the door, shaking her head delicately.

"Nr, wil hij niet om het even wie zien." The girl continued speaking with the interpreter for a few minutes, but the negative nature of the response was already obvious. Finally, the girl retreated into the home, closing the door behind her and the interpreter descended the steps.

"What did she say?" Mark asked.

"She zay he vill not zee any-bodee. Not sinds his dooghter *moord.*"

"Moord? What's that?"

"Moord. Eh...moordered."

"Murdered?"

"Ja. She is muhrdered. De criminalz throw her in de canal. De Rabbi go back to home soon in Bacharach."

***

May 17th 1649, 4:07 PM - Amsterdam, Holland

They needed the Rabbi's cooperation. Sure they could shift into his house and take whatever they wanted, but that wouldn't help much. They had no idea which book they were looking for or where the Rabbi kept it, and even if they found the right one, they couldn't read Dutch or Hebrew. Not to mention the fact that only the Rabbi knew everything the Rabbi knew. There might be things about the Silver Scroll he'd heard but had not written down.

If they could find a way to ingratiate the Rabbi to them, he might just tell them everything they needed to know. Saving his daughter from being murdered seemed like a good way to start the relationship.

Of course, it wasn't quite that simple. They had to do it in a way that didn't involve the daughter seeing them shift in and out of time like temporal ghosts. That would be counter-productive. Especially in witch-hunt prone 17th century Europe.

So, it was time to scrape the rust off some of their combat training moves. As much as they tried to avoid it, they'd become somewhat addicted to the ease of the escape-by-shifter strategy. From time to time, Mark found himself slipping into a dependence on his shifter instead of his training to get himself out of jams. He and the others had discussed the problem ad nauseum.

They didn't want to lose their edge. The shifters could stop working at any moment. They didn't want to ever take them for granted, especially when they didn't even understand their origin. What if your shifter suddenly shut down in the middle of a battle? Then what? If you'd gotten rusty, well, one false move could get you killed.

So, as much as possible, though they might shift into a fight, they tried to finish them without having to engage in a premature shift-out.

They followed Rabbi Hertz's daughter for more than a mile as she meandered back home from one of the markets near the edge of town. It was late afternoon, and she looked to have been buying some harder-to-find items in preparation for dinner later that evening.

The air was especially chilly, more chilly than Mark would have expected for May. The girl, her name was Rachel, hugged her shawl more tightly around her shoulders, huddling against the cold as she made her way down the street.

A canal filled with dark water ran parallel to her path. Rows of tall, slender brick homes similar to the Rabbi's lined both sides of it as far as the eye could see, which wasn't that far as the canal and accompanying streets were curved.

A pair of ruffians ahead were carrying on and making a ruckus, laughing at something in the water of the canal. Mark and Hardy had already watched this entire scene play out several times before in preparation, so they knew what was in the water. It was a dead pigeon.

Their mocking of the dead bird said a lot about the men, who were probably in their early twenties. What they would do next proved it beyond a shadow of a doubt.

17th Century Amsterdam had a large crime problem, though most of it resided outside the city limits. The city had an unusual criminal justice system. It had no jails to speak of and did not imprison criminals. Instead, all criminals were banished from its limits. If they ever reentered, the penalty was severe, often death.

The result was gangs of outlaws who dwelt on country highways right outside the city limits, preying on travelers and smaller villages. And if a criminal was dumb enough to come back into Amsterdam, all his inhibitions were thrown to the wind as the probability of death was already strong.

These two men were drunk. They had stumbled back into Amsterdam for who knew what reason, maybe out of rebellion, maybe for the thrill of taunting the authorities.

In a few moments, these two hoodlums would snatch Rachel Hertz as she passed by and drag her into an alley, clamping their filthy paws over her mouth to keep her from screaming. They'd kick out some boards covering an abandoned home's basement window and cram her through the opening. They'd have their way with her for several hours and then dump her body in the canal when they were done.

And they would get away with it.

At least they had gotten away with it in the former version of history. That was about to change.

"Are you sure you want to watch this, Savannah?" Mark asked. "It's gonna be up close and personal this time."

The episode with the Apaches had been fought with rifles from a distance and ended swiftly. Such battles could seem bloodless to the distant observer, the permanency of the brutal death inflicted not seeming real. Hand to hand combat, however, was another story. It was in your face, bloody, and violent.

"I'll be fine, Mark," she said. "I can take it. I want to see this girl saved as much as you do."

Mark nodded. He still had in mind to spare her, and Rachel Hertz for that matter, from as much as possible. He positioned Savannah safely behind some crates in the alley and gave her a pistol. She could observe from there and back them up if needed without being seen.

As young Rachel approached, one of the men slapped the arm of the other to get his attention, and they scanned the streets to see if anyone was around. Mark and Hardy had concealed themselves out of sight. They had to let the attack begin or Rachel would never know she'd been saved.

The murderers rushed Rachel as she passed. She threw her arms up in sudden fear and tried to scream, but they were upon her before she could. Her groceries tumbled to the cobblestone and rolled in all directions. She struggled, trying to bite a dirty hand as it suffocated her mouth, but another yanked her arms painfully behind her back until she was helpless.

The men pushed and dragged her toward the alley.

Her eyes were wide with panic. She knew she was seeing the last moments of her short life.

Mark waited until they got her into the alley, counted to three, and then signaled. In under a second, he and Hardy were racing toward the scene of the crime. They rounded the corner at full speed and saw the men had almost gotten Rachel to the boarded up window.

Hearing the unexpected sound of Mark and Hardy's feet upon the rough pavers, the men jerked around and tried to face them, their grip automatically loosening on the girl. She fell to the pavement.

Both men were armed, but neither was ready. They scrambled to draw their crude pistols from their belts, but Mark was on his man before he could lift it out and Hardy slammed a punch into his target's jaw even sooner.

Mark slapped the gun out of the first thug's hand, who then went for a knife tucked in a hidden scabbard between his shoulder blades. Mark sent that clattering too. A few more well-placed punches to the solar plexus and Mark's guy fled the alley heaving for breath. Hardy's followed suit.

They could have put them out of commission for good right then and there, but they wished to protect both the young woman's and Savannah's sensibilities. They weren't about to let such evil men back into society's mix though, free to hurt someone else, so Mark and Hardy would catch up with them later, further down the street and out of sight.

"Are you okay, Miss?"

Terror reigned in her eyes. The girl trembled, her pupils darting back and forth between him and Hardy. She made a strange gulping sound as she tried to regain control over her breathing and battled the tears already welling.

On cue, Savannah emerged from behind the crates and gently laid her arm around the girl's shoulders. Rachel jerked at the touch but when she saw it was another woman, she relaxed. The reality of her salvation was fully dawning on her now.

"Are you okay, Miss?" Mark repeated.

She dared lock eyes with his for a flash of a moment.

"*Ich verstehe nicht.*" She shook her head.

Mark recognized German when he heard it, not that his German was much better than his Dutch. Still, he knew a few words.

"*Du bist* safe," Mark said. He waved his arms like an umpire to underscore the meaning of the word 'safe'.

"What, you think she's going to understand baseball?" Hardy

laughed.

Mark realized his folly. "All right, wise guy. Let's see you talk to her."

"Savannah seems to be doing a pretty good job of it already."

Savannah had gently lifted the girl from the pavement to a standing position, rubbing her shoulder in comfort. Rachel leaned her head against Savannah and let the tears she'd been fighting fall freely.

Savannah looked to Mark.

"Let's get her home."

Mark nodded. He was grateful for the outcome. He never knew when fate was going to rear its ugly head, forcefully blocking his efforts to save someone. Seeing this pretty young woman breathing, crying, *alive*...it made him thankful, even if for just a moment.

Chapter 25

That's a chin held high as the tears fall down
A gut sucked in, a chest stuck out

Something to be Proud Of

~ Montgomery Gentry

"Papa!"

"Rachel, was ist los?"

Rachel Hertz ran to her father and hugged him. She clung to him, gripping the sleeves of his robe in clenched fists. The Rabbi looked suspiciously upon Mark and friends, unsure if they were the cause of her stress, or her saviors from it.

After a few moments, she calmed enough to recount to him the story and he realized they were the latter. A broad smile broke out onto his face and he released his daughter, who was now smiling herself. Rabbi Naftali Hertz threw his arms wide to embrace his guests.

"Danke, danke. Danke schön." He kissed each of their cheeks in warm greeting.

"Deutsch nicht," Mark said, holding his hands up in a helpless gesture.

"Nederlands dan?"

"English?"

"Angelisch? Yes, I spreke zome Angelisch. Zank you very much for save my dooghter."

"It was nothing. She was in trouble, so we helped."

"Yes, it big thing. Zank you, zank you." He shook Mark and Hardy's hands and kissed Savannah's cheeks again. "Von't you stay fur zupper?"

They agreed to stay for the evening meal and soon an arousing blend of wonderful aromas were wafting in from the kitchen. Rachel and the young servant girl they'd seen before dedicated themselves to preparing the repast. Hertz's wife was laid up sick in bed and the rabbi apologized for her absence. He stoked the fire in his study until its warmth flooded the whole room. Books lined the walls on all sides.

He insisted on seating them in plush chairs and had them put their feet up on ottomans. He brought them cups of hot tea and the servant girl entered with a plate bearing four ginger cookies.

"*Vier? Aaghie, verkrijge meer koekjen,*" the rabbi said.

She left and returned a minute later with eight cookies on the plate.

"Ach, zat girl vill be zee death of me."

He rose and took her elbow, guiding her back into the kitchen. After a moment, he returned.

"Sorry, Dutch thriftiness, hard to overcome," he said.

Aaghie returned this time with an overflowing plate and a reddened face. She placed the cookies before them and withdrew back into the kitchen.

They conversed lightly with the rabbi, inquiring into his work and what he was doing in Amsterdam. He explained that he was German by birth, born in Frankfurt. He'd married his wife, Esther, who was from Bacharach, Germany and they'd settled there. He was a student of ancient Jewish texts. When they pressed for details, he explained that during his studies, he had discovered something he called the *Massakhet Keilim*, which was basically an ancient scroll which told the whole story of Jeremiah and the other men of God hiding the Ark and how they recorded the hiding places on the various scrolls.

"So, why did you come to Amsterdam?" Mark asked.

"I vant to publish my book. Zehr is no other city vhere I can preent it. Only Leipzig. Leipzig too far."

"Have any of the ancient texts you studied given you a hint as to where any of those scrolls are?"

"Ze Marble Tablets, I not know. Ze Copper Scroll and ze Vellum Scroll are said to be together, somevhere east of Jerusalem, but I not know vhere."

"Have you ever heard anything about the Silver Scroll? Where it might be?"

"Maybe. I zink so. I vould have to search my papers."

"Would you mind looking?"

The Rabbi looked puzzled.

Mark laughed to lighten the moment. "I'm sorry, it's just that I also am a student of history and this is not the first time I have heard of this Silver Scroll. I've always been curious about things to do with the Ark."

"Vhat have you heard of the Silver Scroll? Eet is not zuch a common thing you know."

"Not much. I've heard it mentioned before."

"Who? Who has mentioned it? I know no one."

"Uh..."

Savannah broke in, "Antonio Fernandez Carvajal is a friend of ours."

"I not hear of him."

"He is a Jewish merchant in London. He works to allow the Jewish people to return to England."

"Eet is a noble thing. Still, I not know him." Apparently appeased, the rabbi got up and went over to his desk where he began rifling through papers. He picked up a couple of journals and flipped through their pages, searching for something.

Finally, he found what he was looking for and scanned it, running his finger along several lines of text. "Ah yes. Here eet is." He looked up at them, tapping the page. "Vhen I vas younger, I met ze son of Rabbi Isaac Luria, who vas very...he know very much. I wrote down something he say to me zen. He say ze vatter of his grandvatter..."

"His great-grandfather?"

"Yes, his great-grandvatter. Zis man speak of Silver Scroll. Vhen he live in Venice, he see a book. A book vhich say vhere eet is."

"Where what is?" Hardy asked.

"Ze Silver Scroll."

"Who saw this book?"

"Ze great-grandvatter."

"When was this? What was his name?"

"I zink it vas Shlomo. Shlomo Luria. I not know vhen. Ze great-grandson vas about forty years old. Maybe Shlomo live around...maybe 1500 AD." The rabbi smiled, pleased with the amount of information he'd been able to provide.

Mark looked at Hardy and Savannah. They weren't so happy with the vagueness of the answer, but smiled anyway. More specifics would have gone a long way. They chatted a while longer and then excused themselves politely. Now that a relationship had been established, they could come back later if more information was needed.

As soon as they were far enough from the house to not be heard, they discussed the developments in earnest.

"Where in the world did you get that name?" Mark asked Savannah. "Antonio..."

"Antonio Fernandez Carvajal?"

"Yeah, that."

Zack Mason

"You know those historical packets you had me prepare a while ago, the ones filled with all the historical data you could ever need to prepare for travel to any era of any country?"

"Yeah."

"You might read one some time. They're full of good stuff." She winked.

Chapter 26

Long before 1525, the Venetian Republic had designated the Island of Giudecca as land where Venetian Jews could live and express their faith as they chose. Giudecca soon came to be referred to as the *ghetto*, referring to the early foundries which had been located on the island and were called *geti* in Venetian. In fact, all later so-called ghettos were named after this one.

No Jew was allowed to live elsewhere in Venice, and Christians were not generally allowed to interfere with Jewish life in their *ghetto*.

The most immediately notable feature to any visitor of the ghetto was the strange construction of its buildings. This island was the extent of the territory the Jews were allowed, so, by reason of necessity, as their population grew, their buildings grew taller and their streets more narrow. Virtually every building was devoid of paint. The construction looked like one story had just been slapped on top of another as demand for living space required, and it was not uncommon for these shabbily built residences to collapse upon themselves from time to time.

In the center of the community was the Scuola, the ghetto's main synagogue. It looked fairly unimpressive compared with other synagogues Mark had seen.

All Venetian Jews were required to wear a circle of yellow cloth sewn on the breast of their outer garment. The sight of hundreds of yellow patches worn by these Jews set Mark back a few steps when he first saw it. It reminded him too much of the yellow stars of Nazi Germany and he hadn't been expecting it.

Savannah reassured him it did not carry the same stigma for these people as then. The Nazis had in fact borrowed the practice from previous eras like this, but in 16th century Venice, it was not a badge of shame, just an inconvenient reminder of prejudice.

Venice was actually known as one of the more tolerant of

European communities toward Jews for its day. Here, they were allowed to work as doctors, bankers, or dealers in second-hand goods, but they were not allowed to serve as merchants dealing with other Christians.

Shlomo Luria, the man they sought, lived on the bottom floor of a five story residence. Less affluent families took the higher floors.

He worked as a low-level loan officer in a bank owned by a prominent Jewish family. By Jewish Law, Jews were not allowed to charge other Jews interest, so most of the bank's customers were Christians from the main section of Venice in search of capital loans.

Mark had decided they would not try to blend in. They would have great difficulty passing themselves off as Venetian Jews with any authenticity. Instead, they would represent themselves as foreign travelers who wished to make a large deposit with the bank. They would ask for Luria by name, claiming he had been recommended to them.

This bank was not like its modern-day counterparts. There was no large marquis sign out front advertising its name. It simply looked like one more building in a long line of tall, narrow, bare-faced tenements. Inside was not a wide-open space filled with desks and teller stations ringed by offices and a vault, but a small hallway filled with a single desk attended by a middle-aged man. Spots of grey streaked the hair at his temples.

Once again, Mark's team had secured an interpreter. Their interpreter of choice spoke perfect English, being an Englishman himself. He'd emigrated from London to Venice more than a decade before, and that made his English very understandable, though his accent was strong. They hoped his Italian would be good enough.

They asked for Shlomo Luria. The receptionist nodded and bid them to wait while he retreated behind a door. He returned and motioned for them to follow. The man led them to a simply furnished office.

Behind the desk, a slender man with angular features stood to greet them as Mark and friends entered. He shook hands with each of them as the receptionist brought in enough chairs for all to sit, though the space felt cramped when he was done.

They held their conversation through the interpreter.

"To what do I owe the pleasure, gentlemen?" Luria said.

"We wish to make a significant deposit with your bank," Mark answered.

They discussed the deposit, its size, and how and when funds would be available should they wish to make a withdrawal. Life in 1525 was not as fast-paced as the 21st century, so it was natural and easy to extend the conversation beyond the business at hand. Shooting the breeze was a part of doing business, building trust through relationship.

Mark inquired about Jewish life in Venice which brought them into a discussion of all things Jewish. They then steered the conversation to Jewish history and eventually the destruction of Solomon's Temple by the Babylonians. Luria was impressed with the knowledge of his visitors. Savannah explained that Mark had been given a copy of the Wycliffe Bible and they had all read it. This impressed Luria even more. As a Jew, he had always been amazed by how few of the Christians in Europe actually knew anything of what their own Scriptures said. Even the priests were mostly ignorant. In comparison, all Jewish boys were trained in the Torah and other rabbinic writings from an early age.

Collectively, the three friends artfully focused the conversation on the Ark of the Covenant, but Luria seemed to have no information. Mark recounted the legend they had heard regarding the hiding away of the Ark, and the documents that had been written about its location. Even when Mark pressed specifically about the Silver Scroll, Luria remained blank-faced.

"I am sorry," he said. "I know nothing of these things."

Mark slumped back in his seat. "That is too bad. It is true we are passing through Venice, but we had heard the Ghetto was a place with much learning at its fingertips. We are students of ancient relics and had hoped to learn more about these things while we are here."

"Sir, I would be more than happy to make you an appointment with my rabbi," Luria said cheerfully. He would probably get a small commission for their deposit and wanted to make them happy. "He may know something I do not."

"That would be great," Mark said resignedly. He took a sack of gold coins from his satchel and placed them on Luria's desk. "Of course, we'll need a certificate of deposit for these."

"Of course, *monsignore*." Luria took the sack and began counting the coins, making scratch marks on a paper as he did. He paused in mid-count and snapped his fingers. "Oh yes! I may know someone who can help. Carlo Lutono. He is a nobleman, from your country, I believe. A great collector of ancient documents."

Mark smiled. "Well, let's go see him."

***

Luria led them through the winding streets of Giudecca to a dock where a ferry picked them up. The wide Giudecca Canal separated this island from the rest of Venice. The ferry deposited the crew in the *Piazza San Marco*. St. Mark's Square was the largest open area in all Venice, bordered on one side by St. Mark's Cathedral and the *Doge*'s Palace on another. Here was the heart of Venice.

There were no carriages or horses within the city limits. Venice was then as it is now. You got around by foot, or by boat, or you didn't go.

As they made their way into the city and neared some of the smaller canals, a distinctive, unpleasant odor reached their nostrils. The dark water swirled with wooden splinters and fruit peelings. The odor, however, was from something much more foul. Much of the human waste in the city was dumped directly into the canals, and the water here did not circulate enough to keep things fresh.

Luria turned right down an even narrower street. He took a shortcut through a side alley and they found themselves dodging clothes hanging out to dry between the buildings.

Eventually, they arrived at an open area, another square, though much smaller than St. Mark's. Luria made a beeline to a large house on the right, four stories tall, and much wider than most of the other homes. The bank officer asked them to wait while he asked for Lutono.

After a minute, they were all ushered up several flights of stairs to a plush study. Red velvet tapestries hung over every section of wall that wasn't covered by cherry-stained bookcases. Only half of the "bookcases," however, were actually designed for the storage of books. The other half housed hundreds of small, diamond-shaped cubby-holes, which were filled with scrolls.

A massive, ornamental stone fireplace took up most of one wall. Another wall consisted mainly of large decorative windows which overlooked the square below. The head of an antlered stag had been mounted on a wood plaque above the fireplace.

Mark, Savannah, and Hardy each took seats in finely carved wooden chairs. The seat cushions were covered in red silk. Overall, it was a very luxurious environment. Lutono was a man of means.

Presumably, Luria had gone to meet Lutono and explain the purpose of their visit.

Hardy studied the books on the shelves and the scrolls. "What's an Englishman doing with a name like Carlo Lutono?" he asked.

"Charles Lutton to a fellow countryman," a voice boomed.

A large, barrel-chested man strode into the study. His silk robes did not reduce his masculinity in the least. He was a force unto himself, a man to be reckoned with. Shlomo Luria entered the room behind him.

He thrust out his hand to Mark in greeting.

Mark took it. "Mr. Lutton, I presume."

The man laughed. "*Baron* Von Lutton, if we wish to be precise, but no matter." He shook hands with Hardy and greeted Savannah with a kiss on the cheek.

"To what do I owe the pleasure of this visit from fellow Englishmen?" He asked.

His accent was clearly British, though distinct from modern British. It was more refined, yet certain words were hard to make out.

"*Sono interessati in libri antichi circa manufatti biblici,*" Luria said.

"So, you are interested in ancient manuscripts, biblical artifacts?" Lutton asked.

"Yes, we are, sir. And *Signore* Luria was kind enough to recommend you as an expert in these matters," Mark said.

"Are you *lollards* then? Where are you from? Your accent is strange."

Savannah stepped in. "We have been raised in Paris." She curtseyed. "Yes, you might say we are Wycliffites, sir."

Lutton laughed. "No offense meant, *mademoiselle*. I too am a Lollard."

"None taken, sir."

They conversed comfortably for a while. Lutton had his servants bring in numerous refreshments. It was reminiscent of their recent visit in Amsterdam with Rabbi Hertz, only this study was much more luxurious.

When he had an opportunity, Mark leaned over and whispered to Savannah, "What's a *lollard*?"

She turned her face toward him and whispered back, her words puffs of feathery breath upon his ear. "John Wycliffe was one of the first men to translate the Bible into English. His followers, or those who read his translation, are called *lollards*. By 1525, the term is a negative one and can mean heretic, depending on who's using it."

"Ah." Mark returned his attention to the conversation at hand. Hardy was asking Lutton about the Ark of the Covenant. He mentioned the same legend of Jeremiah and the alleged records telling where it was hidden.

The baron clapped his hands. "Oh, splendid indeed! It is rare to find such learned gentry. Yes, yes, I know of this legend as well."

"Have you ever heard of the Silver Scroll?" Mark asked.

Lutton stared into Mark as if deciphering his soul, his intent. After a long moment, when the weight of the silence grew so uncomfortable it seemed someone might scream just to break it, Lutton finally spoke.

"It is strange you should inquire about that very document. I, myself, had never heard of such a thing, until recently. Several weeks ago, I acquired a scroll that speaks of this *cosa*. Where did you hear of it?"

"From a Rabbi in Paris," Mark answered. "May we see the scroll?"

Lutton rose from his chair and crossed the room to some of the cubby-holes near the fireplace. He removed one of the scrolls and unrolled it gently on a small table.

"Aren't you worried about keeping these ancient books so close to the fireplace?" Savannah asked.

Lutton glanced at the hearth. "We keep it screened at all times."

Mark, Savannah, and Hardy moved in closer to see the scroll. It was written in medieval script. The header at the top read:

CARTAE

Protectio   Argenteae

What followed was a long series of random letters. In the center of the letters lay a separate scrap of paper filled with a series of roman numerals.

"What language is that?" Hardy asked.

"Latin," Savannah whispered.

"My, you are educated, young lady!" Lutton declared.

She blushed.

"That's Latin? It looks like just a bunch of letters" Hardy looked puzzled.

"Just the top three words," Lutton explained. "The rest is a cipher, a code of some sort."

"Have you deciphered it yet?"

The baron shook his head. "No, it has proven very difficult. The title is intriguing, though, you must admit."

"The Hiding Place of the Silver Scroll," Savannah translated.

Hardy raised his eyebrows and Mark took a sharp intake of breath.

"Would you be willing to sell this?" Mark asked. "We can pay well."

It was Lutton's turn to look surprised. He shook his head. "No, no, I'm sorry, I do not wish to part with such a spectacular item."

"Would you mind if we made a copy then?"

"I'm sorry. This scroll is not for public consumption. I only showed it to you because of our common passions."

Mark backed down, but his face had clouded over. He was frustrated, but Hardy knew that wouldn't last.

Chapter 27

"Remember, man. Venice will be tricky. Be careful before you shift," Mark said.

The skin of Hardy's face was a cold blue in the bright moonlight. The rest of him blended well with the darkness, covered in the black rubber of scuba gear, which they both wore.

The brisk night air was cool and crisp as it blew across Mark's cheeks. The faint odor of human refuse and garbage still wafted into their nostrils, but the strong nocturnal breeze greatly diminished its strength from daytime levels under the summer sun.

Hardy was double-checking the date and time on his shifter in case he had to hit it in a hurry. Savannah was going to sit this round out.

"What do you think is safe?" He asked.

"Set it to tomorrow. The skyline of Venice is constantly changing. The farther we shift from today, the better the chance we have of finding ourselves falling into a canal in the middle of the night."

"Or to the pavement from four stories up."

"Exactly."

Because of water-logged foundation of the city, Venice was known for unstable edifices.

"I'll set it for noon tomorrow, so if we do fall into a canal, at least we won't be dunked in the middle of the night."

"No, set it for this same time tomorrow. If we have to shift out in a hurry, it's best to shift to a time when people are asleep. We won't have a problem with the structural consistency of the buildings after just one day."

"Roger that."

They synched their target time settings for three in the morning the next day.

They had positioned themselves across the canal from Lutton's house. They were going to borrow his scroll — just for a little while. Long enough to make a copy and then return it. If all went as planned, they'd have the scroll back before Lutton even knew it was gone.

"Let's go."

They slipped into the canal, the thickened water closing in around their bodies silently. The odor was much stronger at the water's surface. Mark almost gagged on the stench and vowed to take a thorough shower as soon as they were done.

"Man, it stinks," Hardy whispered.

Mark nodded in agreement and slipped his regulator into his mouth and his goggles over his eyes. Hardy did the same, and then they were slicing through the water.

They weren't headed directly to Lutton's house though. The baron was wealthy enough he could afford to have a guard constantly stationed at his front door, and that same front door sported a heavy iron gate which looked like it might shriek if they tried to pick the lock and squeeze it open in the middle of the night.

Instead, they were going to use the canal to sneak into the house next door. The rooflines of the two homes were about the same height, so they could make their way to the roof of the neighbor's house and then jump over to Lutton's. Then, they'd make their way down to Lutton's study from the roof.

Mark surfaced in a large enclosed pool inside the neighbor's house. It was the Venetian equivalent of a garage, a storage area for the family boat. This family was much less well-off than Lutton, so they had very little in the way of security measures.

Mark pulled himself from the oily water onto a wooden platform. The water dripped in puddles under him. Hardy followed suit and they wriggled out of their scuba gear, revealing dry, unstinking clothes beneath. They folded their wetsuits and stashed them together with their air tanks in a corner of the boat dock.

The stairs to the top of this residence were rickety. Stepping lightly at the edge of each step, they successfully elicited only three squeaks from the rusty nails holding the risers in place on their way to the rooftop. A family or two occupied the bottom two floors, but the upper stories were empty, probably because of the instability of the structure.

Once on the roof, they made their way over to the toe wall at its edge. There was no gap between this house and Lutton's, but there was a six foot difference in height. Mark interlaced his fingers and lowered them for Hardy to step into his palms. Mark heaved him up until Hardy could grasp the rim of the Lutton's roof and lift himself up and over. Then, Hardy stretched out flat and grasped Mark's forearms, hoisting him up until he could do the same.

A rustic wooden structure stood in the center of Lutton's roof. It looked kind of like an outhouse, but it housed the staircase which led down into the cramped mansion. A rusty, oversized lock gripped the door's iron latch, but it was no match for their lock-picking skills and clicked open after just a few seconds work.

The door shrieked loudly as they swung it open.

They cringed.

They dropped low, listening. A couple dogs barked incessantly in the distance. A few more closer to home had picked up the chorus after the door's squealing. Lutton had dogs, but none of them seemed to have been alerted. If they were on the lower floors, the sound might not have reached them.

They squatted and waited.

Somewhere on a nearby canal, a gondolier crooned a lonely melody. Silence was all that met their ears from the house as they leaned in, straining to hear any sounds of movement from its occupants.

Nothing.

They crept into the stairwell and began their descent. One would expect the construction of Lutton's residence to be of higher quality than his poorer neighbor, but the noises their feet extracted from the planks on the stairs here belied that. They shrank back with every squeak and redoubled their efforts to avoid noise.

They were going to have to be quick. With the racket they were making, the whole household might be roused at any minute. Thankfully, Lutton's study was on the third floor, so they didn't have much further to go.

When they reached the study, the faint odor of smoke greeted them, hinting a warning. Mark thrust his arm across Hardy's chest, holding him back from entering. Glowing embers peeked out of the fireplace, but elsewhere the room was too dark to see if anyone was inside.

Mark removed a pair of night vision binoculars from his pack and flipped them on. The device emitted a high-pitched whine when they started up. Almost immediately, ferocious barking erupted from the room below. Mark cursed under his breath.

Mark hastily scanned the study in the green glow of the night vision scope. No one.

He motioned them forward and they rushed to the corner where the scroll was kept.

"It would have been better if you hadn't turned those on,"

Hardy whispered.

"What if Lutton had fallen asleep in a chair in the study? Why did they make that sound?"

"They're my old ones, from my time on Delta. They're 1ˢᵗ Gen. Sorry."

"Well, bring the modern stuff next time."

Several heavy thuds from below meant people were getting out of bed, roused by the dogs. More noise came from the level above them.

"Move it!"

Hardy located the cipher scroll Lutton had shown them.

"Make sure that scrap of paper with the roman numerals is there," Mark said.

Hardy unrolled it a little further. The scrap was there. He rolled it back up tightly and lowered it gently into the water-proof pouch Mark held out. Mark zipped it closed and placed the bag inside a steel, water-tight cylinder. He screwed on the top and dropped the whole thing in his pack.

"Let's go."

As they rushed toward the study's door, they could hear men and dogs racing up the stairs from below. More footsteps thudded coming down from the fourth floor. Mark and Hardy reached the study's exit and turned for the stairs to the roof. The snapping of the dogs was so close behind, it seemed the beasts and their masters must be right on their heels. About halfway up to the fourth floor, they bowled a man over before he understood what was happening. Mark recognized the pale, panicked visage of Charles Lutton as they rushed past.

They poured out onto the roof.

"Here, take this and move out," Mark said, holding out the silver container, "I'll cover you." Hardy took the cylinder.

A sharp explosion rocked the night and Mark twisted in pain. He fell flat.

Lutton's guards had shot him.

Hardy stopped and pulled out his pistol.

Mark grimaced, but warded him off with a hand. "Don't shoot 'em. I'm right behind you." He stumbled to his feet. Lutton's guards were still about thirty feet away, but they'd loosed the dogs.

"Jump across and shift," Mark ordered.

Hardy leapt across to the neighboring rooftop. It was not the same building they'd used earlier, but was another residence on the other side of Lutton's house. Mark heard Hardy's feet hit, followed by the static hiss of his shift.

Mark didn't wait to shift. The dogs were almost on top of him. He hit the button.

***

Hardy landed hard on the lower rooftop. It was about a ten foot drop. He felt the building tremble and sway under the impact of his feet. He gave it a second to settle and then stood. He ran and hit his shifter in mid-stride.

The next thing he knew, he was falling. Falling into blackness.

***

Mark exhaled deeply. They were safe from pursuit, hidden away safely in time. Just one lone dog barked now in the cool night. He heard the shift static of Hardy's entrance from the other side of the ledge. Next, a sharp cry pierced the darkness, followed by a distant crash.

Mark raced to the parapet at the edge of Lutton's roof and peered over. He could see nothing but darkness. And he should see a roof.

The moon was bright enough he should see a roof.

"Hardy?" He called.

No answer.

Mark lit up his night vision goggles again. Hardy lay twisted about three stories below on top of a tangled mess of roof beams and bricks. Incredibly, the house next door had collapsed at some point during the past twenty-four hours. He knew Venetian homes in 1525 were not real stable affairs. Savannah had said building collapses were somewhat a common occurrence, but this was ridiculous.

Mark cursed and ran to the opposite side of Lutton's roof. He jumped down the six feet to the roof of the house they'd used to gain access to Lutton's and bounded down the stairs, two at a time.

Before he'd gone too far, he caught himself and slowed down. No need to complicate matters by waking this house up too.

It took Mark a full twenty minutes to get over to the rubble and climb up the mess to where Hardy lay. His body was mutilated, though he was still alive somehow. Jagged white shards of bone pierced through the skin of both his legs. Blood poured from several gashes in his head. His friend was deeply unconscious, possibly dying.

Mark took note of the exact position of Hardy's body. Then, he shifted to earlier in the day before Hardy fell. He bought a horse and a cart and filled the cart with pillows. The "pillows" were nothing more than canvas sacks stuffed with duck down. He returned to the pile of rubble, staked the horse out, and laid the pillows in thick rows on the spot Hardy would hit. He shifted forward to the moment just before the fall and readjusted the pillows to make sure they were positioned right. They were at least three thick everywhere. Around where Hardy's head would hit, Mark had put four.

Static hissed from the sky above. Hardy slammed into the pillows like a human meteor. The crash expelled the breath from his lungs with a rush of air. Something snapped. Hardy rolled off the thick pillows onto the jagged bricks and groaned. Mark was right by his side in an instant.

"Sorry, pal," He said.

"What happened?" Hardy moaned.

"This house collapsed sometime between last night and now. I tried to cushion your fall with some pillows."

"Lutton?"

"We're fine. We've just got to get you out of Venice."

"I think my leg's broken," he said.

Mark examined it. It probably was. He'd heard something snap, but there was no bone extruding this time, so at least that was an improvement.

"Anything else?" Mark asked.

Hardy rolled back and forth and tried to sit, but gave up, wincing in pain. "Got the wind knocked out of me. Feel like someone beat me with a sledgehammer."

"Is that all?" Mark laughed. "You should have seen yourself the first time."

"What first time?"

"The time you hit without the pillows."

"Don't remember that."

"Believe me, that's a good thing. Let's get you out of here before my past self shows up and I see myself." Mark had a strong aversion to ever meeting his past or future self.

He got Hardy to his feet and Mark helped him limp down the pile of rubble with Hardy's arm draped across his shoulder. Mark loaded Hardy into the cart, careful not to bump his leg.

"You got the cylinder?"

Through gritted teeth, Hardy managed a grin and raised the

silver tube high.

Mark guided the horse away from Lutton's neighborhood. He had no desire to shift around Venice anymore. This town was too unpredictable. Still, Hardy was in a lot of pain and he needed to get him some care quickly.

Once they reached St. Mark's square, Mark reckoned they had gone far enough. St. Mark's was virtually the same now as it would be four hundred years in the future. He placed his hand on Hardy's shoulder and shifted them forward to the future.

The cart lurched and tilted down. Hardy slid forward and Mark had to grab his shoulder to keep him from jarring his broken leg on the pavement. The cart had come with them, but not the horse. Must have been too much mass for the shifter to move.

An Italian policeman stood in front of them, staring open-mouthed at the unexpected phantoms that had just materialized out of nowhere before his eyes.

"Hospital?" Mark asked.

Chapter 28

The *ospedale* was an odd collage of antiquity and modern technology. The policeman had somehow understood Mark's one word question and called for an ambulance. The ambulance turned out to be a water *ambulanza*, a boat specially outfitted for transporting patients. They were taken to a nearby hospital where Hardy was set up in a room by himself and examined by a doctor. After eight hours that is. Oh, the joys of socialized medicine.

Eight hours waiting in a hospital with a broken leg just to get seen. Well, Hardy had to wait that long. Mark had just shifted ahead to the hour the doctor had finally gotten around to seeing them.

According to the physician, it wasn't a bad break. Hardy had sustained a simple fracture in his right tibia, but no other serious injury. The makeshift pillows had done a decent job. As soon as the technician finished setting a cast on his leg, Hardy would be released. Savannah had already sent the corporate jet ahead to the Venetian airport, so they'd be on their way home in no time.

Mark went to fetch them a couple of Cokes. Icy drips of water rolled off the bottles onto his wrists as he rounded a corner in the hospital's hallway. He couldn't believe the prices of soft drinks here. These had cost him nearly five bucks a piece. He was glad he didn't live in Europe, not that he couldn't afford it, it was just the principle of the thing.

Mark reached the room and stopped short. Then, he rushed through the door. Something was wrong with Hardy. A neat, red hole had bloomed in the center of his forehead. His friend stared open-eyed at the ceiling. The window in front of his bed had been torn open by the shot.

Mark dropped to the floor. Hardy's pack laid open on the floor. Mark snatched it and peered inside.

Empty.

The scroll was gone.

He crawled out of the room and raced down the hall, scanning every face for one he recognized. There had to have been at least two men, a sniper outside and someone else inside the hospital to grab the bag.

Rialto.

With a shifter, it could have been just one guy. Still, they would have wanted back-up.

Mark stopped short of the street, holding position inside the entranceway to the hospital. He would be a target too. After taking the first shot, the shooter would have shifted to another time to avoid detection. He probably would have used a jammer too so Mark couldn't track him.

Mark set his shifter to a couple of hours before Hardy was shot so he could scout around prior to the event. About an hour before, he saw a familiar figure entering the building across the street from the hospital carrying a long black case. Vincent Torino.

Torino hadn't seen Mark, but then he hadn't appeared to be worried about being seen either. Graves was probably out there somewhere backing Torino up. And Rialto had probably sent Cook or someone else into the hospital to grab the cylinder with the scroll.

Mark had no desire to get into a firefight with Rialto right now, but he had to find a way to undo what had been done. No matter how often it happened, you never get over seeing your friend's dead body, even if you can undo it.

A newspaper stand in the hall about ten feet away caught Mark's eye. The paper on display blared the headlines for the day. A story at the top, right-hand side of the front page jumped out. There was a picture of the policeman they'd encountered the previous night when shifting into St. Mark's Square.

Mark studied the headline, trying to make it out:

Due uomini appaiono misteriosamente in Piazza San Marco

The Italian was too difficult. He grabbed the nearest nurse he could find.

"*Parli Inglese?*" He asked.

She didn't, but she got another nurse who spoke some broken English. Mark jabbed his finger at the newspaper headline.

"Eet...ah...eet say, 'Two men appear meesteeriously in *Piazza San Marco*. St. Mark Square."

"Thanks."

She walked off, eyeing him weirdly. The policemen had

blabbed the story all over town and the newspaper had picked it up. The hospital staff had to be aware of it too. Amazing there wasn't a flock of reporters hovering around the building. Likely, the policeman hadn't been fully believed. This paper was probably more of a tabloid type publication than a regular paper.

Still, it had been enough for Rialto to locate them.

***

Mark shifted back to the previous night and caught the policeman after he left Mark and Hardy in the water ambulance. The patrolman looked astonished to see Mark again. After all, he'd just watched him leave in a boat with the man with the broken leg.

Mark motioned him over to an empty café table under the colonnade in the plaza. The officer sat tentatively, expectantly, and crossed his legs with a haughty look on his face. Still being the middle of the night, the square was empty except for the two of them.

Mark slapped a briefcase on the table and opened it. It was filled with stacks of Euros. The policeman's eyes widened in surprise.

When the officer's eyes fixed back on Mark, Mark held a finger to his lips as if to say "be quiet" and pointed at the money. Then, Mark laid his pistol at the other end of the table and raised his eyebrows questioningly. He'd shown the carrot, he'd shown the stick, and he hoped he'd communicated what it was he wanted. He pushed the briefcase toward the officer and put his finger to his lips again.

The officer looked back and forth between the money and the pistol and then nodded. He closed the briefcase and took it.

Mark re-holstered his pistol and shifted out right in front of the officer, as if to punctuate the transaction with an exclamation point. *We have powers you can't dream of, so don't mess with us.*

When he got back to the hospital, Hardy was fine and dandy — and still thirsty. There was no newspaper story, no bullet hole in Hardy's forehead, and the scroll was back safe in the pack again.

"Good to see you, friend." Mark said, smiling.

"Don't know what's so good about it. Where have you been anyway? Where's the Cokes?"

"Sorry, I forgot. I'll go get them now."

"You should have let me shoot Lutton's men. This leg hurts like the dickens."

"They were only protecting their property."

"Jump across and shift, you said...I should remember not to

listen to you."

"Not in a good mood, are we? It's a beautiful day outside."

"Doc says we're free to go."

"Good. The jet's waiting at the airport."

Chapter 29

"Man, you're gonna be impossible until that cast comes off," Mark said.

He laid a steaming box of pizza on the table in front of Hardy, who had his leg propped up on another chair.

Hardy looked awfully smug as he extracted a slice of pepperoni and raised it to his lips, trying not to crack up.

Savannah burst out laughing. "You've created a monster, Mark. You never should have apologized to him."

Hardy interrupted, "Hey, he yelled 'Jump!' I jumped. Next thing I know I'm lying face down three stories below on a pile of bricks."

"On a pile of pillows," Mark corrected.

Hardy jabbed a finger toward his cast, pointing out his evidence. He grabbed another piece of pizza. He was going to milk it for all it was worth.

"So, what you got, boss?" He said.

"Savannah?" Mark turned to their resident historical expert.

She tucked a lock of her hair behind an ear as she began to explain. Mark had tasked her with researching the scroll they'd taken from Lutton's house.

Savannah gently unrolled the scroll on the conference table and pinned its corners with a stapler and a couple of paper weights.

CARTAE

Protectio   Argenteae

aqeArtyriopcasdafghDkeleezxicCbevlbantmuqsnpeerrtqyuiionpqausedufghiopasdfg hk[zRisesdtmlsbtkncrfzekncrfpdtmlsxveigasdtmlsxvrplmryihYgedtmlsbtDioplmryi hrdtmlsxveigapkncrfadtmlsbtrnckçeeigatdtmlqtLvrmryihSYgudtmllbFzomryihDiu sdtmlsxvplmryihisepdtmlqTlhpmryihiseedtmllbFzomryihiserdtmlqTlvrmryihiseqdt mlsbtplmryihiseudtmlqTLvrmryiheigaadtmlqTlhpmryihisetdtmllbFzomryihisetdtml

*qt£vrmryihiseudtml sxvplmryihnxfodtmlqtlhpmryihiserdtmlkxFzomryihkncrfTodt
mlqt£vrmryiheigaedtmlsbtplmryihkncrfrdtmlqTlhpmryihkncrfgdtmlqTlvrmryihknc
rfuplmryihdtmlsbtkncrfmplmryihdtmlsxvkncrfiplmryihdtmlsxvkncrfbzbdtmlsbtpl
mryihiseedtmllbFzomryihkncrfxdtmlqTtHpmryihkncrfuplmryihdtmlsbtkncrfmplmr
yihdtmlsbtkncrfeplmryihdtmlsxvkncrftdtmllbFzomryihkncrfadtmlqTLvrmryihkncr
fedtmlsbtplmryihkncrfnplmryihdtmlsbtkncrfeplmryihdtmlsxvkncrfuplmryihdtmlsbt
kncrfsdtmlqTlhpmryihkncrfpdtmlqTLvrmryihkncrfrdtmlkxszomryihkncrfodtmlqTl
hpmryiheiagapbeipimhtrareigoioYgeMzriseozoeigrMrbedtStisenzrnxfizieigtntuDii
ziiseczcnxfszsYgceielseigirziuruDizqcqzqissezsnuxfzugeokgeitgabednpnmhteyeYg
cgzkncrrfkncrAfeigaialMeamrrmaoCrrienpduuso*

Ty whistled. "How in the world are we going to decipher that? It's just a bunch of letters."

"Tell 'em what the title says," Mark said.

"The Hiding Place of the Silver Scroll," Savannah answered.

"In other words," Mark said, "if we want to find the silver scroll, we have to decipher it. Did your guys have any luck?"

Savannah took a deep breath and released it.

"Well, this was not an easy task. I figured the code was most likely to be in Latin, so I had to find some medieval experts who are fluent in Latin to look at it. It wasn't easy to get their interest over at Harvard because the dean of my department is convinced it's a recent forgery. The scroll doesn't show enough aging to have been written seven or eight hundred years ago."

"We know why that is," Mark interrupted.

"Of course." She flashed a smile Mark's way.

"I pushed them to date it based on the script, and the universal consensus was Central Europe, 12th or 13th century.

"The problem with most college professors is they are not flexible thinkers. You need people like you'll find over at the CIA to decode something like this, not medieval historians."

"If we need to get the CIA involved, the president can set that up."

She creased her brow and shook her head. "It's okay, no need. I thought we weren't going to get anywhere at first, but Professor Sandburg found the key. He's actually a mathematician. Latin is just one of his hobbies.

"The most obvious issue is the long series of random letters. The only legible part is the three words at the top. We assumed any medieval cipher was going to have a somewhat simple key used to encode it. Sandburg thought it could be a substitution cipher. That's when every letter is replaced consistently by another. For example, every *x* could represent a *d*.

"He ran the string of letters through a deciphering software program that checks for that, but got nothing, no matter what letters were substituted. So, he thought it might be an ELS pattern."

"What's an ELS pattern?"

"Equidistant Letter Sequence."

"And that means?"

"You skip a certain number of letters repeatedly. For example, you would count every fourth letter and see if any words show up."

"Did that work?"

"We did find something, but it wasn't easy. There's no apparent key."

"C'mon, Savannah, what did you find?" Mark said, exasperated.

She smiled.

"Sandburg tried skipping every other letter, then every two letters. It was when he skipped at three-letter intervals that a couple Latin words showed up which made sense. The cipher read *Arca Dei.*"

"*Arca Dei*? What does that mean?"

"Ark of God."

Mark took a sharp intake of breath. They'd been pursuing the Ark long enough that he was emotionally invested in finding it now. Ty sat forward in his chair expectantly. Hardy started to do the same, winced at the pressure it put on his leg and changed his mind.

"So, that's definitely it, then. It's an ELS sequence."

"Yes, but the words *Arca Dei* don't even take up half of the first line of the cipher. There's much more code in there. The first problem we encountered was the letters that follow *Arca Dei* are **e-a-u-p-r**."

"Which means?"

"Nothing. That's the problem. Sandburg guessed that the ELS distance might have changed or reset after *Arca Dei* and he was right. Skipping one letter instead of three after that revealed *Celatus per quinque,* which means 'Concealed by Five'."

"That would be the five men who hid the Ark?" Ty asked.

"That has to be it," Mark said.

"Presumably," Savannah replied, "After that, however, we were stuck. He tried skipping basic intervals of letters, but nothing popped out, and we were still in the first line of the cipher. We needed the key. Then, Sandburg noticed something."

The sleeve of her blouse slid smoothly across the skin of her arm as she pointed to the scribe's writing. It was a lightweight, sheer material. *Probably rayon*, Mark thought.

He shook his head, realizing he'd gotten distracted and refocused on what she was saying. Her lips were full and pink. Mark squeezed his eyes shut and refocused again, taking a deep breath. What was the matter with him?

"Look closely at the title of the scroll," she said.

CARTAE
Protectio   Argenteae

"It translates 'Hiding Place of the Silver Scroll'. The first word of the phrase is *protectio*, which means 'hiding place', but *cartae*, is on a separate line above it. Notice anything else unusual about *cartae*?"

"It's in all caps," Mark said.

"Yes"

"What does *cartae* mean," Ty asked.

"Letter or scroll. Here's the thing. If you were to read these lines normally, from top to bottom, it would translate 'Scroll of the Silver Hiding Place', yet because of the declension of the nouns, that doesn't even work out grammatically."

"Not sure what that means, but I'm following you," Mark said.

"So, 'Hiding Place of the Silver Scroll' is the only possible translation grammatically, but then *Cartae* should be on the same line as the other two words, in between them. That and the fact that *Cartae* is in all caps told us there was something special about that word.

"Professor Sandburg hypothesized that *CARTAE* might be the key to the cipher. 'C' is the third letter of the alphabet, and to get *Arca Dei*, we skipped every three letters. 'A' is the first letter of the alphabet, and we had to skip one letter to get the second line of the cipher. So, if the theory was correct, and 'R' was the next part of the key, then we needed to skip every 18th letter.

"Also, remember the scrap of paper with the roman numerals on it?"

She opened a small manila envelope and shook it gently until a small piece of paper fell out onto the table.

"We estimated it was very probable this scrap had some sort of connection with the cipher, or it wouldn't have been stored together with the scroll. Sandburg noted that the first line *Arca Dei* had two words, and the next line we deciphered had three words. He guessed the roman numerals were an extra help included for anyone decoding the scroll, revealing how many words would be in any translated line. If true, there would be a total of six lines to decode."

"And?"

"Nothing. When we skipped every eighteen letters, the result was all gibberish. We tried skipping the same number of letters as the roman numerals, but that didn't work. We tried starting over at the beginning, but nothing. We went home that night very frustrated, thinking the theory was wrong.

"But then Sandburg called me in the middle of the night all excited because he'd remembered that the Latin alphabet didn't have a 'J'. That meant the 'R' in *CARTAE* would be an instruction to skip every seventeen letters, not eighteen."

Savannah grinned victoriously. "And *that* worked. The Roman numeral theory also seems to be correct. They seem to represent the number of words in each line."

She saw Mark was about to burst with anticipation, so she went ahead and distributed a sheet of paper to each of them with the deciphered text on it.

"Here's what we got."

Arca Dei
Celatus per quinque
Reseratus per quattuor
Tergum ibexum et aeneus prope Succaca
Marmor in duo

The Ark of God
Secreted by Five
Revealed by Four
Ibex and Copper near Succaca
Marble in two

They studied the paper for a couple of minutes.

"*Succaca* is the ancient Hebrew name for the area around Qumran, which is where the Ibex skin scroll and the Copper scroll were found."

Mark looked puzzled. "But...it doesn't give the location of the 'Marble in two,' which I assume is referring to the two Marble Tablets. It clearly says where to look for the Ibex and Copper scrolls, but not the other?"

"That's true."

"We're saying the "secreted by five" means the five men of God who hid the Ark at Jeremiah's direction, and the 'Revealed by Four' presumably means the Ark's location is revealed by four documents, but if you count the Marble tablets as being two separate documents, then they together with the Ibex and Copper scrolls are four items. Yet the title of the scroll refers to the hiding place of the *Silver Scroll*, and this does not mention the Silver Scroll at all. That and it does not say where the marble tablets were hidden."

"Exactly," Savannah said, nodding her head vigorously. "Something appears to be wrong. We also established that the Roman numerals on the scrap corresponded to how many words were in each line. According to it, there should be six lines and we've only deciphered five. Also, the marble tablets line is supposed to have five words, not just three."

"Any ideas?"

She shook her head. "No good ones. We thought maybe the scroll was incomplete, that it had been torn. But there's no evidence of that. The last word, *duo*, is encoded at the very end of the cipher, so this appears to be the entire encoded text."

"Did you try continuing again at the beginning?"

"Yes, but we found nothing. The only thing we could imagine is that this scroll was an incomplete copy of an earlier scroll that had more text.

"You have *got* to be kidding me." Mark laid his face in his hands.

Hardy grunted. He was not pleased either.

"So, we're going to have to go back and find the monk who wrote this scroll and get the original he copied from?" Mark asked.

"I'm afraid so." Savannah shrugged her shoulders.

"Don't shrug like that — you remind me of Hardy."

"Hey!" Hardy objected.

"Any idea when or where this scroll was written?"

"No, not beyond what I already told you. Central Europe, 12th or 13th century."

"That's a two hundred year span."

"Like trying to find a needle in a haystack," Hardy commented.

"Well, there can only be so many monasteries in Central Europe during that time. We could just knock on all their doors until we find a monk who knows something about it."

"True."

"Or we could go back and ask Lutton where he got the scroll."

"Yeah, we can make Lutton talk," Hardy said.

Mark grimaced at the veiled threat. "You're just sore because his men chased you off the roof."

"I jumped off the roof because *somebody* told me to," he laughed.

Ty interrupted the banter.

"Hey, Savannah, did you guys try going backward?"

"What do you mean?"

"Well, the 'Marble in Two' line is the fifth line. So, it corresponds to the second 'A' in *CARTAE*, which means you were skipping one letter to decipher that line, right?"

"Yes. That's right."

"Well, looking at it, if you start at the end and go backwards, skipping every other letter, you get the word *super*. Does that mean anything in Latin?"

Savannah snatched the scroll and turned it around, forgetting to take her normal care with the document. "*Super* means 'on top of'."

She ran her finger over the last line of the cipher, her mouth moving silently as she counted letters and sounded out the words in her head.

"It says *super Carmeli*. You're right, Ty. It does go backward! That means 'on top of Carmel'."

Mark smiled. "The Marble Tablets were found on top of Mt. Carmel. Let's keep going."

"And that matches the roman numerals again. When you add *super Carmeli*, there's a total of five words, which is what we expected," Savannah said.

"So, the last line will have four words and we'll skip every five letters to find it?" Ty asked.

"Yes." Savannah grabbed one of the papers with the partial translation on it and scribbled rapidly as she took notes from the scroll. After a minute, she looked up, satisfied. She then turned the sheet of paper around so the rest of them could see it.

Arca Dei
Celatus per quinque
Reseratus per quattuor
Tergum ibexum et aeneus prope Succaca
Marmor in duo super Carmeli
Argenteus quiescit intro Moria

The Ark of God
Secreted by Five
Revealed by Four
Ibex and Copper near Succaca
Marble in two on Carmel
Silver lies in Moriah

"Moriah?" Mark asked. "Where's that?"

"Moriah," Ty stated flatly. "We've been there already."

"Mt. Moriah is the mountain where God commanded Abraham to offer his son Isaac as a sacrifice, only to stay Abraham's hand before he actually did it. It was a test of faith," Savannah explained.

"So, where is that mountain?"

"You know it as the Temple Mount."

Mark sat back in his seat.

Hardy dropped his leg from its resting place to pay closer attention.

"Ow, ow! Oh, man...that hurt," he said, rubbing what portion of his leg he could reach in spite of the cast.

"That was dumb," Mark chided.

"What can I say, I forgot. Man alive." He continued to rub his leg gingerly, leaving it resting on the ground.

"So, according to this scroll, the Silver Scroll is buried somewhere in the Temple Mount?" Mark's brow creased.

"It would appear so."

"It doesn't say the Silver *Scroll*, though, just 'silver'. Could it mean there is just some silver hidden there?"

Savannah shook her head definitively. "No, not in this context. *Argenteus* can be translated as 'silver' or as 'the silver one'. The cipher says that the Ark's hiding place is revealed by four, and then proceeds to list each piece of writing and where it was hidden. We know what the Ibex, the Copper and the Marble refers to. Also, the title of the cipher says "The Hiding Place of the Silver Scroll", not just 'silver'.""

"That Temple complex is huge. The tunnels under it go in all directions and they're filled with rubble. We saw how much effort the Templars were going through to clear them."

"We could shift back to Jerusalem before it was destroyed by the Romans," Ty offered.

"What year was that?" Mark asked.

"70 AD," Ty responded.

"Those tunnels were most likely filled in with rubble at the time of the Babylonian destruction six hundred and fifty years before that," Savannah said.

"It's worth a shot," Ty countered.

Mark pulled the laminated time delay chart from his pocket. "If we travel back to 70 AD, our shifters will shut down for more than a month. And that's assuming these calculations Prescott made are accurate," he said, waving the card up and down. "Out of the question. We'll have to find another way."

Hardy looked like he was going to try and stand up and then thought better of it. "Could someone go in my room and get my backpack?" he asked.

Ty got up and went to get it while Mark and Savannah continued to discuss the cipher and where in Moriah the Silver Scroll could be. Ty returned shortly and handed the pack to Hardy. He unzipped it and pulled out a large piece of paper. He studied it for a second and then leaned forward, pushing it onto the table in between Mark and Savannah.

"What do you think of that?" He asked. Back in Hertford, England, before joining back up with Mark and Ty, he'd returned to make a charcoal impression of the second inscription he'd found down in the Templar tunnels. He'd forgotten all about it amidst all their other journeys, but something about Mark and Savannah's conversation had sparked his memory. He'd remembered the inscription mentioned something about silver.

IN BENGEO HERTE
HÆR RESTE IN PART
HOLI FATED
AWEI REMEVED
GREAL SILVER SHADED

FRO STONCROS
TWOE UNDRED PASE
STEORBORD A TEIME AND TEIMES
HEVEN SHEUETH THE WEI

Savannah's eyes widened as she examined it. Mark's narrowed.

"I could only make out some of it, but it mentions silver."

"Where did you get this?" she asked.

Hardy filled them in on the details of what he'd found in the tunnels under the Templar castle in Hertford back in 1307. He'd already shared some about the treasure and the booby traps, but he hadn't mentioned the inscription yet because it had seemed like they were on a better trail.

"What does it say?" Mark asked.

"It's in Middle English," she said. "If you say the words out loud, most of its meaning will become clear." She began writing a translation on a blank piece of paper, mouthing the words as she did. Her eyes grew wider with each line.

> *In Bengeo's heart*
> *Here rests in part*
> *Holy fated*
> *Away removed*
> *Silver Grail shaded*
>
> *From Stone Cross*
> *Two Hundred Paces*
> *Starboard a time and times*
> *Heaven shows the way*

"What in the world does that mean?" Mark asked.

"I'm not sure," she said. "*Bengeo* is either a place name or some word I don't know. I'm going to have to get an expert to look at this." Her eyes lit up excitedly. "But, Hardy, I think you may have found something of tremendous value!"

"Why?"

"Many of the legends surrounding the Templar Knights spoke to their quest to find the Holy Grail. This doesn't say 'Holy Grail' per se, but it calls a 'silver grail' holy."

She pulled out a seat and sat down. Her legs had grown weak all of a sudden.

"You mean while searching for the Ark, we may have stumbled on the Holy Grail?" Hardy was incredulous.

Savannah looked more surprised than any of them. "I don't know, I've just never heard of an inscription like this, referring to an actual location of the grail."

"So it doesn't have anything to do with the Silver Scroll?" Mark asked.

"Maybe it does. The Templars cleared out the tunnels in *Moriah*. Maybe in their search for the Ark, they found the Silver Scroll, and that is what they're calling the 'grail' in the engraving."

"Why would they call a scroll a grail? Why wouldn't they call it a scroll?"

"Well, a grail is a chalice, a container, if you will. The scroll is the container for information on the Ark. Maybe that's the connection."

Mark stood up. "Where's Bengeo?"

"We'll find out."

Chapter 30

"Say not thou, What is the cause that the former days were better than these? for thou dost not inquire wisely concerning this."

- Ecclesiastes 7:10

Bengeo turned out to be a small village on a ridge overlooking the town of Hertford. Bengeo had since been absorbed into the Hertford community as the town had grown over the centuries, but there was still a large piece of undeveloped property nearby called Temple Farm. In medieval times, the farm had been owned and operated by the Templars.

It was Templar knights from Bengeo that the King of England had imprisoned in Hertford Castle in 1309 in an effort to discover the massive Templar treasure.

Hardy couldn't do much with a broken leg and didn't want to stay cooped up while they went treasure hunting, so Mark helped him get back to Abbie's cottage in the 1600's. She'd do a better job looking after him while he healed than they would anyway. And he'd be off Rialto's radar.

Once Mark had dropped him off, he, Ty and Savannah took ChronoShift's jet to London and then rented a couple of nondescript vehicles to drive to Hertford.

After so many centuries, Bengeo was still a small community. It was mostly a series of smallish two story residences built of reddish-brown brick. A few pubs, a school, and the ancient Church of St. Leonard were the most unique structures to be seen. There were a number of moms out walking with their children, so they asked around about Temple Farm and were soon pointed in the right direction.

On the far side of the fields, they found a grove of trees isolated enough from view they could change into more era-appropriate, medieval clothing, which they'd brought along in a duffel bag. Mark and Ty tucked weapons of various types and sizes wherever they could hide them. Savannah's eyes widened at the sight of all the guns, but she said nothing.

"You never know..." Mark offered. She nodded.

They chose to shift to the year 1300 AD, since that would likely be a year late enough that whatever treasure the Templars had found in Jerusalem would already be stashed in the place the engraving referred to, yet it was before the persecution began in 1307. They had no idea what the Templars would have done at that point. They very well could have taken the silver 'grail' with them as they evacuated, leaving an engraving in the tunnels of Hertford that pointed to nothing.

Savannah gently gripped Mark's forearm so she could shift with them. The light touch of her fingers sent electric tingles across his skin. He glanced at her. She returned the look, a delicate smile gracing her lips.

Involuntarily, he was finding his attention drawn more and more to her. He tried to maintain a sense of professionalism when he was around her, but her emerald eyes would pop into his mind at the most inopportune and surprising times.

For some reason he didn't understand, he also found himself subconsciously resisting the attraction, determined to not allow it to take root, but the subtle romantic excitement her presence elicited was winning the contest like low waves rolling relentlessly upon a seashore.

They shifted and were immediately faced with wider, more open fields and two much smaller, more primitive communities in both Bengeo and Hertford. The few residences up on the ridge in Bengeo were all medieval, one story, and much more rustic.

The Templar farm was much bigger, and they were in luck. No workers were out in the fields.

Dark rolling clouds overhead dimmed the light, implying a heavy storm might break within the hour. Perhaps that was the reason for so much inactivity.

The fields here were not level like they were in the future. You never really thought about all the changes that took place in a community over the centuries until you saw the differences with your eyes. In the future, the owners of these fields would level them at some point to make them easier to farm, probably after the invention of bulldozers and the like.

The trees were sparser and stood in clusters scattered sporadically across the tilled land.

The engraving Hardy found underneath Hertford Castle had referred to "Bengeo's Heart," which they had interpreted to mean the center of the Templar farm. If they couldn't find anything there, they would have to search the center of the village instead for some indication of a hiding place or tunnel.

They walked across freshly overturned dirt toward the center of the main field, taking note of several piles of large rocks. Scrawny trees and scraggly bushes sprung up among them. It soon became apparent the rock and tree groupings were even more prevalent than they'd first thought. A few of them were extensive enough they were too big to call a grove, but not near large enough to call woods by any stretch of the imagination.

More interestingly, many of the rock formations were big enough to create natural caves, their entrances hinting at potential tunnels that might extend deeper within. By modern times, these rock groupings had been removed.

"Those look like the best place to start looking, but which one?" Ty asked.

They moved about, inspecting each cluster closely, looking for a clue, something out of place.

"There." Savannah pointed to a rock grouping that laid in such a way it appeared to form a Neolithic doorway, like a tomb or one of the Pi shaped structures that made up Stonehenge. The rocks were set into a small round hill covered in brush. Trees and large boulders on both sides of the grouping created a narrow pathway one had to traverse to get to the hill. Because of this, you had to be right on top of the "doorway" in order to see it. The opening between the Stonehenge-like rock pylons was pitch black, a space of mystery that could go anywhere.

Carved high on a large boulder which stood to the left of the entrance was a Templar cross that measured about one foot square.

"From stone cross, two hundred paces...," Savannah quoted out loud.

A sense of wonder filled the air as they advanced toward the darkened opening. They could be about to discover a holy object historians and adventurers had sought for centuries.

Savannah stopped by the cross. She began counting out steps, but then halted.

"One of you guys should probably do it," she said. "It's probably two hundred *male* paces, not female."

Ty stepped forward and counted out as he walked. He and Mark whipped out Maglite flashlights before they reached the pylons. The framed opening really was the entrance to a short cave leading into the hill.

At thirty paces, they found themselves at the top of a long run of stone steps descending into more blackness. Ty lifted his foot to count out the thirty-first pace. Mark grabbed his shoulder, halting him.

"Remember — Hardy said the tunnels under Hertford were booby-trapped, and whatever is down here was important enough to separate from the rest of the Templars' massive treasure. If they rigged those tunnels under the castle, it's a guarantee there'll be some nasty surprises here too."

Hardy had described in detail the booby-traps he'd encountered and what they should look for.

A third of the way down the stairs, Mark noticed the next step had a stone with an odd hash mark on it. One of the stones in every step below that had a similar mark. The rest were all unmarked. Mark made sure Ty and Savannah saw it.

Ty stepped down, carefully avoiding the marked stone. A sharp crack pierced the air followed by the rumbling of Ty's collapsed form sliding and rolling down the stairs the rest of the way. The groans began after his body finally came to a halt at the bottom. He'd left a wake of tumbled stair stones scattered randomly along the steep slope. Every stone in the staircase below had been left loose on purpose, held in place weakly by a few frail sticks. If a person placed their weight on one of the stones, the stick broke, the stone tumbled forward, and the hapless victim cascaded down the stairs, taking all the other stones with him. Just like Ty had done. It wasn't necessarily designed to kill, just to injure and seriously dissuade.

"You okay, Ty?" Mark called out.

"Yeah. Barely," his friend croaked back. "First Hardy, now me, huh?"

"Looks that way. You break your leg too?"

"No, I think I'm all right." He stood, dusting himself off. "I'm not taking the lead anymore."

"Fair enough."

"Well, what are you waiting for? Come on down."

Most of the stones left intact were the marked ones. Instead of a warning, the hash marks had actually been a sign of where it was safe to step.

One at a time, Mark and Savannah gingerly used the hash mark stones to join Ty at the bottom and had no further trouble.

"If you hadn't pointed out those marks, I probably would have stepped on them instead and been fine," Ty lamented, rubbing his hip.

"You would have stepped on the wrong one eventually."

"Like I said, I'm not leading anymore."

Further down the tunnel, they came to a large pit in the floor. It extended from wall to wall and looked to be about fifteen feet across.

Too far to jump.

Mark dropped to his belly and leaned over the edge, raking his flashlight across the pit's bottom.

After a twenty foot drop, pointed iron spikes rose up menacingly like sharp fingers, ready to puncture whatever came their way.

"We *really* don't want to go down there," Mark commented.

"How are we going to get to the other side?"

"The Templars must use some special boards they have to get across." Mark thought for a minute. "I'll be right back."

He bounced back up the stairs, hopping from marked stone to marked stone.

Ty half expected him to return with some 2 X 12's or something similar, but when he came back, he just had a backpack in hand. Mark pulled some rock-climbing gear from it. He tossed a couple of harnesses Ty and Savannah's way and laid out a long rope, which he looped through the buckles of his own harness.

He took out a hammer and some lengthy pitons and proceeded to pound several of the pitons deep into the cracks between the stones in the tunnel wall, both at the foot and the hand levels. There were now steel rods sticking out about eight inches from the wall, which would be enough to stand on, and had loops in their ends that a rope could be run through. Mark stepped onto the first of these pitons and hammered more in as he moved over the chasm. Once he was safely on the other side, Ty and Savannah followed suit.

They discarded the gear, but left the pitons in place for the return trip.

"So...did they count paces as they walked across their boards, or were we supposed to stop counting and pick up again on this side of the chasm?" Ty asked.

"Good question," Mark said. "Let's assume they counted as they crossed."

A pace was generally considered to be about two and a half feet, so Ty mentally added another six paces to his current count and continued. They began to pass openings in the tunnel walls on both sides, but they only paid attention to those leading off to the right. *Starboard a time and times.* Starboard was the right hand side of a ship.

The problem was that every twenty feet or so, there was a new tunnel on the right. When Ty finally stopped counting, they stood exactly halfway between two tunnels.

"Great," Mark grumbled.

"Which one?" Ty asked.

"No idea."

"We can try them both, I guess."

"Ty, you're a big guy, so your paces might be a little longer than the average Templar. I'd bet it's the tunnel we just passed, not the next one. Nobody back then would be bigger than Ty."

"What if we weren't supposed to count the number of steps to get over the pit?"

"Then, that would probably mean one of the next tunnels is the right one," Savannah said.

"Let's assume we were supposed to count the steps over the pit and go with this one," Mark said. "We can always come back and try others."

They retreated to the last tunnel they'd passed and began making their way cautiously down it. That they'd guessed correctly seemed to be indicated by some suspicious flagstones in the floor in perfect alignment with rows of unusual holes in the walls.

Mark was reminded of Hardy's description of one of the booby-traps he'd encountered. If it was the same kind of trap, then a spiked, iron portcullis would explode from the wall as soon as one of them stepped on one of the "special" flagstones. Whoever stood in its way when that happened would be killed, and if not killed, trapped on one side of it or the other. Hardy had never found a way to reset his trap after he'd sprung it, so they could not count on pushing the iron gate back into the wall.

If this was a similar trap, then they had just walked into a virtual minefield. There were at least a hundred of the unusual flagstones littering the floor ahead of them, and at least ten separate vertical rows of holes in the walls.

"Do *not* step on any stone that looks uneven," Mark whispered to the others.

Ty halted his friend with a hand. "What if it's like the stairs? What if the raised stones are actually the ones we're supposed to step on?"

Mark searched the floor for a loose rock, one large enough it had some weight. He tossed it onto one of the normal flagstones.

Nothing happened.

Mark entered the danger zone, taking extreme care where he placed his feet. His guess had been right and not Ty's. The bad stones were the ones that stuck up a little and didn't look even. He made it across without incident and the others followed.

They came to another break in the right hand wall — a side tunnel that extended deep into more blackness. They took it.

Abruptly, they came to a third right hand tunnel not thirty feet further in. Yet, their current tunnel continued past it.

"What are we supposed to do?" Mark asked. "What exactly does *'Starboard a time and times'* mean?"

Savannah spoke up. "In poetry, it would simply mean to turn right twice, which we've already done."

Ty shook his head. "In the Bible, when the phrase 'a time and times' is used, the 'times' means twice by itself. It means we're supposed to turn right once, then twice more. The Templars would have been influenced by the Bible."

"That's true," Savannah nodded.

"Let's go straight," Mark decided against their advice. "If we don't find anything, we'll come back here."

Mark led the way. Ty grumbled something about people who were ignorant of Scripture, but moved forward anyway.

They'd traveled about seventy feet when the tunnel suddenly ended.

Mark moved closer to see if there was anything carved into the end wall, but something gave way under his foot. He pushed back and tried to regain his footing, but the whole floor seemed to be caving in underneath him. The cracks of old wood breaking echoed off the tunnel walls. Heavy flagstones in the floor thumped and bumped as they were jostled out of place.

Mark tossed his flashlight back toward Ty and Savannah as he twisted for salvation. The groaning accelerated as the entire floor finally gave way under him, though he was right at the edge of the disaster.

It had been a false floor suspended by thin, rotting boards over a deep pit, which was probably filled with more of the deadly iron spikes.

In spite of his rushed efforts, Mark dropped. His chest slammed into the side of the newly revealed pit, his arms draped up over its edge, fingers digging for a hold in the cracks between the stones in the still stable portion of the floor. His quick turn and desperate grip were all that saved him from disappearing into the blackness below, but he was slipping.

Ty and Savannah ran forward. They threw themselves onto their stomachs, grasping his forearms tightly to keep him from sliding further over the edge.

A tremendous snapping rang out from the depths. Ty turned the beam of his flashlight down into the hole to see what was going on. Its beam did indeed reveal vicious looking spikes imbedded in the bottom of the pit, but that was not the worst of it.

One of the falling stones from the false floor had struck a thicker beam lower in the pit hard enough to put some serious cracks in it. The beam must have had something heavy exerting tremendous pressure on its ends, because the snapping sound had been it rupturing violently.

Growing tremors shook the surrounding walls in a thundering crescendo. Clods of dirt and dust rained down upon their heads.

Ty and Savannah gripped Mark's arms and heaved backward in unison, pulling him up enough he could kick his way to safety.

The tunnel was collapsing. They raced back the way they came dodging falling debris on all sides.

Remembering the mine field ahead, Mark hastily ducked into the side tunnel they'd neglected to take a few minutes earlier and the others followed.

The overwhelming roar of falling rock came like an assault on their ears. Dust rolled up the tunnel in thick, billowing clouds and threatened to fill their lungs. They tugged their shirt collars up over their mouths and noses to block it out. The smell of musty, wet soil permeated the air.

After the rumbling subsided and the dust settled, they made their way back toward the dead end where the floor had collapsed. While that entire section had caved in, the rest of the tunnel was intact. The dead-end had been designed as a death trap for someone. A large boulder, larger than an SUV, sat atop the pit Mark had almost fallen into.

Whoever stepped on the false floor was supposed to have fallen into the pit, pierced themselves on the sharp spikes, and then been buried under a ton of loose dirt with a massive boulder sitting on top, like the proverbial cherry on a gigantic, booby-trap sundae.

The fact the Templars had been able to engineer such a thing was incredible in of itself. The fact that they had *chosen* to go to so much trouble spoke volumes about the value of whatever lay hidden in these tunnels.

The trio returned to the side tunnel they'd passed up before.

"Looks like you were right, Ty," Mark offered.

"As usual," Ty smiled, performing a mock bow. A layer of grey dust covered his face.

"You don't look so good," Mark said.

"You're one to talk."

Mark ran the back of his hand across his forehead. It came away grey, grimy with sweat and dirt. Savannah shook her hair out, trying to dislodge whatever dust had lodged in it. Mark imagined she must be just as sweaty and uncomfortable as he, though she didn't look it.

"You're a sport, Savannah."

She looked at him, pursing her lips, dismayed by how she must appear.

They advanced down this side tunnel slower than ever, alert for new and even more dangerous traps. If their revised interpretation of the engraving was correct, this would be their last turn.

About halfway down, they came to a very unusual feature. The floor of the tunnel took a dramatic dip downward until it was about ten feet lower than their current level. It ran at that depth for about forty feet before the path ascended again to the previous height. A giant dip in the road.

At the other end, an iron grille blocked the exit from the ramp. The grille was unusual in that it lay at an almost flat angle, its far end even with the floor on the other side. Whoever went down in the dip would not be able to get past it without a key. The grille was about fifteen feet long, so climbing around it would be no easy feat either.

Another iron grille, a vertical one this time, had been imbedded about ten feet in front of them and extended from wall to wall. Its bottom, however, stopped where the floor would have been if it did not dip down so low. A man descending down into the dip could easily walk under that grille. Its only purpose seemed to be to prevent someone from climbing on the walls to bypass the dip like they'd done at the first pit.

That grille was to force you into the dip, the other was to keep you in there.

"That's weird," Ty said.

"Yeah." Mark ran his flashlight back and forth, scanning every surface for signs of possible danger. "You think something might be waiting for us down in that dip?"

"I'd bet my life on it. No idea what though. I'll go," Ty offered.

"You sure? I thought you weren't going to lead anymore."

"Yeah, just watch my back."

Gingerly, Ty stepped onto the ramp leading down into the dip. Once he was fully down in it, he walked even slower, running the beam of his Maglite over every surface he could find. He'd gone about twenty feet when he paused.

"What's the matter?" Mark asked.

"Something's wrong. I...I don't feel so good." He turned around and took two steps back toward them before he collapsed to the floor unconscious.

Chapter 31

Mark and Savannah raced to Ty's side, momentarily forgetting possible iron portcullises primed to burst from the wall or false floors ready to collapse.

They each grabbed an arm and hauled Ty back up out of the dip.

"It smelled funny down there," Savannah said.

Mark had noticed the slight odor too. "It's some kind of subterranean gas."

Mark checked Ty's pulse. It was there, but weak.

"We need to clear his lungs," she said, then turned away and covered her mouth as she broke into a fit of coughing.

Mark took a couple of deep cleansing breaths, coughed some too and then began partial CPR, blowing clean air into Ty's lungs.

After a few rounds, Ty coughed and groaned. In less than a minute, he was conscious and fully alert again.

"Wow, what happened." He shook his head, still dizzy.

"Some kind of gas down there," Mark explained.

"Well, we knew it'd be something."

Mark re-examined the whole dip in light of what they now knew. "Even if somebody raced through there at full speed, they'd be stopped by the locked iron gate on the other end. Once more, ingenious."

"How did they get a gas down here?"

"It's not uncommon for subterranean gases to build up in cave systems of unused mines."

"But how do they make sure it stays down in that dip?"

"It's heavier than air, so it would lie lower, but they'd still have to vent this tunnel from time to time. No idea how they do that."

"How about we blow the vertical iron grille with some explosives and use the rock-climbing gear like we did before?" Ty suggested.

"You want to set off an explosive in here after what we just went through in the other tunnel? Really?"

"Yeah, I guess not."

"I'm gonna get some gas masks," Mark said.

"I'll go." Ty stood. "You went last time."

Mark and Savannah sat opposite each other on the stone floor with their backs to the wall while they waited for Ty to return. Sweat and dirt streaked Savannah's face and had transformed her hair with earthen highlights to shades of dirty blonde. She'd never looked so beautiful.

Mark felt his heart leap as if lifted by butterflies, but he slammed it back into place. He had to stop falling for these women in his life so easily. Savannah was a friend. She worked for him. She trusted him. He would not allow some fleeting puppy-love attraction ruin that.

He turned his face away.

None too soon, Ty returned carrying another duffel bag. He'd been gone about three minutes. He set it down, unzipped it, and pulled out three gas masks and a couple other miscellaneous items.

"How are you guys getting this stuff so fast?" Savannah asked.

"Fast?" Ty grimaced. "You're kidding right? I had to drive all the way to London to get this, and even then I thought I was going to have to fly home. Took me all day." He held up his shifter and tapped it.

Savannah nodded understanding. The effects of the shifters could be confusing, even for those who were used to them.

They put on the gas masks and made their way back down into the dip. No other apparent traps or dangers stood out. The Templars had assumed the gas would be enough to stop most people. The iron gate on the opposite end was indeed locked, but it wasn't complex.

Burning or cutting their way through would not be wise. They had no idea if the gas was flammable or not. Ty extracted a lock-picking kit from his pocket and had it open in less than thirty seconds.

The tunnel then wandered uneventfully for another fifty feet before ending abruptly. Mark grew wary, remembering the last dead end tunnel.

"There's nothing here," Ty said, stating the obvious.

"We followed the instructions to a tee. There's got to be something here." Mark ran his flashlight over every surface.

"Maybe the Templars already took it out, whatever it was."

"Look at the back wall," Savannah noticed. "It's full of pockmarks."

Mark stepped closer, lightly, almost on his tiptoes. He was

hypersensitive the floor might give way any second.

"Those aren't pockmarks," he said, "They're little stars carved into the stones."

Savannah unfolded the paper with the Hertford verse on it.

In Bengeo's heart
Here rests in part
Holy fated
Away removed
Silver Grail shaded

From Stone Cross
Two Hundred Paces
Starboard a time and times
Heaven shows the way

"*Heaven shows the way,*" Savannah breathed. "The last line."

"Quick, back up. Everybody shine your light on the wall. Let's illuminate the whole thing."

"Look, the pockmarks glitter a little bit when the light hits them just right."

"Like stars," Savannah said.

Mark examined a couple of the star-shaped holes closer up and saw that little pieces of shiny quartz had been embedded in each hole so they would reflect light when it struck at the right angle."

Ty pointed. "There's a torch on each wall."

They lit both torches and soon the whole rear of the tunnel was flooded with a warm, flickering light. The pockmarks twinkled like a thousand stars in seemingly random patterns. Yet, after a time, some familiar ones crystallized as memory banks recalled forgotten things learned in school.

"These are constellations. I recognize some of them," Mark said.

"Yes, there's Ursa Major, Orion, Leo..." Savannah ran her fingers over the holes, tracing out patterns from her memory.

"You know your stars too," Mark laughed. "You're like a walking library."

She blushed and dropped her finger.

"There's the Big Dipper," Ty said.

"That's the same thing as Ursa Major." Mark laughed even harder. Exhaustion was making him giddy. Or maybe it was the gas.

"Kind of," Savannah corrected. "The Big Dipper stars are part of Ursa Major." She looked puzzled. "There is something off here. I may not be remembering right, but I could swear that Orion is supposed to be facing the other way. I think his bow is supposed to be on his right, but here, it's on the left. See." She pointed at a curved line of "stars" that resembled a bow. "And there's a line of marks that looks like an arrow in the bow. I don't think there's an arrow in the real constellation."

"I guess we could go outside, shift to nighttime, and check to be sure."

"We've been down here so long, it's probably already night," Ty said.

Heaven shows the way.

"Where is that arrow pointing?" Mark asked.

Orion was twisted counter-clock wise about thirty degrees, which caused the arrow to point toward the base of the left wall. Mark dropped to his belly and examined the stones there, each of which measured about a foot and half tall by two feet wide in this section of the tunnel. He tugged and pushed on the stone butting up against the pockmarked back wall, to no avail.

He tried the stone to the left of that one. Nothing seemed amiss, but when he tapped on it, a hollow sound echoed behind it. He pushed hard and felt it give.

Ty handed him a Bowie knife which he used to scrape at the mortar surrounding the stone. A satisfied smile broke out on his lips when he saw the mortar was only an inch deep. Enough to hold it in place, but not nearly enough for solid wall construction. This wall had been built with a hole in it on purpose. This stone had been laid in later.

After a few minutes, he'd removed enough mortar to really move it. A loud grating ricocheted off the walls as he shoved it further into the wall.

The trio cringed momentarily, sure the echoing sound had been enough to summon any wandering Templars nearby, but if the falling boulder hadn't alerted them, the scraping of one stone on another wouldn't either.

"Hand me a flashlight," Mark said.

Ty gave him one. "Be careful, Mark. We may not be done with the booby-traps. Remember the gas."

"I know."

He wriggled through the small hole he'd made in the wall. It was just wide enough to allow his shoulders to pass through. His beam of light pierced the darkness ahead, illuminating suspended particles of dust as they wafted about, having been disturbed for the first time in years.

The wall was about two feet thick, so his small hole opened into a much larger space almost immediately. A hidden room.

Mark studied every crack and crevice before moving into it. He rolled over, as much as his confined space would allow, and shone the flashlight toward the ceiling of this new chamber, examining in length any object that looked in the least way suspicious.

Satisfied nothing was going to get him if he stood up, he did. The air in here was cool, damp, and smelled of wet earth. He continued stroking his light about the room, which measured about twenty feet deep by fifteen feet wide. It was empty, except for one lone object on the back wall. A very exciting object.

Mark bent down and called through the opening. "All clear. Come on in."

He waited while Ty, then Savannah, crawled through the hole and emerged into the chamber with him.

"I think we may have hit the jackpot," he said, focusing his beam on the object at the back of the room.

The three of them scoured the chamber with their flashlights, searching for any sign of a hidden trap. Trip wires, loose flagstones, suspicious holes. There was nothing, but still they hesitated. They were gun shy, especially skittish after everything they'd gone through so far.

"It can't be this easy," Mark said.

"You call those tunnels back there easy?" Ty snorted.

"All right, let's do it."

Mark led the way, gingerly stepping on one stone at a time, careful to not let his foot hit anything that he'd not examined and re-examined thoroughly.

When he reached the halfway point, Ty grew exasperated.

"C'mon, man." Ty strode briskly across the floor to the back wall, passing Mark who froze in place, open-mouthed, staring at him. "If there's a trap here, let's just set it off and go. Personally, I think they're done."

He made it the whole way without incident.

Encouraged, Mark picked up the pace, but still studied the floor warily as he went. Ty was already studying the object.

"Wait there, Savan..." Mark trailed off. She was already standing beside them, grinning sheepishly.

"All right, fine."

The object that held their attention was a small, tightly rolled, metallic scroll. It looked sooty black with hints of another color underneath. The scroll was suspended about four feet off the floor, held to the wall by a pair of iron hooks.

Mark shone his light closely on every side of the scroll, examining in a particularly careful way the space behind it and the hooks for any sign of a trigger if they removed it. Seeing none, Mark reached out...picked it up, and...

...nothing.

Collectively, all three breathed a sigh of relief.

"It's definitely metal," Mark said, hefting it to get a feel for its weight. "Hard to tell if it's silver or not with this black coating over it."

"When silver tarnishes it can look black," Savannah said.

Mark studied it in silence.

"Well, let's get it back to headquarters. Can't really analyze it here."

Chapter 32

The mood in the conference room was glum.

Mark, Savannah, and Ty sat around their round table staring at the silver object lying in the center of it. Hardy still had his leg in a cast, so he'd chosen a more comfortable, leather recliner closer to the pool table.

Savannah had taken the scroll to Bobby Prescott who had conscripted a top team of scientists to clean it up, though he insisted it had been a fairly simple process. Something about running an electric current through the scroll while it sat in the right chemical solution.

The fact the scroll was made of silver was a blessing in of itself. When the Copper Scroll was discovered in the 1950's, scholars argued for years about how to open it. Copper is known as an anti-corrosive metal, but it does corrode, especially over a period of two thousand five hundred years. At last, it was decided to cut that scroll into thin strips to prevent random cracking as the scroll had become quite brittle.

Silver, however, is even more resistant to corrosion. When exposed to normal atmospheric conditions, it develops a heavy black coating of silver sulfide, but this same patina actually ends up protecting the silver from further corrosion, especially when exposure to sunlight is limited. Humidity in the air had no impact at all.

The benefit of this was their scroll was still quite flexible after it had been cleaned, flexible enough to unroll without damaging it. Jumping the scroll from the 14th to the 21st century hadn't hurt either, saving it from another seven hundred years' worth of corrosive influence.

Their surprise — no, it would be more accurate to say their shock — was what the text said when they unrolled it. Their initial excitement unraveled into disillusionment after several experts in biblical Hebrew from Fuller Theological Seminary had analyzed it.

Savannah uncrossed her legs and then crossed them again the other way, smoothing her blue cotton skirt over her knees. She'd selected this outfit with Mark in mind, in spite of the way she knew the day would go. Still not comfortable, she re-crossed her legs for the third time. She started to lean forward, then thought better of it.

She had expected Mark to react much differently. There had been no slamming of fists on the table, no spilling of chairs as he stood angrily. Not even a hint of the furious flame she'd seen kindled in his eyes so many times before. He was either learning to control his temper...or he was giving up. If so, *what was he giving up on?*

Mercifully, the phone system in the center of the table chirped, announcing an incoming call. Mark leaned forward and hit speaker phone.

"Hello?"

"That you, Carpen?"

"Yes, Mr. President. I'm here with Ty Jennings, Hardy Phillips, and Savannah Stanford."

"I hear you've got something."

"We *thought* we had something — not so sure now." Mark filled the president in on their research so far, that they suspected Professor Rosenberg over at Harvard might be an agent for Mossad, how he had sent them on a wild goose chase after the Templar Knights. He recounted how they'd met Professor Zahavi in Israel and what he had taught them about Jeremiah hiding the ark around 580 BC. He explained about the Copper Scroll, the Ibex Scroll, the Marble Tablets, about the Silver Scroll that had not yet been found and their theory that it might be the key to locating the Ark.

He told of the search for the Silver Scroll, starting with the escapade in New Mexico 150 years ago, through Amsterdam and Venice, until they'd come to the conclusion the Templars might have been involved after all. He explained about the results of the cipher they'd decoded, the connection between Moriah and the Templar mount, and how they'd connected it with the inscription Hardy had found engraved in the tunnels under Hertford, England. Finally, he relayed their trek under the fields of Bengeo and the way they'd discovered the silver scroll.

"It sounds like you've found a lot!" The president said.

"Well..."

"Is there any chance Rialto knows any of this?"

Mark looked across at Hardy and Ty and then at the scroll on the table. "I have no idea, sir. He could be on a completely different path from ours."

"Can we be sure?"

"We certainly haven't seen him or his crew except for the one time in Jerusalem and then later in Venice. They tried to kill us in Venice." He explained how the newspaper article had tipped Rialto off to their position. "After I undid that, however, they didn't show up again."

"Man, I didn't know all that," Hardy complained.

Mark waved him off, pointing back to the speaker phone. "That and the fact we found the cipher and this silver scroll means he doesn't know what we know."

"That's good." The president sounded relieved.

"But that doesn't mean he doesn't have better info, sir. Another trail to follow that could lead him to Ark more surely than ours."

"Carpen, are you trying to give me an ulcer?"

"No, sir."

"So, what's the problem?"

"It's what the scroll says, sir. It's not what we expected."

"Spit it out, son."

"We expected a long text, similar to the Copper Scroll, detailing treasures from Solomon's Temple and where they are hidden."

He glanced at the scroll.

הספר שימר במקום אחר

"Instead, it's just a single line of Hebrew text."

"What does it say?"

"*The book is guarded elsewhere.*"

"What does that mean? Where is 'elsewhere'?"

"We have no idea. Not yet anyway. Just got the report back from the experts this morning. To be honest, we're a bit discouraged."

"Well, you have done an amazing job so far. Keep it up. You'll find it. I don't have to remind you how explosive a situation we're facing if this Ark is found by the wrong people and put in Arab hands."

"What do you want us to do with it when we find it?"

"We'll cross that bridge when we get there. Hate to cut this conversation short, but I've got a meeting with the Secretary of State and need to go over a briefing first. Good luck and God bless." He clicked off.

Mark rubbed the palms of his hands over his face, as if stimulating the skin of his cheeks would help him think.

"I don't get it," he said. "Is *this* the Silver Scroll or not?"

"I don't think so," Savannah answered softly, hesitantly. "I think we failed to pay attention to the first part of the engraving Hardy found."

In Bengeo's heart
Here rests in part
Holy fated
Away removed
Silver Grail shaded

"We now know for sure the phrase 'Silver Grail' is referring to a silver scroll. I mean we found a silver scroll at the end of the instructions in the second stanza. The line 'Here rests in part' seems to be saying it is not the entire scroll. 'Away Removed' is clear enough if you interpret it in light of what we now know. Originally, I thought it meant the Templars had removed it away from Jerusalem to England, but it is probably saying the Silver Scroll in the tunnel is not the real one, that the original had been removed.

"I can understand that part," Mark said. "So, what does the *shaded* line mean?"

"*Shaded* is a reference to a shadow or a ghost. For example, in the New Testament, St. Paul describes things of this earth as being mere shadows of things existing in Heaven. 'Silver Grail shaded' would mean it is a mere representation of the original, not a full copy. I'm sorry I didn't see that sooner."

Mark stood up and began pacing. Ty went to the fridge and started passing out sodas. He tossed one to Mark, who caught it with one hand absent-mindedly.

"So, who removed the grail and where did they move it to? Did the Templars take it somewhere else and leave this copy in its place? Or did someone steal it from them and so they made the copy? Or was the original removed from the Temple Mount before the Templars ever got there and what they found was this copy?"

"The Hebrew script on this scroll is good Hebrew, grammatically speaking," Savannah answered, "Some of the Templars were scribes and scholars, but they generally would not have been experts in the study of Hebrew like the monks of some of the other orders might have been. Still, they could have sought the help of Jewish scholars to create this shadow scroll.

"However," she continued, "Ancient handwriting samples can be dated to specific eras based on the styling of the letters. The experts who looked at this dated the Hebrew to Roman era Palestine. In other words, the time of Jesus. It would have been very difficult for the

Templars to duplicate the letter style of a previous era, and why would they have felt the need?

"Also, the Templars set up some pretty hefty booby-traps to protect this copy of the scroll. If they had created a mere copy and secreted away the original, why all the traps? Why go to such lengths to protect something that isn't real?"

"Maybe they set up the traps while the real scroll was still in there and just left them in place later," Ty offered.

"Why make a copy of the original at all?" Savannah countered. "It doesn't make sense. No, that fact, combined with the dating of the script style, tells me the original scroll was switched out at some point around the time of Christ. The Templars found this copy while digging under Moriah eleven hundred years later. That is the only reason I can think of they would have venerated this shadow scroll at all."

"Then, *who* made the copy?" Mark asked. "Who switched them out and where did they put the real Silver Scroll?"

Savannah pursed her lips and dropped her gaze. "I don't know," she breathed.

Mark stopped pacing and gripped the back of his chair hard enough to turn his knuckles white. "All right. Any ideas? Anybody?"

"There is one more thing that may help," Savannah said. "Something I didn't mention before because I didn't want to get the president's hopes up."

She stood and turned the scroll over so they could see its back.

"Look right here." She pointed at the lower right corner. They could barely make out a small circular indentation that appeared to have some faint writing in it.

"It's a personal seal, stamped into the metal rather than engraved. More importantly, there's a name running inside the outer border. Mattatiyah HaLevi. Translates to Matthew the Levite."

"Who was he?"

"No idea. But we'll try to find out."

Hardy spoke up for the first time. "Here we go again."

Chapter 33

"You may delay, but time will not."

- Benjamin Franklin

Mark flicked the lid of a metal lighter open and shut absent-mindedly. He'd found it on the bench where they now sat.

"You don't seem yourself, Mark. Something wrong?" Ty looked at his friend.

Mark kept his gaze on the milling pedestrians in front of them. It was lunchtime and Aachen, Germany was a bustling city.

"We've never gone back this far before. I don't like it."

"Yeah, I know. The shift delay."

"Prescott says we'll be stuck for almost four hours."

Savannah had sought out several experts in Jewish history to analyze the seal they'd found on the back of the scroll. The only Mattatiyah HaLevi they could find reference of was an obscure scribe mentioned in the writings of a Jewish scholar who lived during the reign of Charlemagne. Charlemagne was the supreme ruler over most of Western Europe between 768 and 814 AD. Nothing else was known of this Mattatiyah. Which meant, if they were going to find him, they would have to shift to the era of Charlemagne.

The problem with that was something they referred to as shift delay. Whenever they shifted between years, their shifters would become inoperable for a specific period of time. The amount of time a shifter shut down increased exponentially with the number of years traversed. Normally, this was not a problem. They could shift back to 1800 and only be shut down for 4 seconds. The more years they crossed, however, the worse it got.

Until now, they'd never traveled to a time earlier than 1100 AD, and then, their watches had shut down for around twenty minutes. In Jerusalem, they'd gotten rid of one of Rialto's men, Randolph DeCleary, by taking advantage of this feature and sending him back to 1000 BC with his own shifter. They calculated DeCleary's device would have shut down for at least 400 years, forever trapping him in the past. And sure enough, they had not seen the man again.

Bobby Prescott, their resident physicist, had studied the shifters in depth and helped create a number of gadgets they could use in conjunction with them to protect them during attacks by Rialto. Prescott was also the one who had created the chart that told them how long a shift delay they would experience during a shift. He'd determined that if they traveled back to the reign of Charlemagne, their watches would shut down for 3.78 hours, to be exact.

It wasn't the four hour delay that bothered Mark as much as the increased potential to be trapped somewhere in the face of the un-expected. They had come to rely on the shifters as a reliable escape mechanism. Four hours stuck in an unfamiliar time amid a semi-barbaric culture was a long time in which something could go very wrong.

"You know, I remember the good ol' U.S. government used to send me into active war zones all the time and I didn't have a shifter then. I don't know about you, but I never hesitated. I just did my job and got out. It'll be like that again."

Mark picked up his coffee and downed the rest of it. "You're right. I know. But there's still something different about being locked in the past. Something claustrophobic."

"What's the plan then?"

"We'll negate the shift delay as much as possible. We'll drive until we're out in the country and then shift. We'll hang out there until the four hours are up and then make our way back here to Aachen. As long as we're not around people, our risk should be minimal."

Charlemagne's palace and court had been located in Aachen, Germany, though back then it was considered more of a French town. The Jewish scholar they sought would have been a member of the emperor's court, so logically, he would be found there too.

Ty agreed on the plan, so they drove out of Aachen for about five miles until the countryside looked sparse enough to suit their needs.

"You think we're far enough out?"

"I would imagine so."

The green pasture extended for hundreds of yards in all directions. European towns didn't experience the same suburban sprawl that you saw in the United States, partly because their extraordinarily high taxes discouraged investment, partly because of a strong and oppressive environmental movement, and partly because Europeans traditionally don't share the American pioneer spirit, so their cultural preference is for a life in the city. The result was a plethora of country manors that had not changed for hundreds of years.

"If anything, Aachen is bigger now than it was twelve hundred years ago when it served as Charlemagne's capital. We should definitely be in the middle of nowhere after we shift."

They walked well away from the highway to find a suitable spot for the transition.

Mark and Ty pulled some early medieval clothing from their duffel bag and changed into it. Originally, Savannah's mother's company had only fabricated historical attire for them that went back to the Renaissance. They'd had to place a special order with her for these.

What they'd gotten were a pair of rough woolen pants dyed beige and off-white tunics for their upper bodies. On top of the tunic they wore another garment that looked like a beige poncho.

Unfortunately, they had no way of being certain these outfits were accurate. Documented cultural data from the 8th century was very limited, and what images they had of contemporary clothing was usually that of nobility or priests. Mark and Ty had determined to go disguised as peasants to maintain a low profile, but they could not be sure of how well their attire would fit in. To complicate matters, clothing styles changed from region to region.

Mark rummaged through another duffel checking their weaponry.

"What do you want to take?" Ty asked.

Mark straightened. When it could be helped, they tried to avoid contaminating history with modern items.

"I'm going to feel naked without a pistol. How about we each take a Glock, an Uzi, a couple of flash-bangs, and some clips." He tossed a couple of extra ammo clips to Ty.

They slung their Uzis across their backs underneath the ponchos using leather straps that hung around their neck and shoulders. They stuffed whatever else they could in various pockets, hidden or otherwise.

Sufficiently armed, they stashed the duffels under a tree, not that they would be gone from this time for more than a few seconds, but it never hurt to be cautious.

Mark checked his gear again. "Remember, the immediate goal is to stay hidden for four hours until our shifters reset. We'll begin the actual mission after that. *Then*, we'll head to Aachen and find this scholar.

"Even after the shifters reset, don't shift at the drop of a hat like we're used to. Every time we do, we'll have to wait four hours to shift again. Until we've completed this mission, we try to forget we've got shifters. Agreed?"

"Roger that."

One more gear check and then they faded into time.

Mark was immediately dismayed, because he was falling. When shifting between a large gap in years, it was common for their feet to drop or be pushed up a little because ground levels change over time. This time, however, he fell about five feet before slamming into the ground below. Since he hadn't been expecting such a large drop, he hit badly. He landed at an angle and fell over, collapsing onto his shoulder which absorbed most of the impact. It knocked the breath from his lungs, and he laid there gasping like a fish out of water.

Ty's shifter's safety mechanism kicked in and he felt himself being automatically shoved to the right so he wouldn't materialize in the middle of a tree. Then, he fell a good seven feet. He landed on his feet, but hard, which shot sharp shock waves up through his shins and knees. He lost his balance and tumbled down a short incline, rolling to an abrupt stop against a medium-sized rock that was entirely too pointed for his taste. He jerked back from the sudden, jabbing pain in his ribs.

Both men staggered to their feet.

"This is *not* a good start," Mark said dryly when he could breathe again.

A stick snapped sharply under the weight of someone's foot. They dropped instantly into a crouch, silently swiveling in every direction, seeking the noise's source.

The 21st century pasture had transformed into an 8th century forest. They were in a small gully carpeted in yellowed autumn leaves. Thick trees ran in all directions as far as the eye could see.

The terrain was not nearly as flat as in modern times. At some point in the future, after this forest was cleared, somebody would level this area out to create more arable farmland. So, what was flat in the future, was a gully in the past, and thus their fall. It was one of the many risks of shifting into the unknown.

The noise had come from the other side of a ridge directly in front of them. It didn't take long to discover the cause.

A small female face poked up over the top of it. Her head was covered in a dark brown hood. She'd probably been nearby when they shifted in and had come to investigate the strange, crackling static hiss that accompanied their shifts.

Which actually made her quite brave. Mark could only imagine that most 8ᵗʰ century peasants probably would have scrambled off, screaming of ghosts and witches.

The female took a few more steps until she was almost fully visible above the ridge line. Her attire was simple. Her hood and cloak made her look like a brown version of Little Red Riding Hood. Or one of Robin Hood's merry men. Underneath the cloak was more simple, brown, peasant clothing.

Mark glanced at his own clothing and winced. The type of material was glaringly different from hers. The needlework and finely woven nature of the cloth used in his attire was visibly distinct from the coarse wool of hers. Mark looked at his shifter in vain. The display glowed just as red as they'd expected.

The woman's eyes grew wide in fear, but not because of Mark's clothing. She hadn't had time to take that in. No, she was fixated on Ty.

She screamed something at the top of her lungs and ran away back down the ridge. As the echoes rang in Mark's ears, his mind processed the strange sounds, informing him she'd probably yelled "*Moor!*"

Mark grimaced. He hadn't taken Ty's skin color into account. He hated to even consider that as a factor, but traveling through history and varying cultures demanded it. Ty looked embarrassed. He realized what the problem was too.

"So much for the element of surprise." Mark slapped Ty on the back, trying to lighten the moment. "Let's go see where she went."

After they climbed the ridge, their hearts fell. They were not in the middle of nowhere, not in the 8ᵗʰ century. The ridge on which they stood was a hundred feet away from a road. On that road was a formation of thirty men dressed roughly in the manner of soldiers. The woman ran toward them screaming unintelligible things until the soldiers reacted. The formation turned and began moving toward the ridge. Once she saw the soldiers were moving to intercept the threat, the woman changed directions abruptly and fled toward a small cottage about two hundred yards away on the other side of the road.

"Man, we have the worst luck," Mark lamented.

"So much for hiding out for four hours," Ty said. "How do you want to play it?"

"We evade."

The braying of several hounds floated in on the cool morning air. Mark tightened his jaw and muttered a profanity.

"We're not going to be able to hide from those dogs," Ty said.

Ty was right. The hounds would be trained trackers. The lack of underbrush had already made the possibility of evasion seem difficult. With dogs on their trail, it wouldn't take long to be pinned down or treed.

"Keep a few items, we'll stash the rest."

They ran back down the ridge into the gully and tore at the leaves by a tree. It would still be a minute or two before the soldiers topped the ridge. Mark threw his Uzi and flash-bangs onto the ground. Ty scooped them up and hurriedly buried them under a couple inches of dirt while Mark stabbed at the tree with a knife to mark it. Both men shoved their pistols into the waistband at the back of their pants where they hopefully wouldn't be discovered. Each kept one flash-bang in a secret pocket inside their tunic.

As soon as he was finished, Mark flung his knife as far away into the woods as he could. It would look too modern. They raked the leaves back over the burial site and straightened up, tugging on their shirt sleeves to make sure the shifters were covered.

"Ready?" Mark asked.

Ty didn't have time to respond before the first soldiers topped the ridge. The dogs and their handlers were still a few minutes away.

Mark raised his non-shifter hand in salutation. The soldiers hesitated and yelled something back down the other side of the ridge.

Which man was their commander was obvious by the way he held himself. He appeared behind his men and the entire group descended on Mark and Ty. Within moments, were surrounded by a group of thirty men and two large hounds of a breed they didn't recognize.

Mark briefly contemplated shooting the dogs and making their escape, but too many of these men were outfitted with bows. They would know how to use them too.

Most of the soldiers wore a long brown tunic covered with a shirt made of thin chain mail. They each had an iron helmet with a small piece of iron extending down between their eyes as a nose guard. Under the helmets, they wore a hood made of chain mail that covered them down to the shoulders. Their calves were wrapped in a web of leather straps. Each man had an elongated, oval-shaped shield and a short sword that looked like it could double as a knife. Many had bows and quivers filled with deadly looking arrows. All of them had a small axe strapped to their leather belt as well.

The captain's shield was different from the others. It looked like it was made of leather. He carried a long spear in addition to the sword and axe attached to his belt. He stabbed the earth with the spear as he made his way toward them. The butt end of it wobbled back and forth in the air behind him.

His face was pockmarked, lined with greasy stubble that butted up against a thick mustache. His eyes were dark brown and looked like they could relent in mercy just as easily as they could narrow in judgment.

He scrutinized Ty, but spoke to Mark.

"Thu pist thar?"

Mark glanced at Ty, but shook his head.

"Thu pist thar?" He repeated. *"Quisnam es vos?"*

He'd switched languages, but Mark still had no idea. The captain repeated himself several times, jabbing his finger vigorously Ty's way.

Savannah had done her best to prepare them linguistically for this time period, but no one knew for sure what language Charlemagne and his court spoke. Official business was conducted in Latin and it was rumored the king himself was fluent in Greek, but those would not be the vernacular of the common people. The best candidates were Old High German or Old Franconian and there weren't enough manuscripts preserved in either language to fully reconstruct it.

Still, Savannah had done her best to equip them with certain key phrases and vocabulary that would help in most situations. The problem was that even if this man were spewing the words right off the list in Mark's pocket, he doubted he'd be able to make them out among the thick guttural accents.

"Elilenti," Mark said, shrugging his shoulders. It was a word that meant 'alien' or 'foreigner'.

The captain's face turned a shade redder. *"Wanana lantes?"* He pointed animatedly at Ty's chest. Mark guessed he was asking them where they were from.

"Australia," Mark said.

"Aws-trael-eea," The captain tried to repeat the name.

One of the soldiers slammed the butt of his sword into the back of Ty's neck and Ty collapsed unconscious to the ground. Mark stepped forward to intervene, but something hard slammed into the back of his neck as well and everything went black.

Chapter 34

Mark awoke cold and stiff. They were in a dark, musty room that smelled faintly of human filth. Cool hard stones pressed up uncomfortably against his prone body. He struggled to sit up. His hands were bound behind him, probably by manacles. He could feel the hard heavy metal squeezing his flesh, biting into his wrists.

His entire back ached from whatever abuse he'd suffered while unconscious. His head was pounding. He pressed his back to the wall, letting the coolness of the stones seep into his spine. It brought momentary relief.

A faint glow shone in a hallway in front of him. The light of a small torch burned bright enough he could make out the outlines of his surroundings. They were in a small cell surrounded on three sides by walls built of large stone blocks. Thick, flat iron bars formed the fourth wall in front of him and blocked off any possible exit from the small prison.

To his left lay Ty, still unconscious. His arms were twisted behind his back just like Mark's. Mark tried to kick out at Ty's leg to shake him awake, but the effort sent shooting pains up and down his back. He recoiled his limbs into as comfortable a position as possible.

Mark studied the cell for any way they could escape. They were underground and the only way out was through the ironwork at the front of the cell. The bars seemed solid. They had no rust that he could see, though the light was limited.

The moan of an iron hinge echoed up the hall, followed by hollow footsteps. Two greedy looking guards moved into view at the front of their cell, blocking most of what little dim orange light they'd had. The guards muttered and bantered in that same guttural tongue the captain had used.

One raised a slim black rod that he'd been holding down by his pant leg. The other one laughed as the first went to the torch and held the tip of the metal rod in the flame.

The second guard unlocked the cell door and then both came

inside. The tip of the primitive branding iron had grown so hot it glowed in the darkness.

The second man stood guard by the door, eyes watching Mark for any unexpected move, while the first hovered over Ty and inched the brand toward Ty's face. He intended to scar Mark's friend.

Mark shot his hips forward, landing on his back on top of his manacled arms with a thud. He ignored the flashes of intense pain that flowed through his shoulders, wrists, and back as his legs wrapped around the brander's neck. He began to squeeze.

The second guard reacted, wrapping his forearm around Mark's face, trying to get it under his chin so he could pull Mark off his companion. Mark bit down hard into his arm and did not let go. The guard let out a bewildered scream of mingled shock and fear. Mark jerked his legs in a twisting downward motion and snapped the first guard's neck, ending all motion from that direction.

Ty awoke in the middle of Mark's struggle with the door guard. His teeth had dug deep into the man's flesh and he wasn't about to let go. He had no other purchase, no place to get leverage against this man. Ty swung his legs out and struck the guard in the ankles, sweeping the man backwards to the floor with a hard thunk. The momentum of the fall ripped his arm from Mark's bite.

The guard jumped to his feet, eyes wild with panic. He gripped his limp arm in a failed attempt to alleviate the pain, glanced at his fallen comrade, and fled the cell.

More soldiers flooded the dank hallway, the captain among them. He moved forward, examined the scene, and barked some orders at a couple of men who dragged the body of the brander from the cell by his arms. They carted him down the hall and out of sight while the captain re-locked the cell and left them alone.

Which was surprising. Mark had expected much more reprisal than that.

"You okay?" He whispered.

"Yeah, what happened."

"They were going to brand you. I couldn't let them mess up your pretty little face, so I stopped him."

Ty moaned. As the adrenaline wore off, some of the expected aches and pains were seeping back in.

"My hands are cuffed," Ty said.

"Mine too."

"Hey, they left the branding iron."

The faint glow of it was visible in the corner.

"Can you get it?" Mark asked.

Ty shuffled over and managed to grab the cool end with his trussed hands. Mark scooted around until his back faced Ty.

"Press the hot end against one of the links of my chains," Mark said. "Where the link is joined."

Ty did so for several minutes as the brand cooled. Mark hoped the heat would transfer enough to weaken the link so they could break it. He rolled onto his stomach.

"Stick the rod into the link and leverage the other end down."

Ty did so, lying on the rod with his stomach and chest. Mark's hip acted as a fulcrum. He'd pulled his hands apart as far as possible, keeping the chain taught. The pressure on his hip was incredible. He thought his hipbone might crack, but the chain wouldn't give.

"All your weight, man."

Ty lifted himself up and then fell on the rod like a dead man. A sharp clink announced their success as the link snapped open.

Mark sat up and wrestled with the chain until he'd freed one end of it from the other through the new gap in the weakened link.

He finally got his hands free. Pulling them around, he was ready to massage his wrists in relief, but the large manacles were still in place. The wide cuff on his left hand completely covered his shifter. It pressed tight and wouldn't budge. He couldn't even slip a finger under it. Until he got it off, he wouldn't be shifting anywhere, whether the four hour delay was up or not.

Luckily, his pistol was still stuck in his waistband at his lower back. He withdrew it and pointed the barrel at the ground in front of Ty.

"Turn around," he said.

Ty's eyebrows rose. "Are you crazy, man? I ain't gonna let you shoot at my wrists."

"What? You afraid I'll to miss?"

"In a word — Yes."

Mark grimaced. "Have you ever seen me miss?"

"There's always a first time..."

"Fine." Mark turned to the cell door. "Get back."

He pulled the trigger twice, punching two neat holes in the simplistic lock mechanism. The iron door swung limply ajar.

There was no time to free Ty with the branding iron. The sound of the shots would bring soldiers rushing into the jail any minute.

"Let's move."

They flew up a flight of stairs and heard footsteps clambering down more flights above. They ducked out of sight into a side hallway.

A group of eight soldiers passed by without seeing them. As soon as the guards had turned the corner, Mark and Ty finished running up the stairs.

One lone guard stood by the exit, which was a large steel grille embedded in the stone wall. A small door set in its middle was the only way out and it would no doubt be locked.

Mark rushed the guard. The man opened his mouth to yell for help, but Mark reached him first and slammed the heel of his palm into his iron nose guard. The blow dazed the man.

Mark wrapped his arm around his neck and squeezed until the soldier went limp. Mark snatched a large key from a ring on the guard's belt and moved to the gate, but it swung open when his hand touched it.

"Figures," Ty chuckled.

It hadn't been locked.

"Glad you're in such a good mood."

Mark glanced around the room hurriedly. He spied the ax attached to the guard's belt and grabbed it. They raced from the jail.

Immediately, the bright morning sunshine blinded them. Holding a hand over his eyes like a salute to dampen the effect, Mark led Ty toward a stable across the street.

Once they were safely inside, they leaned their backs against the wall and took a minute to catch their breath.

"Trust me with an axe?" Mark asked, holding the hatchet up.

"Do it."

Ty turned and laid the chain binding him across a wooden beam separating two horse stalls. Mark swung as hard as he dared. He was not practiced in the art of controlling such a heavy blade.

"Seriously, man. You know I'm better with a gun."

Five blows later, one of the links broke. They yanked on both ends of the chain with all their might until the gap widened enough to free Ty's hands.

"Hey, you still got that key?"

"Yeah."

"Try it on the manacles."

It didn't work.

The soldiers were now spilling from the jail into the square outside the stable, barking orders and issuing rallying yells.

Mark and Ty crept to the back of the stable and exited from the rear. Ty still had his gun too, so now that both their arms were free, they could take a stand and fight, but they had no desire to kill these men. They had no beef with them, other than the one who had tried to brand Ty.

What they needed was a blacksmith shop and fast. Priority number one was to get these manacles off so they could use their shifters at will.

A horse was tied to a post about a hundred feet away. Mark ran to it and untied him. He leapt onto the horse's back and turned for Ty.

Something hard slammed into his chest and knocked him from the horse. He sprawled helplessly on his back in the dust. Then, the prick of something very sharp against his Adam's apple froze Mark in place.

He slowly swiveled his eyes up to see a tall, stately man wielding a long, deadly broadsword. Its point pressed into the flesh of Mark's throat. One moderate thrust would end his life.

The man was incredibly tall and muscular, with an unusually thick neck. His bushy mustache and long locks were a pale blonde that was turning white. Vibrant, energetic eyes spoke of supreme confidence in his abilities.

From twenty feet away, Ty stood in the marksman's stance, legs apart, pistol raised and braced with both hands. He was pulling the trigger repeatedly, but the gun's hammer kept falling on emptiness. The resulting series of hollow clicks produced visible confusion in Ty.

Mark did not take his eyes from the man standing over him as he called out to his friend.

"You can't kill Charlemagne, Ty."

Chapter 35

A wave from the Holy Roman Emperor's hand was all that saved Ty from being pierced by several high-velocity arrows. Though the emperor's personal guard could not understand the strange black device in Ty's hand, it was obviously a weapon. That it was ineffective was also obvious. Charlemagne was a warrior at heart and seemed to understand Ty was just trying to protect his friend.

Ty dropped the gun to his side.

Charlemagne flicked his blade up and slipped it into a scabbard on his hip. Unconsciously, Mark rubbed the prick where the point had met his neck.

Charlemagne turned away and motioned for Mark and Ty to follow. His guards did not lower their weapons.

Their destination was Charlemagne's palace and the magnificent cathedral he'd commissioned. The cathedral and palace grounds were surrounded on all sides by acres of clipped green grass, an unexpected paradise in the so-called Dark Ages.

Mark's mind raced back over what he remembered from the briefing Savannah had given them regarding the history of this era. Charlemagne had begun his reign as a lesser ruler of half of what would be modern-day France. Through a political marriage and several conquests, which he initiated in defense of the Pope, he very quickly found himself ruler over all of France, much of Germany, and northern Italy. From there, he just expanded further. His establishment of the Holy Roman Empire was the foundation for Western Europe as we know it today.

Charlemagne spent most of his life battling the Saxons to the east and the Moors in Spain to the south. He'd defeated both repeatedly, but the Moors were the only ones who had ever achieved a victory over Charlemagne in the battlefield.

Mark made a mental note to pay much closer attention to Savannah's historical briefings in the future and consider *all* the potential impact a historical setting could have on their mission. They should have realized Ty would be mistaken for a Moor before coming.

Charlemagne's throne room was full of splendor, though the king did not match its luxurious appearance in his own personal attire. While the noblemen and other court attendees wore elegant, embroidered robes, Charlemagne's clothing seemed to be just a slightly higher quality version of that of a commoner. To even a first time visitor, it was apparent he was not a man given to materialism.

A simple marble throne rose up from one end of the long hall, several feet off the floor. A short series of stone steps led up to it. Several colonnades lined both sides, drawing the visitor inevitably to the throne.

Instead of ascending the steps to take his traditional seat, however, Charlemagne stopped short of it and grabbed a wooden chair. He twirled it to face Mark and Ty and sat down. He did not offer for them to do the same.

Clergy and nobles lined the hall on all sides. Many had heard about the visitors and strange happenings in Aachen today. Charlemagne's guards had put away their bows, but their hands remained on the hilts of their swords.

"*Quisnam es vos?*"

The emperor's voice was commanding, though slightly higher-pitched than one would expect.

Mark guessed he was being asked again where they were from.

"Australia."

Ty glanced at Mark. "Why Australia?" he whispered.

Mark ignored him, fixing his gaze on Charlemagne.

The emperor looked to the captain of the guard who'd originally captured them. He'd materialized from somewhere during Mark and Ty's arrival. The captain nodded.

"Aws-tray-lee-ah," Charlemagne repeated, almost sounding like Mark. "*Qua est?*"

Ty shook his head in wonderment.

Mark finally broke his stare and shot a glance Ty's way. "It's the only place I could think of they definitely wouldn't have heard of," he muttered.

"What about America? Wouldn't that have been easier?"

Charlemagne asked them several more questions in Latin. Mark helplessly held up his hands to show he did not understand. Charlemagne broke into a more guttural language, the same language the soldiers had spoken. When that didn't work, he tried a little Greek.

The noblemen hovering around the scene were rapt with

attention. Foreigners had arrived from a land no one had ever heard of. A Moor together with a man who looked like them, and they seemed to be on friendly terms. It was clearly the intrigue of the month, something that would be talked about for some time to come.

Charlemagne turned to the modest crowd, looking over their heads, seeking someone.

"Einhard!" he called.

The crowd parted as a smallish, scholarly man approached the throne. His manner with the emperor was one of humility and submission, yet strong familiarity. The two spoke out of hearing for a moment, Charlemagne probably explaining the translation difficulties they were having.

Einhard turned and posed them several questions in Latin to which Mark responded with more apologies in English for their inability to understand. Einhard listened intently, head tilted to one side, as Mark spoke. He stared after Mark ceased, not in rudeness, but as if the wheels of thought were turning behind his eyes.

Finally, he turned back to the emperor. *"Alcuin,"* he said.

"Flaccus?"

Einhard nodded and left the court. The king motioned for Ty and Mark to have a seat while they waited for whatever it was Einhard had gone to get.

Fifteen minutes later, a taller, frail looking man in his late sixties entered the court. The emperor referred to him as Flaccus, but others alternated between Flaccus and Alcuin.

This man approached Mark and Ty and attempted conversation. It was immediately apparent he spoke a dialect that was much more familiar to their ears. It sounded a lot like Middle English, which Mark had become accustomed to during his stints in medieval England, but there were enough archaic terms and strange sounds thrown in to confuse a good bit of the man's meaning.

Still, after some trial and error, they found that if both sides stuck to very simple phrases and words, and spoke very slowly, a rough conversation could be held.

"Where are you from?" Alcuin asked.

"Australia," Mark said. "Some people call it America."

Ty grimaced.

"We have heard of neither," Alcuin said.

"It is a country very far away. On the other side of the Great Sea."

"There is nothing on the other side of the Great Sea."

"If you know where to sail, there is land."

Alcuin turned and translated this to Charlemagne. A number of gasps and sounds of exclamations went up from the crowd. Charlemagne did not react, but Einhard nodded silently as if this was something he'd always suspected.

"Why have you come here?" Alcuin asked.

"We come in peace."

"You killed one of the king's guard and attacked others."

"The one we killed was going to harm my friend. We were attacked and imprisoned without reason."

Alcuin translated this and Charlemagne nodded. He had already been informed of the circumstances. He barked questions at Alcuin, who in turn posed the translated Old English versions to Mark.

"What is your mission? Why are you here?"

"We seek a scholar, a man of knowledge."

"Which man?"

"He is a Jewish Scholar named. Baruch ben Elishama."

Alcuin translated and Charlemagne burst into hearty, roaring laughter. He slapped his knee in amusement, a large grin enveloping his handsome, ruddy face. *"Baruk? Mus?"* The king laughed some more. He called over his shoulder to someone they could not see. *"Apportame Mus!"*

"What does *Mus* mean?" Mark asked Alcuin.

Alcuin squinched his nose. *"Mus,* you know, little animal. Cats eat it."

"Ah, mouse."

"Yes, we know Baruch. King Charles calls him 'Mus.' He gives names to those he loves."

"Why does he call him Mouse?"

Alcuin shrugged. "He is not a big man, likes to be alone, always has his nose in books."

Charlemagne barked something else at Alcuin.

"The king wants to know why you want to see the Mouse...eh, Baruch."

"We have heard that he has much knowledge of the land of Israel and we wish to learn from him."

"How do you know this?"

"A trader came to our land and told us."

Alcuin reported all this to the king, who then replied, his brow creased severely with another question.

Alcuin's tone took on a slightly more stressed tone. "The king wants to know why you travel with a Moor. The Moors are enemies. How can he know you are not spies?"

"Ty, perhaps you should speak for yourself?"

Ty stepped forward and bowed at the waist before the emperor in a courtly fashion. "Your highness, I am not a Moor, but I come from America, the same as my friend. We are not here as spies, but as seekers of knowledge. Marcus and I are friends."

Ty faced the king while Alcuin translated every word.

"Is this true?" Charlemagne asked Mark. "Are you friends with the Moor?"

"He is not a Moor. Yes, we are friends."

"He is black, so he is Moor."

"He is not a Moor," Mark countered. "He is American."

The king studied Ty for a long time, as if trying to peer into his soul. He finally relented, his posture changing from alert to slightly relaxed.

"You do not speak the language of Moors," he allowed.

Ty bowed again.

The crowd parted once more for another smallish man who'd entered the court. He was rounder at the belly than Einhard. A heavy, wild beard covered his jaws and he was starting to bald around the crown of his head.

"*Mus,*" the emperor greeted him, explaining in Latin everything that had been said. He turned back to Mark and Ty.

"Are you Christians in Ah-mehr-ee-ka?" he asked. "Or Mosolman?"

"Yes, your highness, we are Christians." Ty responded confidently.

"Good." Charlemagne nodded. "In that case, Baruch will help you as much as you desire. He is Jewish, so you must treat him well, yes?"

Mark assured him they would. The emperor ordered Alcuin to continue to translate for them. He requested that Mark and Ty convey his good treatment of them to the leaders of America once they returned to their land.

Baruch ben Elishama and Alcuin led them out of the palace grounds and down several twisting streets until they came to a cluster of narrow, two-story homes with thatched roofs. Elishama's home was a humble abode filled with what must have been considered upper middle class furnishings for the time period.

Warily, Baruch answered every question they had that could be understood through the medium of their rudimentary translator in Alcuin. The constant puzzlement that dwelt in the lines of his face throughout their encounter was directly due to the bizarre nature of Mark and Ty's visit.

No doubt, when the Jewish scholar had gotten out of bed this morning, he had no clue the ensuing day would soon make him the center of attention of Charlemagne's entire court, nor that he would entertain in his home a strange, tall foreigner who befriended moors and came from a land no one had ever heard of. He certainly had no idea the name Baruch ben Elishama was known outside of the city of Aachen, much less outside the Holy Roman Empire, and especially as far away as this unknown place called America. Baruch was a nobody.

Later on, he would have to answer endless questions from the emperor about the odd visit and why the strangers came looking for him of all people. His puzzlement masked a deeper worry that lurked beneath, a concern that he might become suspected of collaborating with Charlemagne's enemies because of the Moor. Charlemagne was a good ruler, not given to paranoia, but still...

For now, his only option was to help these strangers as the emperor had requested, posing questions of his own and taking note of any helpful detail he might pass on to reveal their purpose and belay some of the suspicion from himself.

Mark and Ty, however, were holding their cards very close to the vest. They had no intention of revealing any more than they had to, and that meant not much since Charlemagne had commanded full cooperation.

The day's events had turned around quite nicely. From prison to Charlemagne's court, all within the span of an hour, and without even being able to speak the language.

After numerous diversionary questions, Mark explained to Baruch their desire to learn more about Mattatiyah HaLevi. They told Baruch that his reputation for knowledge of all things Jewish had preceded him even to the shores of America.

Still, the puzzled creases in Baruch's forehead did not lessen. He did not buy their cover story, nor their explanation of how they'd heard his name.

Nevertheless, he rose and left the room, returning with several scrolls and a few loose sheets of legal-length paper. Tender hands unrolled one scroll after the other as he gently ran his finger down lines of endless Hebrew script, silently searching for the information they had requested. His manner toward the writings was almost loving in nature.

Finally, his finger came to a stop and he lifted his face toward them.

"*Mattatiyah HaLevi...*" He continued, speaking in Old High German, but they had no idea what he was saying.

Alcuin, translated, "He says this man was a scribe who lived in Israel before the destruction of Jerusalem."

"When specifically?"

"About forty years before Jerusalem was destroyed by the Romans. In the seventeenth year of Tiberius Caesar."

"Who was this scribe? What is he known for?"

Alcuin translated the question. Baruch studied the document further and rattled off several short answers.

"He says the scribe was associated with several of the high priests and wrote a treatise on the sacrifices in the Law. Other than that, he knows no more."

"Ask him about the Ark of the Covenant?"

The wrinkles in Baruch's forehead deepened. He shook his head as Alcuin interpreted.

"He says he knows nothing of the Ark other than it was lost when the Babylonians conquered Judah."

"Was Mattatiyah associated with the Ark in any way? Has Baruch heard of the Silver Scroll?"

Baruch shook his head again sternly, but then his eyes lit up as if he'd suddenly remembered something. He grabbed another scroll and examined it. Then, he rambled on to Alcuin for a few minutes.

"He says he knows nothing of a silver scroll, but that there is a legend of the Ark. He says once a barbarian king attacked a city called Arcadiopolis. Before the attack, a Jewish scribe went out to this barbarian king and begged him not to destroy the city as it held many historic treasures. As an example of the artifacts, this scribe showed the king a small scroll which told of the location of the Ark. The barbarian confiscated the scroll and destroyed the city anyway, but he did spare the scribe's life. Legend says this king later had his sword specially fashioned so the scroll could be stored inside its hilt."

"Who was this king?"

Baruch answered Mark directly. "*Flagellum Dei.*"

Chapter 36

"Who?"

"*Flagellum Dei.*"

Mark looked at Ty. "Who's that?"

"No idea."

After a few more rounds of questions, it became clear Baruch knew nothing more than what he had already told them. They quickly wrapped up the discussion and Alcuin accompanied them back to Charlemagne's court.

The emperor grinned from ear to ear upon seeing them again. Curiosity burned fiercely within.

He interviewed Alcuin in private for several minutes, presumably about what kind of questions Mark and Ty had asked Baruch.

After he returned, Mark and Ty happily bantered jovially with Charlemagne for several minutes until a natural lull laid itself across the conversation, at which point Mark held up his wrists, reminding the king of the manacles that still bound their wrists.

Charlemagne laughed heartily and slapped both of them on the back.

"I will take you to a smith who can take those off," Alcuin said.

Mark and Ty bid their farewell to Charlemagne, who entreated them to stay the night in his palace, but Mark insisted they must be on their way. He requested they send more delegates from America to visit his court and they said they would see what could be done. The emperor was reluctant to lose such a sure source of entertainment and intrigue, but since his suspicions had been allayed, he graciously thanked them for the visit and let them go.

The blacksmith shop was a few blocks away from the palace. It was another humble structure topped with a thatched roof. A superheated forge inside made the air definitively uncomfortable.

The blacksmith was a greasy, oversized man lathered with sweat. He was about to begin hammering at the pins holding Mark's manacles shut when a soldier showed up with the key. In a few moments, their wrists were finally free and they were on their way.

They left Aachen on foot, returning to the spot where they'd shifted in for the simple reason that they'd left their car there in the future.

A cool autumn sun warmed their faces as they walked. Light breezes rippled their tunics and funneled brightly-colored leaves upward in unpredictable spirals alongside the path.

They came to the cottage that belonged to the woman whose screams had given them away to Charlemagne's soldiers.

It was a crude, low-roofed hovel. The straw of its thatched roof was a dull, dark grey, dotted with moss. Two smallish windows bordered either side of the front door. Clean, white curtains hung behind both. A dainty hand tugged one of them back, creating a dark triangle through which someone could peer out at the road and observe whoever was passing by. Most likely the same woman.

"Let's go see her," Ty said.

"She's not going to want to see us. She's scared."

"Let's go," he urged, bobbing his head up and down several times.

Mark sighed in assent. As soon as they veered off the path toward the cottage, the curtain dropped back into place. Whoever had been spying was trying to hide.

The vegetable gardens around the cottage were well kept, free of weeds, but Mark saw some squirrels or other arboreal foragers had been nibbling at her produce. If she lived by herself, it was a natural frustration that she probably had difficulty fighting and could mean tragedy under the wrong circumstances.

Ty knocked softly, but firmly. No response. He tried again.

"C'mon, man. She's not going to answer."

"Wait. She'll come."

He knocked several more times and finally went and sat down upon a rock to wait.

"This is silly," Mark said.

At long last, the front door cracked open. A trim figure peered out, hesitated, then opened the door the rest of the way.

Of course it was the same woman. She wore the same brown cloak, but now the hood was pushed back and laid in folds behind her neck, revealing long, raven black hair. Her skin was pale like cream, her eyes the color of chestnuts.

Ty stepped forward and she retreated. Then, she turned aside and motioned for them to come inside.

The interior was swept and well-kept, neat and tidy, but poor in every other respect. A chair, a table, and a crude bed were the only furnishings. Two small stacks of firewood lined either side of the hearth. Mark hoped she had more stashed behind the house. He hadn't seen any out in front and winter was coming on.

The woman was young, perhaps in her early thirties. Her eyes were wide and her breathing heavy.

She was pretty. Slender jaw line, high cheekbones. Her clothing was made of rough wool, brown and worn. She fell back from them, her lower lip trembling.

She could not know their intentions, but hoped their reemerging freely from Aachen indicated they had been released by the emperor. Still, they might want revenge for her alerting the soldiers.

Yet, if they'd wanted to, they could have kicked the door in. It was barely on the hinges anymore anyway. Their gentle knocking spoke of another purpose and common sense said she should show hospitality.

She retrieved a wooden bucket from the floor and dipped a wooden cup into the water inside. She offered it to Mark with a shaky hand, fearful eyes locked on Ty. She got a second cup and handed it to Ty. This time, her eyes were glued to the floor. She stepped back and looked around her home, searching for something else she could offer them, but she had nothing.

"We can't talk to her, man."

"Give me the sack of gold," Ty said. He held his hand out without taking his gaze from her.

Something moist was welling in Ty's eyes. There was an expression on his friend's face Mark had not seen before. He gave him the gold.

Ty held the small pouch out to the woman, but she hesitated, afraid to get closer. He jingled it, the clinking of coins revealing its nature. That overcame her reluctance. Warily, she reached for it.

She peeled open the mouth of the sack. The gleam of the coins widened her eyes in shock, fear renewed. What could these men want in return for so much gold? She'd never held a gold coin in her life, much less this many of them. She shook her head and tried to thrust it back into his hand. Ty waved her off, assuring her through gestures it was okay.

"Let's go chop her some wood," Mark said.

Ty smiled. "That sounds like a good idea."

***

It turned out *Flagellum Dei* was Latin for "The Whip of God" or "The Scourge of God". As soon as they gave her the title, Savannah knew exactly who they were talking about.

"Attila the Hun," She said. matter-of-factly. "He died in 453 AD."

"*Attila the Hun!*" Mark exclaimed. "You've got to be kidding me. One of the cruelest men ever born has the secret to the Ark stuffed up his sword? And how long will our shifters shut down if we go back *that* far?"

Hardy studied his laminated time-delay card. "Two days," he reported gleefully.

His broken leg was propped up on the table. He lifted the cast for a second and let it fall back down on the wood with a low thunk to emphasize the trip wouldn't be any skin off his nose.

"We can wait till you've healed," Mark commented.

"No," Hardy waved his hands in the air. "By all means, this is something that can't wait. You need to take care of it now."

"What if we go back to the time of Christ and find this scribe, Mattatiyah HaLevi. How long would the shut-down be?"

"Two months."

"*Two months!*" Mark stood and began to pace the room. "We almost got killed when we were shut down for four hours."

"Maybe we're slipping," Ty smiled.

"Well, you guys certainly seem to be taking this whole thing lightly. Why am I the only one worried here?"

"What's there to worry about? It is what it is," Ty said.

Mark grunted. "Don't start in with that 'fate' crap, man. I'm not in the mood."

Ty laughed. "Well, maybe it's because Hardy's laid up and after our last experience I doubt you'll want to be taking a 'moor' along again. Looks like this one's in your court."

Mark cursed.

"He really wasn't all that bad, Mark," Savannah offered. "The Romans gave him a nasty reputation, but he wasn't as brutal as everyone thinks. I could go with you to help translate the Latin."

"Ha!" Ty could barely contain himself. "Not even a girl's afraid of little old Attila. What are you so worked up about, Mark?"

"Shut up."

Hardy burst out laughing at that. Savannah blushed, but smiled in spite of herself. Mark finally relented, seeing the humor in the whole thing.

Between a two day shutdown and two months, the choice was obvious. Who wanted to lose two months of their life stuck in the past? Even though that lead seemed a little more reliable than the spurious legend of Attila and his sword, the time difference was too great not to give Attila a try first.

Mark returned to his seat. "All right. Savannah, looks like we're going to meet Attila the Hun." He turned to the others. "I'll tell you what, though. The No-Modern-Contamination rule is hereby suspended. I'm taking every weapon I can carry. Especially if Savannah's going."

Chapter 37

*If I gave you my hand would you take it
And make me the happiest man in the world*

"Would You Go With Me"

~ Josh Turner

Eastern Hungary

The fields of old Hungary were wide open and green, inspiring a beautiful sense of freedom.

He couldn't help but stare as the wind lifted her hair in short, cascading waves while they moved through the prairie. Her auburn tresses flowed up and down, back and forth, swaying in tune to the dry grass rolling before the breeze. Unconsciously, he kept a few steps behind so he could watch the dance, fascinated.

Then, he shook himself out of the reverie, moderately surprised by his strange fixation.

"Uh...this should be far enough."

The Hungarian countryside looked like the southern United States. Lush green grass spread out in all directions. A low line of hills ended the flow of green on one side, a dense forest and the Tisza river capped the other.

Mark slung his black duffel from his shoulder and set it down.

Savannah knelt to the ground, modestly sweeping her skirt under her with one hand in a distinctly feminine way.

Well, it wasn't really a skirt, more like a silken tunic/toga combo modeled after common female attire of the 5th century Roman Empire. Mark was dressed similarly, but with a cape and a thick leather, military-style belt around his waist. They'd taken pains this time to make sure the quality of the material in their clothing would not be modern looking to a keen observer in the past.

They had dressed as Romans because not much was known about the Huns or their empire. Only a few words had been preserved from the Hunnic language and even less was known of their culture. It was generally believed the Huns had migrated from further east in Asia until they'd settled in what was now modern Hungary. Even the actual location of Attila's palace was still a mystery to modern historians.

With some exhaustive research, Mark and Savannah had been able to narrow the possibilities down to a specific region around the Tisza River. Still, once they shifted, it was very likely they'd have a good bit of exploring to do.

Unless they stumbled upon some of the Attila's men. That would either set them on an express path to a meeting with the head honcho himself, or to a very unpleasant outcome.

Mark didn't plan to let this mission slip out of his control. Not with Savannah along and the magnitude of the shift delay they would experience. So, they'd explore, but they'd keep their distance from any soldiers for as long as possible.

"Are you going to explain to me what all this stuff does?" She asked.

"Sure. I may need your help in a pinch, though I hope it doesn't come to that." He squatted next to her and went over the different kinds of explosives he'd brought. He taught her the differences between the various types of guns and what kind of situation each was best for, all while trying to ignore the faint scent of her perfume tickling his nose. It reminded him of lilies.

He made sure she knew where the safeties were on each weapon.

She stood, placing her hands on her hips.

"Looks like we're all set for a mercenary picnic," she said.

"I'm not a mercenary," Mark grumbled.

"I know," she soothed, smiling. She laid her hand lightly on his shoulder to reassure him. "It was a joke."

An electric tingle lingered for several minutes after she withdrew her fingertips, the afterglow of her gentle gesture.

"Are you sure you want to risk this, Savannah? It really *will* be dangerous."

"I'm sure. I love history. How could I pass up an opportunity to go back and see it firsthand."

"I can take you to a thousand other times. There's a lot safer places to visit than the land of Attila the Hun while he's on the warpath."

"It's okay, Mark. I'm ready."

She was certain.

He turned away and double-checked the equipment again. "You're not trusting in that same fate crap Ty preaches, are you?"

She didn't respond immediately and he didn't wait for the answer.

"All right, let's go. You stay by my side at all times. If I say get down, you drop. If I say run, you run."

She nodded.

He slung the duffel bag over his shoulder and took her hand. He hadn't intended for it to be an intimate gesture, but tenderness just seemed to slip into it. The hair on the back of his neck tingled. In that moment, his whole world centered on the electricity created by the dry brushing of their skins against one another.

Imperceptibly, he shook his head to break his mind free from the distraction.

This was ridiculous. He'd proven his unreadiness — his unworthiness — to be in a relationship. She could not, would not, be interested anyway — nor would he be good for her. He was a rough, undisciplined man, tormented by grief, sorrow and guilt. She was a breath of fresh air, young, beautiful, and untainted by the world.

He'd been through these emotional gyrations with Laura and Abigail. He knew himself a little better now. His heart had never really healed since Kelly left. Not to mention the massive rips torn into it by the deaths of Daniel and Brittany. He'd grasp after any female who showed him the least bit of attention, like a beached whale tasting a drop of water.

The growing affection he felt was nothing more than desperation masquerading as desire. It was an illusion. His attentions would only harm her. To think she would even welcome an advance from someone like him was ludicrous. She trusted him.

This time, he would discipline himself and protect her, protect their friendship.

He pushed the red button on his shifter.

The earth tilted and dropped beneath their feet, twisting them off balance, but nowhere near the levels he and Ty had experienced when they'd arrived in the time of Charlemagne.

As soon as the shift finished, he dropped her hand like a hot potato. She noticed, but pretended not to, masking her hurt.

He'd forgotten to have a pistol ready. He drew one and braced himself in the firing position, swiftly swiveling in every direction in search of threats. Seeing none, he lowered the weapon and reholstered it.

From where they stood, not much looked different. Same lazy river, same field, though the tree lines had shifted in places.

"What do we do now?" She asked.

"We walk until we find somebody we can communicate with. Do you want to be husband and wife, or brother and sister?"

"Husband and wife. We don't exactly look alike."

"Works for me. I want to warn you though, dear. No one's taking us prisoner this time."

***

I wanna stand out in a crowd for you, a man among men,
I wanna make your world better than it's ever been,

"Making Memories of Us"

~ Keith Urban

They soon found a well-used path, but the only person they encountered during the entire day was a lone tinkerer, a half-crazy, babbling hermit who migrated from village to village fixing things and doing odd jobs for a living. He couldn't understand a word they said and didn't care to take the time to try. He just kept walking. So, they did too.

As night drew on, Mark picked a spot close to the river where they could camp. It was far enough away from the trail they'd be out of sight from the casual passer-by.

He laid some rocks in a small ring and started a moderate-sized fire. Knowing they'd be stuck in the 5th century for several days, they'd packed a decent amount of rations, some of which he broke out and began to cook. Soon, the thick, enticing aroma of hot lasagna rose up tantalizingly from an oversized tin baking over the flames.

When it was ready, he divvied it up onto two plates and they dug in. The only thing they'd had to eat all day up to that point was granola bars.

The night air was crisp, but not so cool as to be uncomfortable. The gentle rippling of tiny waves in the river acted like soothing music to accompany the meal, and warmth from the crackling logs combined with the light of the stars to stoke the atmosphere. Every now and then the fire popped, followed by a shower of sparks spiraling upward from the flames.

Mark was uneager to dissipate the charged nature of their meal.

"I think this is the best Italian restaurant I've ever been to," she said.

"Yeah." He laughed awkwardly.

Any levity dwindled like sand through fingers.

"Is something wrong, Mark?"

He turned to her. Orange light flickered across the sweep of her chiseled jaw and high cheeks, twinkling in her eyes. She'd swept her hair up into a pony tail, which revealed the fullness of her slender face, but he remembered how it had looked earlier in the fields. Bouncing waves of auburn glory in the afternoon sun.

A strand of it had strayed, and now fell loosely against her cheek. Unconsciously, he reached out and tucked it behind her ear, brushing her skin with the back of his fingertips.

Realizing what he'd just done, he froze and dropped his hand back to his side.

"Uh...sorry. I didn't mean to do that," he said.

"It's okay, Mark. What's the matter?"

"I'm sorry," he repeated. He was visibly shaking.

She leaned forward and took his face between her hands, forcing his eyes to fix on her own.

"It's okay, Mark. It's okay."

"What's okay? What do you mean?"

Her eyes enveloped him like a medicine. He felt the overwhelming urge to kiss her, but refrained. His heart was struggling against the bars he'd built around it.

Images of Kelly's pained face as she walked out the door for the last time flooded his mind. Images of Laura laughing with Hardy on a sailboat. Of Abigail holding his face in her hands, just as Savannah was doing now, in that grove of birch trees near her cottage, holding onto him as she rejected him.

Of the men he'd killed in the line of duty as a soldier — and since. Disgust with himself for things he'd desired, and for other things he should have, but didn't. Images of his filthy hands, too dirty to contaminate such a white flower. The stains were inevitable.

Of his children giggling and playing free and alive only to be suddenly whisked away by death. Of their gravestones which marked the end of all hope for him, for love. The death of his freedom.

He twisted his eyes away. They fell on his wrist. The shifter was like a sleek, silver manacle, binding him to a fate not of his choosing.

The pain was too great. He broke the moment, grasping the backs of her hands in his own and pushed them away.

"I know. Yes, it's okay. I'm okay. Sorry."

Her moistened eyes had looked deep within his soul and she'd seen much. She'd understood his torment.

She retreated to her dinner.

He dug into his own, the taste of sweet marinara filling his mouth.

That falling lock of her hair would linger in his mind for days to come. And the feel of her skin against his fingers.

Chapter 38

You've been looking for love all around the world...
Your Kentucky girl's been waiting patiently, why not me?

"Why not Me?"

~ The Judds

The night lay still under a blanket of nocturnal peace.

Still awake, Mark gazed at the twinkling stars overhead. They looked like sparkling diamonds strewn randomly across a black Jeweler's cloth. The illuminated swath of the Milky Way was clearer than he'd ever seen in his home time. Here the night was crystal clear, free of all earthly pollution or electric street lights muting the view.

The gurgling of the brook floated faintly through their camp, a soothing lullaby in harmony with vigilant cicadas. Yet, sleep evaded him.

His eyes would not close. Their campfire had descended into a pile of weak embers, their orange glow only hinting now of the fire that once had been.

Her smooth, pale cheeks were bathed in a faint blue as she slept, cozy in one of the down-filled sleeping bags they'd brought along. Her breathing was clear and rhythmical, a faint murmuring the only indication she might be dreaming.

He wished he could trust like that. So peaceful.

She trusted in him. He hoped that trust wasn't misplaced.

Too often, he'd taken her for granted over the past few years. He suddenly realized how much he depended on her, how many times she'd been there for him. Without her knowledge of history, they would never have accomplished so much. Without her faithful presence, he might never have made it through Laura's break-up, or been strong enough to handle Abigail's rejection.

She held a quiet strength, a resoluteness so hidden he'd overlooked its full power. He thought back over everything she'd done at his request, never questioning, never balking at whatever work load he dealt her.

He'd paid her handsomely of course. She and her mother were multi-millionaires now, but she kept on working for him, doing whatever research he asked, promoting their cause among her colleagues at the university. Why *was* she working for him?

It was because she believed in what they were doing. She believed in *him*.

She couldn't want him too, *could she*? Why was he feeling such a strong attraction for her all of a sudden? Wasn't it just another of his desperate infatuations on this broken road within his heart? How arrogant did he have to be to think a pure heart like hers could want his?

A snap of wood cracking in the brush slammed those thoughts to the side. He tensed, fully alert, his ears strictly attuned to sourcing whatever had caused it.

It had been something heavy.

Silently, Mark slipped from his bag and moved out of the faint glow emanating from the coals. In the shadows, he circled on his tiptoes toward the far side of the camp, toward whatever it was.

He peered into the darkness, searching for a sign of movement. His pistol was out and up, braced with both hands.

Suddenly, an enormous black bear burst from the brush and slammed into his chest, knocking him off his feet. He crashed into the loose dirt on his back. The beast was heavy, snarling, vicious in intent. From all sides, sharp warrior cries rose up and pierced the night. His vision swam. The gun was slipping from his grasp.

***

The wild hollering startled Savannah awake. She sat bolt upright and saw Mark struggling on the ground with what looked to be a big black bear. Shrieks and cries echoed all around as painted barbarians swarmed into the camp from every direction.

She scrambled for Mark's duffel bag, trying to remember everything he'd shown her. She managed to get it unzipped enough she could get a pistol out. She stood and was taking aim when something hard and sudden wrapped around her throat. One of the barbarians had gotten behind her and was pressing his forearm into her larynx, choking off her breath.

She watched as Mark wrestled with the dark, snarling beast. He arched his back and sent a powerful punch into the bear's skull, smashing the side of its face right at its lower jaw. The bear's head snapped back.

It lurched, and its skin flapped up in the air freakishly like a tent billowing in the wind, revealing not muscle and sinew underneath, but a man. It was just another warrior who'd draped himself in a bear skin.

The "bear" wobbled and collapsed onto its side, freeing Mark, who leapt to his feet, scooping his gun from the dust as he did. Besides the bear-man, there were five other warriors, not including the one holding Savannah. They were on Mark in an instant.

He slammed the heel of his palm into the face of the barbarian in front of him and sent an elbow back into the face of one behind. He pivoted and kicked a third in the solar plexus, leaving that one gasping for air. The fourth and fifth stepped back warily, trying to regroup in the face of Mark's unexpected ferocity.

Turning, Mark saw her attacker had wrapped his forearm around Savannah's throat. Worse, he saw the gleam of a crude knife in his other hand.

"Drop," he said firmly, eyes fixed on hers.

She'd never seen such coldness in those eyes before now. Anger, sure. Pain definitely, but this was beyond any of that. At this moment, he was a merciless, calculating soldier who would do the job at any cost.

If I say get down, you drop, he'd said back in the field.

She dropped.

Mark flipped his pistol up and caught it by the barrel. He flung it whirling end over end through the air. It struck Savannah's would be kidnapper in the middle of the forehead, and it might as well have been a ton of bricks. He flopped unconscious to the ground like a limp noodle.

The bear-man was out cold. Numbers one, two and three were back on their feet and moving to surround Mark along with numbers four and five.

Savannah's breathing came in sharp, panicked intakes of air, but she forced herself to calm down. She had never been in combat before and the adrenaline rush was more than she'd anticipated. She remembered the gun in her hand.

She lifted it and took aim at one of the barbarians, but Mark waved her off.

"Don't," he said simply, not looking her way, but at the attackers.

He waited until the warriors had regained a modicum of their initial bravery and pressed in once more. As soon as they were within range, his arms and legs became a blur of motion. He swept one warrior from his feet with a roundhouse that struck him in the back of his knees. Cries of pain and panic alternately shot up from each of the barbarians like a cacophony of wounded seals. In a matter of thirty seconds, Mark had four of them out cold on the ground and the fifth was on his knees begging for mercy in a babble of unintelligible syllables.

"Hun?" Mark asked.

The man nodded, terrified.

"Good. Take us to Attila."

Chapter 39

Mark bound all seven warriors by tying their wrists behind their backs with strong rope. He also tied cords around their ankles with enough length they could walk but not run. He slapped the unconscious ones until they woke up and once they were on their feet again, he knotted all their bonds together. They would walk in front of Mark, single file, each one of them tied securely to the others.

All seven men wore the same style leather pants and linen tunics. The most curious feature of the troop, however, was that every single one of them had a long, deep scar running down his right cheek.

These Huns had stashed their larger weapons in some nearby brush before the ambush to avoid making noise as they'd approached Mark and Savannah's camp. Mark collected all their weapons and bundled them up in his sleeping bag, which he dragged along behind them.

After Mark had repeated the barbarian king's name a number of times using several different pronunciations, they had finally understood what he wanted.

They would lead him to Attila the Hun. If they tried to run, they knew they wouldn't get very far. Mark had demonstrated the power of his gun on a tree trunk to further ingrain the futility of flight. They walked all night and finally arrived at the Hun's headquarters right after dawn.

Attila's palace was an enormous, multi-level wooden structure which stood several hundred feet off the Tisza River. It sat atop a low circular hill covered in cropped green grass and was surrounded by a full moat. Numerous walkways and bridges crossed the moat at different points around the perimeter, some of which disappeared into large, gaping, stone-rimmed tunnels that led deep underground.

The primary entrance was a grand covered walkway that led straight across the moat, up the hill and into the center of the enormous structure like the trunk of some alien elephant. A large wooden dome crested the building where the peak of the skull would be. The elephant's eyes were two thick wooden turrets topped by steep conical roofs that could have rivaled the best Victorian homes. A curved overhang jutted out significantly at the upper levels, circling the palace all the way around like a fold in its skin.

Two mirrored paths wound their way up the hill from the moat on both sides. White linens were stretched as canopies across these paths, held aloft by wooden poles lining each side. A throng of people flooded the right-hand path and that was where they were headed.

As soon as Mark's party drew near, a squad of barbarian soldiers surrounded them. After a short discussion between them and Mark's captives, who apparently gave a sufficient explanation of Mark's intent, half the soldiers moved in front as a menacing escort of sorts while the other half fell back behind them to ensure Mark didn't try anything funny.

Mark reiterated his desire to them, just in case it was not clear, by firmly repeating "Attila" several times. The new guards nodded sternly and continued.

Which man was Attila was not hard to figure out. Those surrounding him moved in deference to his position.

He was a short man, shorter than Mark had expected. Barrel-chested and stocky, his brawny arms told tales of tremendous strength. His skin was a dark bronze, and his nose was flat. His features hinted of at least some Mongol heritage. His eyes sparkled with determined ferocity.

The crowd parted to allow Mark, Savannah, and their captives through. Attila watched their approach warily, an amused smirk twisting his lips. His hand did not move toward the hilt of the small sword slung horizontally across his belly, but the charged atmosphere made it clear he could do so at any moment.

"Attila?" Mark asked, remembering from their experience with the captured warriors to put the emphasis on the first syllable so it came out "AH-til-la."

The barbarian king spewed a long chain of unrecognizable language at them in response. Mark shook his head and looked to Savannah.

She stepped forward.

"Non sumus romani."

She glanced at Mark and explained "I told him we aren't Romans. I think that's important for him to know."

Mark waved theatrically and took a step back. "By all means, say whatever needs to be said so he doesn't kill us."

Attila's demeanor visibly relaxed as she explained more and tried to convince him they weren't Romans, yet he nevertheless remained cautious and hostile. The Roman Empire was Attila's primary enemy and they didn't need him believing they were there to negotiate on the empire's behalf. Attila responded in Latin and he and Savannah exchanged sentences several more times.

Attila said something to her while looking at Mark that he obviously thought was humorous and then yelled it again loud enough the entire crowd could hear, which caused everyone to burst out laughing.

Savannah turned back to Mark. "I told him we are from a land far away, but that we have come to meet him because we have heard of his greatness."

"Sounds good, but why are they laughing?"

"He asked me what kind of a man allows a woman to speak for him."

"Tell him the same kind of man who can subdue seven of his warriors without breaking a sweat."

"Uh..."

"Tell him."

She blushed, but turned back to the Hun and translated.

Next, it was Attila's turn to grow red in the face. He grumbled and shouted something curt, then puffed out his chest in defiance. Mark simply waved his gun in the direction of his prisoners to emphasize his point.

"Tell him that we do not wish him, or his people, any harm. That these warriors attacked us at night without provocation, yet we have shown mercy by not killing them. Tell him that I may have a gift for him should we be received well."

Attila's eyes narrowed as he listened. He grunted more Latin back at Savannah.

"He says he can take all that he wants from you by force, but what is this gift?"

"Explain that it is a weapon that may help him against the Romans. I will demonstrate, but he should not become alarmed."

Attila nodded once to indicate Mark should proceed.

Mark took his pistol and aimed at a nearby tree trunk about thirty feet away. He pulled the trigger and the wood splintered explosively.

As the crack of the shot echoed across the valley floor, Attila's eyes grew wide in unexpected awe. Several barbarians squealed and dropped to the ground. Attila eyed them with disdain, but returned his focus quickly to the amazing weapon that had just been demonstrated. He spoke to Savannah again, but this time, his tone was much quieter, more subdued.

"He says that is an amazing weapon. One that you must give him now."

"Tell him it will be a gift to him should he receive us well."

"He says he can take it by force."

"Tell him that I can kill him and many of his warriors before they even get near us. That he would do better to invite us to dinner."

Attila laughed uproariously. He gestured toward his palace in dramatic fashion and waved off the warriors glaring at Mark.

"He says you are a bold man. I think he likes that."

"I figured he would."

"He says we are to eat with them. He's been married today and the feast is tonight."

"Great! So, he's in a good mood."

Savannah looked concerned. "Yes, but Mark — this is 453 AD. Attila married several times, but he only married once in 453, to Idilco, the gothic princess."

"So?'

"So, according to history, he will get drunk at the feast today and then retire to his bed chamber with Idilco. Tonight, he'll pass out and hemorrhage blood through his nose. He'll be dead by morning, having drowned in his own blood."

"We'd better move fast then. Let's go."

***

The feast was a tremendous, bawdy affair. The barbarians made every effort to live up to their name, and if this celebration was any indicator, they'd earned their reputation several times over. Plates of goat meat and lamb and steaming seasoned vegetables were repeatedly thrust under their noses, but the general stench of the unwashed soldiers filling the tents stole their appetites. Mark took a sip from a mug filled with golden drink and discovered it was some kind of mead or beer. He licked his lips. It was quite tasty actually.

"I'm sorry about all this." Mark motioned toward the drunken, womanizing party-goers stumbling around them. "Do you want me to take you outside?"

"Don't worry about it," Savannah said. "I'm safer with you in here. Besides, this is a chance of a lifetime."

While Mark was disgusted by their barbaric behavior, she was studying the clothing of both the women and men, the tent materials, the way the food was prepared, and hanging on every word that was spoken.

She leaned toward Mark. "You don't understand, but there is very little known about Hunnic culture. Only three words of their language have even survived to modern day. Very little was recorded for posterity, yet here I am with a front row seat to Attila's wedding feast."

"You really get a kick out of this, don't you?"

She nodded enthusiastically.

"I should take you on more of my trips."

She smiled.

The crowd began to thin out. Most of the drunken noise-makers were younger and moving outside to continue their festivities. After a time, the noise level inside the tent fell to normal levels and the feast transformed into a more formal dinner. The remaining guests were older and looked to hold important offices. They were seated around a couple of long, rectangular tables, probably in a specific pecking order from Attila's seat in the middle.

Next to the Hun king sat his new bride, Idilco. She was fair-skinned, blonde, and beautiful. The features of her oval face were finely-chiseled and spoke of a quiet, unrecognized strength.

Servants entered carrying poles with incense burning on top. The fragrant aromas washed away the pungent odors left behind by the previous revelers. The change in atmosphere was complete.

"That's weird," Savannah said.

"What?"

"Attila doesn't seem to be drinking much, not like the officers around him."

"So?"

"In recorded history, he gets very drunk tonight and passes out after retiring to his bed chamber with Idilco. At some point during the night, a blood vessel hemorrhages inside his nose, but because of his drunken state, he drowns in his own blood. Idilco is found weeping over him the next morning."

"But, he's not drinking."

"Right."

"Let's keep watching."

A few minutes later, Attila ordered the seats to his left vacated and he signaled for Mark and Savannah to come sit beside him. They did.

Idilco slipped out of the tent while her new husband conducted business.

"He wants to see the weapon," Savannah relayed.

Mark held it up. Attila reached out to take it, but Mark drew it back out of his reach. The barbarian's face darkened dangerously.

"Explain to the king that I will gladly give him this new weapon as a gift if he will allow me to hold his sword for a moment."

She translated. Attila grinned. He placed his hand on the short sword crossing his belly as if to ask if Mark meant that one.

"No, tell him I mean the long one hanging from his chair."

The king shook his head.

"He says that is the Sword of Mars that was given to him by the gods as an omen. No man but he may touch it."

"I do not believe in any gods, but I have heard the sword is special. That is why I wish to see it."

"He says for you to hold the sword in front of his people would be a sign of...uh..."

"Weakness?"

"Yes, a sign of weakness. Sorry couldn't quite figure that word out."

"Nevertheless, tell him that is my price."

Attila was not pleased with Mark's firmness in bargaining. The Hun king was not known for ceding any point at the bargaining table, but perhaps he recognized a familiar determination in Mark's eyes that matched his own, or perhaps the temptation and fear the gun's demonstration provoked resulted in a more temperate response than normal. Whatever it was, the man grunted something, stood, and left the tent, taking his sword with him.

"He says he will think about it."

"That probably won't be soon enough."

"What happens next?"

"He'll retire with his new wife soon and then he'll die."

"What happens to his sword after that?"

"It's buried with him."

"Where?"

"No one knows. According to legend, his men take his body to some unknown location along the Tisza River. In order to deter grave robbers, they divert the river temporarily and bury him with all his treasures under the river bed and then release the river back into its normal path, but no one knows where along the river that was. Even if they did, you'd have to divert an entire river to get to his body."

"And we won't have much access to his body after it's discovered, will we?"

"Not likely."

"We'll have to figure something else out."

From outside the tent, Attila gruffly yelled something unintelligible at some unseen soul. A moment later, a panicked servant scurried back into the tent and hastily scooped up Attila's mug filled with mead. As the servant was about to leave the tent again, he was stopped by one of Attila's bodyguards who took the cup from him and waved the servant off.

After the servant had scampered away, the bodyguard glanced around and then nonchalantly turned his body to block the view of the cup. Mark could still see well enough to know the guard had put something in the drink.

"I think we just found out the real reason Attila died," Mark said.

"I think you're right," Savannah agreed.

Chapter 40

"Shouldn't we try to save him?" Savannah's eyes were wide. This was the first time she'd been confronted with a decision between life and death.

"We can't," Mark replied coolly.

"Yes, we can. You can get out of this room without them knowing."

She and Mark had been left under guard. Two guards to be specific. Savannah was right. They wouldn't be a problem. Attila had remained suspicious of them, but he apparently still didn't fully appreciate the full threat someone like Mark represented. Granted, the Hun had not been expecting a visit from foreigners today. He was distracted by his wedding to beautiful Idilco.

"It isn't that, Savannah. We *can't* save him. We'd just fail. It's like my kids."

She was shocked.

"How can you know that?"

"Just like I couldn't stop the Lincoln assassination, or a million other major historical events. Whatever's out there ruling this universe won't allow it. We can change small things, things that affect only us, but not the big events...and certain other things that don't seem so big in the scheme of it all."

"How can you know this is one of those cases?"

"Because Attila the Hun's death changed history fundamentally. If he had survived another few years, he might have conquered Constantinople hundreds of years before its time, or caused the Roman Empire to fall early. His survival would change the entire history of Europe, and thus the United States, and the rest of the world. The impact would be so great...there's just no way this force we keep encountering will allow us to prevent his death."

"We can't just let a man be murdered under our noses and not do anything about it."

"We're not *letting* anybody do anything. We couldn't stop it if we tried. And he's not that great a guy anyway. He's murdered his fair share of innocents."

She brooded on his reasoning. She understood the logic, knew he was right, knew how often they ran into situations they couldn't fix. She'd just never been faced with the reality of it before up close and personal.

"I *am* going to get us out of here though. Being strangers, we'll be the first to be suspected in the morning, and the best chance I've got to get a look at his sword will be between the time he passes out and when Idilco wakes up in the morning."

"What do you want me to do?"

"Get them closer." He flashed his eyes the guards' way.

"Okay."

She thought for a minute, then tilted her face up.

"*Custos...*" she called out softly.

Both of the soldiers turned to look at her. She continued to speak softly, almost seductively, but in a tone so low they couldn't make out her words. Inadvertently, both men took several steps closer to try and make out what she was saying.

Now within reach, Mark threw a punch into the solar plexus of the closest guard and knocked the wind out of him. Bracing himself with his hands on the bench where they sat, he swiveled and swung his full body weight up into a long, double-footed kick that landed on the side of the second guard's head. That soldier's unconscious body immediately dropped limply to the ground.

Mark slipped behind the first guard who was still stunned and pressed his forearm into the man's throat until he too had passed out. Not a sound had escaped the room other than the thud of the one guard hitting the floor.

Savannah shook her head in disbelief.

Mark just grinned at her.

"Let's move."

No other guards were posted outside the room which spoke poorly of Attila's security measures, or said something about his arrogance.

Mark found a place in the brush for Savannah to safely hide while he went to work. He moved into the shadows along the perimeter walls surrounding the large wooden palace. He found a point of entry where he could ascend unobserved and he scaled the wall. Next, he did the same with the palace itself.

He was now on a balcony up on the third floor just outside

Attila's bedchambers. The suite was located under the dome that looked like the crest of the elephant's head.

He could hear Attila's brusque movements from inside, along with the lighter sounds of a female.

Mark peered through the linen curtains, careful to keep from being seen.

Attila was struggling to maintain consciousness. He stumbled in several different directions. His young bride merely watched from the side of the room, making no effort to help him. Her face was white as a sheet. It was not difficult for her to avoid his clumsy advances in his drugged state.

After a minute, the hun gave up, stumbled to the bed, and collapsed onto it. After another minute, his breathing deepened, indicating he'd fallen unconscious.

Attila's sword was in its scabbard and hung by a strap on the corner of a chair next to the bed.

Mark could not move to it, however. Not until Idilco fell asleep herself or left the room.

He was no stranger to lengthy stakeouts, but this time he felt impatient, unusually so. For some reason, this wait was one of the more excruciating he'd had to endure.

The young bride just stood there against the wall, pale as a ghost, for a full hour. The only indication she wasn't a statue was the shallow heaving of her chest with each rhythmic breath.

After what seemed an eternity, she finally approached the bed. Attila was still breathing. The drug had apparently just knocked him out rather than kill him.

Satisfied he was out cold, she crossed to the door and opened it. The same bodyguard who'd drugged Attila's cup entered.

He paused, glanced around and then went to Attila's side. He withdrew a long dagger with one hand and pressed on the sides of Attila's cheeks with the other, forcing the Hun's mouth open. He slowly inserted the sword and made a large cut in the back of Attila's throat, the true source of the "nosebleed". In a few minutes, Attila would drown in his own blood, with no one the wiser to the foul play that took place.

The bodyguard shut the barbarian king's mouth, cleaned the dagger on his tunic and exited the room.

Idilco closed the door behind him and slipped to the floor, where she curled into a fetal position and stayed there. An hour later, she finally fell asleep, more than likely exhausted from the constant anxiety the plot had wrought in her all day.

Mark swept the curtains aside, watching her for any sign she wasn't truly asleep. He felt bad for Attila. It was a strange feeling to have for such a brutal man, but he felt bad all the same.

Quietly, he lifted Attila's long sword from the chair. Its hilt was covered in gold with small gems embedded in various places. Mark grabbed the hilt's bottom and twisted.

Nothing happened.

Please, after all this trouble, don't let this be another dead end.

He twisted again, this time using his full strength. Again nothing. He tried twisting in the opposite direction.

Finally, he tugged at the end and it simply popped off like the top to a lipstick, revealing a small hollow compartment built into the hilt. Inside, a small, tightly-rolled scroll peeked back at him. Mark pulled it out and stuffed it into his pocket.

He double-checked to make sure nothing else was inside the compartment and then closed it back up. He hung the sword in its scabbard on the chair again by the strap and turned to leave.

He froze.

Idilco still lay on the floor curled into a ball, but she was staring at him in wide-eyed fear. They locked eyes.

Seeing she was more afraid of what he might do to her than ready to call out for help, Mark stepped back onto the balcony and disappeared.

***

You know we can't afford to let one moment pass us by
'Cause it's a short piece of time

"Long Trip Alone"

~ Dierks Bentley

Mark and Savannah snuck out of the camp, avoiding all the sentries until they were hidden deep in the woods and moving south at a brisk pace. It was a tense thirty minutes or so before they were at liberty to talk.

Once he was sure they were clear, Mark released a great sigh of relief having gotten Savannah out safely.

"You okay?" He asked.

She nodded.

"You're very good at what you do," she said.

"Thanks." He felt his face flush and hoped she couldn't see it in the darkness. He checked his shifter. Still glowing red.

"You really are. I've never seen you in action before."

"I had a lot of training...and hard experience." He changed the subject. "We've got to avoid contact with anyone for another ten to twelve hours. My shifter won't work again till then. At least, that's the theory. We're trusting Prescott's predictions are accurate. I've never come back this far before."

"I'm sure we'll be fine."

"Thank you for coming along, Savannah. I couldn't have completed this mission without your help."

"I'm sure you could have."

"No, without your Latin, I doubt I could have communicated with Attila. Plus, having a female along probably softened their response to me attacking his men."

It was her turn to change the subject.

"Have you ever considered what it is that might be stopping you from changing these events in history?" She asked.

His face darkened. "Future too. There are some things in the future we can't change either. Like Ty's death."

Solemnity draped their conversation like a thick funeral shroud. Light-hearted debates about fate versus free will were for those who couldn't prove it one way or the other. Mark had to deal with the *reality* of the age-old conundrum. Being slapped in the face with the loss of your children and the murder of a dear friend and then being stopped from saving them by some mysterious force imbued the discussion with a whole different tone.

Fate was no longer just a hypothetical, some whimsical theme to enliven the conversation around a campfire. No, to him, it was deadly reality. An unavoidable, undeniable force. A force of immense strength that made gravity look like child's play.

"What do you think it is?" she asked again.

"Ty says it's God. He's never doubted that. Says he even expected it. Hardy used to rail against Ty — and God for that matter. He said it was just a safety feature of the physical universe, a protection measure that prevented paradoxes of time from being created. Haven't heard him say much about it though since Abbie got her hands on him."

"Abbie's a very nice girl."

"You're right."

"You think Hardy's changed?"

"Yeah, something's different. Sometimes I think Abbie might have made him into a Christian. He certainly doesn't disagree with Ty much anymore. He's nicer too."

"You never said what you think is behind this 'fate,' this force. It seems to me it would have to be something intelligent. An unintelligent feature of the universe couldn't manage the intricacies of the space-time continuum like this."

Mark didn't answer. He just stared into the woods ahead of them.

"Do you think it's God?" she probed.

"I'm not willing to consider that."

"What else could it be?"

"I'm surprised you would believe in such a thing."

"I've never told you what I believe."

He took the verbal slap in stride. "True. Sorry."

"Are you afraid to think it might be God because that would mean God killed your kids?"

He stopped in mid-stride, tense. She'd hit a nerve and known she would. Sometimes a nurse has to inject the needle to heal the patient.

He clenched and unclenched his fists several times.

"I'm not going to answer that," he growled through gritted teeth.

"I can't imagine the pain that must put you through," she said, not apologizing.

"Just follow," he snapped, cutting off the conversation.

He moved in front of her, leading them through the dense brush until they reached the edge of a clearing.

He silently made their camp, without a fire. Her question had opened a deep, twisting wound. He struggled to put a cap on the flood of pain and hurt that seeped out of it.

Flashes of her beauty slipped through the bouts of inner turmoil. He stared at her delicate hands as she helped him unroll the sleeping bags. Her hair shone in the moonlight as she rolled away from him to fall asleep.

Slumber evaded him for a long time. Her voice, her words haunted him like an insistent melody in the cool, night air. His wound wouldn't close this time, nor would visions of her pretty countenance dissipate from his mind's lens.

The light scent of her perfume lingered in the air.

Chapter 41

Trails of dust spewed up and then hung lazily in murky clouds behind the jeep as they rode. Alexander Rialto scanned the hills surrounding the City of Jerusalem. The city had developed tremendously over the last decades, but there was still plenty of undisturbed land surrounding it, hills and vales that had remained untouched for centuries.

Stanley Graves slowed the jeep to a crawl and then brought it to a halt right in front of a large pile of rubble imbedded in the side of a low hill.

"You sure this is the right spot?" Rialto asked.

Vincent Torino double-checked the GPS device in his hand. He nodded.

Torino, Graves, and Laura Kingsley followed Rialto out of the jeep

Randolph DeCleary had disappeared suddenly while on mission in Jerusalem. Luckily, Rialto had installed passive GPS tracking devices on the underside of each of the shifters before handing them out to his recruits. He wasn't as concerned about their well-being as he was his shifters. Those devices were invaluable.

Still, even though he could easily track the devices using satellites, figuring out which transponder signal was the correct one was no walk in the park, not even for their resident physicist, Stanley Irvine. Since they tended to jump around between years, DeCleary's most recent signal, chronologically speaking, would not necessarily be his actual "last" signal.

After much study of the records, Irvine had finally identified one particular signal of DeCleary's outside Jerusalem that was stationary regardless of the year. Good news for Rialto, bad for the former knight.

He didn't know how Carpen could have pulled it off, but he suspected his nemesis had figured out some way to get rid of DeCleary. That the knight was dead and buried didn't seem to be in doubt. How else would a shifter stay in exactly the same place for decades?

He wasn't really so much concerned about DeCleary's welfare, but the fact that Carpen had managed to permanently kill the knight bode badly for the rest of them. Killing a man with a time shifter in a way that his teammates couldn't rescue him was a feat and a half.

Rialto could find someone else to take DeCleary's place and that might actually be a positive change. He'd recruited DeCleary because the man had already harbored a strong resentment toward Carpen when he found him, but DeCleary had been rattled by all their modern technology, which had caused issues that had somewhat offset the benefit of a predisposed hatred for the other side.

What really bothered him was the loss of DeCleary's shifter. The shifter was priceless. If he couldn't get it back, he couldn't recruit anyone else.

Rialto studied the pile of rocks. The formation looked ancient. According to the GPS signal, the shifter was buried somewhere in that hill, about ten feet in.

Understanding slowly dawned on Rialto. Sparks of anxiety intruded like beams of dangerous light through new, seeping cracks in his confidence.

He shook the thought from his head, not willing to consider the possibility.

It couldn't be.

"The GPS must be off."

Torino walked around the large mound studying the device. Laura followed.

Cook and Plageanet had remained back in the U.S. As soon as Rialto realized Carpen had knocked off DeCleary with no way for them to track the knight's disappearance, he'd given orders to stay divided into at least two groups at all times.

"Nope. It's behind those rocks all right. Ten feet in," Torino answered finally.

"Get the equipment."

Torino and Graves moved back to the jeep and began unloading picks and shovels. It took them most of the morning to make any significant progress. At one point, a policeman interrupted their work demanding to see their permit to conduct an archaeological dig. A wad of cash stuffed into his fat fist quickly dissipated the official's need for documentation and he left them alone.

Rialto's fears magnified, as they progressed. However the shifter came to be under this hill, it was clear it had happened a long time ago.

Finally, they broke through to something that looked like a tomb. After much effort, they cleared enough debris away they could get at the edges of the large round rock that appeared to block its entrance.

"Look," Laura said, pointing to an inscription engraved in the stone above the slab.

Rialto waved her off. He was not here out of archaeological curiosity, nor did he care about any ancient curses. Randolph DeCleary, his employee — make that *former* employee — was buried inside that tomb and he'd taken Rialto's property without permission.

He tossed a crow bar to Torino and the two of them began prying the slab away from the tomb. It cracked under the pressure. They jumped back a step as the top half tumbled down, slamming into the ground in a plume of dust.

Torino leaned forward into the gaping hole, sniffing for any toxic gases that might have stored up over the centuries.

Nothing.

Not that all such gases were detectable by smell, but Rialto wouldn't want to wait. The brief hesitation was the only precaution he would likely allow.

Rialto and Torino grabbed a pair of flashlights and moved in while Graves and Laura waited outside. Laura folded her arms across her chest and stared out at the arid land.

Inside, the air was dank and dark. Stale. Several niches had been carved in the side walls, niches that had been intended for bodies, but had never been filled. One niche, however, in the center of the back wall, was not vacant.

As Rialto's light beam passed over it, glints of metal flashed back. One of them was the shifter.

The skeleton in the cut-out was intact. It was dressed in regal attire, like a king from some ancient time. The man had been very tall and the shifter wrapped loosely around the wrist bones told Rialto he was looking upon the physical remains of Randolph DeCleary.

Torino sucked in a sudden gasp of air. Rialto glanced his way. For the first time in their professional relationship, he'd seen the assassin look surprised — and a little afraid.

"How long has he been here?" Torino breathed.

Rialto leaned over and slipped the shifter off the skeleton's frail wrist. The display looked normal now, but it must have once glowed red for a very long period of time.

"It's set to 1,000 B.C."

The two men, so accustomed to using violence to get their way, were taken aback. Carpen had done something inconceivable. Somehow, he'd set DeCleary's shifter to three thousand years ago and sent the knight back against his will, knowing DeCleary's shifter would shut down for a length of time greater than the man's life. Mark Carpen had created a living prison built with bars of time.

Rialto shuddered.

The first thing he did was change the setting on DeCleary's shifter to the current year so the tragedy would not repeat.

He held it in his hand for a long time, staring at DeCleary's bones laid out on the stone bench. Torino stood to the side in silence. Watching. Awaiting instructions.

Rialto had intended to use the shifter to recruit someone else to replace DeCleary. The revelation of what exactly Carpen had done to the knight changed all that. He couldn't risk the same thing happening to him.

He sat on the stone bench next to the skeleton and took off his shoe. After rolling down his sock, he inserted his foot into the loosened shifter band. It hadn't looked it, but somehow, it was big enough to slip over his heel and onto his ankle. Once in place, it whirred and tightened till it held snug against his skin, just as it had done on his wrist. He pulled his pants leg back down over it.

It wasn't visible. Good.

If Carpen ever tried to send him back three thousand years, he would have a back-up shifter to get him home again.

He looked to Torino. "You'll keep your mouth shut about this."

The assassin nodded.

***

ChronoShift Headquarters, Boston, Massachusetts

Tension hung in the air so thick it felt like a tangible force, and Mark was the source of it.

Savannah had just finished debriefing them on the results from the analysis of the scroll Mark had retrieved from Attila's sword.

In short, the little scroll, written in Latin, had nothing at all to do with the Ark of the Covenant. It was actually a written record of the peace terms Attila had extorted from the rulers of Constantinople the first time he'd threatened the Eastern Roman Empire. To confirm the agreement between the barbarian and Rome, the Romans had written the terms down on a small parchment. Attila had preserved the rolled-up parchment in the hilt of his sword as a symbol of his first victory.

This "covenant" with Rome, hidden in the hilt of Attila's sword, had, over the centuries, transformed into a legend about the location of the Ark of the Covenant.

As Savannah related the conclusions of the translation, Mark's face darkened. His fingers tightened around the edge of the desk until his knuckles turned white.

Then, just as oddly, he suddenly released his grip and dropped his fists below the table line, out of sight.

Noticing his reaction, Savannah stumbled in mid-speech, but continued warily. Ty and Hardy looked on with growing curiosity.

Why was Mark so upset? So, the Attila lead hadn't panned out. So what? They'd just keep looking.

Indeed, if they could have peered inside Mark's mind right then, they would have seen frustration spilling over its sides like dark red waters pouring over a dam. A dam holding back a lake well over full pool.

Mark was frustrated with the seemingly endless nature of this search for the Ark. He was frustrated the President of the United States would, and could, pressure them into pursuing it. Frustrated the potential fallout of Rialto finding it first was serious enough to prohibit Mark from just walking away.

He'd led Savannah into an extremely dangerous encounter with the barbaric Huns. Now, it turned out the risk had been for nothing. If the scroll had revealed important information, that was one thing, but it hadn't. It was worthless.

He was frustrated that he was falling in love with Savannah. That her pleasant beauty had grown to occupy the majority of his thoughts. That she was possessing his heart against his will and without her knowledge. Then, she had picked the scabs off his soul's wounds, releasing sharp new waves of pain and regret. Her cruelty belied her beauty. Her beauty shamed his tainted past.

He was frustrated that the only option remaining now seemed to be to travel to Jerusalem and shift back two thousand years. It was a journey that would lock their shifters down for over two months.

To see this through, Mark would have to sacrifice two months of his life trapped in ancient Judea. If, like Attila's sword, it didn't pan out, if they didn't find what they were looking for, that part of his life would be irretrievably wasted, and on a search he didn't really care about. It was time the shifter couldn't give him back.

His greatest frustration, however, was Savannah's words. Her question. Her relentless question that, once spoken, echoed repeatedly through his inner being, churning up dredges of fear and anger he'd so long ago tried to smooth down.

Simply put, she'd asked if he felt God had killed his kids. To be honest, he couldn't even *think* about God without hating Him.

There was too much truth in what she'd asked. *Something* was controlling what they could do in the past. What they could and couldn't change. And that something was obviously intelligent. An intelligent being meant God — so, God must have killed Daniel and Brittany...

Every time that thought reared its ugly head, Mark slammed it back down into the mush of indetermination. He would not allow the thoughts to proceed. Better to not think.

He glanced up, sensing the growing awkwardness in the room. Savannah had ceased speaking a little while ago and they'd been waiting for him to say something. He didn't, and the awkwardness blossomed into full-blown uncomfortable.

Finally, to their relief, he broke the tension.

"Not much else to say, is there? We have to go back two thousand years. To Palestine."

"We'll start planning," Hardy offered.

"No," Mark was firm. "Whoever goes will be trapped for two months. I'm going by myself."

He stood and walked to the door. There would be no discussion.

"Mark," Savannah called out, "You'll let me help you prepare, won't you?"

He paused. After a moment, he nodded. "Tell President James we're gonna have words when I get back."

With that, he left.

Ty whistled. "What was *that* about?"

Savannah looked sheepish. "We had a discussion on the way back from Attila's camp."

"What about?" Ty asked, eyebrows raised.

"I asked him if he was afraid to consider God was behind the strange force we keep encountering during shifts because that would mean God had killed his children."

"Wow." Hardy sat back in his chair. "That would explain it, all right."

Ty scowled at him and turned back to Savannah. "Don't beat yourself up. I've asked him the same thing before. It's a good question. I've already answered it to my satisfaction, even if Hardy hasn't."

It was Hardy's turn to look sheepish. "No, I agree with you," he mumbled.

"What was that?" Ty cupped his hand to his ear. "I couldn't hear you."

"I said, I agree with you." He muttered the admission as low as possible and still be heard. "Abbie's been teaching me a lot."

Ty grinned at Savannah. "Well, anyway, it's good you asked. It's a question Mark needs to answer for himself if he's ever going to heal."

Chapter 42

"Time heals what reason cannot"

- Seneca

"*Lama?*"

"*Lama?*" Mark repeated. "That means 'why?'"

"Yes."

Savannah had been giving him a crash course in Hebrew and Aramaic vocabulary all day. Most scholars traditionally believe Jews living during the time of Christ spoke Aramaic, but recently, a number of others were revising their theories. Too much evidence had surfaced indicating Hebrew may actually have been the common tongue of the region instead of Aramaic. So, to be safe, Savannah was teaching him both.

"You still think we should focus on Aramaic?"

"That's what most scholars think was spoken. It's a safer bet, but it could be either."

"Guess I'll find out for sure shortly."

Mark's destination was essentially Palestine during the time of Jesus Christ. The possibility of encountering the man around whom all of history seemed to revolve was not appealing to Mark. In fact, it loosed a whole new set of anxieties twisting in the center of his mind.

They were alone in the headquarters' library which seemed to have doubled in size over the past year. The light in the room was dim. They'd been studying so long, the afternoon had given way to evening. The last rays of sunset filtered through the windows. Tiny specks of dust danced, illuminated in the golden, dusky light.

The light finally grew so dim it became hard to read. Mark got up and switched on a lamp. He sat back down.

Savannah reached out and delicately rested her fingertips on the back of his hand. Electric tingles ran up and down his arm at the sensation.

"Mark, I want to say I'm sorry for what I said on the way back from Hungary. I had no right to push you like that."

"Yes, you did." He clenched his jaw. "You care about me, that's all. I know that. It's just...it's just I can't answer your question yet. I don't want to even think about it. It hurts too much. On the most basic of levels."

She nodded. "I understand. You'll find your answers when you're ready."

"What do you believe, Savannah? About God, I mean."

She smiled and flipped her book closed. The dull clap of its pages echoed around the silent chamber.

The reddish rays of sun that remained combined with the lamp light to illuminate her hair with a deep, shimmering glow that framed her face beautifully in gold. Her creamy skin radiated warmly in the sunset, mesmerizing him. Her eyes fixed his. Her smile widened.

She reached out and cupped his cheek in her palm.

More electricity.

He longed for her in that moment like never before.

"I'll tell you when you get back."

She leaned forward, brushed his other cheek with a light kiss, and stood to leave.

"Hey!" He called, "That's not fair. What about our studies?"

She turned back enough he could see her smile still remained.

"You're ready. I'll see you when you get back."

Then, she was gone.

Mark swiveled his chair to face the window, battling to keep his head above the turbulent feelings boiling within.

***

He tensed in preparation for the shift, but barely stumbled as it terminated. Dust swirled up around his ankles from the slight drop of his feet. That was unexpected. Two thousand years of dust should have made a difference of several feet at least. He must have picked just the right spot for the transition.

Jerusalem still lay before him, but it was not the same city he'd just left. She was now devoid of all signs of modernity. No paved roads, no concrete homes, no Coca-Cola signs, no power lines. And she was much smaller.

It was pointless to check his shifter, but he did anyway and was not surprised to see the unwelcome red glow on its face. According to Prescott, his shifter would not work again for 56 days, a little under two months.

Well, what's done is done, he mused.

He really hoped this trip would provide them the answers they needed. As much as he hated being pressured into service by the president, there was something seriously wrong with the idea of Alexander Rialto getting his hands on the Ark of the Covenant. Nothing good could come of such a thing.

If for some reason it became necessary to travel farther back in time, Mark wasn't sure they could proceed further. Another hundred years in the past and he'd be stuck for five months instead of two. Traveling to 200 BC would mean a shut down for a full year. 400 BC would be four years. To go back to the very moment the Ark was hidden before the destruction of Jerusalem in 586 BC would require a sacrifice of *twenty years* of someone's life. None of those options were feasible. Two months was about the most Mark was willing to give to this search.

Savannah had taught him a smattering of rudimentary Hebrew and Aramaic, but he still faced huge communication problems. Nothing even closely resembling English existed anywhere in the world this far back in time. He would find no translator.

Which could pose a major problem. Eventually, he would find the scribe he was looking for. However, if his poor Hebrew caused him to make a mistake interpreting some key piece of information the scribe gave him, it could be costly. Another trip back here would lose him another two months to the sands of time.

So, his plan was to spend the first part of his stay learning as much of the local language as possible. Once he felt confident enough he could hold a decent conversation, then he would seek out Mattatiyah HaLevi.

His clothing matched the typical attire of the era and he had enough gold to make his stay in the Roman Empire comfortable and hopefully, complication free. He needed a place to live, though. Ideally, with a local Jewish family instead of an inn. Living with a family would allow him to be constantly immersed in their culture and language, which would greatly accelerate his learning.

On the ground at his side lay a long stick. It looked like it would make a perfect walking stick. He picked it up and began making his way to Jerusalem.

Chapter 43

Mark found a family willing to rent him a small room on their roof. It was a two-story house, but they kept their livestock penned up on the ground floor, so the family's living space was really just on the second floor. Many Jewish families built small corner rooms on top of their roofs just for travelers and guests passing through, and Mark was able to rent this one long term. A separate stairway ran up the side of the home to provide independent access. It was a smart way to be hospitable without putting your family's security at risk.

He spent as much time with them as he could to maximize his immersion. Meal times were warm and full of life.

It didn't take long for him to start picking up on the language. This family, and all the other inhabitants of Jerusalem, for that matter, appeared to speak much more Hebrew than Aramaic, not that there was a huge difference between the two languages anyway.

Hebrew was the language of the religious officials and the common man. Business with foreigners was conducted in Aramaic or Greek, but Hebrew was the most prevalent in their everyday life.

His host family was Levite. The father, Yehudah, was tasked from time to time with performing certain services in the Temple. His sons, Yosef and Shimon, would follow in his footsteps and begin serving once they reached thirty years of age. Yehudah's wife, Miryam, was a quiet, delicately-featured woman who set about the business of the home with a gentle ferocity that would make any level of filth shake in its boots. Still, she always had time for a smile or gentle word for her children. The youngest was a five-year old girl name Rachel who obviously got her looks from her mother. Her future beauty was self-evident. She was a sweet girl, full of laughter.

Mark found himself getting involuntarily choked up every now and then when he looked at her, and he realized she reminded him of his Brittany.

They were a hospitable and accommodating family. Mark enjoyed his time with them, even more so once he was able to converse.

Yehudah was surprised to learn Mark was looking for a scribe named Mattatiyah HaLevi. Mark's pronunciation was off of course. They corrected him, explaining the name should be Matityahu. Since the name HaLevi indicated the scribe was a fellow Levite, Yehudah promised to ask around. Matityahu was a common name though, so he made no guarantees.

One day a few weeks later, Yehudah burst into the home bubbling with enthusiasm. He'd had an opportunity to speak with the great Rabbi Gamaliel. Gamaliel had a student, a scribe, who was called Matityahu HaLevi. He lived and worked in *Yericho*.

"*Yericho*? Where's that?" he asked. They spat the last syllable of the city's name like they were coughing up phlegm.

Yehudah drew him a map on the floor while Miryam looked on. Realization dawned.

"You mean Jericho?" Mark asked.

"*Yericho*," they corrected.

***

The road to Jericho from Jerusalem was dusty and hot. The air was so dry, the back of his mouth felt like it was coated in year-old peanut butter. His tongue was numb and thick, no better than a miniature bale of cotton. Keeping the rocky soil from infiltrating his first century sandals proved an impossibility. Pebbles kept creeping in between his toes and lodging under the balls of his feet. The irritating sensation would easily drive a man crazy if he didn't force himself to ignore it. It seemed like he was stopping every hundred feet or so to shake the little things out.

He still needed to learn the art of walking so your feet didn't get dirty. Not that anyone else here seemed to have mastered it either. Wealthier homes even employed foot-washing servants to cleanse the dust off the feet of guests upon arrival.

The Jericho road wound in and out of round hills that were bare of most vegetation. Hardy desert brush clung to the thin, dehydrated soil like it was trying to revive it, though unsuccessfully so.

Yehudah had warned him the road to Jericho was rich in thieves. They were known for hiding among the low-lying hills and preying on unsuspecting travelers. Thankfully, all he'd seen so far were other travelers on their way back to Jerusalem and a few beggars.

Mark wiped a scrap of linen he'd been using as a handkerchief across his forehead. It came away dirty and sweaty. Bulbs of perspiration kept bubbling up on his scalp and head.

He seemed to sweat a lot more than the local residents. Either they were more accustomed to their climate or he just stayed more hydrated than they. Water could be scarce, and it was always a chore to fetch. You couldn't just turn the faucet on. He liked to keep his palette wet though and his sack of gold had ensured his water pitcher was always full. There were no wells, however, along the way to Jericho.

Suddenly, a stream of stones ran down the hillside to his right. The movement caught his attention, but his reaction was slow.

It could have been the dehydration, but something dulled his normally highly-attuned senses and kept him from perceiving the threat the falling stones represented.

Mark was just wondering why he could not discern what had provoked the miniature landslide when something hard slammed into the side of his head and knocked him off balance. A contemptuous foot kicked him in the side and caused him to fall the rest of way over. The same foot then stomped his lower back and stayed there, attempting to pin him to the ground on his stomach.

Finally, his instincts kicked back in. He twisted and grabbed the foot and accompanying ankle. Leveraging his weight, he flung his attacker into a fall of his own. Instantly, he was back on his feet, primed for a fight.

Ten fierce looking bandits surrounded him. A few wielded swords, many held daggers, and a couple were slowly twirling slings held vertically at hip level.

Mark checked his shifter. Of course, it still glowed red, but checking it had become a fruitless habit.

He was in the time of Christ for goodness sake. He didn't come back here to kill anybody. Granted, these guys were bandits, probably murderers, and hadn't intended to do him any favors. In spite of the prevalence of weapons, he could probably make an escape, but not without hurting all of them and maiming at least a few.

Plus, those slings worried him. They seemed an ineffective weapon to those who didn't know any better, amateurish even, but in experienced hands, and these men would certainly be experienced, such slings could send a small stone sailing through the air with enough speed and accuracy to rival a bullet. Their aim would be dead on, and while the "muzzle velocity" might not quite reach that of a gun, it was enough to kill.

Slowly, Mark raised his hands over his head.

The bandit closest to him slammed a foot into his stomach and shoved him back to the ground again. They grabbed his wrists and roughly wrapped some coarse rope around them. It rasped like sandpaper against his skin.

They yanked him to his feet and one of them poked the tip of his sword sharply into Mark's back, prodding him away from the road and toward a faint trail that disappeared out of sight as it wound its way between the low hills.

Chapter 44

Loud chattering in harsh Hebrew awoke Mark from his coma. As soon as they'd arrived at their hideout, they'd hit him on the back of the head, knocking him unconscious for several hours.

At least he was indoors instead of under the blazing sun. It was actually quite cool inside this shaded hovel.

The bandits were in the adjoining room discussing something heatedly. Probably his fate. He didn't intend to go down without a fight, but his hands were still tied. If he couldn't get them free, even for just a moment, he only gave himself a fifty-fifty chance of getting away.

He rubbed the back of his head. It ached fiercely. In retrospect, he probably shouldn't have been so nice about it. He should have just pulled out his 9mm and shot them all. Sling bearers first. The guys with swords would have been no problem after that.

Oh well. Hindsight is always 20/20.

An eruption of greetings accompanied the arrival of a newcomer to the front room. Mark couldn't see any of them from his vantage point, but from their tones, he could tell the new voice held some kind of authority over the others, though they obviously weren't fully submissive to whatever was being asked.

The voices were muffled which garbled the words, but Mark could make out enough to know the conversation was about him and what to do with him.

After about five minutes of discussion, the curtain to his chamber pulled back. A bright beam of light burst through the crack, forcing him to squint.

Sunlight. His eyes had grown too accustomed to the dark.

A head poked through, evaluated him, and then the body followed. Both belonged to a man of medium-sized build in a beige tunic that reached his ankles. It was similar to the attire of most of the men of this era.

What was different was the fire in his eyes and the dagger in his hand. He moved toward Mark.

Mark prepared to launch his legs up to wrap around the man's torso or neck, whichever he could get a grip on and squeeze. The man knelt beside him.

"*Shimeon?*"

Someone called to the man from behind the curtains. Shimeon stopped and looked to the doorway as the curtain was parted by a second man. He saw Shimeon's dagger and a heated argument ensued, though they were speaking way too fast for Mark to follow.

Shimeon grabbed the rope binding Mark's wrists and heaved upward. The agony this produced in Mark's shoulders forced him to leap to his feet. Shimeon flicked his blade and Mark felt a sudden loosening around his hands.

The man in the doorway yelled something even louder when he saw that.

Mark brought his wrists around to make sure they hadn't been slit and began rubbing the feeling back into them. No blood, and, of course, the shifter still glowed red.

Mark swept a hand over the small of his back. They hadn't found his pistol.

Shimeon caught sight of the shifter and gave it a curious glance before turning his tongue loose on the man in the door, who shrunk back under the verbal assault and retreated into the other room. Shimeon placed his hand in the center of Mark's back and nudged him toward the door.

There were four other men in the entrance room. The man who'd been arguing with Shimeon and another man stood angrily by the front door blocking it. The other two lounged indecisively, waiting to see who would prevail.

Shimeon barked something about gold and held out his hand. The leader shook his head and crossed him arms. Shimeon crossed the room in two steps and popped the man in the face with the bone of his forearm. The man cried out and went down in a heap. He laid there holding his nose.

Shimeon repeated the order at the second man barring their way and held out his hand. This time Mark caught it. "Give me the gold," he'd said.

The second man looked down at his companion and then retrieved Mark's sack of gold from a compartment in the wall. They'd apparently relieved Mark of it while he'd been unconscious. Shimeon took it.

Mark was shocked when Shimeon then held it out for Mark to

take, which he did. Shimeon pointed to the front door and Mark obeyed.

They were in a small village at the bottom of a dry hill. A well stood in the center of the settlement, but there wasn't much activity around it or anywhere else for that matter except for a couple of children playing and a woman walking on the opposite side of the square.

Shimeon guided Mark down a trail that led through the hills.

"Who are you?" Mark asked in his best Hebrew.

"We are *kanna'im*," He answered. He elaborated when he saw Mark's puzzled look. "You know, *zelotes*."

Mark shook his head. "Sorry, I don't understand."

"You are Roman, no?"

"No."

Now it was Shimeon's turn to look puzzled. "You look Roman. You have roman gold. Nice clothes." He pinched the material of Mark's tunic to accentuate the point.

Mark couldn't see much different in his attire from theirs, but he took his word for it.

"No, I'm not Roman."

"Well, no matter. They thought you were Roman. That is why they took you. We, they are *zelotes*."

The term finally clicked in Mark's mind. "Ah, you mean zealots. You're zealots." The zealots were a Jewish political party that actively fought the roman occupation of Israel.

"Zealots? Maybe. *Zelotes*."

"And you are a zealot?"

"Yes."

"But you let me go. Why?"

Shimeon pursed his lips and thought before responding.

"Let me say that I have a new understanding."

"A new understanding?"

"Yes."

"What does that mean?"

"It means I free roman prisoners now instead of killing them or _____."

Mark didn't understand the last phrase. His Hebrew was still very limited.

"Your friends did not agree with you."

"No, they do not. Three years ago, I would have agreed with them. I used to be their leader."

"What changed?"

"We are here.

They'd reached the road that ran between Jerusalem and Jericho. "You should go that way." Shimeon was pointing to the right, back to Jerusalem.

"No, I'm going to Jericho."

"That is too dangerous. You should go back to Jerusalem. I won't be here to protect you when you return."

"I'll be fine. They won't get me again."

"May God be with you then."

He clapped Mark on the shoulder and disappeared back into the hills.

***

The city of Jericho was more extensive than Mark had expected. Herod the Great had rebuilt much of it and the elites of Judea used the city as a winter resort. His giant palace compound dwarfed every other dwelling in the community, and there were plenty of those surrounding it.

The elevation dropped over 3,500 feet between Jerusalem and Jericho. The city of Jericho was actually 1,200 feet below sea level and he could tell the difference. The dry air felt noticeably thicker in his lungs. A few deep breaths dizzied him with extra oxygen content.

Brown hills and mountains flanked the community on most sides, but he'd heard it grew quite green and beautiful during the rainy season.

Palm trees were everywhere and small orchards of date trees greeted him as he approached.

Mark made his way through rows of small houses toward the center of town. After asking around, he located the local synagogue, which was of decent size and had numerous rooms attached.

Inside one of these smaller rooms was a room full of boys, from ten years old to their late teens, all seated at writing tables. Each sat upright while a white-bearded rabbi intoned memorized recitations from the front of the room. After ten to fifteen rhythmical lines, he would pause and then the students would repeat what he had just said in unison.

Mark watched for a few minutes. He was getting used to the slower pace of this world. Being locked in this time, forcibly separated from the internet, cell phones, and television had resulted in a more peaceful, patient spirit. Normally, he would have just walked right up and asked for help and moved on. Now he was content to enjoy the sight of students learning.

After a while, he waved and got the rabbi's attention.

The older man said something to his students and they all took out wooden tablets that looked like a small briefcases. Inside the small cases, the wood was covered in a black wax. The students had styluses and began to practice their writing in the wax as the rabbi walked toward Mark.

"Yes, how may I help you?" he asked.

"I am sorry to bother you, Rabbi, but I am looking for a scribe called Mattatiyah HaLevi."

The old man's eyebrows tilted inward in suspicion.

"You are Roman?"

"No, I am not."

"You look Roman. Your Hebrew is very bad and your accent is worse."

"My apologies. I assure you I am not Roman."

The man scowled.

"Do you know this scribe?" Mark asked.

"He is not just a scribe, he *directs* the scribes here in *Yericho*. He teaches as well."

"So, you do know him."

"I know him. Why do you want to find him?"

"I wish to learn from him. He has knowledge I need."

The man harrumphed. He was a gruff one.

"HaLevi is not here."

"When will he be back?"

"He is in Damascus. He will not return for one month."

"Thank you very much, rabbi. I shall return in one month then."

"Do not hurry."

"Thank you all the same."

Mark turned and walked away, leaving the rabbi to return to his students. In a matter of seconds the young men had begun their recitations again. He didn't bother leaving a message with the rabbi. Not much chance it would get through the grumpy old man's attitude.

Mark inconspicuously checked his shifter. A month wouldn't be bad. His shifter wouldn't quite be back online yet by then. He could come back in a month, find the scribe, get the info, and then a few days later he should be able to shift home. Plus, it would give him more time to improve his Hebrew.

Chapter 45

But when I get where I'm going, and I see my Maker's face.
I'll stand forever in the light, of His amazing grace.

"When I Get Where I'm Going"

~ Brad Paisley

Mark spent his days hanging around Jerusalem. There weren't any cafes or restaurants to speak of. To eat out meant to dine at someone else's house. So, hanging out meant sitting in the city gate watching people pass by, or in the marketplace, or in the Temple courts, which felt like a second marketplace at times.

Herod's temple dominated Jerusalem's skyline. Its thick, gleaming white stones towered high above every other building and could be seen from miles away. Its marble walls were lavishly adorned with ornate golden moldings.

The Temple was clearly the center of Jewish life, not just for the city, but for Jews throughout Palestine — or Judea, as they called it.

The Temple sat upon a foundational structure called the Temple Mount, which in and of itself was an incredible nine stories high in places and covered an overwhelming number of acres. On top of the Mount were the Temple Courts which ringed the Temple like concentric rectangles, each court encompassing another until you reached the Temple itself.

The only court he was allowed to enter was the Court of the Gentiles, which was the largest of the courts. It surrounded all the others. Inside that lay the Court of Women, which all Jews, both men and women, could enter, but from which all gentiles like himself were prohibited. Next came the Court of the Israelites, which only Jewish men could enter. Then came the Court of the Priests, which was reserved for the same. Finally, only the highest priests who actively ministered inside the temple could enter the majestic building itself, and only because they had duties to perform.

The penalty for transgressing beyond the court to which you were limited meant death, so Mark contented himself with remaining in the outer court with the rest of the gentiles.

In fact, the Court of the Gentiles was like a large bazaar. The musty odor of livestock mingled with sweet aromatic spices and fragrant incenses, creating a circus of stimuli for the olfactory senses. Vendors in booths and behind rustic tables sold a variety of animals to be used in sacrifices at the Temple.

Priests dressed in white linen walked to and fro, acting as guides and organizing the worshipers with their sacrifices. The babbling of the buyers and sellers combined with the bleats of sheep so the entire court was blanketed in a dull murmuring.

After several days of sitting in the court, Mark had come to notice a curious practice. Men and women coming to sacrifice would have their animal inspected by a priest, usually a lamb, calf, or doves, although sometimes an ox or full-grown sheep would be brought, but the priest would more often than not shake his head in denial after the inspection and point the would-be worshiper toward one of the animal vendors lining the sides of the court.

Mark's host family had explained that God's law required that only perfect animals without blemish could be sacrificed and that the priests were inspecting for defects. The vendors were selling "blemish-free" animals that had already passed inspection, but their prices were exorbitant.

It didn't take long for Mark to see the priests were corrupt and working in collusion with the vendors. The priests rejected as many of the home-brought animals as they could get away with and then the vendors sold the worshipers "clean" animals at twice the normal market rate, though the vendor would act like he was giving a bargain. In return for this bargain, the worshiper had to give the vendor his "rejected" animal in addition to the high fee.

Once the worshiper had gone on his way, the vendor's assistants would walk the "rejected" animal around to the back of their stall and put it in the same pen with the other "blemish-free" animals. It was now "clean" and would be sold to someone else as an acceptable sacrifice at twice the market rate. Of course, the priest got a hefty kickback from the vendor for his part in the dirty deal.

What made this con especially heinous was the spiritual oppression of the worshiper. Under God's law, the people were required to make these animal sacrifices in order to receive forgiveness for their sins. They could not be forgiven without the sacrifice, and they couldn't sacrifice without the priest's approval of their animal.

The corruption was not limited to the selling of animals either.

Money changers also littered the court with their tables. To purchase an animal, or to pay the temple tax, which every adult Jewish male was required to pay once per year, you had to have Jewish coins, which were not readily available throughout Jerusalem.

In fact, the Court of the Gentiles was one of the few places you could get Jewish coins, and the moneychangers here ripped their patrons off in every way possible, but primarily through a horrible exchange rate. Once again, the priests got a significant kickback. It was religiously sanctioned highway robbery.

A throng of people suddenly entered the court through the Nicanor Gate. They all circulated around one man who walked in the center of them. Mark studied him.

There was something unusual about the man, but Mark couldn't quite put his finger on what it was. He was of average height and build and wore the traditional robes of a rabbi. His stride was confident, secure, at peace with himself.

That was it. He moved with authority. An authority not gleaned from put-on airs, but born of a strong assurance of who he was and what he was about. Those surrounding him must have sensed this as well, which was probably why they followed. Yet...there was something else too...something very different about this man.

Mark straightened his slouch. Few others seemed to have noticed yet, but a distinct tension flowed into the court along with this rabbi.

The man stood still in the middle of the court. Even from this distance, Mark could see fury flaming behind his eyes. The sheer intensity of it terrified Mark like nothing else he'd ever seen. Involuntarily, a tremble shimmered through his body.

The rabbi raised both arms and shouted something. Mark was so taken off guard, he failed to make out the Hebrew very well, but he caught the ending phrase, *den of thieves*. The rabbi ripped a whip from one of the vendor's stalls.

With zealous anger, he snapped the whip and drove the vendors from the Temple courts. One by one, he threw over the money changers' tables. Coins clattered and rolled in all directions across the flagstones. Some tried to object, but a crack of the whip and one look in this man's eyes melted their will to resist. They fled in chaotic lines toward the exits, scrambling to collect as many of their coins as they could before they went.

The sellers of doves were forced to abandon their rustic cages, managing to save only a few on their way out as their tables were overturned. Several of the rabbi's followers opened the cages after they left, freeing the doves.

The herders of sheep and other livestock hastily beat their beasts with sticks to hurry them out of the court before they too lost their merchandise. Many of the would-be buyers fled too. After the last of the sellers had exited the Temple grounds, a quiet hush fell over the entire court.

Scattered coins and overturned tables lay askew along its edges. The rabbi laid his whip down and did not look at it again. The fury had left his eyes, replaced by a satisfied strength.

The rabbi's eyes met Mark's momentarily. In that split second, his gaze seemed to bore into Mark's soul. Then, just as quickly, he turned and moved away.

It couldn't be.

The scene screamed its familiarity from long-forgotten Sunday school lessons and countless history books.

No way. It had to be some other rabbi.

The priests, the *cohanim*, lined the courts walls, frozen in place, astonished by what the rabbi had just done. One by one, they shut their gaping mouths and milled together into a huddle, conferring.

Meanwhile, the rabbi sat down in the center of the court. His followers followed suit, forming a half-circle around him and he began to teach. Mark recognized a familiar face, Shimeon the Zealot who had saved him from the bandits outside Jericho.

Unconsciously, Mark stood and found his body moving to join them. He held himself well outside their perimeter, close enough to hear, but not close enough to take part.

***

There could be no doubt. Mark was sitting at the feet of Jesus.

Most called him rabbi, but he was known to these people as *Yeshua*. "Jesus" was the Greek form of the name with an English pronunciation.

He had to pinch himself several times to remind himself this was real. Mark hadn't set out to find him. It had crossed his mind he was in the same era, the time of Christ.

Well, the truth was it had more than just crossed his mind. Ty hadn't been able to shut up about it before he'd left, but Mark held a healthy skepticism with regards to the Bible. Especially since...well, since everything.

What was worse, God didn't just allow them to die, He'd obviously made it happen. Mark knew the truth. Deep down, Mark had always known the truth. What else could it have been other than God's hand holding him back, preventing him from saving his kids.

A God that gives blessings and then recalls them on a whim. The same God who had then blessed him again with the gift of the shifter, only to yank away any opportunity to use it for the one thing which Mark longed with all his heart, mind, soul, and strength. Like the cruelest of Indian-givers. Mark would never get his kids back and it was God stopping him.

No.

The Bible wasn't reliable...it couldn't be. Mark would not believe. He could not afford to believe.

Yet, here he was sitting as Jesus' feet. And he'd seen him chase the moneychangers out of the Temple with his own eyes. As far as he could remember, the biblical account had been accurate in every point.

Whatever you believed, who wouldn't have their curiosity piqued enough to go and listen for a while?

Mark's Hebrew had improved enough he could follow most of what was being said, though certain phrases and expressions escaped him. The teaching was clear and simple, yet powerful. The man taught through stories, stories whose underlying truth seemed irresistible.

Jesus did not appear special in any physical way. He did not stand out as especially handsome or tall. He certainly did not fit the waifish, manicured image so often portrayed in those Renaissance paintings shown over and over again on the Discovery Channel every time they did an Easter special.

First of all, his beard was not finely groomed, but was rougher, fuller, more like the rest of the Jewish men around him. His clothing was not the ambiguous white toga associated with Romans and Greeks, but the full attire of a 1st century rabbi, tassels and all.

But his eyes.

His eyes were mesmerizing, full of love and compassion, yet they could flash to fire in an instant. During the teaching, Jesus' eyes met Mark's once more. They riveted him in place like he'd been planted in stone, their gaze penetrating to the very depths of his soul. When He finally looked away again, Mark sighed in relief. He'd been unconsciously holding his breath.

The crowd continued to grow as word spread through the city of what Jesus had done. A group of children in a corner of the court began calling out *Hosanna*, which was a religious word of praise that meant

"Save us, please."

Mark sensed they meant it in terms of their oppressors, not just the priests, but the Romans.

Mark sat at the edge of the group for the rest of the day, listening. Hearing. Learning. Jesus' teaching had a way of seeping deep inside, ministering to heartaches and questions he didn't even know he had. It was like drinking cool water from a refreshing fountain. After a while, you thought you'd probably had enough but the water tasted so clear and clean you didn't want to stop.

So, Mark stayed and drank some more.

Chapter 46

An' that preacher whispered: "Can't you see the Promised Land?"
As he laid his blood-stained bible in that hooker's hand.

"Three Wooden Crosses"

~ Randy Travis

One Day Later

Mark raised his hand to block the blinding sun as he emerged from the shadows of the Eastern Gate. Detached, he watched from a distance as Jesus and his followers moved out of Jerusalem toward Bethany, a small village to the east of Jerusalem.

In spite of the sun's brilliance, the day was not hot, but warm and pleasant and without much in the way of humidity. The din of the crowds and the vibrant city smells faded away as they left its walls behind.

It was quieter out here, though that term was relative. Plenty of people still milled about, coming and going, entering and leaving the city. A few vendors of produce and other trinkets littered the roadside, though they were far outnumbered by beggars lining the same.

Mark followed, involuntarily touched by the woeful calls that rose up from the beggars as Jesus approached. They knew who he was.

Most cried for alms, holding out their hands, palms up, ready to receive coins. Jesus ignored them, but stopped when one of the beggars stood and limped toward him. His journey was slow and painful. Something was wrong with his right leg that wouldn't allow him to put his full weight on it.

Jesus waited until he drew near. Then, he crouched and placed his hand over the beggar's knee. The man's eyes grew wide and he stumbled back from the momentous touch.

Jesus stood and continued his walk. The man he'd touched gingerly tested his leg, and then began stepping with more confidence, now without a limp. A joyful expression filled his face as he began to jog a little, amazed at what had just happened. He looked back at his fellow beggars, all of whom still had their hands out, and then looked to Jesus. He turned and followed Jesus down the path.

Mark did as well, all the way to Bethany.

Bethany was a much smaller community than Jerusalem. Mark had checked the reference books he'd brought along with him on this shift and had discovered that Bethany was the home of Lazarus, the man Jesus would supposedly raise from the dead, and Lazarus' sisters, Mary and Martha. All three were close friends of Jesus and he stayed with them during this week in Jerusalem after he cleansed the temple.

What in the world?

Mark jumped back. He scanned the crowd, assessing for danger, senses on full alert.

He had thought he was safe here, but he'd just caught a glimpse of Laura Kingsley emerging from a group of people to the right of Jesus. She was about twenty feet ahead of Mark.

She looked different...clearly something was different, but...no, it was definitely her. Gone were her violet contacts, replaced by the light green hue that was the natural color of her eyes when devoid of modern enhancement. Her hair looked ruffled, a bit unkempt, more natural, like that of someone who'd been here for at least several weeks without the convenience of modern shampoo or conditioner.

Mark retreated several more steps, examining the people behind him at length. He scanned the rooftops and studied every face looking for Rialto, or Torino, or Graves, or some other sniper hidden out of sight. Her presence could only mean an ambush of some kind.

Yet, she did not appear to have noticed Mark yet. Her visage was focused on the crowd surrounding Jesus.

She seemed primed to move forward, but was hesitating. In that moment, she happened to turn her head and locked eyes with Mark for an instant. She looked haunted, a shocking expression he'd never seen before on her face. Twin lines of wet trickled down both cheeks revealing the paths recently fallen tears had taken. Black mascara smudges under her eyes hinted she'd been crying for a while.

She was as surprised to see Mark as he was her. She held his stare for a moment and then turned away abruptly. She broke into a run and sprinted toward the front of the crowd.

What in the world was she doing? Where was she going? What was going on?

Clearly, she had not expected to see him here in this time, in this place. Which meant this was no ambush. So what *did* it mean?

Laura reached the front of crowd, openly weeping. She threw

herself at Jesus' feet, pressing her cheek hard into the top of his foot. She wrapped her arms tightly around his ankles as if her life depended on it. Tears fell in rivers now, streaming down his heel, soaking into the dirt in deep, dark stains. Her chest heaved in and out as she sobbed uncontrollably.

Jesus seemed unfazed by her actions, as if this were a normal everyday occurrence. He stood patiently, allowing her to express her pain and sorrow. He crouched and gently laid his palm on the top of her head. Her sobs finally softened into a weak whimpering.

The crowd fell silent at the unexpected display. They watched, some fascinated, some judging.

Jesus cupped his palm under her chin and lifted her face up until she could look into his eyes. She visibly relaxed, as if the tension had just flowed from her body like a receding wave. He took her wrist and helped her to her feet.

Mark had never seen Laura like this. She was a mess, and not just physically. She was so weak, so broken.

Jesus turned his attention to her other wrist, the one with the shifter. She followed his gaze and shuddered. For her, the shifter had become a shiny manacle, gleaming with tales of her traitorous greed.

Jesus took that hand in his left and gently wrapped his right thumb and fingers around her forearm above where the shifter gripped her wrist.

He never touched the device, but as soon as his fingers came into contact with her skin, Mark heard the soft, familiar whirring of the shifter's band expanding.

Silently, it slid from Laura's wrist and dropped harmlessly to the dust with a dull thud. She stared open-mouthed, rubbing her wrist vigorously where it had been. The beginnings of genuine joy broke out across her face. More tears, happy tears, fell across her widening smile.

Jesus turned Laura around by the shoulders and nudged her toward several women that were waiting by the side of the road. She stumbled off to their welcoming arms.

The crowd began moving on down the road, but Jesus turned back and locked eyes with Mark. Everyone else faded into an unfocused peripheral awareness, oblivious to the magnetic interaction between them. It was as if an invisible wall had risen up around them, separating them like an island from the sea of the crowd.

His expression was a mixture of profound grief and love.

Mark could not tear himself from Jesus' eyes. The magnificent profundity within them was subtle, yet clear, forceful. It slowly grew in mesmerizing strength and his peripheral vision swam, fading into tunnel vision. A humming within his brain eclipsed all other sound until he could even faintly hear the blood coursing through his ears.

Images of Daniel and Brittany appeared in his mind's eye clear as day. They were smiling. And happy. He had not remembered them looking like that for a long time, not without the accompanying memory of shrieking metal and twisted bodies, at which point he always ripped his thoughts in a new direction.

There was none of that this time. Now, they just smiled at him. They were really seeing him. He felt their love and knew they were at peace. Waiting for him.

New images flashed before him successively like a rapid fire slide show. Images of him finding the shifters, of the people they'd helped, the crimes they'd stopped. He saw a little boy playing with some toy cars on a sidewalk. Mark remembered him. That boy had been one of the first people he'd saved once he'd begun intervening in the past to help people. The boy had originally died in a car accident, but Mark had changed history so the toddler would live.

A deeper understanding passed from Jesus to Mark. An understanding that carved itself into the very core of his being.

A jolt of awareness shook him back to reality.

With extended palm, Jesus motioned to the abandoned shifter lying in the dirt. No one else seemed to be paying it any attention. With the unspoken message having been given, Jesus turned his back and moved on toward Bethany.

Shocked, Mark's feet remained rooted to the road long after the crowd departed. He stood alone, staring into nothing, unsuccessfully trying to ignore the silver device that lay in the dust just thirty feet away, drawing his eye like an unwanted magnet. A thick dryness settled on his tongue like cotton, alerting him to the fact that his mouth was hanging agape. He shut it.

With a firm determination, he resisted, but the force of the pull was greater.

Half an hour would pass before he gave in and looked at it. It would be another hour before he took a step toward it. The sun had not quite set when he finally picked it up and slipped it into his pocket.

Chapter 47

Hallelujah, grace like rain falls down on me
Hallelujah, all my stains are washed away...

"Grace Like Rain"

~ Todd Agnew

Several Days Later

Mark's heart was not the same.

He'd felt it crack in that very moment when Jesus had first looked into his eyes. The bitterness he'd harbored for so long oozed from its jagged carbonized walls, replaced bit by bit with a renewed pulsing warmth. It was as if his heart had been hardened into a blackened crust and was now slowly transforming back into red flesh.

He wasn't sure he wanted to let go of the anger yet, but it leaked out all the same. He didn't understand what was replacing it and that scared him. What if he couldn't control it?

He muttered under his breath and kicked a pebble. His emotions were raging up and down like giant waves in a storm.

He still couldn't believe that he'd seen Jesus in person. *The* Jesus. Much less that he'd connected with Him. With just a look.

Mark felt a real affection for Jesus now. A love even.

He'd come to this time period a serious skeptic about God, about Jesus, about all of it. He'd surely had no desire to ever meet Him, but Mark knew now his resistance had been rooted in the issues surrounding his children. Just as Savannah had said.

You couldn't help but be drawn to Him. He was so clearly special, you either fell in love with Him, or you took the route the Pharisees took.

Mark had sat nearby in the temple courts as Jesus taught, amazed by the gentle, yet forceful voice and the words of wisdom that poured forth from it. He'd been shocked by the very real healings and other miracles he'd personally witnessed Jesus perform. He had always believed those stories were myth.

But they weren't. Now, he knew the truth.

And then Jesus had looked into his soul and communicated things so deep, Mark wasn't sure he consciously understood all of it.

He had no more doubt. Jesus was clearly who He claimed to be. The Son of God.

That understanding simultaneously humbled, embarrassed, and elated Mark. The spiritual transformation going on within himself was just further proof of it.

Now Mark faced an unexpected dilemma. He knew what was going to happen next and the historical prep material Savannah had given him confirmed it. Jesus was going to be killed today.

The thought broke his heart. He did not want to be here for the crucifixion. Before, he might have observed the cross with a cool curiosity, but not now. Not now.

Jesus was too gentle, too loving, too awesome. Mark shook his head. He couldn't understand it. How could these people be so blind as to want to kill Him?

Yet, he did understand it. They were where Mark had been just a few days before. Why had Jesus chosen to be merciful to *him*? Why him? Whatever the reason, Mark was grateful.

He itched to get out of town, to get out of this time, to go home and see Savannah. He didn't want to be here anymore, to witness this tragedy play out.

The familiar red glow on his wrist glared angrily at him, affirming he remained a prisoner. Mark cursed.

The crowds of Jerusalem were already bustling about in spite of the early hour. Mark was wandering the streets, trying to resist the pull he felt to go to Golgotha, the place where it would happen.

A woman stepped from a group of people to his right. An all too familiar woman. She had not seen him yet. He grabbed her upper arm and held it firmly.

"Hello, Laura."

She was caught off guard and whipped her head around to her accoster. Her startled expression melted into one of pained embarrassment when she realized it was Mark. Her eyes dropped to the ground, revealing eyelids devoid of colorful eye shadow. No make-up, no hair treatments. She still looked pretty, but no longer exotic.

"Mark…"

"What are you doing here, Laura?" He would not release her arm.

She didn't answer, but glanced in several directions as if hoping someone would come to her rescue.

Mark jerked her back through the crowd and shoved her up against the wall of a vendor's stall. Several Jewish men nearby looked on disapprovingly, their faces stern.

"What are you doing here, Laura?"

"It's...uh...well..."

"Spit it out."

"Rialto sent me. Okay?"

"He sent you? Why?"

"To follow you. See what you were up to."

"He knows I'm here?"

She nodded.

"How? How did he know I was here?"

"I don't know. He just did."

"Who else is here?"

"Nobody. It's just me."

He grabbed her other arm and shook her. "Don't lie to me! Who else did he send? How many of you are there?"

"No one else. I swear . It's just me." Her eyes widened, pained under the weight of her previous betrayal. Hurt tears welled up. He could see she was telling the truth.

He lightened his grip on her arms, but didn't let go.

"Why would he send you by yourself?"

"You know. The time delay. Anybody that comes back here is shut down for two months. He didn't want anybody else tied up for that much time. Especially himself."

"Yeah, he's a selfish turd, isn't he?"

She nodded mutely.

"What? Aren't you happy with your choice?"

A tear escaped, trailing a wet track down her cheek.

"No," she whispered, "I'm not."

"What were you supposed to do, kill me?"

She shook her head. "I was just supposed to watch you. See what you did. What you knew."

"Yeah, right."

She finally lifted her face and to meet his glare again. "No, really, Mark. You have to believe me. That was all he told me to do. But I wasn't even going to do that."

"What do you mean?"

"I didn't want to go back. I don't want to go back. I don't want to be with him anymore. I hoped I could hide here. I was counting on him not wanting to waste two months of his life to come after me. I left you alone."

He dropped her arms and stepped back. "You expect me to believe that?"

"It's true."

"What changed?"

"I...I don't know. What I did to you and Hardy and Ty, it's been eating at me. A lot. I only went with him in the first place because none of you would give me a shifter and he offered me one. I wanted the money, all the nice things I could imagine. And I didn't want to have to depend on anybody for it."

"And now you're here. With nothing."

"Yes," she nodded. "Rialto's evil. He really is, Mark. He's consumed with a lust for power — and hatred for you. I had to get away. I don't want to be a part of that. I was his prisoner. He told me he'd put an explosive in my shifter. He said if I ever did anything he didn't like, he'd kill me."

She massaged her wrist vacantly, remembering. A clear suntan line marked where the device had been.

"...but now I'm free."

She looked back up, the first vestige of a smile breaking out on her lips. "Have you met *Him*?"

Mark took another step back.

"You have. I can see it in your eyes. He changes you, doesn't He?"

She straightened. "It's all different now. I'm different, now. He changed me. And I'm finally free of that stupid shifter. You have no idea what a relief it is to get that thing off your wrist."

He thought he did have an idea.

"For the first time in my life, I feel clean. You don't have to worry about me anymore, Mark."

He stared.

"Really, it's true. I'm never going back. I want to stay here — where *He* is. I'm happy...at last." A new light shone in her eyes.

He knew what she was talking about, though he didn't want to admit it. Nor could he trust her for that matter. She was too slippery.

Still, she seemed sincere. He'd watched her throw herself at Jesus' feet, begging for mercy with her tears. It was an undeniable fact that her shifter was now in Mark's pocket. She couldn't leave or betray him even if she wanted to. And, he didn't think she wanted to. She really was a different person. The flirtatious materialism that had defined her before was gone now. Replaced by someone simpler, humbler, more sincere.

"I really am sorry, Mark. Can you please forgive me?"

He nodded, dumbstruck for words.

"Please tell Hardy and Ty I said I was sorry. I need to go now."

When she saw he wouldn't object, she said, "Good-bye, Mark."

She started to touch his shoulder, then thought the better of it. "Good-bye," she repeated demurely.

"Good-bye, Laura."

Then she was gone, faded into the crowd, like just one more among the throngs of Jewish women in Jerusalem who would all die two thousand years before Mark was born.

Chapter 48

Mark stood lost in thought for a while after Laura left, consumed by contemplation as the streets thickened with people emerging to go about their daily business, swirling about him, oblivious to anything but themselves.

Suddenly, there was a strange stirring among them, an uproar of voices heralding the arrival of something different.

The crowd parted, split in two by a man who moved forward holding a wooden plaque in front of him. The writing on the plaque was in three languages: Hebrew, Greek, and Latin. The man holding it called out loudly as he went, announcing the crime written upon it.

JESUS OF NAZARETH, THE KING OF THE JEWS

Mark unconsciously stepped back, horrified by what he'd inadvertently stumbled into. He thought about running, but it was too late.

A group of Roman soldiers followed, and in their midst was a man marred beyond belief. His face had been so badly beaten he was no longer recognizable, but Mark knew who it was.

Jesus bore a heavy wooden beam across his shoulders, its rough ends bound to his wrists with coarse rope so it wouldn't slide off to either side as he staggered.

Mark recoiled, unable to process, not wanting to process the terror of the sight. Slender branches covered in sharp, spiked thorns had been coiled into several rings and shoved down onto the crown of his head. Blood streamed down his face from the holes it had made and traversed rusty-red splatters of already dried blood from the beating.

As Jesus passed, Mark saw that His back had been flayed so severely it had deteriorated into a mass of raw flesh. The pain and loss of blood must be overwhelming.

Jesus stumbled and fell to a knee. He tried to rise back up, but His strength had bled out.

It did not take the soldiers long to realize that Jesus would not be able to carry the beam all the way to the execution site, so two moved to untie the ropes around his wrists while another commandeered a man from the crowd and laid the beam on his shoulders instead.

The short procession continued through the streets to the city gate, and Mark felt himself compelled to follow all the way to Golgotha, otherwise known as Calvary, the place of the skull.

Golgotha was outside the city walls because by law executions could not take place within them. It was a small rocky outcropping beside the road leading west out of Jerusalem. The road dropped away from the hill as it led from the city, making the escarpment a prominent and preferred place for executions. The purpose of a roman execution was deterrence, and no one coming into or leaving the city from this direction could miss those being made examples of.

The rock face of the hill had been weathered by time in an unusual way that gave it the appearance of a skull. That and the adjacent cemetery were the reasons for its name, and were additional reasons why it had been chosen for its nefarious purpose.

The sixty-pound beam Jesus had been carrying was the horizontal cross piece of the cross on which he would be hung. The longer vertical portion was already lying on the ground, waiting. It had a thick notch two-thirds of the way up it designed to mesh neatly with the cross beam. They laid the cross piece into the notch on the vertical piece and nailed them together.

Then, they extended Jesus along its length while another tried to give him some kind of drink from a coarse sponge, but Jesus refused it.

The crack of mallet on metal was eclipsed by gasps from several of the women in the crowd. Jesus spasmed from the pain of a nail being driven through his wrist, but He did not cry out. His fingers curled up in a way that said some kind of nerve had been severed.

They repeated the process with His other wrist, and then bent his knees up so a third nail could be driven through the tops of his feet into the rough wood against his sole.

Much of the crowd was hostile, spewing insults and mockery, though several women were weeping.

The wooden plaque announcing His crime of being the King of the Jews was nailed to the cross above his head, and then the cross was lifted until the bottom was able to sink into a prepared slot in the rock ready to receive it. It thudded into place with a shudder and Jesus' face twisted in agony as his raw back scraped on the wood and his weight pulled against the nails through his wrists.

Two other men were similarly crucified and their crosses were erected as well, one on either side. Not content with their current crimes, they joined the crowd in hurling insults Jesus' way.

Jesus called out in Hebrew, *"Father, forgive them, for they know not what they do."*

Mark found himself fixated, unable to tear himself away from the scene, even as the crowd thinned out to go about their daily business. A crucified man could take days to perish and most of the action was finished. Still, the chief priests remained to relish in their victory, along with the weeping women and a few other forlorn men unsure what to do with themselves.

The roman soldiers played a dice game to divide up the clothes they'd stripped from Jesus. Those passing by on the highway called out more taunts as they went.

A couple of the women and a man had drawn closer to the cross and Jesus spoke with them, but Mark could not hear what was said.

The blood continued to flow down in slow streams from Jesus' brow and the wounds in his wrists and feet. Lines of it streaked his ribs and flanks and dripped to the rock below.

About noon, the sky darkened and Mark looked up. A large, black object was moving in front of the sun.

Then, the darkness was complete, almost as if it were night. The effect was very distinct from other solar eclipses Mark had experienced.

An ominous heaviness of being settled over all. The mockery from the passersby lessened under the weight of it. Even one of the criminals that had been crucified next to Jesus switched from insults to pleading with Jesus for his soul. Jesus turned and said something to him, and again Mark could not hear it from his distance, but the thief's face relaxed in a new found peace.

Mark could not understand how some could be so blind to continue to mock and taunt in the face of what seemed so obvious.

After several hours, Jesus cried out in a loud voice, *"My God, my God, why have you forsaken me?"*

All other speech ceased and silence reigned. Then, again in a loud voice, Jesus cried, *"It is finished!"* and He expelled His breath.

A deep rumbling erupted from the earth below his feet and grew in intensity. Mark was driven to his knees. Everything shook, the rock, the crosses, his vision, it was an earthquake unlike any other he'd experienced. All others present similarly lost their balance and fell.

After what seemed an eternity, the rumbling and shaking faded away and sunlight returned.

The witnesses milled about, talking excitedly. A centurion

spoke animatedly with his fellow soldiers, gesturing emphatically toward Jesus' body on the cross.

The people had regained their feet now, but Mark still felt the rumbling echoing deep within his heart.

Chapter 49

The curtain parted revealing a much younger face than Mark had expected.

"Mattatiyah HaLevi?"

"Come in, come in. I was expecting you."

"What do you mean you were expecting..." But the scribe had already retreated back into his home. Mark's Hebrew was much better with another month of learning under his belt.

After a few moments, Mark's eyes adjusted to the dim light. It was a humble abode, at least by modern standards. By comparison in the 1st century, however, the Levite was doing fairly well — meaning his home had more than one room.

A young woman stood and pulled some sort of frying pan out of a dome-roofed clay oven. She used a flat utensil to transfer several flat cakes of fried bread onto a couple of wooden plates. Mattatiyah poured red-tinted juice into wooden cups and motioned for Mark to sit. It smelled delicious.

"Miryam has just finished breakfast. You came at the right time."

"You said you were expecting..."

"Yes, I knew you would come. You are *Markos*, no?"

"Uh, it's Mark, but yes."

"See. I knew you would come."

"But how...?"

"You are looking for something, no? Something important?"

Shocked, Mark leaned back on his low stool. It creaked under his weight. Mattatiyah reached out a hand to steady him.

"Yes, but..."

"We'll talk soon. For now, eat. Eat." The man pushed a plate full of fried bread and boiled eggs. It looked good and Mark didn't need a second invitation. He dug in, complimenting the cook, who blushed and left the room.

When they were finished, the Levite stood. "Let's go."

Mark followed him out the door into the bright morning sun. "Where are we going?"

"I'm going to show you what you are looking for."

"What?" Mark was stunned again. Was this man talking about what he thought he was talking about? *Could it really be this easy after all this time?*

"Patience. We'll speak of everything in due time. For now, let's go."

He led Mark out of Jericho to the east. The road continued to drop at a rapid pace until they'd gone about five miles and reached the Jordan River. There were several boatmen there ferrying people across the river. Mattatiyah clinked a couple of coins into the palms of one of them and they crossed.

Once they reached the other side, Mattatiyah led the way.

"What is it you're taking me to see?" Mark asked.

The scribe glanced around making sure no one was nearby to hear and then turned back to him.

"Why the Ark of course. Isn't that what you're seeking?"

"Well...uh...yes. But how did you know I was looking for it? And how did you know I would come?"

"He told me." The scribe stared Mark in the eyes coolly, gauging his reaction.

It took a minute to register. "*He* told you."

"Yes, He told me in a dream. He is Messiah and knows all things. In my dream, He told me a man named *Markos* would come. That you would be looking for the Ark and that I was to hide nothing from you."

"I cannot believe that...it makes no sense...why would he...?"

"You do not know Him very well, do you?"

"No. I would have liked to know Him better."

"You will."

"How? Don't you know what happened?"

"You will."

They walked in silence for a few miles as Mark digested this new revelation. It was beyond his comprehension that God, that Jesus, would consider anything Mark did of importance.

"How do you know where the Ark is?" He finally asked.

"I come from a long line of scribes. Many years ago, our father, the prophet Jeremiah, removed the Ark of the Covenant from the Temple to protect it from destruction by the Babylonians. He hid it in a cave that I will show you.

"Every generation since, one scribe has been trusted with the knowledge of its location so that it would never be lost, but only one so it would never be found. At least not until the right time. I am that scribe for this generation."

"But you are sharing the knowledge with me."

He stopped and faced Mark. "Do not make light of this. I only do so because *He* instructed me to. Otherwise, I would die before the secret escaped my lips."

"I'm sorry. You just seemed so willing."

"Do not mistake obedience for willingness."

"Where are we going?"

"To the mountain where Moses died."

"Mt. Nebo?"

"Yes."

"Many people have looked there and never found it."

"It is a big mountain."

The road began rising under their feet as they neared the mountain. They ascended about a third of the way up the slope and circled around the perimeter until they were well off the beaten path. The Levite stopped in front of an inconspicuous rock.

"Here."

"Here?"

Mattatiyah squatted and leaned into the rock, rolling it over with some effort. Underneath was a dark hole that descended into the mountain. It measured about a half a foot across.

Involuntarily, Mark trembled at the sight of the hollow circle leading down into mystery.

"The Ark is down there in a cave. The cave entrance was sealed centuries ago. This is the only access."

Mark stared. Now that he was faced with the reality of the Ark, an unexplained fear entered him like nothing he'd ever sensed before. It *was* down there. He could feel it.

With trepidation, he leaned his face over the hole and peered into the blackness, but could see nothing. He considered using his flashlight, but decided against it.

He held a static GPS locator in his palm over the hole. Bobby Prescott had specially designed it for them. It was coated in layers of plastic and ceramic and could resist weathering for thousands of years. It would remain dormant wherever he put it until a modern satellite sent an activation signal to it.

Granted, it still needed some kind of power source, albeit a small one, but no battery would last that long. So, they'd designed it so current would flow when exposed to a strong magnetic field. When he returned to the future, they would flood this area with large magnetic field generators that would induce power in the locator. Simultaneously, a satellite would send the activation signal and pinpoint its location. All after sitting dormant for two thousand years.

He couldn't bring himself to drop it inside the hole. It just didn't seem right. Who was he to contaminate the holy site below?

He stood, pulled a folding spade from his pack, and began digging about five feet away from the hole.

The Levite jumped to his feet. "What are you doing?"

"Don't worry. Not going down very far."

Once he'd dug down about a foot, he dropped the GPS locator into a Zip-Loc bag, sealed it and dropped both into his small depression. *Time to see if those environmentalists were right about plastic lasting forever.* He doubted it. He scooped the dirt back over it and packed it down to look undisturbed.

"What was that?" Mattatiyah asked.

"Something to help me find this place again." Mark scanned the mountainside, memorizing the view and the landmarks. "I don't suppose you'd let me carve anything in these rocks."

The Levite shook his head. "No. That would draw the attention of others." He drew an elongated pouch from his travel satchel. "Here. This is what you really need." He held it out to Mark.

Mark took the pouch and turned it upside down so the contents would spill onto his hand. A narrow, tightly coiled silver scroll slipped out into his palm.

"Is this...?"

"The Silver Scroll? Yes. You know of the other scrolls?"

Mark nodded.

"Why do you have it?" Mark asked. "Why did you remove it from the Temple Mount?"

"As the scribe charged with the protection of the Ark and the Temple treasures, I know where all the scrolls are...and the tablets too. In another dream, I saw the Temple in Jerusalem burning, destroyed by the Romans. I do not know when, but it is just a matter of time. I switched this scroll out with another that looked like it in order to protect it. The false one now lies under the Mount...though somehow you already knew that." He looked at Mark quizzically with his head cocked to the side.

"Why are you showing it to me?"

"It is yours to take. You will need it."

"How can you give it to me? I am not a scribe."

"You are now."

***

August 11ᵗʰ 2014 - Jerusalem, Israel

The prime minister's office was not overly ornate. Its clean features spoke of simple, unassuming authority. Prime Minister Alon leaned forward with his elbows on top of his mahogany desk, intensely hanging on to Mark's every word.

Over a secure line, President James had fully explained Mark's shifting capabilities to the prime minister. At first, Alon had, of course, been incredulous. Then, once convinced of the truth, his security forces had refused to allow a meeting for fear of not being able to control Mark. President James urged Alon to accept the meeting, explaining it was vital to Israel's national security. He also pointed out that Mark had the ability to show up in Alon's office whether he wanted him there or not.

So, the meeting had been agreed to, but they weren't alone of course. The office was ringed with agents from Israel's secret service, the Mossad. Mossad's Director, Shabtai Arit, sat in a chair next to the prime minister. As Mark had discussed his shifter and its capabilities, he'd watched a greedy little light growing in Arit's eyes as the man considered the wealth of benefits Mossad could glean from such a device, but he detected no similar spirit in Alon.

Mark told them about Rialto and his demand for submission from the U.S. He explained about Rialto's threat to set the Middle East ablaze using the Ark of the Covenant as an incendiary tool to incite the Arab nations against Israel if the U.S. didn't acquiesce. He shifted in and out in their presence and showed them a newspaper from several days in the future to prove the reality of time shifting. Though he only let them keep it long enough to examine the headlines so they wouldn't get any ideas about playing the lottery or some such. Though he imagined Alit had already made plans for several stock purchases, or to sell short.

Mark walked them through their long journey in search of the Ark, and all their stops and starts along the way. A stenographer was typing furiously to keep up and it looked as though Alon's eyes might bug out of his head at several points during the story. It was an amazing tale, one that they couldn't quite grasp as being real, no matter how much their head accepted the premise of it.

Finally, Mark got to his trip back to 1st century Israel. He told them of his encounter with Jesus, but they just stared at him glassy-eyed through that part. He recounted his walk with Mattatiyah HaLevi to Mt. Nebo and what he'd told Mark.

The prime minister held up a hand.

"So, the GPS locator didn't work?"

"No, it didn't. Though we're not sure why. We tried to activate it with a magnetic field generator, but we couldn't get the satellite to detect it. I know we were very close to the same general area, but the rocks have shifted somewhat over the centuries. To be honest, we didn't spend a lot of time on it because we think it should be the Israeli government who finds the Ark, not us.

"I think this is all you'll need to locate it." Mark pulled the elongated pouch from his pack and laid it on Alon's desk.

The prime minister picked it up and turned it over. The narrow silver scroll fell into his hands.

"What is this?"

"That is the long lost companion to the Copper Scroll," Mark said. "We have not opened it yet, but we believe that together with the Copper Scroll it has all the information you need to find the Ark."

Alon's eyes widened in shock and surprise. He took it gently by the ends and laid it back on the desk on top of the pouch. He looked to Alit.

"Did you know of the existence of this Silver Scroll?"

The head of Mossad nodded. "It was thought to be lost."

"Well, now you know why it was missing," Mark said, "I had it." He laughed and they joined in nervously.

"Gentlemen, that's about it. I will give your men as exact a location as I can for the cave, but I think with that scroll you have all you need to find the Ark. Do you have any questions for me?"

"I'm sure we do," Alon said. More nervous laughter.

"If you have need of me, you can reach me through President James."

Director Alit spoke up. "Such a device could be very useful to Israel, Mr. Carpen. We could compensate you for your time." The pun was unintentional.

Mark smiled. "Your offer is flattering but I'm already a billionaire and content to be my own boss."

Arit's eyes narrowed. "If you do not work with us, such a

device could be considered a dangerous threat to Israel."

"Have I not just acted in Israel's interest? Let me assure you gentlemen, no government, not even the United States, will control me or my team. If any attempt is made to force us into service, or to forcibly remove our shifters from us, we will fight back, and even an army cannot stop us then. I have friends and we watch each other's backs."

Arit's expression was grim.

"Back off, Director," the prime minister interrupted, "Mr. Carpen has already sacrificed much for our benefit. We owe you a debt of gratitude, sir."

"Thank you, sir." Mark stood to go. "As I said, if I can be of service *once in a while*, please feel free to contact me." They shook hands all around and Mark exited the office flanked by Mossad agents who would ensure he left building swiftly.

Once he was gone, the prime minister turned to Alit.

"Do you believe his story?" he asked.

"The evidence is hard to dispute. The man did just disappear and reappear in front of us. If it's not, I don't know what kind of intelligence game the U.S. could be playing, or for what purpose. It's very odd."

"I guess we'll know in a few days if those headlines come true."

Chapter 50

*"Why slander we the times? What crimes have days and years that we thus
charge them with iniquity? If we would rightly scan,
it's not the times are bad, but man."*

- Dr. Joseph Beaumont

Randall Cook was not a very disciplined man. Presumably, Rialto had left the sailor in Jerusalem to keep a vigilant eye out for Mark's return.

He'd apparently decided to neglect his duties because they found him living it up at a 5-star, luxury hotel just outside the walls of the Old City. Cook had gotten sloppy, charging tens of thousands of dollars' worth of liquor and escort services on accounts with his name on them.

A cyber investigator they regularly employed to track any of Rialto's transactions they could find had alerted Hardy and Ty to Cook's activities and they'd flown out immediately to intercept Mark before he left the city.

Mark told them about Laura and they decided to follow Cook to see what he was up to besides a spree of debauchery.

The arrived at Cook's hotel and found him trying to assault a pretty young maid who had rejected his disgusting advances. He'd pressed her into a corner in a back hallway and was attempting to force a kiss on the unwilling woman who was doing her best to turn her face every way in which his was not.

Instead of intervening personally, they maintained their cover and shifted back a few minutes to call hotel security as well as the Israeli police so they could arrive in time to stop Cook before he was able to harm the maid.

Cook used his shifter to escape an arrest, traveling back one day, though he didn't bother to hide before he did so and left the security officials staring in shock as he faded out of sight.

The sailor also didn't bother to employ his jammer. He was sloppy all around. Mark thought Rialto must regret ever bringing him on board.

Mark followed him back in time and made sure Cook caught sight of him in the hotel lobby. Then, Mark hopped in a taxi and took it to Ben Gurion airport in Tel Aviv. He booked a commercial flight back to Boston under an alias. As expected, Cook followed him the entire way. Also, as expected, Cook did not check in with Rialto before getting on the plane to follow Mark. He'd donned a baseball cap and large sunglasses, believing the cheap disguise would keep Mark from recognizing him.

Of course, Hardy and Ty followed Cook, but they made sure to remain undetected by their prey. They boarded the plane before Mark and were already seated out of sight in first class when Cook got on. He never saw them.

Mark sat in the middle of the plane on purpose. Cook took a seat a few rows behind so he could keep an eye on Mark unobserved.

Once the plane was in the air, though, the sailor couldn't help taking advantage of the in-air alcohol service. He ordered several cocktails, one after the other. Mark waited until he got up to go to the restroom and then slipped a mickey in the half-full mojito Cook had left sitting on his tray. After he finished the drink, Cook would quickly fall unconscious. Mark had been sure to not overdo it, however. He wanted Cook awake again in a few hours.

The plane was nearly empty. Before boarding, Mark and his team had shifted back several months prior to the flight and bought up many of the tickets under the names of various individuals who did not exist and thus would never show up for the flight. They then canceled a few of their reservations right before Cook went to buy a ticket so he could get on.

That left a few stragglers who'd bought theirs more than three months ahead of time, but those guys were all seated toward the front.

Now, Mark moved to the seat across the aisle from Cook who was snoring open-mouthed. His head was tilted up against the back of the seat, drool dribbling down his chin.

Mark took a roll of duct tape from his backpack and unrolled a long strip as silently as possible. He cringed when he slipped and accidentally released too much. In the closed space, the noise sounded like a mini-jet's tires hitting the runway. Thankfully, of the few passengers at the front of the plane, none had heard and turned around.

He wrapped the duct tape around Cook's forearm, careful not to cover up the shifter, securing it firmly against the armrest.

He didn't know what the target time was on Cook's watch, but it didn't matter.

Mark leaned over and poked the former purser's shoulder several times. Cook jerked awake with a choked off snort. Mark smiled grimly as the man struggled to make sense of his surroundings and rub the blurriness from his eyes with his free hand. Finally, confusion broke into hatred as Cook recognized the face before him.

He lunged forward but was jerked back into his seat by the unexpected resistance of the bands of duct tape holding his arm to the armrest. Mark's smile grew.

"You!" Cook sneered.

"Yes, it's me," Mark answered. "Ty and Hardy are here too." He pointed behind the sailor. Cook strained to crane his neck back to see but couldn't turn enough to get a full view because of his restraint.

Ty and Hardy both waved and smiled. "Hey, Cookie-Baby," Hardy said.

Cook snorted derision. "What do you want?" He strained up with his forearm again to no avail. He reached with his other hand to undo the duct tape.

"Ah-ah," Mark waved a finger reproachfully. "Sit still."

"What do you want?" He repeated.

Mark withdrew a piece of paper from his pocket and unfolded it.

"Randall Cook, you are a kidnapper. In fact, that is how we first met you, when you shanghaied us into service on board the HMS Huntingdon. You were responsible for the kidnapping of hundreds of other American men during the war of 1812, many of whom were thrown overboard when they were no longer able to serve.

"You are a murderer. You've murdered dozens of people since Rialto gave you that shifter, and those are just the ones we know about. We've been able to save some of them, some we couldn't.

"You've declared war on the United States of America, both back in the War of 1812, and now in this time through your conspiracy with Alexander Rialto to extort the President.

"We've just discovered you're also a would-be rapist, though that doesn't really surprise me..."

"Who do you think you are, some kind of judge?" Cook snarled.

"We have to be. No jail or prison could hold you as long as you have that shifter. Do you deny the charges? The penalty is death."

"Ach, ah spit on yer charges." And he did just that. His rough, 19th century British waterfront accent was returning under the stress. "Rialto'll come fer me, ta be sure."

"I doubt it. You're not worth the trouble I'm guessing."

Cook visibly paled a shade, somewhat deflated for the first time since they'd met.

"Do you have any last words?"

"Ye do not hav' ta do this," he pled, "Ah can be of service ta ye." Fear was finally starting to sink into his thick skull, though he still hadn't grasped the nature of the threat.

"Hardy?"

"My pleasure."

Hardy pulled a long wooden stick from behind the seat.

"I'd make sure you're not touching his seat first," Mark advised.

"What? What are ye...?" Cook desperately jerked his head from side to side trying to see what Hardy was doing.

Ty leaned back and lifted his hands from the top of the seat back. Hardy stepped into the aisle and before Cook could react, he'd used the pole to press the button on Cook's shifter.

The next thing Randall Cook knew he was tumbling head over heels through the air. He had no idea what year he was in, but it didn't matter. Whenever they'd sent him, there was no longer a plane to hold him up. Perhaps if he'd had the presence of mind to immediately use his shifter again he might have wound up back in the plane's cargo hold or something, but he hadn't, and now it was a moot point.

He plummeted through the air like a defeathered bird. The height of the fall was great enough that as he rocketed toward the Atlantic Ocean below, he had several minutes to straighten himself out and contemplate the certitude of his fate before impact. He realized his only hope lay in Rialto coming to his rescue before they shifted him out of that plane.

His last thought before the surface tension of the ocean's water ended all thought was how unlikely that was.

***

Back on the plane, Mark was pleasantly surprised to see Cook's seat had not disappeared with him. Being bolted to the plane's infrastructure, the shifter had apparently interpreted the whole mass as one big structure, too large to shift. So, Cook had fallen into the ocean by himself.

The sizzle of the shift's static was unusual enough that the few passengers up front turned their heads to see what was going on and a flight attendant came back to investigate, but the duct tape had disappeared with Cook, and Hardy had already sat down several rows back and inconspicuously slid his wooden dowel under a seat. She came with a stern frown, but seeing nothing amiss, left them alone. Once they landed, the airline might or might not realize one of the passengers had disappeared, but that was neither here nor there. They'd be long gone by then with no way to connect their aliases to their real identities. Or to Cook's for that matter.

Mark twisted around to his friends.

"We need to fabricate some kind of protective faceplate covers for our shifters so no one can do that to us," he said.

"Good idea," Ty agreed, "Why didn't we think of that before?"

"Shouldn't be hard for Prescott to design," Hardy added, "Hey, Ty and I are gonna head back up to first class. See you on the ground."

"Thanks a lot," Mark laughed.

"Our pleasure. We appreciate the little excursion."

"Well, at least Rialto's down by three now. We're evening the odds."

***

Hugh Plantagenet, former plantation owner, now modern time traveler, watched the flow of passengers exiting the plane into the airport terminal from behind a newspaper. Rialto kept warning him about Carpen's proficiency in all areas regarding undercover operations, and you never knew when or where those guys would show up. So, he kept the newspaper high and watched through a tiny camera on his phone that displayed an image he could see behind the paper. That kept his face out of view.

Rialto had sent him to figure out why Laura and Cook had both gotten on the plane from Israel to come back to the U.S. without calling to check in. They were both supposed to be following Carpen in Israel and weren't supposed to return to the U.S. until they knew something, but GPS showed their tracking signals were on this flight.

The most likely scenario was that Carpen was on the plane and they were following, but that did not explain why they hadn't checked in by phone beforehand. Thus, Hugh was ordered to keep a low profile, observe, and report back.

Most unsettling was that Rialto had just called to inform him that Cook's transponder signal had ceased transmitting midway across the Atlantic. They had no explanation for that as yet, and none of the possibilities were good ones, unless Cook had found a way to disconnect the transponder from his shifter. If he had managed to do that, perhaps he could show Hugh how to do it as well. He'd give just about anything to be out from under Rialto's yoke. No amount of money was worth being a slave to someone.

Plantagenet stiffened. Carpen and Phillips emerged from the tunnel, followed by that cursed slave they called Ty.

Hatred like a white-hot stew of rage boiled up within, threatening to pour over the edges of his control. He hated that slave and Carpen. They'd killed his father and tried to kill him. He had no beef with Phillips by himself, but he was a part of them, so he'd have to die too. Someday.

He couldn't do it now. Not with three against one. The newspaper trembled slightly in his hands as he followed their movement on his camera's video screen. He couldn't help but dip the corner of the paper as they passed to watch them directly. Now, he could only see the backs of their heads. He wished he could put a bullet in all three, right here, right now.

With luck, Rialto would want to set up an ambush for them here now that they knew when and where all three would be together.

He waited until every passenger had disembarked, but there was no sign of Cook or Laura anywhere, which was very confusing. GPS showed them getting on the plane and moving along with it across the ocean.

He needed to contact Rialto.

Something was wrong.

Chapter 51

Plantagenet waited until they moved a considerable way down the concourse before following. It was a crowded time of day, so he had no trouble remaining invisible. Dark sunglasses helped deflect recognition as well.

His phone buzzed.

"Yeah, boss." It was Rialto returning his voice mail.

"Where are you?"

"Still at the airport. I'm following all three of them right now. Cook and Laura never got off the plane."

"Hold on."

Plantagenet overheard a muffled conversation as Rialto turned to ask somebody something on the other side of the line. Then, he came back to the phone.

"There's no sign of Cook's shifter, but GPS shows Laura is in the airport."

Hugh turned in all directions. "I don't see her. She definitely didn't get come out of that tunnel. I waited a long time."

"Where exactly are you in the airport right now?"

"Near the baggage claim."

"She's right in front of you, about a hundred feet ahead. She's moving from the terminal to the curb outside."

"I tell you I don't see her. That's where Carpen is."

More muffled conversation.

"I want you to slip outside without being noticed," Rialto said. "Stay a good distance away and tell me the exact moment they get in a vehicle and it pulls away from the curb."

"Will do."

Plantagenet walked to the far end of the baggage claim before exiting to the outdoor pick-up lane. He could see the three men waiting several hundred feet away. After a minute, a black SUV pulled up to the curb and they hopped in. It rolled away.

"They're moving out now. Headed west."

"Wait a second..."

After a few seconds, he heard Rialto let loose a long string of profanities.

"What's the matter?" Hugh asked.

"Carpen's got Laura's shifter on him. Who knows what he did to her. He must have Cook's too. Neither one of them ever got on that plane. Somehow Carpen killed both of them and got their shifters. He must have discovered the GPS transponder on Cook's and disabled it mid-flight."

"Should I follow them? We could shift back in time and set up an ambush for them as soon as they get off the plane."

"Absolutely not! If he disabled Cook's transponder, then there's only one reason he didn't disable Laura's too. He *wants* us to track him. He knows we're following the signals and so he left Laura's signal alone to lure us into some kind of trap. That's got to be the whole reason they got on that commercial flight in the first place instead of their private jet. Get back here immediately."

"But..."

"No buts! They've taken out three of us without batting an eye and now they've got something planned for the rest of us. We can't risk it. Get back here now."

"Yes, sir."

Plantagenet disconnected the call. It went against everything in him to let Carpen go. Something told him they might not have such a good opportunity as this again.

Still, he had to learn patience. That's what Torino kept telling him. Torino said he saw a lot of potential in him, and Hugh definitely had a lot of respect for the Italian assassin and his skills with a gun. Torino had even mentioned taking him under his wing to train him in the art of sniping. Now, *that* was a plan that got his blood moving.

For now, he would obey and head back to meet with Rialto. He knew the date and time when they came out of that airplane. He could come back and surprise Carpen any time he wanted. And some day, he would.

***

"It's good to be back, guys."

Mark sank deep into his favorite leather chair. He leaned his head back, enjoying the feel of the air conditioning on his face. "I missed that," he said, pointing to the vent. After more than two months in antiquity, he was still getting used to modern comforts again.

"It's good to have you back," Ty said. He, Hardy, and Savannah all beamed at him from around the conference table. Mark looked healthy, more vibrant. His skin had been bronzed by so much time under the ancient sun.

"You seem happier," Savannah commented. "I can't remember the last time I saw you with such a genuine smile on your face. It looks good."

"I do feel better."

"Well, man, don't beat around the bush, tell us what happened."

Mark had not told Ty and Hardy much of the details yet, preferring to wait until they were all safely inside their headquarters and away from prying ears. Now, Mark leaned forward and told them the whole story, from beginning to end. A palpable hush fell over the room when he got to the part about seeing Jesus and the miracles he observed.

Savannah started to cry when he told them about Laura and how the shifter had slid off her wrist at His touch. Ty and Hardy turned to each other wide-eyed when Mark told of Jesus' signal that he was supposed to pick up her shifter. It was one thing to believe God was the mysterious force directing things behind the scenes. It was entirely another to have firm confirmation that God was not only aware of their group, but that He'd intended these shifters for them specifically.

And that He'd begun this plan over two thousand years ago.

"That's unbelievable," was all Ty could say.

Hardy exhaled. "It really is."

"Is it?" Mark asked. "I thought you guys were the ones pushing faith on me."

"But this is so far beyond...it's just...what was *He* like?"

Mark recounted every detail he could remember from his encounters, answering endless questions from all three.

He told them about finding the scribe Mattatiyah, how he'd led Mark to the cave where the Ark was hidden, and the Silver Scroll he'd given him. He further explained about his meeting with Prime Minister Alon and that he'd turned all the information over to Israel.

"Did they find it?" Savannah asked

"President James called me on the way back here to headquarters. He said that he'd spoken with the prime minister, and that they'd found the cave in question. The GPS locator never did work, but the Silver Scroll turned out to be the key. It had all the information they needed."

"So they found the cave. Did they find the Ark?"

"The president said Israel could neither confirm nor deny

whether they'd located anything of interest inside the cave, but that they wished to pass on their eternal gratitude to us. They said that if the State of Israel can ever be of service to us, that we should not hesitate to call on them."

"That means they found it."

Mark nodded. "I'm sure they did."

"But they're going to hide it away again in some warehouse, like in *Raiders of the Lost Ark*?"

"They're definitely not going public with it for the time being. The important thing is that we beat Rialto to the punch."

"What do you think they'll do with it?"

"The president seemed to think they were waiting on something before they revealed it to the world, but he didn't know what."

The team sat in silence for a time, reflecting over all the effort they'd expended to locate the ancient artifact, all the periods of history they'd visited, and the close calls.

"So, what now, Mark?" Hardy asked.

"We're going to finish off Rialto and his crew and get back to our lives. I've got to do something first, but I'll get back to you with specifics."

They all stood as the meeting came to an end.

"Sounds good, friend." Ty slapped him on the back and walked out.

"Good work," Hardy called as he strolled out the door after Ty.

Once they'd left, Savannah asked, "Do you think Laura was going to be okay, Mark?"

He smiled. "Yeah. I think she was more at peace than at any other time in her life. Savannah?"

"Yes."

"I'd...eh...I'd like to go to dinner with you some time."

It was her turn to smile. She took his hand.

"How about now?"

Chapter 52

Clear blues skies shone overhead in Cleveland, Ohio. Hugh Plantagenet relaxed on a park bench facing the Cleveland Public Library, enjoying the strong breeze coming in off the water to his back.

He'd rather be going after Carpen than sitting here, but Rialto had sent him to Cleveland on a mission of a different sort. After losing so many of his team to Carpen, Rialto had come up with a new plan to consolidate more power into his hands.

The man was insatiable. He already had more money than a person could spend in a lifetime, and with a shifter, he could control people. He could take life with impunity or give it back at will. He could force individuals to submit to him in whatever way he wanted and Rialto took full advantage of that every chance he got.

Not that Hugh blamed him. If he were in Rialto's shoes, he would do the exact same thing. In fact, thoughts of how to get out from under Rialto's thumb dominated every waking moment of Hugh Plantagenet's days, and once he did, he would start to build his own empire.

Alexander Rialto, however, went beyond a normal lust for power.

He had two mortal enemies: Mark Carpen and the United States government. He could understand Rialto hating Carpen, of course. Being a son of the confederacy, Plantagenet could also understand a hatred for the U.S. government, but in Rialto's case it was kind of ridiculous, considering the only thing they'd ever done to the man was fire him.

Still, underneath the skin of antipathy was the heart of the matter — a desire to control the world. Rialto had no hope of ever commanding an army — he was not a natural born leader — but if he could control the leaders of the world through extortion or violence, he could logically control the world. And the best place to start was with the U.S. government. They and Mark Carpen were the only things standing in his way.

But now Rialto had been rebuffed. He'd thrown everything he

had at destroying Carpen and had not only failed, he'd lost three of his people. When he'd first recruited Plantagenet, Rialto had been cruel, cold, and calculating. Now there was a streak of wildness, a twinge of unspoken fear that underlay everything the man did. When he'd heard that Carpen had beaten him to the punch on the Ark of the Covenant, a strange light had flickered behind his eyes momentarily, hinting of something dangerous.

Having failed dramatically in a direct approach to control President James, Rialto had decided to take a step back and try a new tactic. Political control didn't have to be rushed, not when you had a shifter.

His new plan was to begin much further in the past. Rialto planned to blackmail or extort as many industrial and political leaders as he could in the late 19th century. Men like the Rockefellers, the Carnegies, the Vanderbilts, and the Roosevelts. He would accumulate influence and power among these and a plethora of lower level bureaucrats and other law-makers, but he would limit his exertion of that power in order to allow his presence to settle deep into the psyches of Wall Street and Washington.

He would continue the process over the next century and a half so politicians and power brokers of every ilk became used to him as the invisible hand who rarely appeared, and even more rarely requested, but who must be obeyed absolutely on those occasions when a request was made or face Rialto's inevitable wrath.

He had sent Hugh Plantagenet to Cleveland because that was the city where Rockefeller had established his Standard Oil Company. Hugh was supposed to travel back and pay John D. Rockefeller a visit before Standard Oil was formed. He was supposed to make some simple demand of the industrialist, shift out of his office in front of his eyes, and then follow up on his threats if Rockefeller did not submit. They could kill family members, friends, key employees, plant embarrassing information with the media, or even manipulate bank accounts and property records.

Plantagenet just wasn't ready to go back and see the oil baron yet. It was too beautiful a day here in modern times and he was tired of doing Rialto's bidding. What would he get out of this deal anyway? More money? He didn't want any more money. He wanted to be his own man.

He feared Carpen too. No one understood what he'd done with Cook or Laura, but it might just be a matter of time before they got to him. He should probably distance himself from Rialto for a while.

For now though, Rialto's ruthlessness and unpredictability still cowed him. He *would* go see Rockefeller, of course. In just a few minutes.

You have got to be kidding...

Unbelievable. Sometimes he just couldn't stand the things they allowed in modern times.

A tall, full-figured black woman was swaggering down the street like she owned it. Her bright red dress was plastered to her body like someone had painted it on. And it was entirely too short. Back in his time, no slave woman would have dared dress like that...or walk like that. And if they had, well he knew how to put them back in their place.

To make matters worse, this woman had the gall to actually look him in the eye as she approached. *That* made his blood boil. She should be looking to the ground in humility, fearful to meet the gaze of someone so clearly her superior.

He had to keep reminding himself that these people were not slaves in this time. He knew how the War for Confederate Independence had ended and the history that followed. It broke his heart how the South had been raped and oppressed following the war. The aggressive northern Republicans had just continued their conquest over the next century and a half. His one consolation was that the policies of those feeble-minded northerners had actually kept the blacks virtually enslaved to the government. Their so-called War on Poverty had decimated them. It had been a nice side effect.

Of course that had been the work of the Democratic Party, his confederates, and he had to believe it was intentional. The Republicans were the ones who'd voted for that Civil Rights crap.

Served them right. A lot of men in power in the Confederacy had spoken openly of abolishing slavery. One of the first things Jefferson Davis had done was outlaw the importing of new slaves, which had infuriated him at the time. It was almost better the south had lost seeing how badly the slaves had fared under northern authority.

This woman was something else though. She was still staring at him. His eyes burned with anger. He had the sudden desire to rise up and slap her across the face, but he had to suppress the urge, as satisfying as it would feel. It would draw unnecessary attention to himself, and Rialto would not tolerate any mistakes. No, he had to focus on the task at hand. He turned away so he wouldn't have to look at her.

The distinct smell of artificial strawberries wafted in as she passed. He heard a spitting sound and felt something wet strike his cheek. He jerked and wiped it away with his fingers. She had spit on him!

Disgust and indignation boiled his blood. A seething roared through his veins like a wild beast as he watched her move away down the sidewalk like nothing had happened. He could not let her get away with it. He had to teach that prostitute a lesson she would never forget.

He assessed the area and cursed when he saw a police officer patrolling near the corner across the street. He hesitated, then moved after her, keeping a distance of fifty feet between them.

She glanced back and saw he was following. A flicker of fear darkened her face before she turned forward and hastened her pace.

He smiled. Good. Let her be afraid. He would follow her until he found a place he could get her alone. She'd regret spitting on him like nothing else she'd ever done in her worthless life.

That swagger of hers was infuriating. It felt arrogant even when she was so obviously petrified. She had to be a prostitute. She certainly looked like one. He followed her for several blocks before she snatched another glance back his way.

She hastened toward a huge squarish monument that rose up in between the office buildings like something out of ancient Rome. It was so large it took up an entire city block. Its square base sat at the top of many stairs in the middle of a park like area and could be approached from all four directions. The base was several stories high and looked big enough to hold a large group of people. The round stone column towering up from the center of its base was topped by an enormous statue and looked to be at least a hundred feet tall. A placard said it was called the Soldiers' and Sailors' Monument.

The monument's grounds appeared deserted and he couldn't believe his luck when the woman disappeared inside the massive open doorway. He hurried to catch up to her before she realized she had trapped herself.

It took a second for his eyes to adjust to the dimmer light, but then he saw her standing with her back to a massive square column in the center of the room. She had her hands crossed at her waist like she was ready to fend him off. Her eyes were wide with fear. He thought he detected a slight tremor among her muscles and the thought was delicious.

The place was empty. The groundskeeper must have stepped out for some reason, but if he showed back up, Hugh would take care of him too.

She panicked and ran around the column and out of sight. If he rushed after her, she'd circle around the other way and try to escape through the doorway, so he moved to the center column and slowly peeked his head around instead.

"Come to papa, little girl," he called.

At the moment his eyes cleared the corner, something big and flat and hard slammed into his forehead. He blacked out.

Mark Carpen stood over the fallen man. He handed the woman a wad of cash, which she took and stuffed in some secret fold in her skin-tight dress.

"You're a pretty good actress," he said, "You really looked scared."

She smirked. "I was. How'd I know you'd really come through? That man was mean. You never told me he was so mean."

"Well, he is. You probably don't want to be here for this."

She patted the wad of cash hidden on her hip, looked around and hurried out of the monument.

Mark crouched and lifted Plantagenet's wrist. He changed the target year to be one Plantagenet would be sure not to appreciate. 800 BC to be precise.

Mark withdrew a wooden dowel from his backpack and started to press the unconscious man's shift button with it, but then changed his mind.

Instead he took a water bottle from his pack and emptied it on Plantagenet's face. He sputtered and coughed. The sensation jerked him back to consciousness since his body thought it was drowning.

Mark stepped back and dropped into a shooter's stance, pointing his pistol at Plantagenet's chest. Plantagenet scrambled backward on his hands and then leapt to his feet, terrified by the sudden appearance of Mark with a gun.

"I wouldn't shift if I were you," Mark said.

Plantagenet moved his finger toward his shifter, but hesitated.

"Don't," Mark warned, "If you shift, I'll shoot."

Out of apparent options, the former plantation owner cackled crazily and pushed the button.

Only after the ground settled beneath his feet did Hugh Plantagenet think to check the target time on his watch. It glowed red and a deep sinking feeling hit his stomach as he blinked his eyes repeatedly, thinking he must be misreading the setting.

He wasn't and no amount of rubbing his eyes would change the nightmare.

He stood in the middle of a pristine forest. One that looked like it had never been touched by human hands.

Echoes in his mind of Rialto's warnings about traveling too far back into the past set his heart racing. Now he knew what Carpen had done to Randolph DeCleary.

He let loose a long string of curses. He snatched up fallen branches and logs and slammed them over and over again into the trunks of surrounding trees, sending splinters of shattered wood flying in all directions. He kicked at saplings until he hit one thick enough it sent a painful shock wave up his leg.

He was in 800 BC with no idea how long he would be stuck here, but he'd be willing to bet it would be a long, long time. That cursed Carpen must have reset his shifter while he'd been unconscious.

He realized he still had that laminated card Rialto gave him. He scrambled to fish it out of his back pocket and then stared blankly.

88 years.

He was going to die here.

Hugh Plantagenet felt defeated for the first time in his life. He sank to the ground, rested his head on his knees, and wept. It was the first time he remembered crying since he was a boy and he wouldn't stop any time soon.

An hour later, Plantagenet tried to pull himself together and gather his bearings. He still couldn't cope with the enormity of it. Was he really stuck here? It just didn't seem real. Were there even any people living in Ohio in 800 BC?

As if in answer to his mental wondering, something moved in the bushes to his right, and whatever it was, it wasn't small.

He briefly considered fleeing to the left, but then he saw something else had disturbed the vegetation in that direction. A moment later, an American Indian stepped from behind a tree directly in front of him, and two others emerged from the bushes on either side.

All three were naked except for a bone-colored cloth wrapped around their loins which made them look like old pictures he'd seen of Egyptian slaves. They were tattooed extensively over the chests and arms, and their hair was pulled back into conical, tee-pee shaped formations on the top of their heads. Long pony tails wrapped in bleached animal skin flowed up and then hung down like animal tails reaching the nape of their necks.

Grizzly bear claws dangled at the tops of their thighs, hung from the cloth wrapping their hips. Golden colored metallic discs encircled their knees and elbows, held together by rawhide straps, and the leader had a larger gold disc in the center of his chest.

Plantagenet's eyes passed over all these details, however, and instead riveted upon the large long bows held in all their hands — and the quivers overflowing with arrows slung across their backs. Each hip also sported a large flint knife and a nasty-looking war club.

Plantagenet raised a hand in a plea for mercy while his other scrambled behind his back for the gun he'd stuffed in his waistband. It wasn't there.

He cursed again. Carpen must have taken it.

"Wait...who are you? What can I..."

The lead Indian swooped his war club up and slammed it into the side of Plantagenet's skull. Amidst the sudden stars swimming in his vision, Hugh collapsed to the ground, stunned. He couldn't seem to move his arms or his legs. His mouth opened and closed like a fish out of water, gasping for the right word that would never be understood by these men.

He felt someone yank his arms forward and then one of the Indians wrapped a strong piece of rawhide around his wrists like primitive handcuffs. Once they'd secured him, he was jerked to his feet and shoved toward the bushes.

It was the beginning of a long march. A long march to their home village in what would someday be called southern Ohio.

And so, eight hundred years before the birth of Christ, Hugh Plantagenet, former slave master, became a slave himself.

Chapter 53

So maybe you could walk with me a while
And maybe I could rest beneath your smile

"Long Trip Alone"

~ Dierks Bentley

The way the wind moved among the tall grasses, bowing them back and forth in rolling waves, returned him emotionally to the Hungarian fields where he'd first watched the sun dance upon her hair.

Mark craned his neck back to see her face. Savannah was beautiful. He never tired of the delicate lines along her jaw. Her little ears, her high cheekbones highlighted by just a hint of rose coloring. Lying here with his head in her lap brought him a peace he hadn't felt in a long time...perhaps he'd never felt such a peace before.

She stroked her fingers along the sides of his head through his short hair. Between that and the feel of the breeze across his face, it was difficult to keep his eyes open.

On their first date, after dinner, he'd taken her to some romantic comedy at the theater, but he couldn't remember the name of it to save his life. He'd been too engrossed with stealing glances her way to pay much attention to the plot.

It was like something pent up had been released deep within his heart. She had freed up something down in his core, something so fundamental it still shocked him how much lightness of being he now had. It was as if he'd never really been able to love before.

His marriage to Kelly had been a good one. He'd loved her, he knew that. He still felt a strong affection for her. But something basic had been missing when they lost their kids. Whatever it was that allowed a couple to endure such a tragedy and come out the other side stronger, they had not had. And they hadn't made it.

Now, he understood that the loss of his marriage had torn a hole in him, leaving him so lonely that when he'd found Laura, he'd instantly fallen head over heels for her. He'd thought it was love at the time, but now he saw more clearly and realized it had just been physical infatuation stoked by loneliness.

His attraction to Abigail had been another subconscious attempt to fill a need he didn't know he had. Her purity, her inherent goodness stood in such sharp contrast to his own unrecognized self-condemnation, that he'd mistaken his desire for that purity for a desire for her. She was good, and that goodness is what he'd wanted for himself. She'd seen and understood this and wisely deflected his muted advances.

But now, it was real. There was a connection between him and Savannah that he'd never experienced before. She made him feel whole.

Each date had been more amazing than the one before. How could he have overlooked her for so long? He was still kicking himself for being so stupid. Maybe he'd just felt so bad about himself for so long that he hadn't allowed himself to consider someone as wonderful as her.

Over the past weeks, he'd taken her on many of the typical dates that new couples do, but they'd had a few unconventional ones as well. Shifting her back so she could attend the opening nights of both *Gone with the Wind* and *Casablanca* had been a big hit. Savannah loved history like nothing else.

On their seventh date, he'd shifted her back to Times Square on August 14, 1945, the day they announced WWII was over, so Savannah could see in person the iconic couple that had been pictured in *Life* magazine, live. Of course, after the sailor dipped the nurse in the famous extended kiss, Mark had followed it up with a long kiss of his own, leaving Savannah red-cheeked.

Today was their first picnic. He'd chosen this field because just over the ridge was a spectacular view that he wanted to surprise her with later.

Her lilac summer dress matched the pockets of purple wild flowers popping up here and there throughout the field, though that was pure coincidence. He'd picked several and given them too her. Laughing, she'd tucked one behind her ear and practically skipped over to the tree where they now lay.

For lunch, she'd packed them ham and Swiss on French baguettes, potato salad, fresh grapes, and strawberry shortcake to top it all off. Full of good food and a spirit at peace, Mark gazed upon the wisps of white puffs lazily crossing the summer sky, enjoying the silence and the soothing feel of her fingers in his hair.

"Mark?"

"Yes," he replied sleepily.

"Tell me about Jesus. What was He like?"

He thought before answering.

"It's hard to put into words. He truly was as amazing as everybody says. I saw him heal people with my own eyes. I mean cripples, beggars, the dirty forgotten of any city. He'd touch them and a new light would come into their eyes. Their broken bodies would straighten, or the blind could suddenly see. It was amazing..." He trailed off.

"I told you about Laura. He just touched her. Then, she started crying and her shifter slid off her wrist. With all of our modern expertise and understanding of physics, Bobby Prescott still hasn't found a way to get a shifter off of someone's wrist short of cutting their hand off. Yet Jesus did it with just a touch."

"So, who do you think He was?"

"The Son of God, just like they say. God in the form of a man. There's no doubt."

"Did you get your answers?"

He nodded and a lump formed in his throat. "When I looked into His eyes...it was like waves of compassion passed into me with just that one look. I saw He knew me, knew my heart.

"He showed me Daniel and Brittany. I saw them in Heaven..." A tear spilled over. Mark quickly wiped it away. "I don't know how to explain it, but I know they are happy now — and at peace, probably more than they ever would have been on earth. It may sound corny, but when I saw them...it was just so real. I know it's real. I know they're okay.

"He showed me other things too. I saw flashes of all the people we'd helped and the things we'd changed for the better with these shifters. Somehow, He put a new understanding in my heart. I don't know why I couldn't see it before. It was like I was blind or something, but now it's so clear."

"What did He show you?"

"That my kids were in their real home with Him now and that if He hadn't taken them when He did, I never would have found the shifter and we never would have helped all the people we have. I realize now He gave me a number of great years with them and that was His blessing. Dwelling on the years we're apart isn't good. I'll be with them again someday, and then, it will be forever."

"So, you're finished grieving?"

"No, not really." He choked up. "It's...ah...it's still hard for all that head knowledge to settle in deep. Plus, I...ah...I...I saw Him die. It was just like the Bible says. It was horrible. To see the pain He was in, to know how much He loved...and what we did to Him...to watch Him, to know He was dying to pay for my sins. He sacrificed himself for me. How can I not sacrifice a few years with my kids for Him?"

"You've changed, Mark."

"You already knew all that, didn't you?"

"Well, I could tell you were different. You've been much softer ever since you got back."

"No...I mean, you knew all the things He showed me before I ever went, didn't you?"

"I'd guessed as much."

"You've always been a believer?"

"Since I was a kid."

"Why didn't you tell me before?"

"You weren't in a place where you were ready to hear it. Plus, I knew you'd find your way at some point."

"How could you be so patient?"

"I don't know," she whispered, " I just knew I should be."

They fell silent, enjoying the afternoon, neither wanting it to end.

He knew it was time. He'd been waiting his whole life for this day, but he hadn't even realized it until now.

"Savannah?"

"Yes?"

"Come with me." Mark reluctantly stood. "I want to show you something."

"What is it?"

She followed him to her feet. He took her hand and led her across the field toward the long ridge at its far side. The summer grass swept at their calves like thousands of tiny fingers, rustling dry like continuous, faint applause.

When they reached the top of the ridge, she gasped.

"I wanted you to see this," he said.

"It's so beautiful."

The ridge where they stood dropped off sharply turning into a deep valley that ran out from its base until it reached the ocean. A ways away, waves crashed onto the beach, their faint roar bounding in rhythms like a distant orchestra. Several crystalline creeks bubbled their way through the grassy valley floor until they emptied into the sea.

"I thought you'd like it."

She turned to him and smiled.

To her surprise, Mark dropped down on one knee. He held a black jewelry box in his right hand. He would never forget this moment, how beautiful she looked with the sun in her hair like ribbons of gold.

"Savannah, will you marry me?"

Her mouth fell open. He'd thought she must have guessed this was coming, but maybe not today. He had caught her off guard. Little butterflies took wing in his gut at the possibility she might say no.

She took the black box from his hand and opened it.

Inside, was a watch set in silken padding like any other watch. A watch with an all-too-familiar design. A shifter.

She removed it and turned it over, examining its shape.

His butterflies were flying in a furious frenzy now. He felt queasy.

Savannah understood what this watch meant, why Mark had felt the need to propose with it instead of a ring. For someone to truly be Mark's life partner, they needed to be able to shift with him, to live the life he lived.

She had wondered before what it would be like to have a shifter like them, but only in a fleeting way. Now, she considered the full responsibility taking a device like this would mean. The risks, the commitment, the sacrifice. Was it worth the cost?

She knew what her decision was as soon as she asked the question.

A tear broke rank and spilled onto her cheek. It was followed by an enormous smile.

"Yes, Mark." She nodded vigorously and the tears became a flood of happiness.

Mark jumped to his feet and pulled her tight against him, wrapping her in the best embrace of his life.

He stepped back and took the shifter. She held out her hand.

He started to put it on, but stopped.

"Are you sure, Savannah?" He looked into her eyes.

"Yes, Mark, yes." She wiped a tear of his own from his cheek with the back of her hand.

He slipped it over her hand and onto her wrist. It immediately began to whir as it self-constricted until it was snug against her skin. She was committed now.

"I did bring this as well," he said. He pulled another jewelry box from his pocket, a slightly smaller one.

She opened it and a glistening solitaire diamond sparkled back at her. It was a beautiful stone in a delicate gold setting. Very high quality, but not too gaudy. He could afford to buy her the moon, but he'd known she wouldn't have liked anything too flashy. It was perfect.

She smiled and held out her hand again. "And for a minute there, I thought you'd lost your romantic streak."

He laughed. "What? The view wasn't enough?" He slipped the ring on her finger and it felt like something essential was now complete.

"Of course it was." She threw her arms around his neck and they held each for a long time, enjoying the rhythms of the wind.

Chapter 54

Hey love, is that the name
you're meant to have for me to call?

"Gravity"

~ Vienna Teng

"Congratulations, you two!" Ty slapped Mark on the back and hugged Savannah.

"I always knew this was coming," Hardy said.

Mark laughed. "What do you mean you always knew. How could you know if we didn't know?"

"Oh, come on, man. It was so obvious."

"What are you talking about?"

"Yeah, it kind of was," Ty agreed, nodding.

Savannah blushed. Mark could only shake his head.

"Wow," Ty whistled loudly. "Look at this, Hardy," he said, taking Savannah's wrist and turning it for Hardy to see.

"A shifter? Are you kidding? Is that real?"

She blushed harder.

"Yes, it is," Mark answered. "It's the one I brought back from Israel."

"You mean it's the one that fell off Laur..."

"Geez, man," Mark interrupted, "You don't have to..."

"It's okay," Savannah laughed. "I know..."

Ty turned serious. "Did he make you put that on? I swear if he did, I'll..."

"No," She laughed even harder. "I put it on of my own free will. I know what I'm getting into."

Ty turned to Mark. "So, what is she going to do? Help us with our missions?"

He looked at his new fiancée. "Well, we haven't really talked about it yet, but I guess so. I don't want her going on any of the dangerous ones though, okay?"

"Um...let's make that a 'no' on both counts," she said.

"What do you mean?"

"I'll help you sometimes if you need me of course, but I had something else in mind."

"What exactly?"

"I want to use my shifter to liberate women and girls that have been sold into slavery. I want to fight sex trafficking."

Mark blinked several times. Ty and Hardy looked at each other, eyebrows raised.

"Uh...we haven't talked about this," Mark said.

"You didn't say *how* I had to use my shifter when you gave it to me, did you?"

"Well, no. But it's..."

"And you guys will be there for me if I ever get into trouble, right?"

"Yes, but..."

"Then, it's settled. That's what I want to do."

Mark stared at her, processing.

"Okay. Ty, Hardy, she can count on us being there if she gets in a pinch, right?"

"Sure."

"Absolutely."

"Then it's settled."

"All right!" Ty clapped his hands and got some Cokes out of the fridge which he began tossing to each of the others. "So, when's the wedding?"

"We haven't really set a date yet," Mark said.

"Why wait? Why don't you just hire a wedding planner and we all shift forward six months to the day of the big event?"

Mark and Savannah looked at each other.

"Uh..."

"Sounds fine to me," Savannah said.

"Let's do it then!"

They all started talking at the same time.

"Hey, what about you and Abbie?" Ty asked. "Are you guys getting married any time soon?"

"Two weeks."

"Wow, congratulations to you too!"

"What about a double wedding?" Savannah suggested.

"I'll ask her," Hardy replied, "But she wants her friends and family to be there. As much as she loves you guys, I think she'll want to have it in her village back then."

"So, what about you, Ty? Any prospects?"

"I might have someone in mind."

"Well, I'll be," Mark said. "This is just like the Love Boat."

***

The three of them spent the next few weeks doing what they could to train Savannah for what she wanted to do. They clucked over her like a gaggle of worried hens until she finally pushed them off, stating that she was more than ready.

She was not planning to confront the pimps. She would simply identify a location where trafficking victims were being held, and then she would shift inside their makeshift prison and shift back out with the girls in tow. In most cases, the girls would be all gone before the pimps were any wiser.

She hadn't wanted to carry a gun, but after ceaseless pressing by Mark, she finally agreed to take a small .22 in a hidden holster — just in case.

She wanted to jump in feet first in some difficult place like Mexico, but Mark wouldn't let her. He insisted she get started in easier cities like Atlanta and Denver, which she agreed to temporarily.

And so far, she'd had great success. To date, she'd successfully liberated over 21 girls without a single confrontation.

Mark was on a mission of a different sort right now. Ever since he'd returned from Israel, he couldn't put Kelly, his ex-wife, out of his mind. She needed to know what he knew, that Daniel and Brittany were okay.

He had not contacted Kelly since they'd divorced. He'd shifted back from time to time to watch her from afar, during years when they'd still been married. It had been a masochistic exercise of his back then, something he did to stoke the pain and basically torture himself needlessly. It had seemed like such a good idea at the time.

After the divorce, however, he'd purposefully never tried to find her. Knowing where she was or what she was doing, or worse, to know that she was doing just fine, had been a possibility he wanted to avoid. The idea of knowing where she was today had seemed like it would somehow shatter the frozen memories he'd guarded of their life before the tragedy as if they were fragile porcelain collectibles.

Now that unhealthy spirit had left him, he was no longer bound by such subconscious manacles. He found himself wanting to know how she was, that she was okay.

Finding her had not been difficult at all. She'd gone back to work as a teacher and he was happy to see she'd become quite successful. She'd dedicated herself to her work so much that the school board had promoted her to principal within a couple of years. She was a rising star among her colleagues and had received commendation after commendation.

He'd gone to her school, but the receptionist informed him she'd been at home with a cold for the past two days.

So, he went to her house, but when she opened the door, he was shocked by her state. For a moment, he didn't even recognize this woman who had been his wife. It was definitely Kelly, though new lines in her face showed she'd aged some since he'd last seen her. This woman who had always taken such care to look her best and well-groomed, greeted him with no make-up and mussed hair that was so tangled in several spots it looked like a lion's mane.

Her eyes opened wide when she realized it was him. Hastily, she ran her hand through her hair and tried to straighten it out, though unsuccessfully. Red, puffy eyes betrayed any attempt to smile weakly. She'd been crying all day, probably for two days. Since today was Tuesday, probably all weekend too.

"Mark?" She tried regain her composure, but couldn't quite muster the energy and her attempt at a smile faded. "What are you doing here?"

"May I come in, Kelly?"

She hesitated, then finally stepped aside, motioning for him to enter.

The house looked like it hadn't been cleaned in months. Crumpled Kleenex littered the end tables in the living room and spilled over onto the couch and floor. She took a seat in a clear spot on the sofa. Mark took a chair across from her.

"Why are you here, Mark?"

How to begin?

"I...uh...I felt like I needed to see you."

"Why? Did someone tell you I was falling apart?" She waved at the piles of magazines and Kleenex.

"No, actually..."

"Why then? I haven't seen you since the divorce."

"I know." He hesitated. He couldn't tell her about the shifters and everything he'd been through. First of all, it would take too long and she would never believe it, not without him taking her on several shifts, which she definitely was not in the mood to do. Second, it wouldn't help, if anything it would just open new questions for her instead of the resolution he hoped to deliver.

"Kelly, I had a dream."

Instantly, the tears burst forth like waters bursting uncontrollably through a dam. Her shoulders shook with the depth of her grief. He knew she was crying for them. He'd felt what she was letting out for a long time.

"Kelly..."

He waited until she'd calmed enough she could focus. She was on the verge of breaking down again at any minute.

"Kelly, I thought you were doing okay?"

"That's what everybody thinks," she choked out. "I've put up a very good image. I even believed it myself."

"So what happened?"

"Saturday night, I had a dream too. I know what you're going to tell me."

What? For a panicked second, he checked her wrists for a shifter, wondering if God had taken her down the same path as he, but they were bare.

"Was your dream about Daniel and Brittany?"

"Yes. I saw them, clear as day. They were in Heaven, playing, and they were happy. So happy."

"Why are you crying then?"

"Because I didn't believe it. I thought it was just something my mind had made up to ease the grief. Instead, it released the floodgates." She paused. "Did you have the same dream then?"

He nodded.

She began to cry again, but this time the tears seemed to be more of relief in nature than grief.

"Kelly...I can't really explain how I know...it'd be too long a story, but God has made it clear to me that Daniel and Brittany are okay and they're happy. They're waiting for us — at the right time. In His time."

"God?"

"I know it sounds weird coming from my mouth, but it was definitely God who gave us these dreams. Trust me."

"Why did He have to take them then?" Her crying intensified.

"That's what faith is, Kelly. Trusting that He has very good reasons, even when we can't see them."

"How did you get to be the expert on faith?"

"Like I said, long story. I can't give you the answers you're looking for, but I know He can. He might take a while, but some day He will. I know in my case, I was angry at Him for a very long time. Very angry. I can't explain it to you, but He showed me why. At least the why that made sense for me. He's probably got another why for you."

Slowly, the sobs lessened and finally dried up. She grabbed some clean tissues and wiped at her eyes and blew her nose.

"Ha, ha. Very attractive, huh?" she said.

"Is that really important right now?"

"No, I guess not. I don't want you to remember me like this."

"I won't. I'll remember you as you were when we were married. Beautiful and alive. You'll be that way again."

"Promise?"

"Believe me, I will. I'll always remember you as we were."

Her eyes were a little brighter, her shoulders a little lighter. "I believe you Mark, I do. I don't understand it, but I do. Now, I know my dream was real and they're okay. I wouldn't have if you hadn't come. Thank you."

"It's nothing. I thought you needed to hear it." He stood.

She grabbed his hand. "Mark? I'm sorry for the way things ended."

"I know. It wasn't a good thing...but it was also part of the plan, just like our kids."

Her eyes welled again, but she nodded, holding the tears inside this time. "I understand."

"Are you going to be okay?" he asked.

"Yes...I'll be okay now. Thank you. You?"

"Yes, I'm doing much better now."

She stood to walk him out. He rested his hand on top of her forehead and then brought it down to her ear. He kissed her lightly on the forehead and said good-bye.

He'd check on her from time to time to make sure she was okay, but this was finally a real good-bye.

***

Alexander Rialto was steamed and he didn't have anybody he could take it out on. He sensed Torino and Graves were about fed up with his abuses and he knew he had to let up on them a little if he didn't want an open rebellion.

After Laura's and Cook's disappearance, they'd pulled out all the stops to find out what had happened to them by tracking their shifters. Then, Plantagenet had also disappeared, which of course also had to be the work of Mark Carpen. Their search now intensified to the point of being frenzied. Torino and Graves could sense as well as he that Carpen and his friends were picking them off one by one.

So far, they knew Carpen had Laura's shifter, but the tracking signal had jumped around after he'd left the airport and they hadn't been able to locate it since. Since it was not stationary in one place like De Cleary's had been, they had no idea which signal in which year to follow. For the moment, they were stymied on that one.

They'd found Cook's shifter, a half-mile off the Azores Islands in the middle of the Atlantic. The tracking device's signal had been weakened by the depth of the water, so Rialto's resident physicist, Stanley Irvine, had to up the sensitivity of the receiver just to detect it. Then, the ocean floor had been so deep there they'd had to take a submarine down several hundred feet to recover it. Once below, they'd had to scoop up every small rock within the limited radius indicated by the tracking device and bring them to the surface. There had been no sign of Cook's body, of course. Carpen had obviously shifted Cook from the plane into the past.

Back on the surface, the tracking signal revealed which rock was the right one and they began chipping off the barnacles encrusting the device. Amazingly, when they were done, it looked good as new. It was as if nothing could tarnish its metal.

He was furious. Furious that Mark had gotten the jump on them and been able to eliminate his entire advantage of superior numbers in such short order.

They'd already found Plantagenet's shifter buried in the side of a hill in southern Ohio, which eliminated any possibility he'd skipped out on Rialto. That meant Carpen had successfully taken him out as well. Who knew how far back Carpen had sent him?

Rialto's ankle tingled where his second shifter gripped it, the one he'd taken from DeCleary's tomb. It gave him the shivers to think it was the only thing preventing a similar fate from befalling him. If Carpen sent him back like that, Rialto would be able to use his ankle shifter to return, but then both watches would be shut down for the rest of his life — which was the same as not having them.

No, he had to keep Carpen away.

Or did he? Having two shifters gave him an advantage. Carpen could only shift 6 times before shutting down, but he could do 12...that could definitely work in his favor.

Now that he had Cook and Plantagenet's shifters back in hand, he was very tempted to keep a third one for himself, or to go and recruit somebody else to fill their shoes, but the fabric of the space-time continuum wouldn't let him. He still had to take Plantagenet's device back to recruit Cook, and then he had to take Cook's device to recruit Laura Kingsley.

Originally, he had decided not to, but then he had suddenly found much of the power structure he'd built undone — and much of what had been in his bank accounts gone. The simple reason was that his recruits had played a big role in building his invisible empire and so any decision he took to not recruit them resulted in parts of his empire not being built.

The bald-faced truth was that as much as he thought Cook was a buffoon, Rialto was tied to the sailor now for eternity. He had to recruit him, or Rialto would hurt himself. And while he was fairly indifferent about Plantagenet versus some other hate-filled mongrel, the same held true in that case. It also meant that his ability to recruit more workers had come to an end with Randolph DeCleary because Rialto had put DeCleary's shifter on his ankle. He couldn't give it to anyone else now.

He was stuck. And that infuriated him more than anything.

Even killing Ty and Hardy would not yield new shifters since he'd already killed them in the future and their shifters had served as the seeds of his recruiting efforts. Basically, Ty's was the one on his wrist, and Hardy's was now on his ankle.

The only way he could truly begin to rebuild was through new recruits, and the only shifter left he could use for that was the one on Mark Carpen's wrist. He had to kill Carpen to recover from the damage that had been done.

Even though he had not recovered Laura's shifter yet, he knew he would at some point. If that weren't going to happen, then DeCleary's shifter would have disappeared from his ankle a long time ago.

He decided for now that he would keep Torino and Graves busy building his power base within the elitist structures of America and Western Europe. They would all keep trying to locate Carpen, but for the time being, his entire focus would be on finding Laura's shifter. Her shifter represented his security, which was more important than anything.

Chapter 55

Savannah studied the run-down building across the street. Its faded purple paint was peeling, revealing truth — a bare, ugly concrete block wall beneath. A neon sign in a grimy window flashed "Girls, Girls, Girls."

She still didn't understand how men could visit such a place for pleasure. It screamed disease and filth and disgust. Yet, she knew they did.

She was here because Toledo, Ohio was rated the fourth worst city for human trafficking in the United States and she'd gotten a reliable tip about this establishment. Ostensibly, it was nothing more than a seedy bar in a bad part of town, featuring watered-down whiskey and women past their prime who danced for desperate men. The cops knew that behind the bar were rooms where more went on than dancing for a price, but they did nothing as the women involved were adults and there voluntarily, at least, so they said. Savannah knew it was never voluntary, sometimes the master was a pimp, sometimes it was drugs, but it was never voluntary.

Most likely a few of the cops were clients. She had run into that several times already.

But what the cops didn't know, or perhaps they did but wouldn't admit it, was there was another hallway behind those rooms which led to a locked door that opened into a forgotten warehouse. In the front of that abandoned facility were rows of stalls that afforded barely any privacy for the twelve to fourteen year-old employees working against their will.

Every time she thought about it, her throat constricted in sympathetic terror.

She'd collected all the evidence she needed for her purposes. Mark had given her infrared imaging scopes, which had helped her determine where exactly the girls were kept during the day, which is when she would go in.

She knew from public records that these properties had been built in the early 1950's. They'd once housed a paper company and before that there had been an empty field here.

Savannah shifted herself back to 1955 and walked into the front office of the paper company. She finagled her way past the secretary and into the warehouse where she managed to get alone for a minute so she could orient herself in the right spot.

Then, she shifted forward to her target time and landed in a dilapidated room devoid of paint or decor of any kind — save one single immature coloring drawn in crayon and taped to the wall. It was of a broken heart.

Though it was daylight outside, the room was steeped in prohibitive darkness, except for the muted wash of red light emanating from a cheap lamp plugged into a wall socket. Seven girls were scattered across the floor, some trying to sleep on thin, dirty mattresses, a couple whispering to each other in a corner.

Those two turned their attention her way immediately upon hearing the static hiss of her shift. They reared back in fear and she knew she had to get them first before they inadvertently alerted their pimp, not realizing she was there to help.

The girls were small enough she could take two at a time, which she did whenever she could. She moved quickly and just as one was about to scream, grabbed both by the wrist and shifted back to 1952, before the paper company was built.

Now, the girls were half-standing, half-kneeling in an empty field with her, screaming, but suddenly aware their setting had magically and dramatically changed in front of their eyes. The result was a gradual, astonished dying off of their cries of alarm.

She let go of their arms and stepped back. Then, she shifted forward again, disappearing before their eyes. In a few seconds, she'd returned with her hands resting on the backs of two more sleeping girls. That was all she could do before her shifter would shut down, so it was enough for today.

A nondescript white van pulled up to the curb and a couple of smiling nurses got out. They shuffled the confused girls to the van who were too shocked to resist. The van would take them to an aftercare facility.

In every city Savannah targeted, Mark set up accounts for her filled with millions of dollars that she used to establish, train and fund aftercare facilities that could handle these special kind of victims. These centers were equipped to care for and nurture victims of trafficking safely back to health. Once the girls had made significant progress in their physical, emotional, and spiritual healing, which sometimes could take a year or more, her centers would place them in a loving home where they could be adopted.

Mark's money facilitated all this, but she had studied the needs of these victims before when she'd worked with several anti-trafficking ministries.

She would leave them back here in the early 1950's where they would be forever out of the clutches of their perpetrators. Who knew? Maybe the time shock would help them relegate their previous life to the realm of fantasy. Some had family back in modern times, most did not. Those who did have family, and actually wanted to go back, she would help do so after the restoration process.

She would sleep in a motel tonight. Tomorrow, the van would meet her here in this field again, at the same time, and she'd have three more girls for them. In the future, the pimp would keep getting new girls to replace the lost ones, so Savannah would keep going back to rescue them, and the van would keep meeting her here in this field.

Eventually, the pimp would give up and change locations or be spooked by the female ghost that kept disappearing with his slaves. If he changed locations, she'd simply follow and see where he went.

She was fully aware she had a fatal flaw in her plan. There was an endless supply of runaways and other young girls available to these pimps, and as long as nothing happened to them, they would keep on abusing them.

She needed to talk to Mark about a possible solution. It was definitely not her style to go in blasting away with guns like Mark and Ty and Hardy did, but she needed to stop the pimps somehow.

For now, she would just keep rescuing girls. She'd figure out the rest later.

*****

The Toledo warehouse worked itself out after all was said and done. The head pimp's name was Zhi Chen and he apparently belonged to some branch of the Chinese mafia because after Savannah liberated the first group of girls, he was visited by a group of unpleasant-looking, wealthy Chinese businessmen.

She discovered that Chen's boss was a well-known local businessman by the name of Hong Liu. It was amazing what bartenders would let slip to an innocent young woman who didn't look like she could hurt a fly. Especially when they were trying to impress her.

It didn't look to her that Chen had done a very good job of

convincing his superiors that he didn't know how the girls had gotten away because when he appeared in the doorway as they left, his face was battered and bruised.

She was surprised to see a Chinese network behind this place, considering the girls had been a wide variety of nationalities. Sure, several were of Chinese origin, but just as many were Filipino, Hispanic, or even White runaways from the countryside.

When Savannah removed a second group of girls the following night, Hong Liu's patience with his underling apparently came to an end. She observed Chen hastily packing his bags and other belongings into the back of an SUV the next day, but Liu's henchmen showed up before he could escape. They shoved him back inside the building and he didn't come out again. They set the warehouse on fire (Savannah shifted in to make sure no other girls were trapped inside) and then drove off in Chen's car.

This sparked an idea.

She had already identified several other establishments around town run and managed by the Chinese mafia. So, she used her shifter to free the girls from their oppressors in those locations, and in each instance, she painted a big, bold symbol in black paint on all four walls where the girls had been held.

It was the number four. The Chinese could be very super-stitious about the number four, believing it was an omen of bad luck and could portend death or misfortune. Many avoided it as much as possible. The color black was also bad in their eyes.

After she raided two more brothels, Hong Liu suddenly disappeared from the social scene. A new man, Hui Woh, showed up to replace him as head of all his legitimate businesses. Liu had apparently been permanently recalled by his superiors for failure to manage the unsettling crisis.

She continued the raids and heard through the grapevine the Chinese were striking out randomly at the Russian and Colombian mafias since they couldn't identify who was behind it. The ghost stories were getting to them though. Inevitably, a few witnessed her coming and going, and though their stories were not believed, the seed of doubt had been planted. That and the black number fours painted on every wall eventually drove the Chinese mafia out of Toledo, Ohio and the trafficking problem virtually ceased.

The powers that be back home in mainland China had decided Toledo was not worth the trouble or the destruction of morale among their employees. They would just move their operations to a new city.

But she would follow. Eventually, maybe they'd give up on the United States all together. For now, a city freed from the scourge of trafficking was victory enough.

***

"What is it, Anton?"

Anton Gavrikov rubbed his hands together in frustration. He didn't enjoy being subservient to this man, but he had to. He feared no man, but Alexander Rialto had powers he couldn't hope to overcome. Thankfully, Rialto hadn't asked for more than a 20% cut of his enterprises' profits and a random favor every now and then.

"Someone is stealing our girls in Las Vegas."

"Your girls, Anton. Your girls. I am just your consultant."

Gavrikov pursed his lips. "Well, someone is stealing *my* girls," he said through gritted teeth, "And it's going to impact *our* profits."

"Why are you bothering me with this? Why don't you just replace them? Probably one of those anti-human trafficking organizations."

"It's not. My men say it's a ghost doing it."

Rialto almost spewed his drink in laughter. "A ghost? That's a good one, Anton." He turned serious. "If this is some scheme to try and get out of paying me my..."

"It's not." Gavrikov held up a DVD. "I have it on video. May I?" He pointed to Rialto's entertainment center.

Rialto waved flippantly as if to say go ahead and Gavrikov popped the DVD in the player.

A grainy image of a dingy room appeared on the screen. Seven or eight girls were visible laying around the room on various cots or mattresses strewn on the floor. After a few seconds, a woman appeared out of nowhere in the middle of the room, pulled two of the girls to herself and then disappeared along with the girls like a phantom.

Rialto sat up straight and put down his cup.

A second later, the woman reappeared without the girls and did it again taking two each time. This repeated until the room was empty and then the "ghost" did not return.

Rialto stood and moved closer to the screen.

"Whoever it is has powers like you," Gavrikov said. "*That* is why I'm bothering *you* with this."

Rialto pressed his face closer and replayed the short video several times. He could see a thick grey band on the woman's wrist that had to be a shifter, but who was she? It wasn't Laura. He knew Laura's shape, her look. This woman was shorter, more slender, and her hair was a light dirty blonde — a natural color Laura Kingsley never would have accepted.

As far as he knew, there were only three shifters, those worn by Mark Carpen, Ty Jennings, and Hardy Phillips. In the future, Rialto would kill both Ty and Hardy and take their watches. He had used one for himself and given the second to Torino. Then, he'd traveled to Torino's future and killed him, taken his shifter off his wrist and given it to his second recruit, Stanley Graves. Rialto had continued the process, recruiting more and more soldiers into his army until Carpen had sent his last recruit, Randolph DeCleary three thousand years into the past, locking the knight there forever.

This had scared Rialto enough that when they had recovered DeCleary's shifter from his tomb, Rialto had put it on his ankle so Carpen couldn't do the same thing to him.

But then, Carpen had somehow gotten Laura's shifter. She had been his second-to-last recruit, the one right before DeCleary.

If he didn't get Laura's shifter back, he'd never be able to recruit DeCleary, which meant the ankle shifter would disappear from off his leg — which would leave him vulnerable to Carpen. He had to get Laura's shifter back from Carpen, and whoever this woman was on the video, she probably had it.

Who was she?

He tilted his head from side to side like a parrot considering a puzzle. There was a quick way to find out. He was going to Vegas.

Chapter 56

The girls had been ordered to lie down and stay still as if asleep. Rialto had checked the time stamp on the video and knew exactly what time the woman would shift in. He also used the recording to position himself behind the spot where she would appear in the next few minutes.

The idea that this woman's shifter could be a new shifter, one not associated with Carpen, excited him to no end. He thought it unlikely, but what if there were other time shifters out there? Groups of people doing what he did. Come to think of it, that might not be such a good thing after all. He wouldn't be able to control people as well if he had more opposition. His only power over others was the uniqueness of his shifter.

Still, something about this whole thing gnawed at his gut, telling him one way or the other, Carpen was involved.

***

Savannah readied herself for the shift. No matter how many times she did it, Mark had warned her to always be vigilant. Getting into a routine meant forgetting the ever imminent danger coiled in the corner and ready to strike as soon as you got sloppy or let your guard down.

Mark had also taught her to use the "peer" function on her watch before committing to the actual shift whenever she could. The "peer" function was something Mark had accidentally discovered the shifters could do. If you depressed the red button slightly without letting it make full contact, a window to the past would open, allowing the user to see into the target time before actually going there. It really was an indispensable function for avoiding nasty surprises. The only downside was it only seemed to work for target times that were within twenty years in the past. Bobby Prescott theorized it had something to do with the amount of power required to perform the function, but the feature remained curious since moving a person through time seemed like it would require more energy than just seeing through time.

This particular building had been vacant until recently when the current bar/brothel had moved in, so she was lucky in that regard.

She depressed the shift button, careful not to push it down all the way. A large "window" with nebulous borders appeared. She could see the girls lying on the filthy slabs their masters called beds. Slowly, Savannah turned around 360 degrees to sweep the entire room with her time window.

She gasped. The face of a man came into view right behind where she would have shifted in. His menacing expression was terrifying. She shuddered involuntarily as recognition solidified. Alexander Rialto.

She let the button up and dropped her arm. There would be no shift today.

Somehow, Alexander Rialto was affiliated with this brothel. That didn't surprise her as far as his character went, but how did he know she'd be here? Had rumors of the ghost woman reached him?

She needed to get back to Mark and regroup.

***

The time for her arrival passed and the woman did not appear. Rialto cursed and one of the girls pretending to be asleep on the floor winced in fear.

Whoever she was, she'd been tipped off. On a hunch, he picked up his cell phone.

"Torino," The assassin answered gruffly.

"Check our satellite tracking records and tell me if Laura's shifter has been at this address since we put it in the sky." He gave Torino the coordinates.

"Hold on."

It was a long shot. He was just guessing this woman might have Laura's shifter. And even if she did, if she'd been shifting into this room from some time before the 1980's, his satellite wouldn't have been around before then to record the signal.

After a few minutes, Torino came back to the phone.

"Yeah. It shows her at that location on June 3rd 1997. Between 3:29 and 3:37 PM."

"Excellent."

***

She heard the static hiss behind her but didn't have time to react before he'd grabbed her by the wrist. Panicked, Savannah hit her shifter to escape his grasp.

She felt the twisting sensation of the shift, but was dismayed when the pressure of his hand on her did not release. She jerked her wrist back and forth, trying to rip it free from his grip. She was in the brothel now. The girls were sitting up, staring wide-eyed at the people popping in and out of their reality.

He would not let go no matter what she did. His glare was hate-filled and determined.

She went to shift again, hoping to escape.

"Don't bother," he sneered. "I'll just go along for the ride again."

She gasped.

"What do you want?" she asked.

"You know what I want. Who are you?"

She pressed her lips together tightly in silent defiance.

His eyes lit up. "Oooh, I *do* know you. You're Carpen's secretary. Savannah something, right?"

She glanced away and said nothing.

He saw the ring on her finger and smiled even bigger. "Aha! Maybe you're a little more than just his secretary now, huh? Wow. Looks like I've got myself quite a weapon now, don't I?"

She shot daggers at him with her eyes.

"He'll stop you. You know that, don't you?" she said.

He swung a fist at her head. Electric bolts shot through her mind and then the blackness came.

***

Take the very breath you gave me, take the heart from my chest...
Take me out of this world, God, please don't take the girl

"Don't Take the Girl"

~ Tim McGraw

Mark watched as Rialto dragged Savannah from the dilapidated building and his blood boiled. It was all he could do to keep himself from running down there and tearing the man apart, limb by limb.

When Savannah hadn't shown up at their next scheduled meeting, all three men had immediately hopped on the jet. When any one of them failed to show up on time, they knew something was wrong, and with their favorite girl they hadn't wasted a second.

Hardy and Ty continued to warn him off through their comm channel. They'd spotted Torino and Graves set up in multiple sniper nests providing Rialto with cover. This was not a good place for a confrontation. Rialto was already dug-in here.

Still, a feverish anger was distorting his assessment. That was the reason Hardy and Ty had to keep reminding him over and over again of the danger. He was becoming irrational, ready to go off in a flash.

Mark settled his eye onto his rifle scope and depressed the trigger on his small, long-barreled gun. A soft puff followed.

A light projectile sped toward the SUV waiting by the curb. Upon impact, the projectile imbedded a tiny tracking device in the SUV's bumper. A bystander on the ground would have heard a sharp, but soft, *clink* and nothing more.

Rialto certainly hadn't noticed. He hauled Savannah toward the vehicle with the help of some other man Mark didn't know. She was unconscious and he'd put some kind of thick metal bracelet over her shifter so she couldn't escape. Rialto stuffed her into the back of the car and then got in the driver's seat himself. The other man went back into the brothel.

"Do we have the signal?" Mark asked over his comm.

"Roger that," Ty replied.

Mark packed up his equipment and went back to his own vehicle. Ty relayed the path of the tracker over the phone as Mark drove. They followed it to an abandoned hotel on the far side of town. Rialto's SUV was parked in the back, out of sight from the public.

Hardy reported no sign of Rialto's men around the perimeter and Ty confirmed. They swept again with no results. Thermal imaging showed three figures inside the front lobby. The rest of the building was empty.

Mark ordered Hardy and Ty to remain outside and make sure neither Torino nor Graves showed up to protect Rialto. Then, Mark rushed the building, keeping out of sight from the lobby windows.

Normally he would have approached cautiously, scoping out every angle, but here and now, he threw caution to the wind. He could not, would not allow Rialto one more second than was necessary to be alone with Savannah. Who knew what the fiend planned to do to her.

Even if Mark could go back and erase whatever torture she experienced at Rialto's hands, Mark couldn't stand the thought of even a shadow of a memory of it lingering in her subconscious. Nor would he want to remember it himself.

Mark burst through the glass front doors, pistol drawn, and swept every side of the room. The lobby had once been opulent, by 1960's standards, but it hadn't been in use for years. Thick layers of dust muted the once bright colors, and outdated chandeliers and carpets spoke of much more prosperous times.

Savannah was struggling back to consciousness. Rialto had bound her wrists together, tied the bond to a long rope, and then thrown the long rope up and over the large chandelier in the center of the lobby. By hauling down on the free end of the rope, he'd already hoisted her off the floor and into a limp, semi-standing position. The pain in her arms was shocking her awake.

Rialto intended to hang her from the ceiling by the arms like some animal caught in a trap. Mark's nemesis stood before him firmly, sneering and leering at Mark like a wolf considering its prey. Torino was about ten feet to the right of him, also grim and determined. Neither man reacted when Mark burst in, nor did they draw their weapons. They'd either been expecting him or didn't feel he was a threat.

"Well, well. You are a resourceful, cuss. I'll give you that," Rialto said.

Mark swiveled his gun back and forth between Rialto and Torino. Neither moved to counter.

"Did you think you could keep something like this from me, Rialto?"

Rialto sighed. "Ah, well...you never know till you try." He laughed. "No matter, now I know who your little friend is. Ms. Savannah Stanford. If you take her back now, I'll just get her again in the future."

Mark's grip on his pistol tightened uncontrollably, bleaching his knuckles with the pressure. He knew Rialto spoke the truth, that he wouldn't rest until he destroyed everything Mark cared about.

Mark fired.

Nothing happened.

He fired again with the same result.

The bullets were leaving the gun, but they weren't hitting the target, which was Rialto's chest, and Mark's aim was not to blame.

He cursed and Rialto cackled with glee. "I remember that day in DC, Carpen. You and I both know *you can't kill me!*" He laughed uproariously and Mark felt his lunch churning, wanting to come up.

Rialto yanked hard on the rope, jerking Savannah up another foot. She groaned.

"Mark...," She called out weakly.

Fury flooded through him and he let loose a tirade of bullets Rialto's way, advancing upon his enemy forcefully and ignoring his assassin-pal, Torino. Again and again, he pulled the trigger. When the pistol clicked on empty, he changed clips without breaking stride.

Finally, when Mark was only fifteen feet away, a satisfying wet smack accompanied one of the shots. He froze.

The bullet had hit Rialto in the upper arm. The blood drained from Rialto's face and his mouth fell open in shock as he looked down at the blood welling from his unexpected wound.

"Oh...," He said softly, shocked by the development. Then, he touched his watch and shifted out of sight.

With the rope freed from its tension, Savannah dropped solidly to the floor and Mark rushed to her side. Static hissed behind him and he glanced back. Torino had shifted out too, following Rialto.

Mark ran his hands over Savannah's head and back. He checked every part of her looking for wounds, but found none except for the bright bruise on her face.

"Savannah?" He patted her cheek lightly, cradling her head in his lap.

Her eyes fluttered open.

"Are you okay?"

"Yes, I think so."

"Good. Let's go home."

Chapter 57

The wound surprised him like nothing else had in a quite a while. He'd been quite convinced Mark Carpen could not harm him — until he'd been shot in the arm.

It had been an unbelievable adrenaline rush, all those shots flashing by his head, veering off at the last second as if some kind of invisible force field surrounded him. He'd felt their breeze on his face as they'd passed. He had no illusions about Carpen's ability with a gun. The man was an expert marksman.

No, the only reason those bullets had turned off target is because Carpen was not allowed to kill him. The knowledge of that never failed to send thrills of elated joy running up and down his spine.

Still, he had no explanation for the shoulder wound. He pressed his fingers to the bandaged area, relishing the sweet pain it produced deep within his flesh.

He would get his revenge. In more ways than one. For now, he still needed Laura's shifter back or everything would fall apart. Getting it from that receptionist of Carpen's would be much more difficult as long as Carpen himself was around though. The moment she disappeared, Carpen would show up to stop him. That was a given.

Then, a light bulb clicked on in the back of his mind. Hadn't he successfully taken out Ty Jennings and Hardy Phillips in the future? And Carpen had never been able to undo that. Perhaps the future was the key. He would travel to the far off future and get the shifter back, after he killed her, of course. And Carpen wouldn't be able to stop him, just like the others.

At first, he couldn't locate any public record of her in the future. He wanted to shift forward as far as he could to guarantee Carpen wouldn't interfere, but he couldn't get past the year 2029. This wasn't the first time they'd run into this problem. Every time they tried to shift to 2030 or later, they simply bounced off the year like a racquetball off a court wall.

So, he had to settle for 2029, but couldn't find any records of her in that year. Not a death certificate, tax return, bank record —

nothing. Until he realized he'd been searching under the wrong name.

He hadn't considered it at first — he hoped he wasn't slipping — but that big rock he'd seen on her finger meant she had probably changed her name. So, he checked under that alias and sure enough, they'd gotten married and Savannah Stanford had become Mrs. Savannah Carpen. When he searched under that name, the records started pouring in.

Alexander Rialto rubbed his hands with glee. Her shifter was as good as his.

***

After the abduction, they'd returned to headquarters to regroup and plan.

Savannah was okay, which relieved Mark to no end. Rialto hadn't had a chance to do anything to her.

All of them were reluctant to let her go out on another mission again.

"Come on, guys. You can't keep me locked up in here forever. I've got things to do."

"You should at least marry Mark first," Ty said. "Give the man a honeymoon before you give him another ulcer."

"What, you don't think I get worried about you guys?"

"You ain't got to worry about us, ma'am," Hardy said, "We're professionals." He bore one of his characteristic grins to match the bravado.

She blew out through pursed lips in disgust.

Mark re-focused the conversation. "No, you're right, Savannah. You can't stay cooped up in here forever. The work you're doing is too important. It's clear to me our fundamental problem is Alexander Rialto. If we take him out, I don't think his henchman would even bother us anymore. We'd be able to breathe easy again."

"How are we going to do that?" Hardy asked. "We've set out to do it before and couldn't."

"Don't forget we did rid ourselves of four of his people...well, three of them really," Mark said remembering Laura. "Maybe it's finally Rialto's time this time."

"Back in the hotel he said something about Washington DC. What did he mean you couldn't kill him, Mark?" Savannah asked.

Mark explained. He told them of how he'd gone back to a year when Rialto had been much younger and tried to take him out, but hadn't been able to. The room fell under a thick silence. Rialto was a danger not only to them, but to the entire world, and they were facing the very real possibility that they could never be freed of the menace. They had all run into too many cases of things that couldn't be changed to take the idea lightly.

"Remember, I did get him in the shoulder this time," Mark said.

"But how hard did you have to try to even do that?"

"Too hard," Mark admitted.

"I do not believe it's impossible to be rid of Rialto," Hardy stated firmly.

"We're certainly going to try," Mark agreed. "But there are some details we need to take care of first. Savannah, you and I are going to work on a plan — a plan that will work. Ty, Hardy, I need you to do something else before we proceed."

"What's that?"

"I need you to go back and recruit me."

"I'm sorry, *what* did you say?"

"I need you to go back in time and recruit me into this company."

"What in the world are you talking about?"

"You guys don't know this yet, but it was you two," he pointed at Hardy and Ty, "who originally recruited *me* into joining ChronoShift. I was fresh from the loss of my children, and didn't really know what to do next. Then, this pushy man I'd never met before showed up out of the blue and asked me to perform a mission for ChronoShift. That man was you Hardy. I did several missions at his...er, at your request. Then, he introduced me to you, Ty. In fact, Ty and I went to Georgia together and saved Ty's third great-grandfather from a lynching back in 1863."

"*What?*" Ty nearly came out of his chair.

"You heard me. But immediately after that, you two disappeared on me."

Mark stood and walked to the window. The sun was beginning to set, bathing the streets below in pools of orange light. Several shoppers hustled along the sidewalk trying to get home on time to dinner, their arms full of bags.

"After that, I couldn't find either of you anywhere and you didn't come back. I started to get depressed again, but you guys had given me a taste of what could be done with these things." He held up his wrist and shook it. "So, I began saving people at random from miscellaneous crimes and launched a fledgling ChronoShift on my own without you."

He turned to face them.

"Still, it wasn't the same. I missed you guys. So, I did a little research and intercepted you while each of you was still actively serving in the military. Then, I pulled a little time-travel switcheroo and recruited *you*. Didn't you ever wonder how I picked you out of all the people on earth — or why?"

Both men sat back in their chairs, stunned.

"This is crazy," Hardy said flatly

Ty laughed. "Well, I'm glad you did."

"Anyway, here's what has to happen." Mark explained what each one of them needed to do. When and where to find him. What missions they needed to assign him and all the accompanying details. What he would say and ask, and how they should respond. In anticipation of this day, he had prepared a written manual for each, which he now handed to them.

"Well, this should be fun," Hardy grinned.

"Don't worry, Mark. We won't mess with you too much," Ty offered.

It was Mark's turn to grin. "I'm not worried at all. You forget, I already know what you did and said."

"You don't think we can change it up on you?"

"Nope."

"Will you look at that? The cynic's come around full circle."

***

In the end, it had been so simple. Toward the end of 2029, Rialto located a death certificate for one Savannah Carpen, resident of Boston, Massachusetts. According to the document, she'd died peacefully of natural causes in her sleep.

Rialto attended her viewing the night before the funeral. He was surprised and annoyed to see so many mourners paying their respects. Many were young women and teenage girls, probably girls the goodie-two-shoes had stolen from other enterprises like his. He recognized the hollow, haunted look in their eyes, which their fake smiles and healthy skin couldn't hide. Served them right, the ungrateful wenches.

Carpen's woman had not aged well at all. That made him happy. The wrinkles on her dried face made her appear well over seventy, but she couldn't be more than fifty by 2029. Of course, the linear progression of years really didn't relate to one's age any more when you had a shifter.

Rialto peered inside the casket and sucked in his breath. He snatched a glance back and forth to see if anyone else had noticed what he had. Shockingly, the shifter lay right there in plain sight, still encircling her wrist, though it was loose like an over-sized bracelet since her body was no longer producing the electro-magnetic field it needed to remain constricted.

And he'd devised such an ingenious plan to get it from her too. Her mother was still alive in this year, and before he'd found Savannah's death certificate, Rialto had planned to kidnap her mother and threaten to kill her unless Savannah showed up at a certain place, certain time, etc. Once his target appeared, he would have then killed both her and the mother and taken the shifter. No Mark Carpen to save her, no Jennings, no Phillips.

It was a delicious plan, one that he would have relished putting into motion, but then she'd gone and messed it up by dying peacefully before he was ready. He had half a mind to do something vicious to her body right here, right now, just to get even.

He shook his head. It wasn't worth it. He had to stay focused. More and more he found his mind wandering down dark, distracted paths.

Inconspicuously, he slipped his hand inside the casket and slid the shifter off her wrist. Nobody was paying him any attention. He stuffed it in his pocket and left the funeral home with no one the wiser.

***

"Why don't we just forget about Carpen?"

"*Why don't we just forget about Carpen?*" Rialto mimicked in a mocking tone. He wagged his finger in Torino's face. "You will call me 'sir' when you address me, is that clear?"

Torino remained stone-faced and didn't back up an inch as Rialto pressed in aggressively. He shot Graves a look who shook his head almost imperceptibly, but knowingly.

"Okay," Torino repeated through tight lips, "Why don't we forget about Carpen, sir? You're already establishing your power throughout Washington and the rest of the world and soon you'll be so entrenched no one can stop you. We've got all the money we could ever need. Why don't we just enjoy it and leave him alone. He's like a wasp's nest. We're fine until we start stirring him up."

Rialto's face turned a striking shade of bright red scarlet and then descended into a more violent purple. A vein pulsed in his temple like a pressure gauge warning its boiler was about to blow.

His chest heaved in anger, but he managed to spit out through clenched teeth, "You idiot, don't you know that Mark Carpen won't rest until he's killed us all. We have to beat him to the punch!"

"But didn't you say that he can't kill you?"

"Exactly! That's exactly why we have to kill him first."

"That doesn't make any sense."

"Of course he can't kill me, but that doesn't mean he can't kill you two. I'm just trying to protect you."

Torino shook his head. He didn't believe the crap Rialto was feeding him for a second.

"Listen," Rialto waved his finger again petulantly. "If you don't do as I say and help me kill Carpen..."

"You'll *what*?" Torino stepped forward.

Graves reached out and touched his shoulder, looking to Rialto. "Don't worry, Boss. We'll help you get him."

"You'd better. Now get to work!" Rialto stormed from the room.

Torino let his chest fall and exhaled heavily. This was the first time Graves had ever seen anything get to him.

"He's losing it," Torino asserted.

"I think you're right," Graves said. "His hatred for Carpen is blinding him."

"We need to bail from this thing before we go down with the ship."

"What about these?" Graves lifted his shifter.

"I don't know. I'm not so sure there really are any explosives built into them. What if we could have just walked away this entire time."

"I'm with you, but are you sure enough to call his bluff?"

"Not yet. Maybe soon."

Chapter 58

Alexander Rialto furiously paced his luxurious office. He had to kill Carpen and he had to do it now. He could be patient long enough to devise a plan though. A good plan. One that had to work.

The key must lie in the future. Every time he went into the future, things went great. It was only in the past that Carpen seemed to get the better of him.

That was *it*. That had to be it. The future.

Rialto shook his fist at the sky in silent victory. He would kill Mark Carpen in the future. It still had to be a good plan though.

And he had to do it soon. He could feel the fledgling empire he'd built crumbling under the touch of his fingers. Sure, he was beginning to bring families like the Rockefellers and the DuPonts and the Carnegies under his thumb, but he couldn't rely on Torino and Graves to manage it for him. They were becoming rebellious. They were too powerful. He had to kill them too.

The frustration was overwhelming. He'd built this incredible machine of wealth and power, but he had no one to show it to. Torino and Graves couldn't even be trusted with that much. For example, why weren't they here right now to calm him down? Because they were falling down on the job, that was why. He had to kill them so he could get somebody good to help him run things before everything fell apart.

He could feel his hold on things dissolving as if the ground beneath his feet were crumbling away. His power was tenuous. He had to solidify it, make it last. He had to kill Mark Carpen. As soon as he did that, everything else would be fine.

***

February 2nd 2017, Washington D.C - The White House

Stephen Holdstadt had been in the Secret Service for over twenty years. He hoped to retire in another ten. His oldest had just graduated high school and it wouldn't be long before all his kids were out of college and married.

Katherine had turned out to be such a great mother. Not to mention she'd put up with his crazy hours and travel schedule over the years. She deserved a break. Once he retired, he would take her on that world-wide cruise she'd always dreamed of taking.

He'd gotten up this morning at 3:00 AM, just as he did every morning, shaved, grabbed a bagel and some coffee, and headed out the door. He'd had enough time to get in a short work-out at the gym and then a ten-minute run before having to report in for duty at the White House.

The day had begun normally enough — but now this guy had shown up.

It was never a dull day guarding the President of the United States, but most days were free of the crazies. Apparently, today was not one of those days.

The guy had raised his hackles from the moment he'd walked through the White House guest entrance. Something didn't feel right about him. Holdstadt was stationed at a desk between the front door and the security checkpoint. Two more agents were behind the scanners. One manned the X-ray belt machine, another stood with a wand ready to sweep anyone who set off the detectors as they walked through. A host of other Secret Service were in hidden offices right outside the foyer, ready to burst in at the first sign of trouble. Not to mention the vast numbers of others walking the grounds and guarding the president himself.

Holdstadt glanced back at the two agents behind the checkpoint to see if they'd noticed him too. They had.

The guy approached the desk.

"How may I help you, sir?" Holdstadt asked. His finger hovered under the desk next to the silent alarm. His other hand was slipping up toward his weapon.

"Alexander Rialto, here to see the president."

Holdstadt saw the craziness floating in his eyes. Not to mention the insanity of the request.

Great. He depressed the alarm button.

"Identification, please," Holdstadt stated without mirth.

What should have happened next is the man should have pulled out a driver's license or something similar, only to be tackled by a flood of agents emerging from hidden doorways. Instead, he evaporated into thin air.

Holdstadt drew his weapon and leapt forward, leaning over the tall desk to see if the man had simply dropped down out of his line of sight. Out of the corner of his eye, he had time to see the man reappear, now with gun in hand, behind his fellow agents manning the checkpoint. He did not have time, however, to warn them before a cold knife slipped into the back of his neck, ending all sense of awareness and his life.

***

As of today, President Alton Jefferson had been president for exactly thirteen days. Before running for the highest office, he'd served as a democratic senator from Illinois for three terms.

It had been a tough election. Nelson James, the previous occupier of his office, which is how he viewed the man, had been a popular president.

Luckily for him, his party controlled the House and the Speaker of the House was a personal friend. She had hired some high-priced call girls to seduce a couple of James' cabinet members and then extorted them with video evidence of their affairs to fabricate lower level scandals within their own departments.

Of course his campaign had ensured these scandals hit the news one right after the other as nasty little October surprises a month before the election. The result was a severe drop in the polls for James as people lost confidence in his ethical leadership. The Speaker made sure any congressional inquiries took the roads the DNC wanted them to take, and it didn't hurt that the national media was on his side. Ninety percent of them voted democrat every election like faithful lapdogs, so it wasn't like he had to really work to get their favor. The media would cover up a multitude of sins for him as long as they thought he was advancing their liberal agenda.

Still, even with the choreographed scandals, his opponent had almost taken the election. An incumbent is hard to beat. They'd thought they had Florida, but it was getting harder for a democratic candidate to take that state what with the DNC's coziness with the Palestinians and socialists the world over.

If they hadn't controlled several Secretaries of State in key states to manipulate voting results, he probably would have lost. Over the years, the DNC had learned the limits of ballot box stuffing. They could pad election results by about 5% in their favor without anyone taking issue. Commentators would just conclude the polls had been off slightly more than the margin of error, but more than that and people grew suspicious.

Which was all fine and dandy since there were always a number of states guaranteed to be close calls and that 5% made all the difference in the world. In the end, just tipping the scales in a few key voting districts in Nevada, New Mexico, and Ohio had been enough and lo and behold, Alton Jefferson had become the next President of the Unites States.

His heart skipped a beat every time the men of his protective detail simultaneously touched their hands to their ears to better hear whatever alert was coming over the wire. This time, however, his heart didn't settle down a moment later, but only raced faster when he saw the unwelcome signs of fierce determination settling into each agent's face. His Secretary of State, his Chief of Staff, and the Chairman of the Joint Chiefs who were sitting on a couch across from him in the Oval Office had not noticed the activity yet, and the president only had a second to register the changes in the agents' stances that would precede them whisking him from the room in a flurry, when it started to happen.

What, exactly, *it* was that was happening, he wasn't at first sure. The lights flickered out, leaving only the dimmer sunlight to illuminate the suddenly darkened room. Numerous electric hisses like static voltage discharging crackled from all sides of the office at once. Secret service agents began sliding lifelessly to the floor, some silently, others with cries or groans, but all fell within two seconds of the first.

Through it all, President Jefferson saw flashes of a man. A man with a large, gleaming knife who appeared and disappeared behind the agents spread around the room. He was the cause of their fall and he was as sudden as he was terrible. None of the president's detail had even been able to draw their weapons before thudding to the floor.

The lights flickered back on and then the man remained, disappearing no more. The gleam of his big white teeth matched that of his knife, which looked long enough to be a miniature machete.

His eyes were crazy...and evil. Alton trembled at the thought of what this man might want — and what powers he must have to be able to do what he'd just done — for surely he wanted something or wouldn't he have killed all of them by now?

He took comfort in the fact that the outer doors to the Oval Office would burst inward any second with a flood of agents coming to his rescue.

The man walked to the doors and opened them. He peered out and then turned back to the president and his officials, shaking his head.

"Tsk, tsk, gentlemen. You weren't expecting anyone to come to your aid, were you?" He laughed. "Why don't you take a look, Mr.

President?"

Warily, the president stood. He looked to the other three men. His Chief of Staff was glued to his seat, eyes wide with fear. The Secretary of State lay flat, unconscious. At first, President Jefferson thought this man had killed him too.

"No, sorry," The man said, as if reading his thoughts, "I didn't touch him. I think he just passed out." That evinced more laughter.

The general stood, angry, fists clenched, ready to protect his commander-in-chief.

"Please don't, General. I'm not going to hurt the president — at least, not at this time. I'd hate to take you out prematurely. I much prefer you hear this."

President Jefferson made his way over to where he could see out the doors and gasped. Seven more secret service agents were visible, all of them strewn chaotically across floors down the hall and through the outer office space. Massacred.

"Who are you? What do you want?" The president demanded.

"My name is Alexander Rialto," he hissed, "And what I want is simple. Your full and undivided cooperation."

"What does that mean?"

"Sit." He motioned to the couches and the president grudgingly returned to his seat.

"The first thing I want is for you to wire $100 million dollars to my account..."

"Money? You want money?" The president interrupted, incredulous.

"Not really. That amount is just a symbol of your willingness to cooperate. I have all the money I could ever need already. It needs to be in my account by early tomorrow or I'll have to come back and do worse than this.

"Second, I want a 20% stake in the Federal Reserve Bank."

"But..."

"Just tell the guys over there at the Fed that I know who owns it, and I know where their families are, and that I'd really hate to have to do a repeat of this demonstration for them. I'll give you till the end of the week to get that done."

Both the president and the general paled visibly.

"Lastly, I want you to bring the full weight of the government of the United States of America to bear on this man throughout your presidency." Rialto handed the president a thick manila folder. He opened it.

"Who is Mark Carpen?"

"You don't know him. Nor do you have any reason too. He's unimportant as far as you're concerned, other than the fact that I want him dead. Inside this folder is all of his information, his known accomplices, known addresses, etc. I want you to persecute him worse than President Bush did Osama bin Laden. Is that clear?"

"I can't imagine why..."

"It's not important why, just that you do it. And I'll know if you don't. Do we have a deal?"

Alton Jefferson stared at the vacant doorway helplessly.

He could not hear any sirens wailing in the distance, no pounding of feet in the hallway. Every minute that passed without aid increased his sense of panic tenfold. He felt the potency of his presidency melting away like snow in summer.

"No one's coming, Mr. President. And if they did, I could dispatch them before they got into the building, before they even knew I was here." He sneered.

Frustrated tears welled in the president's eyes. Not for the fallen men around him, but for the loss of power he'd coveted so long. He'd only been in office for a few weeks! How could this happen? How could things change so fast?

"I'm not asking for the moon, Mr. President. You can still push forward with your agenda. In fact, if you scratch my back, I can scratch yours. Wouldn't it be nice to get things done for a change? You've seen what I can do. Imagine my power in your hands. You'd be like none of your predecessors. All I want are those three things. Do we have a deal?"

Suddenly, Alton had new visions. Visions of his political enemies vanquished and the rest quivering at his feet in fear of what he might do to their careers. No one had to die of course, but blackmail was a wonderful tool. Surely this man could dig up dirt on people even easier than he could kill them.

He locked eyes with Rialto. "We have a deal."

The general was shocked. "Mr. President, you can't be serious..."

President Jefferson waved him off, keeping his eyes on Rialto. "What do we do about this?" He waved at the fallen men.

"Tell them it was a terrorist attack."

"And what terrorist shall we say did it?"

"You'll find a patsy." He pointed to the general. "If he gives you any trouble, let me know. I know where his family lives too."

The general stiffened and his mouth clamped shut like a vice. The chief of staff had his eyes scrunched tightly shut. He was humming some mindless melody as if it would make the bad dreams go away.

Chapter 59

"Mark, you need to see this." Savannah swept into the room and laid a newspaper article on the table in front of him.

MASSACRE IN DC: 203 DEAD! the headline blared. The date at the top said 2023.

"Where did you get it?" Ty asked.

"It was taped to the front door when I came in," she answered.

"Rialto," Mark muttered, staring at it.

It described a scene ripped from a techno-horror movie. The article detailed how the previous night an unknown terrorist had gotten hold of some kind of advanced, gigantic "battle-suit" and wrought havoc on downtown Washington DC. Police had assaulted the machine with every weapon they'd had at their disposal, but to no avail. The mech-bot suit had been layered with hardened armor that had resisted their bullets completely.

The mechanical monster had torn through their ranks and ravaged the public they'd been trying to protect. Men, women, children had been killed. Homes, cars, and businesses destroyed. The Pentagon denied any knowledge or planned development of such a weapon. The technology, they claimed, was decades ahead of anything they were capable of.

"How do we know it's Rialto?"

"Who else is it going to be? Who else would tape this to our door? It's the final showdown. He's as determined as we are to end it once and for all."

They stared at the newspaper clipping on the table.

"Are we going to take the bait? I mean, he's obviously already chosen the turf and set things up exactly how he wants them."

"Yes, but it's the only when and where we know he's going to be. Are we all on board?"

Each nodded.

"I'll do some recon first," Ty offered.

"Good."

***

"As soon as he gets here, we'll go for it," Vincent Torino said.

"Are you sure?" Stanley Graves asked, one eyebrow cocked upward. "It seems too soon."

"It's time," Torino answered definitively. "He's lost it. I think he's approaching levels of true insanity. If we are ever going to be free of him, we have to kill him, and we have to do it now. It's just a matter of time before he tries to off us himself."

"I know. You're right."

"Listen, we'll stand on either side of him and then each of us can grab a wrist to keep him from shifting out. If we can manage that much, the rest will be a piece of cake..."

They were interrupted by the static hiss of a shifter entering their present.

Alexander Rialto was smiling the first genuine smile his lips had borne in years. When he spied Torino and Graves together, it only grew wider. He was reflecting over his many recent successes.

While President Nelson James had always resisted Rialto's efforts of extortion with a will of steeled resolve, his democratic successor, Alton Jefferson, had proven to be cut from the opposite cloth. James had operated under some kind of misplaced banner of honor, refusing to give in, no matter what it cost him. He'd called Rialto's bluff and in the end, Rialto hadn't been able to carry out any of his threats, not with that mysterious force protecting James like some kind of invisible force shield. He'd hated the man at the time for it. Republicans always seemed harder to deal with for some reason, claiming higher principles as their guide. Still there were enough slimy members of the GOP, it didn't matter. The principled ones were easy to work around.

Thing were very different now, however. In 2016, the country would elect a new president, an opportunistic man with none of the ideals of James. Manipulating President Alton Jefferson had been as easy as slicing heated butter. Who knew? The man might have even caved without extra incentives, but when Rialto had offered to use his shifting power to advance Jefferson's agenda in Congress, the politician had melted in front of the possibility of having so much brute power at his disposal.

The $100 million had in fact been wired into his account the next day. And by the end of the week, for the first time in his life, Alexander Rialto had powerful men within the U.S. government — and members of certain elite social circles — at his service, inviting him into secret meetings he never would have been privy to before. He was given the 20% ownership of the Fed as he'd requested, and he loved how they'd given it to him — divided up among a variety of private holding groups so no one could tell who owned what.

The best part, however, was the persecution of Mark Carpen. President Jefferson would throw the full weight of the federal government into the search, fabricating false charges to motivate investigators from a slew of agencies. According to Carpen's official government dossier in 2016, he was a wanted international arms dealer who had recently sold WMDs to an Al Qaeda cell inside the U.S. That meant the CIA, NSA, FBI, ATF, ICE, and even the IRS was after him. That last agency was the most delicious for him personally of course.

The feds had raided Carpen's headquarters and every other address Carpen had ever used, and his name was at the top of every wanted list across the country. Really, the world.

Rialto had no illusions they might actually get their hands on Carpen. There was simply no way regular mortals could trap the man. Not while he had a shifter.

What Rialto had accomplished, however, was a temporal sanctuary for himself. Mark Carpen could shift all over time as much as he wanted, but it was in his best interest to stay out of the years between 2017 and 2024. As long as Alton Jefferson was president and under Rialto's thumb, anything Carpen did during those years would be complicated by governmental surveillance and persecution. It meant Rialto had a haven, a period of years where he could relax and kick back, reasonably assured Carpen wouldn't bother him.

Things were proceeding nicely. It had taken a lot of effort, but he was slowly gaining control over everyone and everything with any influence in the world. The spider web he'd woven was so interconnected, most of the players didn't realize who was running who, and certainly no one understood just how much control he'd accumulated so far. For the first time in his life, things were finally looking up. And it was exciting.

The only dark cloud was Carpen's shadow hovering in the background of his mind. He had to be rid of the man or it would always be possible for all his work to be undone.

He looked at both Torino and Graves expectantly. They were growing uneasy with the length of time he had stood here, silently churning thoughts in his head with a vacant grin on his face. He started to open his mouth to say something.

Instead, he closed it and shot them. First, Torino of course, who was the better shot of the two. He was proud of himself for having been able to peg the assassin right in the middle of the chest while using his left hand. His right wasn't far behind though and Graves went down too. They hadn't seen him raising the guns. It was as if they'd been blinded by thoughts of something else.

He crossed the floor to them. Torino was struggling to get his weapon free. One last grasp at revenge, but it was useless. Rialto kept his weapons trained on them as life drained from both men.

"It was just a matter of time, guys," he stated matter-of-factly.

He closed his eyes, hearing the familiar whir of shifters loosening their bands.

***

Ty finished his recon and the report wasn't pretty.

"It happens just like the newspaper said, but worse. It's going to be a regular bloodbath."

"Can we stop him?" Mark asked.

"I've got some ideas, but the armor on that suit he's got is something else. It's just like one of those futuristic mech-bots from a sci-fi flick."

"What do you mean?"

"It's like a giant robot. He's sitting in a bullet-proof compartment about seven feet off the ground. And when I say it's bullet-proof, I mean it's bullet-proof. I took a couple of pot shots with a .50 cal just to see what would happen. Nothing."

"Ain't much that can hold up to a .50 caliber for long."

"We'll see. I think he controls the thing's movements with sensors strapped to his arms and legs inside the contraption. He's got multiple 20 mm rotary cannons attached to each arm, along with grenade launchers, and some other futuristic weapons I didn't recognize.

"This thing is like nothing you've ever seen. And DC law enforcement certainly didn't know what to throw up against it. I don't know where he got it. If we can't go past 2030, then I can't imagine he can either."

"He probably stole some top secret project the Pentagon was working on," Mark offered.

"Maybe. Regardless, who knows what else he's got up his sleeve. This could be just door number one with more to follow."

"What about Torino and Graves?"

"I didn't see any sign of them. Or any other supporting staff for that matter. Rialto may have done this one solo."

"Ty, get with Hardy and secure the equipment we need. I'm going to try and talk Savannah out of going with us. As of this morning, she was still determined to help."

"There are a few additional complications," Ty said.

"Like what?" Mark asked.

"It may be just me, but have you spent any significant time in the future yet?"

Mark thought long and hard about that. "Uh...not really, I guess. Just a short shift here and there. I spent a lot of time trying to save you, but that's about it."

"Same here. I'd be willing to bet Hardy hasn't either."

"What are you getting at?"

"Well...I'm still trying to pin down exactly what is going on in the future, but it appears we are all personas-non-grata as far as the U.S. government is concerned. At least after the year 2016."

"What happens in 2016?"

"New president. I think Rialto gets to him somehow. Gets him to agree to turn the government loose on us."

"What do you mean? Is the Pentagon trying to get the shifters for itself to study?"

"No, nothing like that. We're classified as domestic terrorists. In fact, after Rialto finishes this attack with the mech-bot, the government officially blames you for it," Ty explained.

"So, let me get this straight. While we're trying to stop Rialto from killing a bunch of D.C.'s police, the same police are going to be trying to arrest us on behalf of the president."

"You got it. Plus, we can't shift around town."

"Why not? Rialto's apparently installed shift detectors all over the city and has a monitoring system set up to alert the authorities any time a shift signature is detected. Every time I used my shifter anywhere near the city, I had police sirens after me within fifteen seconds. So, we've got to do our shifting outside the beltway and drive in."

"I am *really* getting tired of Rialto," Mark said, "We need to put an end to him once and for all."

Chapter 60

*It don't matter where you bury me,
I'll be home and I'll be free.*

"All My Tears"

~ *Jars of Clay*

The jet-black machine was truly monstrous. Its thighs were as thick as four telephone poles. Street light glinted off the inky armor as it moved, like oil on water under a bright moon. The sounds of its hydraulics whirred and clunked like something out of a Terminator movie. Small tremors accompanied every step, which inevitably cracked and crushed the asphalt beneath.

It was just a shell — the true monster sat inside the driver's seat — yet, he still found himself intimidated, shivering at the thought of taking on the Goliath-sized robot. He surveyed the weapons lying at their feet. They had brought the best of their armory, which was considerable, but he still felt naked before the mechanical beast.

The sheer weight of it must have been tremendous. One of its feet came down on the hood of a car and crumpled it so badly the rear end was lifted off the ground and the wheels remained spinning in the air after the machine was gone. More amazingly, the beast did not lose its balance when this happened, but kept moving as if nothing had gotten in its way, which testified to the highly advanced technology underlying it.

Rialto was approaching a busy section of downtown DC. He was headed to the grassy mall area. Tourists and locals alike were screaming, fleeing in full panic like Godzilla had just emerged from the bay. Though this was worse than Godzilla. Godzilla didn't have bullets.

In just a few minutes, Rialto would deliver his first round of destruction. He'd let loose with the rotary cannons on his arms, driving scores of innocent civilians to the ground with bullets in their backs. Police were hastily forming a barricade at the end of the street with their vehicles to try and stop the monster.

Rialto appeared to be in no hurry. He was either waiting on more police to show up to maximize casualties, or he was waiting on Mark to get there. Or both.

They knew the choreography of this tragedy inside and out by now. They'd viewed it repeatedly to gather intelligence, and they knew where most of the victims would be. As a last resort, they would make as many individual saves as they could, but in the meantime, they knew they had roughly three minutes before he started shooting to try and take him out.

Mark could barely make out Rialto's face through the smoky bullet-proof visor, but he could tell the villain was enjoying himself. He directed the machine to kick and it did, sending a BMW sailing twenty feet in the air like a child kicking a can.

"Get out the M-2s," Mark said. "Let's get to it."

Ty and Hardy threw themselves into setting the .50 caliber machine guns up. Mark settled down into position behind one. Ty took the other. Hardy withdrew an RPG launcher from the last oversized duffel for himself.

.50 Caliber rounds could pierce up to 1 inch of hardened steel armor. There was no way Rialto had anywhere near that thickness on that machine. Mark took aim and pulled the trigger. Ty followed suit and they unleashed a barrage at Rialto.

Incredible.

The armor piercing rounds ricocheted off the robotic suit like they were .22s hitting a tank. Mark narrowed his aim to the visor, but the result was similar...which was inconceivable. Even the joints where the armor looked weakest resisted their shots.

Mark sat back, not believing his eyes. He'd seen armor in action plenty of times. This was no normal armor. It was as if the suit had been covered in some kind of super shock-absorbent coating. He'd heard rumors of efforts to engineer such a chemical coating, but he'd never heard of anyone being successful.

"Let loose, Hardy."

The RPG shrieked from its launcher and hit Rialto dead on, exploding powerfully on the left side of the suit's chest plate. The smoke cleared and the beast took another step. Then, another. There was no apparent damage to it other than a black charred spot where the grenade had hit. The thing hadn't even stumbled under the force of the explosion.

"Plan B!" Mark called out.

The three scrambled to a case of explosives and began tossing packs of C-4 down in its path. They had to be careful not to overdo it. The surrounding buildings had plenty of people in them. Too much plastique and the shock wave could take out more than just Rialto. For now, Rialto had not yet reached the zone where anyone would be endangered, but they didn't have much time left to act.

Four satchels landed within ten feet of the mech-bot. The machine did something very odd then — its legs settled, as if it were preparing to jump, but remained crouched as Mark hit the detonator. The blast sent a wave of heat up the face of the building on which they stood, and the shock shattered glass in the lower levels of every other building nearby.

An American flag on a pole extending from the side of an office building was on fire. Its fabric curled in bright orange light and showered the sidewalk below with dying embers.

The machine swayed slightly under the force of the explosion, but again there was no damage. For the first time, panic rose up in Mark's throat.

"We can't stop it, Mark. It's just like before. For some reason, we're not allowed to kill Rialto."

Jaws clenched, he glared at the maniacal weapon controlled by his nemesis.

"It's not like that," he growled. "It's not fate stopping us this time, it's the thing's armor. That's all." He turned briskly. "Hardy, Ty, get down there and start saving people. We're out of time."

They'd already seen the devastation unfold many times and had taken note of where every victim would be when they were killed. Plan C was to use the shifters to save as many as possible.

"What about you?" Ty asked.

"I'm going to stop him."

"How?"

"I don't know."

He looked his friends in the eyes. They didn't let go.

"It's suicide, Mark."

"Go!" He ordered.

This time, they obeyed and ran toward the stairs that would take them to street level. Mark followed.

Hardy and Ty faded away as soon as they'd reached the bottom, having shifted out. They were off and under way with the mission.

Mark pushed through the glass front door and ran into the street just in time to see the machine lifting its arm to begin its first assault. The only weapon Mark had was a pistol in his right hand. He glanced at it, realizing the futility of anything he might try, but no longer caring.

He only knew he had to intercept Rialto and nothing more. Huge, monstrous, car-smashing machine or not, he had to stop the man.

Mark ran forward and planted himself in the middle of the machine's path, which was still forty to fifty feet away. More than a hundred feet behind him was the first line of police cars the machine would tear through like tissue paper.

The massive 20 mm cannons mounted on the beast's arm began to spin and then spewed a flurry of rounds up the street, their thunderous reports terrifying to the ears. Chips of brick and mortar flew in all directions along with deep thunks that accompanied every round that struck a vehicle.

Five people originally died in this first round. Two cops and three civilians. Thankfully, it looked like Ty and Hardy had pulled all five of them out of the way and into safety for now. They couldn't keep that up though. Saving over two hundred people, and then saving them again from secondary and then tertiary bullets would be a herculean effort. Plus, Rialto wouldn't stop until he'd successfully killed a lot of people. Eventually, Mark, Ty or Hardy would catch a stray round.

Mark reached the center of the street and waved his arms.

"Rialto! You coward! Over here!"

Mark fired a couple of shots at Rialto's smoky visor, which of course dinged off harmlessly. He flailed his arms again and shot a few more times until he knew Rialto had seen him.

The monstrous arm swiveled to point directly at Mark, the rotating guns accelerating their spin in preparation to fire.

He dove for cover behind a parked car just as the bullets began to fly. Hundreds of metallic impacts rang out in rapid succession as the multiple machine guns tore into the car's body in search of Mark. The barrage stopped.

Silence.

Slowly, the car's passenger door creaked open. A young woman was trying to crawl out to safety, but it was too late. Blood poured out from far too many wounds, so much it streamed down the door onto the sidewalk. She moved her mouth in an attempt to speak, but she could form no words. Then, she collapsed.

Mark hadn't known about her. She must have been hiding in her car and made it safely through in the original scenario.

Mark hit his comm mike. "Ty, you see my position?"

"Affirmative."

"There's a lady here needs evacuating about a minute prior to now."

"I'm on it."

All of a sudden reality changed. Ty was moving down the sidewalk and away from the car, carrying the woman to safety in his arms. She was alive and well, without a scratch. Ty had shifted back and gotten her out before Mark dove behind the car. *Amazing.* Like magic. The effect still made him marvel sometimes, the way they bent time.

The beast's thunderous footsteps thudded closer as it moved to crush the vehicle and get at Mark.

Instead of waiting for its arrival, Mark raced from cover and headed straight toward the machine to get behind it, hopefully avoiding the long gangling arms in the process.

The machine guns opened up a third time and bullets tore into the asphalt inches behind Mark's heels as he ran. Thankfully, Rialto wasn't that good a shot or he would be aiming slightly ahead of Mark. Instead he was pointing at Mark's present position, which made the bullets fall just a little too late.

Mark put himself behind the machine, where he thought he was out of range of the guns, but the robot's torso spun 180 degrees like some freaky, greased-up carnival ride. Mark darted under its legs again to stay out of Rialto's view.

The torso spun once more in pursuit, arms extended outward. One of the arms clipped a nearby telephone pole. The wood snapped with a sickening crack and the power lines it supported followed, rending into curling tendrils one by one as they fell. Sparks flew in every direction. A live wire slithered and hissed on the ground like a wounded snake.

Once more, a deadly arm rose up and fixated on Mark, this time already activated and fully spinning. He could see Rialto grinning smugly through the small visor in the robot's chest. Nowhere for him to move, no time to get out of the way.

Harsh repetitive blasts rent the air as rounds began clanking into chambers and exploding out toward him in a thick shower of deadly lead.

Mark blinked.

It took a minute to register that he was okay. The rotating guns still hummed, spitting out hot metal like terrible hail, yet he remained unharmed.

Tiny flames appeared alternately in each barrel as it discharged, so it clearly wasn't firing blanks. Stupefied, Mark looked back and confirmed bullets were chewing up the pavement on all sides just a few feet behind him. How could Rialto be missing from so close? He was only twenty feet away.

The whole world seemed to descend into slow motion. In a moment of heightened sensitivity, Mark realized the bullets were actually bending around him. Rialto's aim was not off. Bullets were flying straight toward his face, only to be turned away at the last second, just enough to miss. He could feel their breeze as they passed.

Rialto's face twisted in frustration. He brought his other mechanical arm up and fired both rotators simultaneously. The hail of bullets was so thick it would have shredded a solid slab of sheet metal.

Mark didn't move. He was frozen in place, staring in awe at the turn of events. Memories of him trying to kill Rialto flashed through his mind. Of that time in DC when Mark's gun couldn't seem to hit its target no matter how close he got.

It was happening again, but this time it was in his favor.

The chambers finally fell silent. Several hollow clicks followed. Rialto had tried to launch his RPGs, but they had malfunctioned.

The beast stood there, staring back at him like a stalled battlefield hero trying to catch its breath.

Mark looked down.

Then, he did something of which his mother never would have approved. He threw himself onto the torn electrical cable slinging itself back and forth on the pavement and rode it like a bronc rider trying break his mount.

He stood, gripping the thick black cable in his hands, stunned by his own bravery...or stupidity, depending on one's perspective. He *was* holding a live electric conduit with over fifty-thousand volts to its name.

Rialto glared, hating him.

Mark rushed forward and planted the cable deep into the joint right behind the knee of the machine. The thing popped and sizzled and the smell of burning rubber filled his nostrils. The machine slouched into a state of deactivation.

Mark dropped the cable and stepped back, watching as the suit degenerated from a formidable weapon into a lifeless, awkward collection of robot parts. Its center torso sank lower and lower in the face of loss of power until the whole machine's center of gravity changed enough it toppled over onto its side. The visor popped open with a hydraulic hiss of air.

Inside, Rialto fumbled to unfasten his safety harness, panicked fear lighting his eyes as he stared at Mark. His hand blindly groped for his pistol. It was only a few feet away, but his fingers never found it and he gave up.

Ty and Hardy had seen what had happened and raced to Mark's position. Ty aimed at Rialto's chest and prepared to fire, but Mark stayed his hand, so Ty lowered the gun.

Rialto managed to crawl out of the machine and onto the pavement. He staggered to his feet, facing Mark. His hair was singed, tufts of it standing on end. The nauseating smell of burning human flesh reeked strongly.

Rialto moved his lips silently, looking like a fish out of water. His hands flew up and gripped his chest. Then, his face contorted in pain, and he collapsed.

Ten seconds later, the soft whirring of a shifter loosening its band was music to their ears. That whirring was soon followed by a second. Mark lifted Rialto's pant leg and discovered the ankle shifter. It was just one more surprise they took in stride.

It took a little more work to get that one off of his heel, but he did. He gathered both shifters and slipped them into his pocket.

He looked to his friends. For the first time in days, all three were smiling. Mark breathed a sigh of relief and sat down hard on the curb, eyeing the wreckage. The robot suit was done. Rialto was no more and no one had come to rescue him. There was no sign of Torino or Graves. That meant they were either dead or had abandoned their boss. Either way, the war was over and they had finally won. No more did he have to worry about Rialto doing anything to Savannah or destroying his country.

He felt a taut tension somewhere deep in his back slowly releasing its hold.

The police behind the barricade were still gathering their senses, coming to grips with the rapid succession of events. Several officers, realizing the threat was over, advanced with their weapons drawn.

An overweight policeman in his mid-thirties ran over to them with his pistol pointed vaguely at the middle of their group.

"Freeze!" he ordered.

Mark hit his shifter and Ty and Hardy followed a second later, leaving a stunned officer staring at the empty sidewalk in the wake of their sudden departure.

He stammered, but slowly holstered his weapon. *No one back at the station would believe this.*

Chapter 61

When all is said and done, I'd never count the cost
It's worth all that's lost just to see you smile

"Just to See You Smile"

~ Tim McGraw

Until now, he'd never realized today was the day he had been waiting for all of his life.

Beautiful was the only word to describe her, and even that didn't fully express what the vision of her inspired. Her dress was gorgeous, a pure white adorned in minimalist style with droplets of pearl and delicate stitchings accentuating the lines of her curves. Her natural blonde hair glowed in the afternoon sun under a veil that teased at the beauty beneath.

The forest around them was still pristine, untouched by human hands. Several songbirds lilted their music upon the light breeze, adding depth of sound to a perfect atmosphere.

He couldn't pull his eyes from her. In this moment, it was hard to understand why he had waited so long to ask her to marry him.. Even harder to believe she'd said yes. He desperately wanted to lift that veil.

So, he did, though they had not reached that part of the ceremony yet. Wisps of baby's breath were tucked into the folds of her hair under it, a delicate and unexpected touch. He dove into her vibrant, blue eyes. Their color matched today's sky perfectly. Bright, cloudless, healing. Her pink lips turned up in a gentle smile, lighting his heart with warmth.

He knew this moment was being stamped into his memory. He'd never forget the way she looked right now. The way the sun kissed her skin and wrapped her hair in gold. Tiny petals of white accentuating the face of an angel. A smile framed by shades of cherry blossoms, welcoming him into her heart.

He longed to kiss her. He wasn't sure what would be considered proper back here in the 1600's. Abbie had assured him a good solid kiss at a wedding was considered a good sign.

The minister had finished his sermon on love and was now walking Abbie and Hardy through their vows. In just a minute, it would be Mark and Savannah's turn.

When Abbie and Hardy had first shared their plans to have their wedding in Abbie's home village, Mark and Savannah had jumped at the chance to make it a double wedding. Mark had no relatives or friends outside of ChronoShift he wanted to invite, and Savannah's only family was her mother. In the end, they'd decided they could trust her mother to keep their secret and brought her along on the shift back to this time for the wedding preparations.

Savannah's mom was as much of a history buff as Savannah, if not more. She was naturally mesmerized by the whole concept and frankly, still stunned by the reality of it. Mark had an idea he might be getting some requests in the future from his new mother-in-law for trips to this or that era.

Abbie completed their portion with a firm "I do" and her countrymen erupted in applause. The minister turned to Mark. He repeated the same introductory remarks and then continued.

"Do you, Mark Carpen, take this woman, Savannah Stanford, to be your lawful wedded wife? Do you promise to cherish and care for her all the days of your life, so help you God?"

"I do."

He moved to Savannah. "Do you, Savannah Stanford, take this man to be your lawful wedded husband? Do you promise to respect and love him all the days of your life, so help you God?"

"I do," she breathed with a smile. It was like music.

Both couples exchanged rings.

The minister turned to the crowd and raised his arms high. "Now, by the power vested in me by God, I pronounce you Mr. and Mrs. Hardin Phillips and Mr. and Mrs. Mark Carpen. You may kiss your brides."

Mark had no idea how it went with Hardy, but kissing Savannah was like fireworks going off in his head, celebrating the thrilling launch of a new life, and new love. A lasting love.

Chapter 62

Oh 'cause you move me
You get me dancing and you make me sing

"You Move Me"

~ Garth Brooks

The remaining years flew by, for them faster than most, of course. Their ages advanced more rapidly than others who did not shift for a living. They spent so much time in the past or bouncing around the future that their bodies literally aged two, three, or even four years for every chronological year that passed for the rest of the inhabitants of earth.

Mark's life with Savannah was truly blessed. She was the soul mate he'd been searching for his entire life without even knowing it.

They built themselves a house in the woods of the North Georgia mountains, the same woods where Mark had first found the shifters. It wasn't extravagant by any means, just a refuge in the midst of nature where they could be together. Of all the things that happened over the next years, he loved the time he spent with her in that two-story cabin more than anything else.

He loved being there in a rainstorm, watching rain dribble down the glass of the large, oversized windows in the great room while she painted or did some other artistic endeavor. He would usually read a book, pretending to be engrossed, but really just watching her.

He built her a dance studio up there too, as ballet had always been one of her favorite pastimes. The days she felt like dancing were the best. Light leg lifts, glides and leaps and curling arms, it was like visual music, a melody only he got to enjoy.

She never stopped rescuing children, though she did slow down a bit as she aged. It was her great purpose, the passion of her life, and Mark was more than happy to help her fulfill it.

Hardy spent most of his down-time back in the 1600's with Abbie and by all accounts, they were as much in love with one another as were Mark and Savannah. Abbie rarely participated in shifts over the years, though she was known to take a jump with Hardy every now and then, especially if he needed a really good archer for something. Hardy, of course, aged a lot faster than she did. She said she didn't mind, and he made jokes about having such a young wife.

Abbie continued to serve as protector of her village until all the New England Wampanoag Indians had either migrated west or submitted to the governance of the colonists.

Ty was a different story. Mark wished with all his might that Ty could find someone who would make him as happy as Savannah did Mark and Abbie did Hardy. But it never seemed to happen.

For a while, he did have somebody. He'd fallen in love with the young widow he and Mark had stumbled across when they'd traveled back to the time of Charlemagne. At first, he'd just visited her once in a while to make sure she had enough food and chopped wood to get her through the winter. He chased away bandits, villains, or any other wild animal who tried to bother her. After numerous visits by him, she overcame her general fear of moors, and they'd fallen in love, even before Ty could really speak her language, though he did learn that pretty well over the next few years.

Her first husband had died on a campaign with Charlemagne six months before Ty first met her. She was a shy and meek girl, and without Ty's patronage, she probably wouldn't have survived much longer on her own in the harsh reality of the Dark Ages. Ty cared for her deeply, and they married, though strangely, he didn't exude the same joy Mark naturally felt around Savannah.

Ty never brought her back to modern times, he never even really fully explained the true nature of his shifter to her. He'd bring her a few modern tools or devices from time to time to make her daily life easier, but she didn't like using them.

Rumors of witchcraft and prejudices against consorting with Moors circulated around the neighboring villages, but through it all they held on to each other. She loved her big protector as much as he loved her.

Before her 40th birthday, she got sick. They thought it was cancer, but she wouldn't let Ty bring her on a shift to visit a modern doctor. He brought her some modern medicine, which seemed to help, but the second time, when she relapsed, nothing worked. Ty mourned her death for months and was never quite the same again.

He dated several women from modern times after that, but never married again.

***

Starting New Year's Day in 2027, a depression entered Mark that he couldn't shake until the entire year had passed. A constant lump took root in his throat the day June gave way to July. They all knew July 17, 2027 would be Ty's last day on earth and they'd known it for years. Now that it was here, Mark was having trouble dealing with it.

The day of the 16th, Mark struggled to get out of bed. He didn't know how to say good-bye to his friend. That night, at 1:48 AM, Alexander Rialto would murder Ty in the Boston Common and steal Ty's shifter for himself.

Mark had already tried every trick in the book to save Ty, but it wasn't something they could undo. If fate allowed Mark to save Ty, then Rialto would never get Ty's shifter, which meant a million other things never would have happened that had to happen.

Ty was as resolved to his destiny as Mark. They had coffee together that morning, neither one saying much other than to reminisce over past stories and a brief discussion of fate versus free will. Not that either one of them was in the free will camp any more.

Time was their business. It would not be unreasonable to say they understood it better than anybody else on earth. They'd long since come to understand that it wasn't just events like the deaths of Mark's kids and Ty's coming demise that were predetermined. Everything they did was predestined. Even the things in history they thought they were changing were actually predestined to be changed by them. It was all part of God's great and magnificent plan. A plan that was too complex, too difficult to understand, though every now and then they caught a glimpse of its primary thread.

After thirty minutes of silence, Mark didn't know what else to say. He'd said everything he could, and the things he hadn't, he couldn't. Ty saw the pain in his friend's eyes and knew it was time to go.

"Mark...you know this is not really the end, right?"

"I know, I know..." Mark was having trouble holding back the tears.

"I'm going to a better place."

A tear broke free and the lump grew so thick Mark could barely speak. "I know that," he choked. "It's just hard to say good-bye."

"We'll see each other again in heaven."

"I know that too. It's just...hard."

Ty stood to spare his friend any more grief. "It's time we said good-bye, old friend. It's been a blast. Thanks for choosing me."

Mark coughed a chuckle as they shook hands. "It was you guys who chose me, remember?"

"I don't know if we'll ever figure that one out." Ty pulled Mark into a bear hug and they slapped each other on the back.

"See you soon, Mark."

"See you soon, Ty."

And with that, Ty walked away. It would be a while before they saw each other again.

Chapter 63

"I will sail my vessel 'til the river runs dry"

"The River"

~ Garth Brooks

Over the years, Mark, Hardy, and Ty had conducted hundreds and hundreds of other missions, stopping crimes and tragedies here or there, and doing the occasional favor for the president, and it turned out they hadn't been finished with Rialto after all, though Mark had most definitely killed the man that day in DC.

Of course, though Mark had ended Rialto's life, that didn't mean their future selves would not cross paths with Rialto's past self. In fact, from time to time, they found themselves once more in combat up against Rialto and his crew, Mark and his team always cognizant of the decided past and their enemies blissfully ignorant of their future. It proved to be quite an annoying aspect of time travel — just when you thought you were rid of somebody...

For that matter, Mark got to see Hardy and Ty again once in a while after their deaths as well, though it felt emotionally awkward to connect with their younger selves.

Hardy just disappeared one day. Mark had always suspected that Rialto had gotten his second shifter by killing Hardy in the future just like he had Ty, but Mark had never been sure about that. Once Hardy disappeared though, Mark had searched and discovered the truth. Rialto snuck up one night on Hardy in a rented house Hardy always used to crash in between missions and killed him. That had been the source of Rialto's second shifter, the one Rialto had used to recruit his crew, one after the other.

Mark took a few half-hearted stabs at trying to save Hardy, Ty's death fresh on his heart, but he gave up quickly once he saw it wasn't working. His death was just like Ty's. Supposed to happen.

Mark shifted back to Abbie's time to let her know, but she acted like she'd almost been expecting him. At least, the news didn't break her up like he thought it would. Hardy had apparently traveled into his own future years ago and uncovered his fate. Hardy had kept the truth from Mark, but he and Abbie had already known how long they had together, so they'd just enjoyed every minute. She'd finished grieving long before he even left.

Mark was glad he hadn't known ahead of time. Saying good-bye to Ty had been too painful.

"Are you going to be okay, Abbie?" he'd asked. "Do you need anything?"

She smiled. "I'm fine, Mark. Hardy made sure I was well provided for before he left."

"I think I'll still check on you once in a while, if you don't mind."

"Hardy would like that. I'd like that."

In 2017, they'd had to abandon their headquarters in Boston. That's when President Jefferson, under the influence of Rialto, began his persecution of them. The headquarters had been one of the first places raided, though they'd been ready for it of course.

After that, they'd gone underground, never forming a permanent headquarters again. It proved to be too much trouble keeping it from the government, especially since Rialto's past self could just figure out which flavor of front company they were using that day and spill the info to the feds.

It was then that Mark had built his and Savannah's home in the Georgia mountains, hidden away from the world, though he'd built it in the 1990's, before the time of persecution so they would have plenty of years to live there in peace. It was a home whose floor plan and style were all too familiar since he'd built it from his own memory.

He was in that house now. Holding the hand of his bride who no longer looked like the youthful sprite he'd fallen in love with. Yet, his love for her had only deepened in tune with their wrinkles.

Earlier this day, Mark had inspected the small shed he'd ordered built a few hundred feet away in a small clearing. Thick trees separated that clearing from the main house, just as he remembered.

Mark had constructed that shack seventy years prior, but made sure it was well cared for over the decades, assuring it would have the correct appearance of age to fulfill its purpose.

He had walked through the shack, making sure it matched his memory. He'd had a couple of workmen replace some of the rotting boards the other day and the scent of fresh lumber still floated upon the air inside. The shed was empty of any furniture except a table in its center. Aside from that, some cabinets and a long window seat, there was nothing else inside it, which was exactly as it should be.

He dusted the few horizontal surfaces there were and swept the floor clean of debris. Then, he walked to the window seat and opened it. Empty.

Well, it was time to fix that.

Mark removed the two shifters from his backpack. They were the two he'd taken off of Rialto. Next, he pulled out two small sheets of paper. He'd typed these back in the 1940's on an actual typewriter and brought them forward to today. Every detail had to match. The paper felt old, but looked crisp and new.

The first slip simply read, "This time, put it on." He placed that note inside the window seat. Then, he took one of the shifters and placed it with the note. His fingers lingered for moment on its face before letting go.

This shifter had special significance for him. Or more correctly, it would have special significance for him. In that moment, he fully realized that in reality, *there was only one shifter*. He touched his fingertips to the one on his own wrist without looking at it and then closed the window seat.

Mark laid the second piece of paper on top of the window seat. It said:

1. Insert wrist into band.
2. Using the three buttons on right side of face, set the bottom display to:

010000P-09031890

3. Press the red button.

Then, Mark laid the second shifter on top of that paper. He looked up and studied the interior of the shed one last time, making sure it was just right.

With a deep sigh, he finally let go and walked out.

Now, he was back in his home, with Savannah sitting beside him on the bed. It was getting harder to breathe. He'd caught a glimpse of himself in the mirror earlier in the day. He truly was an old man now, white hair and all. She didn't look as old as he did yet, though with the way she was spending months at a time on any given rescue, that was sure to change. She was still beautiful and always would be to him.

They'd removed most of the furniture from the house earlier in the week, leaving just a few pieces here and there. Savannah wouldn't be coming back here after today.

They'd cleaned it from top to bottom as well, dusting and mopping, leaving the smell of lemon-scented Pine-Sol in the air.

"It's time," Mark croaked with a dry throat. "I can feel it coming."

"Are you okay? Do you want some water?"

"I'm fine."

They sat in silence, holding hands.

"Savannah, darling, I love you with all my heart."

"I know, Mark. I love you too."

"Thanks for putting up with me over the years."

She laughed and then began to cry. He took her in his arms, which no longer held anything close to his former strength. He kissed her lightly on the lips and then hugged her tight.

The embrace lingered for as long as they could, each knowing it would be their last. Finally, Mark had to break it off. Each breath was becoming more difficult.

Savannah stood, tears streaming down her cheeks.

"Here, let me look at you."

She brushed some lint from his shirt and checked his collar. He wore slacks and a dress shirt and had pressed them this morning just for the occasion.

Mark turned and tried to lie down. He felt so weak. Savannah helped him get his legs up onto the bed. He laid flat and she straightened his legs out. He reached out and took her hand, basking in the last feel of her skin upon his.

She bent over, caressed his cheek with her other palm, and hugged his head. Finally, she stepped back and locked eyes with his, still holding his hand.

"Good-bye, Mark."

"Good-bye, Darling. I love you."

"I love you too."

Slowly their hands parted until only the fingertips remained. Then, they released and Mark brought his arm back to the bed. She averted her eyes in pain, but Mark didn't look away. It was his last chance to see her in this life.

Through her tears, Savannah sighed and pressed her shifter.

With a flash of static, she faded away in front of his eyes.

He lay there for a few minutes staring at the ceiling, his chest rising and falling with each labored breath. The hum of the air conditioner was comforting.

He wasn't quite sure what was wrong with his body, but it was clearly failing.

"Hellooo?" A voice called out from below. It was the voice of a much younger man.

Until this day, through all his adventures, in spite of the fact that Mark had spent the better part of his life moving back and forth through time at will, he had always managed to never look upon a former version of himself. Ty and Hardy had seen themselves plenty of times, but Mark had always had a strange phobia about it. Frankly, the thought of it had always freaked him out. Over the years, he'd made sure to avoid seeing himself at all costs and had succeeded.

That changed in an instant as the young man's face appeared in the doorway. It was himself, fifty years younger. Boy, he was more handsome than he'd remembered.

Mark laid there studying himself through barely cracked eyelids. He looked so young and vital, yet so poor in spirit. The pain of Daniel and Brittany's death and the loss of his marriage were still freshly etched into the lines of his face.

It was an odd knowledge. He knew the pain that awaited this man. This man who *was* him, yet at the same time, was *not*. No, this was not him, but this man would grow to be him. He also knew the joy that awaited this younger self.

If he could go back and live it all over again, would he?

No, he decided. Well, maybe certain moments with Savannah, he would. But his whole life? No. He appreciated the journey, even more now seeing this version of himself that had yet to experience the majority of it, but a journey is only exciting the first time you run it. Once you've traveled its path, the magic is gone. Knowing in advance makes the pain unbearable and the joy all too fleeting.

Should he say something? Give himself some key piece of advice that would help comfort over the years? Mark had dwelled on this a lot lately, debating what single statement would be the most effective.

In the end, he said nothing. It was better that young Mark Carpen experience it all for himself as was intended.

His younger self moved into the room and picked up Mark's wrist, checking for a pulse. Mark opened his eyes fully to get a good look at the man. It felt like he was looking at a grown son. He smiled, happy to finally be here. Content to look at life from this end and know it was all going to work out. Seeing himself so young, he felt a warmth, a love for himself he had not allowed before. He understood this man's pain and the reasons he did the things he did. *It's going to get better*, he wanted to say, but couldn't crack his throat open to speak the words.

Instead, Mark reached out and grabbed his wrist. He gripped it tightly for as long as he could manage, staring into his own eyes, trying to communicate everything and getting nothing across. Then, his strength left him. His arm dropped back onto the bed and he felt his eyes closing.

It was okay.

Everything would be okay.

His eyes were now closed, but he could still hear the man breathing. Then, even that faded.

A light appeared at the end of a tunnel. The light grew and neared. He could see his children.

Daniel was there, smiling, full of life, so handsome and waiting for him to come and play. Brittany looked so beautiful. The glimmering light danced on her hair like a halo. She too was smiling, holding her arms out to him. So happy.

A man stood behind them. A man Mark hadn't seen for two thousand years. His face shone like the radiant sun.

He was smiling too.

Acknowledgements

Authors often begin their work inspired in solitude, yet before a novel can be considered complete, it has been aided and touched by many hands, each contributing to its final excellence in their own way.

First and foremost, I would like to thank my wife, Lindsay, for her love and support, for always believing in me, and for loving my books.

My sincere thanks go out to Jack & Barbara Mason, Joel Odom, Daniel Server, Paul Wolak, Charlie Warner, and Lynda Bacon for taking the time to review my writing and for their endless offerings of encouragement.

To Fran Stewart, for her selfless and detailed copyediting, which clearly helped make the *ChronoShift* series a better set of books. To Matt Smartt, a true artist, for designing such a phenomenal set of book covers, and for putting up with my nit-picky perfectionism.

To 12Stone Church, for opening up God's house to allow a writer a peaceful place to craft his work (And to Patti Reiland for keeping him supplied with endless amounts of coffee).

And finally, to all my friends and clients who have voiced their support and helped spread the word, may you receive a multitude of blessings as you continue the journey.

Author's Note

I hope you enjoyed reading the ChronoShift series — I certainly loved writing it. One of my goals was to provide the reader with something more than mere entertainment.

Throughout the trilogy, you will notice that *how* Mark's shifter works is never explained — you just know it does. An author who wishes to take on the time-travel genre immediately faces the challenge of explaining how their character's time-travel device will work. I have yet to read the novel that successfully did this in a satisfactory way, scientifically speaking that is.

Therefore, I decided to avoid the issue altogether. Relegating the device to the background, making it just one more weapon in Mark's arsenal, allows the true story to shine through. Eliminating the power of time allows the real nature of our struggles to be seen.

Too often in life we stew in our regrets, imagining what could have been, if only... We are often held prisoners by our bad decisions, and hold onto the fantasy that if we could only go back in time and fix them, how things would be different.

Yet, would they?

Mark was able to remove the constraints of time, but his problems did not go away. Some were internal struggles, others were from without. Those inner battles are only resolved through spiritual maturity, a maturity that comes with the passage of spiritual time, and the ability to skip through temporal time would never jump start that growth.

For everything else that happens to us – it is not the oppression of time holding us prisoner. Nor are our bars from the prison of poverty. (You'll recall Mark had no limits to his wealth either.) It is true that both money and time do restrain us, but their removal would not remove our struggles, which is the point of the ChronoShift trilogy. Instinctively, we all sense that if we had unlimited resources of both, we would still have problems. So, what is the true source of those problems?

Mark could not save his children. This became his torment, the focus of his heart, at the cost of acknowledging the blessings that were still his. In the face of their loss, Kelly and he could not see the blessing of their love for each other, and they divorced.

Mark could not initially appreciate the full value of his friendship with Hardy and Ty, nor the magical match for his heart in Savannah. Nor could he see what a powerful blessing he'd been given in the ability to rescue others. All of this was eclipsed by his obsession with his loss, an obsession born and cemented in place by pain.

Thus it is with us. All of us bear pain and struggles, yet, simultaneously, all of us also have greater blessings, though blinded by our pain, we often fail to recognize them.

Why do bad things happen to good people? is an eternal question asked by many. The answer becomes easier to see when you understand that people who have no problems become lazy, depressed, self-loathing, and eventually, self-destructive. Hollywood is full of such examples.

God allows us problems because of His Love, to shape us into what He wants us to be, and to allow us to thrive in the midst of our blessings without self-destructing. Challenges make us stronger, the easy life make us flabby, unhealthy. His is a much stronger, more mature love than you and I are capable of expressing, yet it remains love. This is true faith, seeing His love in the face of our problems.

So, *where is God when it hurts?* He is there with us, in the midst of our pain, feeling what we feel. He takes no joy in it, but does what is best for His child, as any good father does.

Why not just give us flat tires and burnt casseroles instead of allowing terrible loss as in the case of Mark and his children? I can only say that His ways are not our ways, His thoughts are not our thoughts. It is His prerogative when to take life as He is the original giver of it. God is outside of time and sees things we do not see.

As Mark found out in the last paragraph of *Turn*.

As for the history contained in the series, I took every care to be as historically accurate as possible with regards to events, dress, and the personalities of well-known historical persons, from Abraham Lincoln to Charlemagne and Attila the Hun.

In *Shift*, Mr. Randolph Vinson, of the famed stolen cravat, is a complete fiction, as is the entire cast of characters and happenings in Madison, GA surrounding the enslavement of Ty's third great-grandfather. However, the story about Sherman sparing Madison on his march to the sea is true.

The circumstances during the battle of Khe Sanh and the level of lawlessness in Juarez, Mexico are accurate.

I have seen a photograph that places Lee Harvey Oswald on the sidewalk outside the book depository at the moment the motorcade was passing, though whether that photograph is reliable remains to be proven. I think the question of who actually killed Kennedy is well answered in "Blood, Money, and Power" by Barr McClellan.

The long list of coincidences cited by Savannah surrounding the Lincoln and Kennedy assassinations is a well-known phenomenon.

In *Chase*, King Philip's War is a real event, quite a significant one frankly in American history, yet do you remember learning about it in school? I have faithfully portrayed its causes and the details of how it began. If you wish to read more about it, "King Philip's War" by Eric Schultz is a great resource.

Geoffrey de Mandeville, Earl of Essex, was a real person and the descriptions of his power and estates is accurate. Though we do not know for sure the nature of his personality, all the powerful magnates such as he serving directly under William the Conqueror are likely to have been at least somewhat domineering and oppressive as they were willing to conquer a free people.

When exactly Robin Hood lived has been a matter of much debate, but I agree with those who place him during the time of the Anarchy (1135 – 1153). Hood is a word that can mean outlaw and thus does not indicate his lineage, but the Anarchy period in England would have been exactly the kind of time when one such as he would have arisen – and there are evidences of him then in the records. If so, he very well could have been a boy at the time Mark meets little Robin.

In *Turn*, the story centers around the search for the Ark of the Covenant. Of course, the number of books and theories regarding its current location are endless. As I set out to write *Turn*, I determined to see if I could, from my armchair, figure out where it really is (I do not believe it has been destroyed.)

Having already been a student of the various Ark theories for years, I was well familiar with them, and my personal favorite was the possible location in Ethiopia. However, the more I researched, the more I came to the conclusion that Ethiopia was not a true possibility. Nor were the Templar claims very convincing, though I have accurately represented Templar history here as well as their presence in Hereford and Bengeo. The King of England did in fact imprison several of them believing there was a great treasure hidden in Hereford.

Everything Professor Daud Zahavi tells Mark regarding the hiding of the Ark by Jeremiah and the various documents that have been discovered revealing its location is true.

Solomon Schechter was a real person and did everything Zahavi says he did. Having Jacob Gould be the source of some of Scechter's information was my own invention, and I thoroughly enjoyed using the character of Gould to have Mark meet Jake Halfbreed in Cottonwood, New Mexico (which many of my readers will remember from another story).

Rabbi Hertz in Amsterdam was a real person, and he did write the *Emeq HaMelekh* which describes the hiding of Ark and cited some sources lost to us now. The criminal situation outside of Amsterdam is also described accurately.

It is known that Rabbi Hertz was a student of Rabbi Isaac "Ari" ben Luria, though the account of Isaac Luria's grandfather seeing mention of the Silver Scroll in a document in Venice is my own invention. The description of the situation of the Jewish people in Venice in 1500 AD is accurate.

The descriptions of Charlemagne, his palace and kingdom are accurate. Alcuin and Einhard were real officials in Charlemagne's court and Charlemagne did have a reputation for treating the Jewish people well.

Descriptions of Attila the Hun and his palace are accurate. Not much is known about Hunnic culture, but what is known is faithfully represented. The circumstances surrounding his mysterious death is also accurate in every detail, and Idilco is suspected by historians of being involved in some sort of poisoning.

The obscure Jewish scribe, Mattatiyah HaLevi, who Mark seeks during the time of Christ, is my creation.

I took extreme care to ensure that every detail of the scenes during the time of Jesus was as accurate as possible, and I believe if you had been an observer, you would have witnessed scenes very similar to what I described.

With the exception, of course, of Jesus' interaction with Mark and Laura. I wrote those chapters with great trepidation. It is no small thing to have Jesus do or say things that are not in the Bible, but I could not avoid them as those very scenes were very much central to the entire point of the trilogy. I must trust He will forgive my liberties and overlook any errors contained therein.

At the end of my research, I came to the conclusion that the Ark of the Covenant is in fact in a hidden cave on Mt. Nebo, in *the Cave of the Column by the River of the Dome* to be specific, though no one is exactly sure where that is, and since Mt. Nebo is currently in Jordan, it is difficult for Israel to look for it. (I was there late last year, but they wouldn't let me dig.)

If any of the time periods or historical events I have described intrigue you, I encourage you to read more! History is full of curious mysteries and lessons to be learned for life today.

It's always a bittersweet feeling to finish a series that one loves. Many of you will be wishing there were more adventures for you to continue to follow Mark, Ty, and Hardy. I know I will miss them as I move on.

Thank you for reading my work, and may you always enjoy the journey!

~ Zack Mason

About the Author

Zack Mason loves the art of the word and the thrill of the story. He has wandered the countryside of Bangladesh, built churches in Costa Rica, roamed the desert in Arizona, hiked the Alps in France, and fought human trafficking in Atlanta. He has been a dishwasher, a house framer, a teacher, a waiter, a salesman, and a businessman, just to name a few. He currently resides with his family outside Atlanta, GA and plans to continue writing for as long as he is allowed to do so.

Want a peek at a Secret Chapter?

The author has installed a secret chapter on ChronoShift's website that can only be viewed there.

1. Go to www.Chrono-Shift.com
2. Use the same login give earlier in this book and click on "Search Archives."
3. Enter a search for "At Peace."
4. Follow the instructions.

www.ingramcontent.com/pod-product-compliance
Lightning Source LLC
Chambersburg PA
CBHW030547260626
47157CB00006B/2215